A Husband's Confession

ZOË MILLER

HACHETTE
BOOKS
IRELAND

First published in 2014 by Hachette Books Ireland

1

Cataloguing in Publication Data is available from the British Library

ISBN 978 1444743203

Typeset in Apple Garamond by Bookends Publishing Services
Printed and bound in Great Britain by Clays Ltd, St Ives plc

Hachette Books Ireland's policy is to use papers that are natural, renewable and recyclable products and made from wood grown in sustainable forests. The logging and manufacturing processes are expected to conform to the environmental regulations of the country of origin.

Hachette Books Ireland
8 Castlecourt Centre, Castleknock, Dublin 15

An Hachette UK Company
338 Euston Road
London NW1 3BH

www.hachette.ie

Dedicated with all my love to three special people
who mean everything to me:
Michelle, Declan and Barbara.

Acknowledgements

It is a privilege to be writing the acknowledgements for this, my sixth book with Hachette Books Ireland, and I would like to extend huge thanks and appreciation to my lovely editor Ciara Doorley and all the team, including Breda, Jim, Ruth and Joanna.

To my wonderful agent Sheila Crowley of Curtis Brown, London, I owe lots of gratitude for unstinting enthusiasm, kind friendship, and steadfast support.

Much appreciation is due to the warm and welcoming Yvonne Fallon of the Queen of Tarts café and patisserie on Cow's Lane (and Dame Street), Dublin, for taking a break from her busy schedule at a particularly demanding time to talk to me about the day-to-day running of a bakery and for treating me to creamy coffee and delicious meringue. Pop in to the Queen of Tarts for some mouth-watering pastries, you won't be disappointed!

Thanks also to Breda Considine, who patiently answered lots of questions, helped with my research and rescued me from falling into a plot hole.

I'd like to pay tribute to my mother-in-law Clare, who was a most enthusiastic reader and a very supportive fan, but who sadly passed away just as this book was finished. We miss her jokes and spirited laughter, but are still surrounded by the legacy of her love.

Thanks, as ever, to my family and friends for huge dollops of love, friendship and encouragement, especially my three children to whom this book is dedicated, as well as Derek, Dara, Louise, Colm, the very precious Cruz, and other little stars waiting in the wings. Along with my extended family, I am so fortunate to have you all in my life.

And thanks to you, the reader, for choosing this book. I hope you enjoy it!

Zoë xx

Prologue

Saturday night

She knows she has made an even bigger mistake than she first thought when the car swerves off the road and veers down a dark country lane. Her hands grip the edge of the seat while headlights illuminate a pot-holed, bumpy surface. They bounce off bent and twisted hedgerows and they shimmer across densely packed woods that tower like a silent phalanx of mercenaries. Her heart ricochets inside her chest.

This couldn't be happening. Not to *her*. Nausea surges into her throat, the sour taste telling her that this is real, here and now. A bubble of fear explodes at the back of her skull.

'Stop the car, *now*,' she cries, her voice thin and quavering in her ears. *If only, if only, if only.*

If only she hadn't agreed to get into this car.

If only she hadn't been so stupid.

If only she could turn back time and be in the safe, warm security of her home and her life, which has never seemed more precious. Although it is barely a dozen miles away as the crow flies, it has never felt so distant. They passed through a huddle of houses about a mile back, so they're not all that far from civilisation.

'I said, stop the car.' Her voice is hoarse.

The car stops so suddenly that it slews across loose gravel and she jerks forward in the seat. She gets such a shock that her trembling fingers have all the traction of soft, running water as they try to disengage the seat belt. Her scalp crawls with spikes of tension. Finally, the belt springs free. She summons whatever shreds of strength she has left and scrambles out the passenger door, her legs shaking as her feet somehow connect with the stony surface of the lane, her face chilled with the flow of cold night air. She slams the door. The car speeds away up the lane. The roar of the engine recedes in the distance, the tail lights vanishing as it rounds a bend. She is alone in the depths of the night, her breath heaving loudly in her chest, her heart thumping in her throat. A thin wind buffets her face. It rattles the hedgerows and whistles through the dark woods rising up on the other side of the lane. Up above her, shredded clouds float like grey ghosts against the coal-black sky. Off into the distance beyond the hedgerows, the darkness is broken here and there by pin-pricks of light from scattered houses, shining like welcoming beacons.

She pulls up the collar of her jacket and begins to pick her way up the lane in the direction of the nearest light, slipping and sliding on the laneway's broken surface, almost losing her balance, her hands flying out to save herself as she steps into a crumbling pothole and staggers headlong. Trailing brambles, reaching out like tentacles, tear at her face, slice through her tights and scratch her legs.

She struggles to her feet, takes off her heels, and tears clog the back of her throat as she hobbles painfully along. She keeps to the side of the lane, her feet sinking into squashy undergrowth, loose stones, and more thorny brambles; her heart racing, her blood pumping, her breath laboured in her chest.

She's almost there when she hears it coming up behind her. A car.

She turns and watches the beams of the headlights as it cruises up the lane towards her. Rescue, surely. Soon she will be home safe. Nothing seems sweeter. Her heart lifts, buoyed on a flood of hope. She flaps her hands. She jumps up and down, uncaring that her feet are cut to ribbons on the stony surface, wishing she had her mobile to provide some kind of signal light. The car comes closer. Just when she expects the driver to spot her in its headlights and slow down, it picks up speed, coming straight towards her.

There's no time to get out of the way. She has a split second to realise she hasn't been so lucky after all. A huge wave of regret chokes her just as darkness closes around her.

Oh God, how utterly, incredibly, stupidly foolish I have been …

PART ONE

One week earlier ...

One

Monday morning

It all started to go wrong on Monday morning, like someone sliding the
queen of hearts out of the middle of a delicately balanced pyramid of cards
so that, one by one, all the central pieces pinning it together came tumbling
down.

Only it wasn't just a deck of cards, it was their lives.

At first, the day seemed perfect, right at the time Ali Kennedy took a
detour through St Stephen's Green, soaking up the early-spring sunlight
fizzling all around her. She wanted to reach out and catch some of the
sunbeams and wrap them in the palm of her hand, just as her mother had
shown her years ago when she was a child, when the sun had streamed in
through the bevelled glass of their front door, shooting colourful prisms into
the hall. After she'd told Max about that memory, he would sometimes wrap
a kiss in the palm of her hand when he was in a soppy mood – or looking
for something, or, her mouth curved in a grin at the thought, apologising for
forgetting the dry cleaning or the refuse bins.

She came out of the park at the top of Grafton Street. After the rain
the night before, the air was rinsed so clearly that, up above, the higgledy-
piggledy stretch of buildings and rooftops running down the street was

brightly outlined against a bowl of sky so blue she thought it looked like a painting. It was the kind of magical morning that made her think something wonderful was around the corner.

Ali cut down through Johnson's Court and on, across to Drury Street and when she reached Booth Street, she paused for a moment, her eyes flicking over the façade of the bakery on the corner. The paintwork around the door and windows was a shade of cobalt blue, with the name painted in silver lettering over the doorway: Booth Street Bakery.

To the passer by, the bakery looked warm and inviting, somewhere you could relax over coffee and warm scones, meet friends for brunch or afternoon cream tea, or sit back against the velvet cushions in the window seat with hot chocolate and a blueberry pastry and watch the world go by.

To the movers and shakers, it was becoming the place to be seen in.

To Ali and Max, it was a second home and the culmination of a dream.

The bakery was already open when Ali strolled in shortly after nine o'clock, passing the bay trees in aluminium containers that flanked the door, the blackboard chalked up with the morning specials. She carried her tote bag on her right arm whilst her left hand reached up to start unwinding her silk scarf. Mouth-watering aromas of freshly brewed coffee and oven-baked bread greeted her. She scanned the counter displays – the tempting assortment of fluffy fresh breads, light, melting pastries, a variety of enticing scones and cakes all invitingly arranged in baskets, china bowls and ceramic stands. All was in order with the bakery this morning.

Later, when she looked back, she wanted to rewind time and go back to that moment – her just entering the bakery, Max in London, Tom and Jessica in school – because it was the last perfect moment, the last untarnished pulse beat in the intertwined lives of Max and Ali Kennedy before all the strands of their life together began to unspool and fray at the edges.

'Morning everyone,' Ali called out. She had no time to respond to the chorus of greetings from staff and nods from a handful of customers because her mobile rang.

'I must have left my notebook behind,' her husband said, the minute she answered. 'Will you have a look?'

Max. Unusual for him to be calling from the London trade fair like this and sounding so irritable, especially when he should have been engrossed in some bakery demonstration about now. And he should still be feeling happy after their love-making last night, Ali thought, recalling with a nugget of pleasure the hot touch of his hands on her hips as she rose of top of him.

'Good morning, mister,' she said. 'I gather your red eye flight was on time, and how are you today?' With her phone to her ear and her tote bag slung over her shoulder, she was already moving down the flagstone floor beyond the counter, up the stairs, and down past the first-floor seating area, into the narrow corridor that held the customer rest rooms and her tiny cubby hole of an office. She put her mobile down on her desk and switched it to speaker mode as she took off her scarf and shrugged out of her leather coat.

'Yes, right, missus – love you to bits and all that,' Max said, his jerky voice telling her he was on the move somewhere. In the background, she could hear strains of energetic music and a disembodied tannoy. 'But the first workshop is just about to start and I can't find my notebook ...'

'Where did you leave it?' she asked, sliding her coat onto a wooden hanger before casting her eyes around, knowing already that Max's precious notebook wasn't going to suddenly magic itself out of the neat environs of her small office.

Compared to the hustle and bustle in the rest of the bakery, Ali's small corner of the building with the barley white walls was an oasis of calm serenity with everything in its place. It was just as well that Ali found any kind of mess aggravating, because the office was far too compact to allow her to indulge in any kind of disorder. She kept her desk free of clutter, apart from her laptop, some trade magazines and a neat pile of paperwork clipped together in a filing tray. There was nothing on top of the filing cabinets along the wall save for a couple of flourishing spider plants.

'I can't remember. I thought I put it in the bag along with my iPad on Saturday evening, before I left Booth Street,' Max said, sounding grumpy. 'That's where I always put it when I'm travelling.'

'Yeah well, are you positive it's not there? I'm a busy lady,' she teased. 'I haven't time for these frivolous distractions, you know.'

He stayed silent. In the quality of his silence, she could picture him clearly, standing very still in the chaos all around him, feeling slightly injured at her throwaway remark. Max had this way of being totally motionless while he absorbed something or turned it over in his mind. On the surface, he was a still, unruffled kind of person, unlike Ali. She liked to think that was why they got on so well and there was a restfulness about him that made her feel totally at peace with him.

She should have known Max would feel out of sorts without his current notebook. From the time he had started out in his career, he had always used a spiral-bound A5 notebook to jot down recipes and ideas. By now, he had quite a collection filled with his award-winning recipes. Ali knew how bereft he would be not to find his current one in his bag, his fingers itching to scribble down tips and advice he would glean in the course of the two-day London cake and bakery show.

'I thought I packed it, but I was so busy finishing up …' his voice trailed off as though he was beginning to doubt himself. 'Will you try the cabinet?'

'Your wish is my command,' Ali said, picking up her mobile. She went across to the cabinet where she kept all the business paperwork and accounts locked in the top drawers, and where Max stored his collection of notebooks in a roomy bottom drawer.

'It's not much good to me there, but at least I'd know where it is,' Max was talking, raising his voice against another upsurge of noise. When the noise receded a little, Max went on, 'I hope I haven't dropped it somewhere, I've lots of stuff in it that I haven't processed yet.'

'Then I can't imagine you put it away. I bet you left it lying around downstairs, where anyone could have taken it.' Mobile to her ear, Ali pulled out the bottom drawer with her free hand. But instead of looking at a pile of Max's notebooks, she was looking into clean, empty space – space that should have been taken up with over a dozen notebooks filled with Max's work, his pencilled scrawls and cookery notes, which were a legacy to his creativity and almost his entire career. She blinked. Blinked again. She put her hand inside and felt around the smooth sides as if to confirm the evidence of her eyes.

Nothing. Zilch. She hadn't been seeing things.

She didn't realise how long she'd been silent until Max said, 'What's up?'

'Max, it's not here,' she said slowly, staring into the drawer. 'Funny thing is, neither are any of the others.'

'*What?*'

'The drawer is empty. Did you clear it out?' Confusion washed over her and a small seed of anxiety lodged itself in her chest. This was odd. She knew in her heart of hearts that Max hadn't touched them, because he spent as little time in her office as he had to. The kitchen and bakery floor were his kingdom. And no way would he have suddenly decided to embark on a spring clean of his horde of precious notebooks or shift them somewhere else without telling her. He did very little without telling her or asking for her advice. As he had said himself on many occasions, she was his oracle.

'What does that mean?' she'd asked him once.

'You must be consulted at all times, without fail,' he'd said, putting on an extra-deep voice like Arnold Schwarzenegger in *The Terminator*.

'I'm so glad you know who's the boss around here,' she'd said.

Now, his voice clipped, 'I didn't go near them. They have to be in there somewhere. You must have moved them when you were doing some of your over-enthusiastic cleaning and—'

'*I* must have moved them? I wouldn't dare mess with your precious work.' Her scalp prickled with uneasiness.

'Okay, okay. Sorry. Will you look around the bakery for me? Please? And thank you, darling.'

'Right, *darling*. I'll call you back,' she said, straightening up and putting down her mobile. She stepped out of her Nikes – essential footwear for her morning walk into work – and slid her feet into her black shoes. She checked all of her cabinets, sliding out drawers one by one, blinking her eyes as though she doubted the evidence in front of her, but all her files and paperwork were in order and there was no sign of Max's current notebook, let alone his entire collections. It was as though they had been spirited away, with everything else undisturbed. She tried to remember if Max had taken out his notebook at home the previous evening. But he'd just watched some television after dinner and they'd gone to bed early, his overnight bag left in the downstairs cloakroom, ready for his 5 a.m. airport departure. She adjusted the silver belt of her charcoal-grey Karen Millen shirt-dress and pasted a smile on her face as she left her office.

They ran such a tight ship, with every inch of space in Booth Street carefully accounted for, that instinct told her Max's notebooks with his award-winning recipes weren't suddenly going to pop up from behind the coffee machines or from under his treasured Hobart mixer.

But they had to be somewhere. It wasn't as if, she laughed to herself as she came out onto the first floor, anyone would have come into her office, opened the cabinets and actually *stolen* them.

Two

Booth Street Bakery had been partly inspired by a patisserie Ali and Max had stumbled on in France, years earlier whilst they were on a camping holiday.

'When we get our own place, it will be just like this,' Ali had said dreamily, as she looked around the welcoming Provence patisserie and stirred her frothy coffee. 'Mouth-watering displays, sweet and savoury aromas, brightly clean and inviting.'

'You mean if,' Max had corrected.

'No, I don't,' she'd said softly, leaning across the table towards him, putting her hand on his, and looking into his blue eyes, trying to convince him with her steady gaze. 'Don't you realise how good you are?'

He didn't.

Sometimes she still had a job convincing him. Despite being a qualified pastry chef, occasionally he said he couldn't understand where his success had come from. Or how it had all happened.

The décor of the bakery was a mixture of retro chic and clean contemporary, themed in farmhouse style, infused with a mix of Irish heritage. It seated fifty and was spread over two floors. Banquettes were strewn with blue and cream cushions, and shelves held jugs of lavender and herbs and spices, as well as baskets of fresh fruit and vegetables. All the counter and serving staff wore blue aprons with the Booth Street Bakery logo over white shirts and black trousers. One exposed, golden-stoned wall ran the length of the bakery, and the remaining walls were painted in pale cream with colourful prints of the Irish landscape: a purply-gold Connemara autumn, a Westmeath lake under high, blue skies, so clear it mirrored the surrounding woods; then Max's favourite, and a nod to his roots, a wide tableau of the Claddagh at sunset, where the River Corrib flowed into Galway Bay.

Ali went downstairs to the main floor. It was quiet at this hour of the morning, when most of the business was takeouts.

'Morning, Ali. How are you today?' Emma, a counter assistant, was busy filling metal holders in the shape of flowers with blue-checked napkins, in between serving customers. Early twenties, Emma was a college graduate unable to find work in her chosen field of teaching, but she was always cheerful.

'Great, couldn't be better!' Ali smiled automatically. She slipped in behind the counter and her gaze darted about the shelves. There was no sign of any notebooks. She went down to the counter holding the coffee machine, hot water and the selection of teas, but the shelves underneath held nothing but cups, saucers and mugs. Then she looked up at the high shelf behind the counter.

'Are you looking for something?' Emma asked, her forehead crinkling.

Ali smiled. 'Sort of. I wish I was about a foot taller so I could see what's on that top shelf.' *Or what's not there.*

'Daniel's doing kitchen porter this morning,' Emma said, blushing prettily.

Daniel. At twenty-two years of age, he was the resident heart-throb of the bakery. He'd tried out his charms on all the staff until they got the measure of his flirty ways. He had been with them just four months, having returned from travelling the world, and while Ali wasn't always happy with the way he chatted up the counter and floor staff, he was good in the kitchen. More importantly, he was Debbie's son, and they couldn't afford to get on the wrong side of Debbie.

Emma turned to look after a customer and Ali came out from behind the counter just as Helena whirled by with a tray of used mugs, plates and cutlery en route to the kitchen.

'Morning, Ali. Lovely day, isn't it?'

'Yes, it's fab.'

'Makes you hope spring is on the way at last.'

'About time.'

She followed Helena down towards the kitchen, and waited in the doorway, watching the busy yet co-ordinated hive of activity as preparations for lunch got under way. Debbie was directing operations in Max's absence, working alongside Zofia, a Polish chef. Their other chef, Estefan from Brazil, had a day off.

'Hi, Ali,' Debbie said, looking up from the counter where she was preparing quiche fillings for the oven. 'How are things? Did Max get off okay?'

'He did—'

'But?' Debbie raised an eyebrow and paused in her work. She knew Ali well enough to guess something was up.

Ali found herself slightly lacking in confidence when it came to Debbie and she wasn't sure where this small insecurity stemmed from. She supposed it was because Debbie had known Max and his older brother Finn from childhood. Long before Ali had come on the scene, they'd grown up close to each other in Galway. Max had trained with Debbie, learning the ropes with her in her mother's Galway bakery before he'd come to Dublin. Then three years ago, just before they'd extended the bakery, Debbie had met Max fortuitously, had come on board straightaway, and been with them ever since.

Max had won several awards for his artisan baking, but was most famed for his organic cranberry bread. The recipe was his trade secret, and had only been revealed to Debbie. Not even Ali knew what exactly went in to his mix; then again, she had long ago accepted that she hadn't a cookery bone in her body. And from the day soon after they'd opened, when she had mistakenly poured sugar instead of salt into the lunchtime soup – Max had kept a straight face as he said it was the most avant-garde soup he'd ever tasted – she'd decided it was best if she kept well away from the kitchen.

Plus Debbie knew exactly how to take charge of the kitchen in Max's absence, supporting him whenever he was there. Tall, dark-haired and brown-eyed, not even her aprons could hide her enviable, curvy figure. Ali sometimes saw her as Booth Street Bakery's answer to Nigella Lawson and she had more knowledge about baking in her little finger than Ali would ever glean in her lifetime. Looking at her lively face, you'd never think she'd been in the bakery since six o'clock that morning, turning on the ovens, preparing the breads and pastries and overseeing the morning deliveries.

'Max didn't leave a notebook around here, did he?' Ali asked.

Debbie searched the kitchen, and Ali watched as she competently and briskly checked around the shelves and presses, high and low, and then she shook her head as she came back out to Ali. 'Nope. Don't tell me he went to London without his precious baby?'

'Seems so.'

'If I find it I'll get the first flight over to him,' she said, smiling at Ali. A timer on one of the ovens pinged and Debbie said, 'Daniel, will you leave the dishwasher for now and get that?'

'I'll borrow Daniel for a moment, when he's free,' Ali said, looking down to the tall, lanky young man who was pulling a tray of organic loaves out of an oven. He deftly transferred the loaves to a wire tray, grinning sideways and winking at Ali as he caught her looking at him.

Daniel had a cheeky look to his face that was fine for Tom, her eleven-year-old son, Ali thought, but a bit immature for Daniel. Still, some of the assistants found him flirty and endearing and now and again during a lull in the day, even Ali had to smile at the repartee bouncing between the kitchen and the counter areas.

'Daniel, the boss wants you, the *real* boss,' Debbie said, winking at Ali before she headed back into the kitchen to prepare her quiches.

Daniel gave her a friendly smile. 'Ali, what can I do for you?'

'I need someone tall for a sec. Have a look and see if there are any notebooks lying around that shelf up there,' she said, indicating the shelf behind the counter.

'Nah, nothing there beyond the jugs of dried flowers,' he said as he stood on his toes checking the shelf. He was almost as tall as Max and he had no problem looking into the back of the shelf. 'Is there anywhere else you want me to check?' he asked.

'No, it's fine,' Ali said. She looked around the rest of the ground-floor area, smiling at customers as her eyes scanned the banquettes and window seats, the dresser in the corner.

When she went back upstairs, Ali closed the door, letting the staff know that she wanted to be alone. She leaned against the door for a moment, breathing slowly and deeply, fighting a sliver of unease. She couldn't bring herself to admit that twenty years' worth of Max's work seemed to be missing.

❁

'Don't worry about it,' Max said, when she called him back, and she knew he had caught the note of agitation in her voice. Or else he assumed she was too busy to have had a proper look. 'They must be there somewhere.'

Like where?, she wanted to say. Both she and Max, along with Debbie, had a full set of keys to the bakery. Although they had a robust security system, she locked her office at night, but she came and went so much during the day that the door was left unlocked. No one apart from herself or Max had any business in there, except during their very infrequent holidays when either Debbie or Emma checked the post and kept things ticking over.

'When was the last time you went to that drawer?' she asked, trying to be practical, telling herself there had to be a reasonable explanation.

'Jeez, Ali, I can't remember,' he said impatiently. 'A month, maybe six weeks ago …' He broke off to talk to someone nearby and then he said, 'Look, I have to go, we'll chat later …'

'Okay.'

A sudden panic gripped Ali, and she hurriedly checked the wall safe, the keys slipping out of her shaky fingers, the office closing in on her, but everything was fine, cash and receipts neatly bundled and waiting to be collected by the security firm, who came in twice a week. Only she and Max had a key to the safe, with the spare key secreted away at home.

She decided to try and get on with her day and opened her laptop. She checked Twitter and Facebook, updating their profile, responding to comments and requests, as well as posting their specials of the day. She texted Max, this time to remind him to send through a couple of photos from the fair that she could upload to Facebook. She mightn't be much use in the kitchen, but she liked to think she was good with the customers and the staff, and she used the best of her marketing skills to push their business out there. But all the time the back of her mind was elsewhere, trying to guess what might have happened to his lifetime's worth of notes.

Next, she went through the business emails.

There were emails for lunch reservations in the coming days and she keyed them straight through their system so that they would be picked up on the terminal downstairs. There were the usual requests for endorsements from reputable companies eager to have the bakery using their ingredients, and offering competitive discounts over trial periods in order to get their foot in the door. She'd let Max have a look at those. The one thing he was passionate about was his policy of using only the freshest ingredients, locally sourced.

'You can make all the rules you like, Ali,' he'd said, when they were starting out. 'But that's my one rule and it overrides everything else.'

She'd grinned. 'Didn't know you could do "overrides"?'

He'd flicked her hair. 'Watch me.'

Early that afternoon Max called her again.

'Any luck?'

'Nothing,' she said. 'I've been keeping an eye out all day. I'll check the house as soon as I get home and call you later.'

'I'm off to a reception now and it could go on.'

'Good for you,' she said, a little testily. 'You'll be swanning around the glitzy fair, networking with all the beautiful people, knocking back bubbly and getting high on adoration, and I'm stuck in the office.'

'It's a work thing. I'll be busy. And you could have come with me if bubbly is what you want—'

'Nah. I don't have to go to London for bubbly, and I'd only be in the way. And I couldn't have left Tom and Jessica at the moment.'

'They would have been okay for a couple of nights.'

'A teenager, an eleven-year-old and a free house? Come on, Max.' Easy for Max to make such generously sweeping pronouncements when he knew he had her to keep his feet on the ground.

'Jessica's nearly eighteen. I miss you tagging around with me.'

'Jessica's head is elsewhere right now with her mock exams coming up and you've described me perfectly – tagging around like a spare piece of string.'

'I'll show you what I think of a piece of string tomorrow night as soon as I'm home.'

'Why don't you tell me now?' Ali dared.

'I don't like phone sex. I'd rather let you imagine it ...'

'Yes, I've nothing else to do this afternoon,' she said, looking at the pile of invoices on her desk and fresh emails appearing in her inbox.

'By the way,' he said, 'we've been invited to Finn and Jo's for a meal on Saturday night. He texted me this afternoon.'

'Finn and Jo's? Next Saturday?' Invitations to Max's brother and his wife's house were rare. The couples didn't get together that often any more. Because of the demands of Booth Street, Max and Ali led hands-on, hard-working lives and mostly collapsed in front of the telly on Saturday nights, whereas Finn and Jo were the beautiful people who swished around in glamorous social circles, thanks to Finn being one of Ireland's most feted television actors and Jo's high-profile career in event management. Over the years, the two couples had drifted apart. Besides, the solid, reliable Max, who was always comfortable in his own skin, had little in common with the edgy, mercurial Finn. And Ali, who sometimes felt she was running around to stay still, found herself a little defensive in front of the graceful Jo. 'What's that in aid of?' Ali asked, perplexed. 'Is there a big birthday coming up?'

'Not that I know of. Finn is still a couple of years off fifty.'

'There must be something up, otherwise they wouldn't be inviting us over.'

'We don't have to go,' Max said. 'We can always say we've something on.'

'Yes, a hot date with a boxset. Still, we haven't seen them since that rushed visit at Christmas.'

'That was their call. Ali, I have to go,' Max said hurriedly. 'I'll talk to you tonight.'

An email pinged into Ali's inbox. It was from TV5.

The television station had already made initial approaches to Max about fronting a six-week run of an autumn bakery programme. He'd laughed it off when he'd discussed it with Ali, deciding it couldn't be a serious offer. Still, word about the proposed programme, featuring Max, had already been leaked to the media, which Ali guessed had to mean something. Max had done some stints of breakfast TV at the station, and he'd been a guest on a couple of foodie programmes, but this was different. It would be prime time and megabucks. She scanned the email and her eyes widened as she noted the key points contained in the proposals. They were serious. They really wanted him.

She'd save this news until he came home from London. This would be huge for Max and propel him into the stratosphere. In recent times, with Max's reputation growing, it was taking him more and more away from the day-to-day business in the bakery. He'd featured in weekend supplements and had been the all-important judge at several food fairs. And now, fronting his own programme with a six-week run on TV5, his name would be up there in lights and Booth Street Bakery would really be on the map.

Ali had little time to savour the glow of satisfaction before her stomach lurched with a disquieting thought. Just as Max was on the verge of pulling off the coup of his career so far, all of his work and his carefully crafted recipes seemed to have vanished. She closed the email and stared into space. There couldn't be a connection, she decided firmly. If anyone deserved his success, Max did. They'd worked so hard together to bring the dream of their bakery into fruition that no one could begrudge them their success.

As Ali looked at the black-and-white canvas prints on the wall beside her desk, her heart swelled. One was of herself and Max with Tom and Jessica, taken a year ago to celebrate their twentieth wedding anniversary. They all looked so happy, jumbled together in a group hug, Max's dark hair a contrast to Ali's blonde corkscrew curls; Jessica, blonde like Ali, only younger and far more beautiful; Tom, dark like his father, his childish, cheeky face beaming like a light. Ali and Max both agreed that far more important than the success of Booth Street was the happiness and contentment of their precious family.

Jessica, at almost eighteen, was already distancing herself from her parents, ready to forge her own exciting path as she moved out into the world after her final school exams. Tom, just eleven, would in time follow his own path, leaving her with an empty nest, but Ali cheered herself up with the thought that no matter how far or high their children might fly, she and Max would have each other.

She'd been married to Max for half of her life. Over twenty years of love and laughter, of squabbles and tiffs, occasional sorrows and deeply felt joys had meshed and moulded them together to form a shared life. Sometimes they overlapped so much that Ali didn't know where she ended and Max began. She couldn't picture living a life without him.

Beside the family group was a canvas print of her favourite wedding photograph; it was a profile of her and Max, she was snuggled into his chest, hugging him around the waist, and his arms were securing her protectively, both of them smiling at the camera. They looked like a clean sheet. New. Shiny. She had the same photograph at home, and the kids sometimes poked fun at it, Tom making a funny noise as if it embarrassed him, Jessica remarking teasingly on how ridiculously young they both had been, that she'd never make the mistake of marrying *that* young.

Ali had been twenty-one, fresh-faced, her flyaway curls running riot around her veil. Twenty-one! Almost a child bride in today's currency. But it hadn't been a mistake. It seemed she had jumped in the blink of an eye from that smiling bride with her whole life in front of her, to being a successful woman in her early forties. She had Max to thank for her happiness and contentment. He had turned her empty life around and given it meaning and colour, as well as filling it with love.

Very occasionally, something dark clutched at her, a terrible fear that it all could be taken away. Twice before, her life had shattered in an instant. But that had been before she met Max . . .

1990

When Ali Brady first meets Max Kennedy, she is nineteen years of age, it is the summer of Italia '90, and the towns, cities and villages of Ireland are gearing up to have a massive, exciting World Cup party. Credit facilities have been extended, pubs and off licences have ordered extra stock, shops are bursting with merchandise and Jack's football army is on the march.

The anticipation of it all flows over Ali's head that spring and early summer as she goes through the motions of life. She leaves the top-floor flat in Larkin House, a council housing block in south inner-city Dublin, at half past eight each morning to walk into her office job in Thornton's department store. Some days, the hours drag by slowly and other days she doesn't know how they have sped by so fast, but all of them slide by her as though she is separated from them by a thin sheet of glass. She comes home at six each evening and attempts to prepare a meal, which more often than not she merely picks at. At the weekends, her friend, the bright, bubbly Linda, who looks after the shoe displays in Thornton's, insists they go to the movies or out for a few drinks.

Ali is just beginning to wonder if she will ever recover her appetite for life, when it all comes to a head one lunchtime.

And it all begins with a cake.

It sits in prime position on the upper shelf behind the glass counter, a confection of pink and white, the edges boasting whipped clouds of soft icing contrasting with delicate lattice work across the top. It has obviously taken hours. And skill. It is so big and creamy and marshmallowy that Ali thinks you could almost lie down and bury yourself in it.

And then as the queue moves along and she gets closer, she sees the inscription in the middle, piped in fluttery pink: 'To the best Mum in the world'. A sharp pain shoots through her heart. She doesn't realise she's all choked up with tears until the lunchtime queue shuffles along the counter in Nolan's bakery and then it's her turn, and when she tries to asks for four doughnuts – a special Friday afternoon treat for the office staff – she begins to cry, huge gulping sobs that shake her slight frame and frighten her with their strength. She thrusts her hand into her bag but, naturally, she'd come out without any tissues.

Through her mist of tears, she sees alarm on people's faces. They move back, give her space. She gulps for air, thinks she is going to choke on the never-ending torrent of tears. She vaguely notices a tall figure detaching itself from the line of assistants behind the counter. She feels a hand on her arm as she is led away from the counter to one of the small tables by the side. A glass of water and a handful of paper napkins materialise on the Formica table in front of her.

He sits down opposite her. 'Are you okay?'

She nods, then shakes her head. She takes a fistful of napkins and pushes them against her streaming eyes.

'It's fine, take your time,' he says.

She cries and cries, mopping up her tears as they fall, trying to drink some water, her teeth rattling against the glass. She is dimly aware of the queue shuffling around, the murmur of conversation, the scent of roasting coffee beans, customers going by with trays, someone with a cloth wiping the cleared tables. Eventually she shudders to a halt.

'Sorry,' she says, her voice thick. She hiccups.

'No worries,' he says.

'It's just—' she begins, feeling some explanation is needed for her monumental crying session.

'You don't have to—'

'It's my mum.' She grabs more napkins and dabs her eyes.

'It's okay—'

'You see, I just realised I'll never buy her a birthday cake. Ever again,' Ali says, the last of her words coming out like a thin, high squeal. Fresh tears cascade down her face, but softer now, more healing.

'That's too bad.' He reaches out and pats her hand. He has long fingers, nice fingers. Her hand looks small and childlike against his. She sits silently for a few moments, allowing her breathing along with the upsurge of emotions to settle back to some kind of normality. She lifts her head and glances around. She catches some eyes looking at her curiously and she tilts her chin and stares back. They look away hastily.

'I'm sorry, I'm holding you up,' she says, a thread of embarrassment finally sliding through her body as she becomes more aware of him sitting opposite her.

She's sorry when he takes his hand away from hers, sensing she is recovering. He says, very reassuringly, 'No problem, I'm due on my lunch now anyway.'

'Thanks for …' she doesn't know quite what to say. Because she's looking at him now as though she's seeing him for the first time, and she finds herself staring. A couple of years older than her, he reminds her a little of David Essex in the video for 'A Winter's Tale', one of the first singles she'd ever rushed out to buy, her money hot in her clenched fist. She shifts her gaze and stares instead at the glass jar with the metal spout that dispenses the sugar. Now that she's getting back to herself, she expects him to get up and walk away, but he doesn't. He buys both of them a pot of tea and a sandwich and instead of avoiding the topic, he asks about her mum.

'She's gone six months,' Ali says with a gulp.

'That's tough. Do you want to talk about her? Or is it too hard?'

'She was a hospital assistant,' Ali begins. 'She helped with meals, brought around the book trolley and made tea for the relatives of the terminally ill ...' she puts her fist to her mouth.

'And?' his voice is tender.

She swallows. 'She was knocked off her bicycle on the quays. On the way home from work.'

'I'm sorry.' His hand covers hers again. For the first time in six months, she is aware of a warmth stealing through the coldness of her bones. She tells him a little bit about her mum, Clara, but nothing too personal that would make her cry again. Things like how much Clara had always loved her – it shone through her eyes – and how, now, Ali feels like her whole world has been demolished. She speaks instead of things that are easy to talk about.

'I still lived at home with her, in a top-floor council flat in Larkin House. Mum used to call it our penthouse suite. Her dream was to have a house with a garden, but there was never enough money.'

'And your dad, is he around?' he asks, his eyes soft with concern.

She shivers and looks away, staring down at the breadcrumbs on her plate. 'No. He went to England when I was six and never came back. He ran off with another woman,' she says, a hard edge in her voice betraying this older hurt and devastation. She glances up at him in time to catch the mixture of empathy and embarrassment in his face, as though he's afraid he has put his foot in it. She shrugs. 'He was never part of my life.'

'Sisters? Brothers? Family?'

'Nah. Mum has two brothers but they emigrated to America, so it was always just the two of us, but we were happy. Mum was a very positive person. Even though it didn't pay very well, she loved her job, she thought it was valuable and important. I'm not as noble as Mum was. I did a secretarial course after school and went straight into the best-paying office job I could find to bring home some decent money so that we could enjoy a few luxuries. And I had high hopes that we could afford to move into her dream house with a garden. But that's never going to happen now.'

She shouldn't have said that. Fresh tears prick the back of her eyes and she forces them to stay there lest this guy thinks she is a real basket case. 'I just feel … God, it's like everything has fallen apart into a big black emptiness, it's all just a daze, and I don't know what I'm going to do with myself or my life.'

'I'm sure whatever you do with your life, your mum would want to be out there, enjoying it, having fun.'

'She always told me to trust in my dream and follow it.'

His eyes are gentle and encouraging. 'And your dream is?'

She flounders. Her cheeks redden. She can't bring herself to tell him that she dreams of meeting someone she could trust with her life, a lover, a best friend, a man she could have wonderful babies with … 'I can't tell you.'

He smiles. 'Okay, but I guess you should just go ahead and follow it like your mum said.'

'What about you?' she asks, changing the subject. 'Do you still have your parents?'

'I never knew my birth mother,' he says. 'I'm adopted. But I have great parents, Margaret and Sean, and, as far as I'm concerned, they're my real parents.'

'Oh, that's good.' She twirls the sugar dispenser around, chiding herself for her inane remark. How could it be good if his mum had given him up for adoption? Still, it doesn't seem to bother him. He looks quite easy about it.

'Where are you from?' she asks, as it's clear from his accent he's not from Dublin.

'I'm from Galway,' he says.

'Galway. It's a beautiful county.'

'It's beautiful all right.' His eyes hold hers until she shifts her gaze.

She folds the left-over napkins in a neat pile. 'I have to get back to work,' she says, making a fuss of picking up her bag, suddenly reluctant to leave his presence, his steady smile and friendly eyes.

'Are you feeling any better now?' He looks as though he's afraid she might burst into tears again.

'Oh, yes, thank you. This isn't normally me. I never used to cry that easily,' she says, fixing him with a look, wanting to explain. 'I'm usually able to cope and get on with things. Until Mum … it's like …' she hesitates.

'What's it like?'

'As though I'm drowning. Other times it's like everything is just pitch black.' She can't believe she's even telling him this. She sounds like a complete twat, yet there is no other way to describe the way her life had collapsed around her. And he's not looking at her as though she's a twat. He looks kind and soft-hearted.

'So where do you work?' The way he asks the question sends a spike of hope through her – as though he's interested in knowing more about her.

'I work in Thornton's, the big department store on Henry Street.'

'I know it. So if I were to, say, drop into Thornton's, just to say hello, where would I find you?' he says.

She feels her face reddening again. He's gorgeous, the way he looks at her like that, eyebrows crooked, his deep-blue eyes kind of flirty. He has thick, dark eyelashes and a long, nicely chiselled nose. *Imagine having his babies*, she thinks, confused and embarrassed. Even though she's had a few boyfriends, she's never slept with any of them. She has never felt strongly about any of them to be that close and special with them. *Was he asking for a date? 'Just to say hello' doesn't sound like a date.*

And the state of her. To judge by the mess of crumpled paper tissues, she hasn't a scrap of mascara left, or any kind of makeup. Then there was the all-important question, the benchmark by which she checked off all her boyfriends – was he the kind of person you could trust? Although she'd already trusted him enough to share some of her heartfelt pain.

'I work in the offices,' she says, annoyed that her voice sounds so stiff with uncertainty. 'Personnel or Accounts, depending on which is the busiest. I'm a kind of Girl Friday, so I get all the crap jobs,' she laughs.

'You must be good at everything.'

She steals a look at him, but he is just being nice and not the slightest bit teasing. 'They say I'm a self-starter, a go-getter … that kind of thing. So you see, I'm not really an emotional wreck. Sometimes …' she pauses, smiling, wanting to show herself in a positive light without bragging, 'sometimes they fight over who needs me the most.'

'Hey, good for you. What's your name?'

'It's Ali – short for Alison.'

'Hi, Ali,' he says, 'I'm Max.'

'Max,' she echoes, liking the definite sound of his name.

When they both stand up she realises she barely comes up to his shoulder. There is something so whole and reassuring, so protective, as well as sexy and attractive about him that she wants to melt into that chest and she feels her face flame.

Later, she has a Friday-evening drink with Linda before they go to see *Pretty Woman* at the cinema. She doesn't tell Linda about Max. But in the cinema, while Linda stares at Richard Gere, Ali thinks of the way Max gazed at her steadily as he said goodbye, and she wonders, with hot embarrassment and snagged breath, what it would be like with him on a piano, or in the bath.

The following week, Linda has the great idea of going to watch the next World Cup match in a pub.

'Are you for real?' Ali snorts. 'That's boring.'

'We're missing it all,' Linda says. 'The night Ireland drew with England the whole pub was hugging and kissing each other. So my brother said. What better place to find a man,' she continues. 'If we put on a green jersey we'll look like sexy Irish goddesses to any hot-blooded football fan.'

'Maybe I'm not looking.'

'Have you something to tell me?'

'Nope.'

'Well come on then, Thursday night it is. Ireland are playing Holland, and it's a ticket affair in the pub. I'll buy the T-shirts.'

'I'm not going to wear it.'

But she does.

By the time Ireland play Holland, Ireland's third match in the tournament, all of Ireland has become consumed with the energy and uplift of World Cup fever. It is the summer when the long, grey eighties are finally over, when Sinead O'Connor has just made waves with 'Nothing Compares to You', when U2 are putting Ireland on the map, and, thanks to the Irish football team, the country is in party mode. Streets, towns and villages are awash with tricolours and bunting. Thornton's have run out of every single item of World Cup merchandise. Even the street hawkers can't keep up with the demand for T-shirts.

The pub is a noisy, chanting sea of green. Ali can't get over the way she is swept up in the electric atmosphere. There is pandemonium when Ireland go one-nil down in the first half. And in the middle of it all, through the forest of waving tricolours, she sees him. And he sees her.

Max.

When Niall Quinn sends the equaliser into the back of the Dutch net, the whole pub erupts in a frenzy of people grabbing each other, friend and foe, hugging and kissing and dancing on the tables. In spite of the stifling heat of the pub, Ali feels a shiver when she sees Max heading towards her with determination, his broad shoulders cutting easily through the jumping crowd. Without saying a word, he picks her up lightly in his arms and twirls her around. Then he takes his World Cup scarf from around his neck and winds it around her waist, before tying it around his hips, securing them together, and then he kisses her.

Four days later, they watch the next match together. Ali ties green ribbons in her hair and paints a tiny shamrock on her face. The joy and excitement of the penalty shootout cascades around them, and he hoists her up onto his shoulders when the final penalty is scored. Afterwards, they walk up O'Connell Street hand in hand, laughing and giddy at the carnival atmosphere, listening to a cacophony of honking car horns, out-of-tune choruses of Jack's Army, and laughing at revellers jumping into the Anna Livia fountain.

Their next date is a quiet meal in an Italian restaurant on Dame Street. She finds out that Max is almost three years older than her and he moved to Dublin from Galway at the beginning of the year in search of work when his job in Galway folded.

'Sisters? Brothers?' she asks.

'One brother. He's in Australia.'

'Since when?'

'Since the end of January. Finn hot-footed it out of Galway soon after me.'

'Hot-footed?'

'Figure of speech,' Max says, immediately. Then, 'Although—'

'Although?'

He doesn't meet her eyes. He fiddles with the black pepper grinder and says, 'We had a … difference of opinion. Sort of.'

'I see.' She doesn't see, but she's not going to pry. 'Do you miss him? Or miss Galway?'

'I did, in the beginning. Home was heaven compared to a single, cramped bedsitter in a noisy building, even if some of the other tenants are my fellow county men. But—' he takes her hand in his. 'I don't miss anything about Galway anymore.'

It is the summer when Ali falls in love with Max, when the city-centre streets as well as their future glitter with heady promise, excitement and hope. A summer when Max picks her up easily into his arms and whirls her around, and tells her that with her blue eyes, pink cheeks and pale blonde curls, she reminds him of a good fairy on top of a Christmas tree. She soaks up his kindness, funny jokes and friendship, and she feels warmed by the way his eyes always light up when they meet after work.

Before long, he is her best friend and she trusts him enough to bring him back to the top-floor flat in Larkin House, where she'd lived all her life, and they begin to do some very nice things in Ali's bed, as well as the bath and other places. He holds her tight and whispers words of love to her and Ali feels she has crawled out of a long, dark tunnel into bright, glittering sunshine.

Three

Monday night

In south County Dublin, in a small, exclusive estate of four-bed detached houses, Jo Kennedy's pale fingers tightened the sash on her silk dressing gown and slid along the top of the mahogany banister rail as she stole down the dimly lit stairs, her slippers making no sound on the thick carpet.

She stopped outside the ground floor den, where a light was still burning. She pushed open the door, but instead of venturing in, she leaned on the jamb. She'd been hoping to find her husband sitting at his desk, engrossed in his laptop, but instead he was slumped back on the squashy sofa, oblivious to her presence. His shoes were off, and his long, jean-clad legs were propped upon the sofa. He had one arm behind his head, and he was watching a programme on the wall-mounted television screen, the remote control and an empty bottle of beer on a low table beside him.

'Are you coming to bed?'

Finn jumped at the sound of her voice and, sitting up, grabbed the remote control, changing the channel as he pointed it at the screen. 'Jesus, Jo. What are you doing creeping round like that?' His dark grey eyes looked at her accusingly.

'I don't want to disturb Grace, she needs her sleep,' Jo said quietly, feeling her face flush as everything tightened inside her. 'What's so great that you can't come to bed?' she asked. And why are you hiding it from me?, she wanted to add, but the words stuck to her tongue.

'You wouldn't like it,' he said. 'Too much blood and guts.'

She stared at the television screen, which was now tuned to a music channel, where half-naked female bodies gyrated suggestively around a small, luridly lit stage and she wondered how that was supposed to be less offensive than blood and guts. She suspected that Finn had been watching reruns of *Reprisal*. For years he'd played the dangerous, rakish character of Larry Boland, the lead role in the long-running, weekly aired Irish crime drama series until his contract had recently been terminated. Or until he'd been axed, which was the more painful way the popular press would put it as soon as word leaked out, something she knew he was dreading. 'In that case,' she said lightly, 'I definitely wouldn't like it. Will you be much longer?'

'Why?'

'I've left on your bedside lamp, and it's easier to sleep when you're with me,' she said, making it sound as though she needed him in bed instead of admitting that, in recent weeks, he'd been so keyed up she could only relax properly when he was sleeping. 'And I've a busy day tomorrow,' she went on.

'Yes, remind me, why don't you?' he said, belligerence in his tone. 'It'll be all very important, I'm sure.'

'Not half as important as you being around for Grace,' she said, injecting as much positivity into her voice as she could. 'Look, Finn, it's just as well one of us is at home while she gets back to herself and recovers. Glandular fever is no joke, and Grace needs one of us to keep an eye on her.'

He remained silent. His eyes were shuttered as they looked at her and she didn't know what he was thinking. Was his dejection because he'd lost his job going to sour everything between them?

'How are you getting on with your book?' she asked.

She silently cursed herself when he looked at her with his eyebrows raised as though she'd asked him if he still believed in Santa Claus. 'Oh yes, my book,' he said in a self-deprecating tone. 'Did I say I was halfway through the first draft? I wonder if I could clinch a six-figure advance on the strength of fifty thousand words. What do you think?'

'What do I think?' she was surprised. He was playing with her. 'I'm not sure how these things work,' she said, struggling to hold on to her patience. 'Although I guess it would take time,' she went on, trying to be realistic. 'I mean, it's not as if you can suddenly decide to paint a masterpiece and it happens instantaneously.'

Finn laughed, shook his head. 'I love your sense of humour, Jo, I always have. But' – he stared at her directly – 'you'd want to make sure if doesn't get you into trouble some day. Masterpiece! You're setting the bar rather high. But I like a challenge.'

He threw her a resentful glance, and Jo felt stung.

Even though Jo had a decent job as a Creative Executive with Dunne and Conway, a leading Irish event management company, moving into this plush home several years earlier, at the height of the Irish property boom, to suit Finn's new status in the lead role of *Reprisal*, meant they had a considerable mortgage to service.

When he'd talked of trying his hand at writing a mystery novel for young adults, she'd been silently delighted that he had found a sense of purpose, now that he had acres of time to fill. She'd encouraged him as much as she could, telling him to channel his imagination along with his empathy.

'My empathy?' he'd laughed.

'You feel things. Deeply,' she'd said. 'I know how sensitive you are beneath your—'

'Beneath my what?'

'Crusty layer,' she'd laughed. 'Get that sensitivity onto paper, somehow.' It would be far better, and more therapeutic, she'd thought at the time, than having him moping around. There could be little worse than coping with a six-foot-two husband doing his best imitation of a darkly brooding Heathcliff.

At first, Finn had been enthusiastic. He'd set up a corner of the den as his office, got a new laptop, ordered a rake of books on the various techniques of fiction writing, and she'd encouraged him to join a few online support groups.

Then three weeks ago, Grace, their eleven-year-old daughter, had fallen ill with glandular fever, right at the time Jo was working extra hours in the run-up to a busy Health and Beauty Fair for one of Dunne and Conway's major clients. While she'd been grateful that Finn had been around to spoil Grace a little and do the necessary ferrying to doctor's appointments, somewhere in the middle of it all his low spirits had taken a downward plunge and his initial enthusiasm for the book had stuttered to a halt.

He didn't talk about it. That was partly the problem. But she knew things had caved in on him because he was spending a lot of time staring into space, his brooding manner invading the house like a thick cloud.

She could only imagine how difficult he was finding it – to have gone from being a well-paid actor, commanding the lead role in the popular series, and all the trappings that went with it, to an out-of-work actor moping about the house, waiting for the phone to ring or an email to arrive. No wonder he looked as though his pride was in tatters.

Jo stepped further into the room and perched on the arm of the sofa. 'Look, love, we can only take everything one day at a time, and it's just as well you're home at the moment, to be here for Grace. That takes priority. It's a huge load off my mind.' She looked at the dark circles under his eyes that told of his lack of sleep, and her stomach contracted with anxiety. 'I know it's not easy for you, for us, right now, but it won't always be like this.'

'What's your problem?'

'I know you're unhappy,' she said softly. 'You can talk to me.'

'I've nothing to talk about.'

There was silence.

'As soon as I can get some time off, we'll have a break away, a long weekend perhaps, in Paris or Rome,' she said, sounding as cheerful as she could.

'And that'll solve everything,' he said, staring at her levelly, searching her face as though he was trying and failing to come to grips with something.

Over the years, he'd looked to her for a lifeline of sorts. At the start of his career, when his insecurities in the precarious world of acting had got the better of him and he'd needed her encouragement in the face of stiff competition and occasional rejections, she'd been more than happy to give him her unstinting support, bolster him up with love and kisses. But tonight, he looked so defeated that she didn't think she could rescue him.

'We have the movie premiere on Wednesday night,' she said brightly.

He stayed silent so she went on, 'We are going, aren't we? You never know who you might connect with.'

'Yeah, sure, I might be able to pitch for a movie deal before my novel is even published.'

Jo couldn't take much more of his negativity, so she turned away. 'I'm off to bed.'

'By the way,' his voice followed her, 'I've asked Max and Ali over for a meal on Saturday night.'

She stopped, her hand on the door. 'You've *what*?' She turned to look at him. He was standing up now, with his arms tucked into the pockets of his grey tracksuit top, a smile on his face.

'Don't look so shocked,' he said. 'He is my brother and we don't see enough of each other. It's not right. Even at Christmas we were just thrown in with a bunch of friends and neighbours for drinks and nibbles.'

'That was our choice,' she said levelly. 'We could have gone out for a meal with them but you cried off. And you didn't want to return the invitation, if I remember.'

She shouldn't be talking to Finn like this given his current frame of mind. Not when she knew he had hardly seen Max at Christmas because he couldn't bear to be reminded of his brother's successful career while his cherished dreams seemed to have come to a stuttering halt. They were scarcely bosom pals, anything but, so it was surprising that Finn wanted to see Max now, when his mood was at an all-time low.

The smile was gone from his face and she couldn't gauge what he was thinking behind his dark look. 'That's why I thought of asking them over on Saturday night,' he said. 'Family is important, isn't it, Jo? I'll cook.'

'Good,' she said. 'That's fine then.'

'I'll be up soon,' he said.

'Okay.'

On her way back up to bed, Jo passed a wedding photo. The two of them, laughing carelessly, entwined against the backdrop of sparkling waves curling across a beach in Sydney. She was wearing a jaunty red straw hat and jewelled flip-flops and was extending her ring finger with the modest silver wedding band to the camera. Finn's deep suntan was set off by his white jeans and shirt, and his white, smiling teeth. His messy, dark hair was riffled in the breeze.

Had they really been like that? The day had been a perfect capsule in time. Carefree, madly in love, Jo just twenty-two years of age to Finn's twenty-seven, both of them looking like the world was theirs for the taking.

The twenty years of their married life had hit a couple of speed bumps, and the early years had been challenging. They might be going through a rough patch now, but they were still together. And that was the main thing, Jo thought, walking into their spacious bedroom. Surely there was some way they could rekindle the spark of that newly married Jo and Finn? It had to be there, somewhere, if she could only peel away the tangled layers that life and living had superimposed on that happy, carefree couple.

Australia, 1991

Jo is living in Australia – in Sydney – when she meets Finn, four months after her twenty-first birthday.

Her friend Mollie insists on bringing her to the Irish bar that night, promising that she'd love the guys who have started to play there on Saturday evenings.

'I can't think of anything worse on a Saturday night than a mad Irish bar in Coogee,' Jo complains. At five feet ten, she has to stoop a little to see her face in the mirror. She pulls her dark, shoulder-length hair into a scrunchie so that it emphasises her high cheekbones. Then she sweeps a kohl pencil around her hazel eyes and glowers at her slightly sunburned face, the legacy of her pale Irish skin.

'Yes, I know it'll be a bit of a scrum, but you'll like these – I promise.'

'I'm trying to stay away from all things Irish,' Jo says, waving her mascara wand. 'I'm here to experience the full-on Australian adventure.'

Mollie throws her a curious grin. 'Yeah, and is that why you've settled for a job at the checkout till in BestBuys?'

'It pays the rent, doesn't it?' Jo quips immediately. 'And it's so busy that the day flies by. Besides, I've new talents. I'm a dab hand at separating the chilled dairy from the meat and veg.' She turns up the dial of the Sydney radio station so that Bryan Adams and 'Everything I Do' flows out across the room. It helps to drown out the memory of her mother's gasp down the phone line when Jo's conscience eventually caved in and she called her to let her know she was still alive and told her where she was working. But it doesn't help to ease the tight soreness in Jo's heart.

'I guess this is the genuine-enough adventure,' Mollie says, glancing around the tiny bedroom they share in the basic flat, which boasts a two-ringed cooker, paint flaking off the shower cubicle ceiling and no air conditioning to speak off on these warm Australian nights.

Jo finds herself unable to reply for a minute. If she hadn't arrived home early from college that January afternoon, she'd still be living in the big house in County Meath, enjoying the privileged life of a third-year college student. She feels a sudden wave of longing for the fresh greenness of the spring countryside, the sight of the lambs in the field adjacent to their rolling back lawns, the luxurious comfort of her bedroom with a view of the gently undulating hills, her father's greeting in the hallway when he comes in from his surgery ...

She turned her back on it all the afternoon that privileged life had imploded around her, running away as far as Australia. She had moved in to share Mollie's flat to help mop up her tears when Mollie's boyfriend had moved. It is a handy arrangement. Mollie is from Scotland, and providing a shoulder for her to cry on also helps Jo to take her mind off all things Irish. They work together on adjacent checkout tills in a supermarket on the outskirts of Sydney, a job that suits Jo insofar as it is a total turnaround for her and a very satisfying rejection of her mother's expectations. A mother who, Jo feels, has no right to see any of her ambitious expectations for Jo fulfilled. Not now.

Jo blinks and takes a sharp breath. She stares at the poster of Sting on the wall to blot out other pictures that are threatening to crowd in.

'Tell me more about this fabulous band,' she says to Mollie.

'I have my eye on the lead singer,' Mollie says, spraying far too much cheap perfume. 'He's a proper ride, Jo. Absolutely gorgeous. And he's the first guy I've had hot thoughts about since …' her voice wobbles.

'Well done, Mollie, that's a fantastic step forward,' Jo says, half-afraid Mollie might start to cry again, but glad of the diversion. She rattles back the curtain that runs across the front of their wardrobe rail and riffles through her meagre selection of clothes. 'I'll come along for the laugh, but you owe me, big time,' Jo says, stepping out of her grey tracksuit bottoms and wiggling into her jeans and white sleeveless top.

The bar in Coogee is exactly the type of place she usually avoids. Run down, unimaginative, yet packed to capacity with a cross-section of the transient, multicultural population that hangs out and parties in Bondi and Coogee. *God knows what they see in this place*, she thinks, with the limp Irish flag idling against the wall, the fake leprechauns on the shelves behind the counter, and the black and white sketches of famous Irish rebels adorning the alcove.

'You must have got those for nothing,' she says to the bar guy, jerking her head in the direction of the sketches as she waits for two beers. He has to be Irish. He has that brooding Celtic look about him. It's in his dark-grey eyes and thick lashes. He is tall and well-built with unruly, dark hair that needs a trim.

'Like hell we did,' he says, throwing her a baleful glance. 'They're originals and came all the way from ye old original sod. Cost a fortune in postage and packing.' He has a slight accent, but she can't quite place it. Not Donegal or Cork anyhow. She'd holidayed in both counties as a child, and she has a sudden memory of diving off rocks into cold, clear water while her older sisters pranced on the sand and collected pretty sea shells.

To her annoyance, a peculiar homesickness washes over her. She takes a sip of her drink and scowls moodily.

'Cheer up, why don't you,' he says, lifting a tray of hot, steaming glasses from the dishwasher with the utmost ease.

Her glance drifts to his strong forearms, dusted with a fine pattern of dark hairs. Her eyes flick back to his face. 'The next thing I hate after fake Irish pubs are pseudo-smart guys who tell me to cheer up.'

'Christ, I was only trying to help a fellow countryman. But that's not a chip on your shoulder, that's a cannonball.' He begins to take out the glasses, piling them on the shelves, effectively ignoring her. Slightly miffed, she turns and saunters back to the table where Mollie is sitting. She puts down the beers and pulls out her chair.

'Whoever that barman is,' she says, putting her elbows on the table and resting her chin in her hands, 'he has attitude problems.'

Mollie cranes her neck. 'He's new. I haven't seen him here before. But whatever you said, he's staring at you, Jo. Wow. I wouldn't mind some hunk staring at me like that.'

'Like what?'

'Hmmm, kind of sexily—'

'Shut up, Mollie. He can stare all he likes, I don't give a toss. And you're going to the bar from now on.'

Jo feels an uncomfortable prickle settle between her shoulder blades. And something else that startles her. A minuscule spark of interest.

No way. She's quite happy drifting along the surface of life, spending her day pushing groceries along a belt, where an Australian voice across the supermarket tannoy is refreshingly different, and coming home to a shoe box of a flat in the evenings, where Mollie opens the beer and spills out her latest romantic disaster. It's all very undemanding and effortless. She doesn't have the energy for any complications like this guy with his dark-grey eyes and dismissive attitude – something she'd never encountered before. Then again, back in Ireland she'd been unmoved by most of the guys she met at university, finding them dull and boring and far too ready to fall at her feet.

❖

The band is surprisingly good. Despite her misgivings, Jo finds herself enjoying the buzzy atmosphere, her consciousness heightened by the thought of a pair of sexy eyes glancing in her direction. She sees him crossing the floor a couple of times towards the staff quarters, skirting around the tables with a restless, loose-limbed grace that reminds her of a supple panther. And when the lead singer picks up his guitar and sings a rendition of Neil Young's 'Heart of Gold', a poignant version that defies the raggedness of his voice, Jo feels something soft easing the tight ribbons around her heart.

Feeling vulnerable against the swell of emotion in her chest, Jo closes her eyes for the final few bars of the song, and when she opens them, she is startled. The barman has come out from behind his counter again. This time he is standing nearby, leaning back against the wooden panelling of the wall, ostensibly to get a better view of the singer, but she knows from the way his gaze suddenly shifts that he's been watching her.

The following Saturday night, Jo is carefully nonchalant when Mollie suggests another trip to the bar.

'I know there's absolutely no hope for me,' Mollie says, adjusting her cleavage so that there is more of it on view at the neckline of her sparkly top. 'I can't compete with the gorgeous-looking girls who were throwing themselves at the band. But I can dream, can't I? No harm in having fantasies, is there?'

'Absolutely not,' Jo says in an encouraging tone of voice, taking a little more care with her eye makeup, and loosening her dark hair so that it flows around her shoulders. There is something to be said for having fantasies. Especially if they take your mind off other stuff you don't want to think about. Like the way nobody except her knows what her holier-than-thou mother had really been up to.

❀

'I thought you hated fake Irish pubs,' he says.

'I do.'

'You must be a glutton for punishment,' he says, pushing two bottles of beer across the bar.

'I've been very bold, you see,' Jo says, her cocky tone of voice covering her surprise at finding herself flirting with this guy.

'Bold?'

'Of the mortal sin kind.' She lifts her chin and meets his gaze head on without elaborating. In the stifling, conventional world of the Harper family it is a mortal sin to crash out of college, and almost sacrilegious to leave home on the morning of your lavish twenty-first birthday party and end up halfway around the world.

'Does that mean you have to do lots of penance? Could we be seeing you in here every Saturday night?'

'What's it to you?' she shrugs.

His dark-grey eyes slowly scan her face. 'I want to make sure I'm not around when that cannonball of yours gets fired off.'

'Prick,' she says under her breath, but she knows by the glint in his eye that he's made out what she's said from reading her lips and to her annoyance, he seems to find it amusing.

'You can get the next drinks,' she says to Mollie when she marches across to their table and sits down with her back to him, the space between her shoulder blades tingling.

'Not again?' Mollie asks, looking across to the bar. 'Hey, is there something going on here?'

'No, why?'

Mollie smiles. 'He's staring at you as though he wants to drag you off to his lair. What did he say to you?'

'Enough to convince me that he's a right prick.'

'Gosh. He must have made a big impression on you.'

'Yeah. The wrong kind,' Jo huffs.

'Still, it's the first time I've seen any guy faze you.'

'I'm not in the least bit fazed,' Jo says mutinously, sitting up straight and squaring her shoulders.

Once again, the bar gets busy, the atmosphere cranking up, the crowd gathering. Then the band comes on and for over an hour they lift the roof with their music so that everyone forgets the crush and the long queue for the drinks. And once again when the lead singer takes over the piano and sings another Neil Young song, Jo finds her heart strings being tugged, and she tells herself it is a mixture of too much booze and the atmosphere and nothing whatsoever to do with the barman, whose eyes she has felt like a laser on her all night long.

When Jo pulls on her jacket at the end of the night, she can't help sneaking a glance in his direction, but he's busy stacking glasses deftly and efficiently, and she shuffles through the departing crowd alongside Mollie without looking back.

Then Mollie meets Sam.

'I hope you don't mind, Jo, he's asked me out next Saturday night.'

'Why should I mind?'

'In case you wanted to go to the bar in Coogee?'

'Nah. Some of the storeroom girls are going to the new nightclub in The Rocks, so I might tag along with them.'

She tags along with the storeroom girls that week, and again the following week, wondering if she's been missed from the bar in Coogee.

The next week, on her day off from the till at the supermarket, she goes for an early-morning walk on Bondi. A sky the colour of duck-egg blue stretches away to infinity, and the glittering sea ripples off to the never-ending horizon, making her think that she, too, could be limitless in some ways. She thinks of the rigid constraints that seeped like undercurrents through the house in County Meath and she takes a deep breath.

He falls into step beside her and she jumps.

'Hey, I didn't mean to startle you.'

She puts her hand up to shade her eyes and keep back her dark blowy hair from her face. 'Didn't you?' she glares at him. 'Where did you come from?'

'I was out for a run,' he says, sounding a little breathless, as though he'd been in a hurry. 'I thought I recognised you.'

She realises that he has hurried to catch up with her. It makes her feel awkward. Away from the bar, he is even more vital. Tall, well built and with a restless kind of energy about him that, much to her irritation, she finds attractive. Even though it is the end of autumn in Sydney it still reaches twenty degrees by day, and he is wearing a khaki-green T-shirt with a Che Guevara logo stretched across his muscular chest and matching shorts. Jo looks away hastily when she finds herself examining him and thinks of Mollie's saucy remarks about being dragged off to his lair. Her eyes flick back to his face and she realises from his amused grin that he knows she was checking him out.

'Shouldn't you be in work, pulling a pint or something?' she says, a little haughtily, annoyed to find herself conscious of her drab grey sweatpants and T-shirt.

'The pub's not open yet,' he says easily, not the least bit bothered by her tone of voice.

'Then shouldn't you be washing glasses or floors or checking the stock?'

He laughs. It has a nice, rich sound. 'I wouldn't like to have you for a boss. What kind of a slave driver are you? Don't I deserve some time off?' His eyes narrow a little as he gazes at her, as though he's trying to figure her out. 'Anyway, what about you?'

'What about me?' she asks defensively.

'How come you're skiving off today?'

'I'm not skiving. I'm on a day off.'

'From where?'

'BestBuys.'

'*Best*Buys?' He looks nonplussed.

'I'm a whizz at the checkout.'

'A whizz. At the checkout.' He shakes his head.

'What's wrong with that?'

'Nothing. I just thought ...'

'Yeah, go on.' She looks at him, head to one side, eyebrows raised expectantly.

He gives a half-laugh. 'I didn't quite figure you for a brain surgeon, but I thought you might work in fashion, or modelling, something like that …' His voice trails away as she looks at him, stupefied, and he makes an embarrassed kind of face.

'That's the corniest, crappiest chat-up line I've ever heard,' she says disparagingly. 'I thought you could do better than that.'

'Hey,' he says, looking mildly insulted, 'I didn't think this was a chat up. If I wanted to chat you up, you'd know all about it.'

Something hot passes across her face at the look in his eyes. She is glad of the fresh breeze flowing in off the sea. 'Would I now?'

'I hope so.' He extends his hand. 'Let's start all over again.'

She steps back from him. 'I liked where we were before.'

'Where was that?'

'You were being a bit of a prick and I had a cannonball on my shoulder.'

He stuffs his hands in his pockets and kicks at some pebbles on the beach. His mouth curves in a wry grin. 'You don't think much of me, do you?'

She shrugs and stares out beyond the glittering sea to the hazy horizon. It's not that she doesn't think much of him. She just doesn't want to think. She wants to float through her days. She doesn't want the challenge that she senses this strong-limbed Irish guy with the sexy grey eyes and alert kind of energy could pose to her carefully boxed-off feelings.

'I think the least you can do is give me a chance to prove your, um, fantastic opinion of me,' he dares, his eyes laughing.

'It could mean firing off that cannonball you said I had on my shoulder and you don't want to be around when that happens.'

'Jeez, I thought I was the only messed-up Irish ex-pat around here,' he says.

'Messed up? I beg your pardon.' She lifts her chin as if to deny the way his words resonate with her. No one could be more messed up than her.

'It might have been a bit of craic to see if we could have a cup of coffee without trading insults, but I know when I'm not wanted.' He strides away with a rueful smile which, coupled with his parting comment, connects with her, makes her hesitate and catch her breath.

'Hey, wait.'

He turns back to her, his eyes squinting in the sun. His solid limbs are a pale, golden brown in the light. He's waiting for her to say something but she doesn't want to mess this up.

'I don't know your name,' she says lamely.

'I'm Finn,' he says. 'And you?'

'Jo.'

She feels on the brink of something risky and exciting when he smiles a slow smile and strolls back to her with that panther-like grace. 'Hi, Jo.'

Four

Tuesday morning

Ali was still awake long into the early hours of Tuesday morning, the bed empty without Max.

With its high, wide bed and antique brass headboard, lots of plump pillows, a thick, fluffy duvet, and a comfy patchwork throw that had been a wedding present and with them all their married lives, Ali liked to think of their bedroom as their special place. It overlooked Dublin's Grand Canal, close to the Charlemont Luas stop, and it had a bay window with a small sofa facing out onto the canal where they could relax and sip coffee or wine, depending on the time of day, and watch proud swans glide by majestically, their feathers starkly white against the rippled surface of the canal.

She could still recall the day she and Max viewed the 'needs-tender-loving-care-but full-of-potential' thirties townhouse, when they were house-hunting for their young family. They had begun their married life in the flat in Larkin House, moving on to a starter home in Harold's Cross six months later, but now with both Tom and Jessica needing more space, it was time to move again.

Max had traced the word 'SOLD' in big letters on the dusty floorboards. Then he lifted Ali and whirled her around in his arms and her laughter echoed around the empty space as he said this top-floor room would be their piece of heaven.

Tonight the cream and gold curtains were pulled across the bay window against the dark night, but despite the cosiness of the room, Ali found sleep elusive.

When she'd arrived home from work, she'd searched the house, and the garage, for the notebooks. Even the garden shed had been gone through, a peculiar low-level anxiety filtering through her veins as she slid a torch around shrouded garden furniture, lawnmowers and hedge cutters. There was no sign of them. His lifetime's work was missing, including the details of his award-winning recipes.

Neither Tom nor Jessica had seen them.

Ali had an arrangement with Linda, her old friend from Thornton's who lived nearby and was married with three sons, to keep an eye on Tom for the couple of hours between school ending and Ali getting home from Booth Street. This evening he'd arrived home later than she had, because of football practice, bursting into the house full of a youthful vigour that Ali silently rejoiced in. It was supposed to be a clear night tonight, he'd said, so after dinner and his homework, he'd gone to his room, busy with his telescope trying to pick out the stars of the Virgo constellation.

At eleven years old, Tom was at that uncomplicated stage in life. He wanted to be an astronaut when he grew up and Ali told him to follow his dream but work hard for it. He filled the house with noise and movement, with his chatter about the night-time sky, the Milky Way, the activity of Venus and Jupiter in the early-evening sky. Ali wished she could stall time for a while, so that he could stay like this for a little longer. Max had texted to say he was going out for a meal with some Belgian pastry chefs. He already had a few ideas for cake and muffins he couldn't wait to try out. She wasn't to worry about his notebooks – he was full sure she'd put them safely somewhere.

She knew she hadn't.

Oh, and he'd texted Finn to say they'd be there on Saturday night.

Saturday night. Ali thumped her pillow and turned in bed. She liked nothing better than to put her feet up on the sofa and chill with Max over a bottle of wine and a boxset. Now she'd have to glam up and make conversation and chit-chat with Finn and Jo and she never felt completely at ease with either of them. Jo never let her hair down or had a glass of wine too many, the way Ali occasionally did with Linda.

Then Jessica had texted to say she'd be late, as she'd been delayed studying and didn't need dinner. Her daughter hadn't arrived home until after ten o'clock, declaring herself bushed after a marathon studying session and she was going straight to bed.

'You're a little pale, love,' Ali had said, stalling her in the hallway, registering the pallor of her face. 'Is everything all right?'

'Why shouldn't it be?' Jessica was on the defensive immediately.

'I hope you're not overdoing the studying,' Ali had said, keeping her tone friendly and supportive. There had been something fragile about her daughter's slumped shoulders that made her careful not to rub her up the wrong way.

'There's no need to fuss, Mum. I'm fine.'

She hadn't looked fine. At almost eighteen, Jessica was on the cusp of womanhood. She had Max's height and his eyes, only Jessica's were a deeper, cornflower blue. She had inherited Ali's pale blonde hair, but on Jessica it swung like a silky sheet beyond her shoulders. Normally she glowed with the beautiful bloom of youth and an aura of confidence instilled by both her parents. She imbued the house with laughter and positivity, seeming to possess the same cheerful sense of humour that Ali's mother had been blessed with, along with Max's even-tempered outlook. Tonight her lovely face was strained, her stance dejected, as though the pressure of cramming for her exams was getting to her.

'Don't forget,' Ali had said, her voice deliberately calm and soothing, 'you're more precious to me and Dad than any exam.'

Jessica darted her a glance and looked as though she was about to cry. 'Thanks, Mum, that makes me feel worse instead of better.'

'I'm just trying to help,' Ali had said futilely.

'You can help by giving me some space,' Jessica had said, plodding up the stairs.

Ali had wanted to sweep her into her arms and hug her tight. Instead she had said breezily, 'Sure if that's what you want.' And had stepped back from the banister.

Jessica had given her a half smile that looked forced, as though she was merely turning it on for her mum's benefit. 'Sorry, I don't mean to have a go at you, and I'm not having a meltdown, I'm just whacked and I need my sleep.'

'Is that all?' Vague ideas had run riot through Ali's head. You heard so much about cyber-bullying these days, it spread its tentacles into the best homes, so much so that parents needed to be on their guard. And at Jessica's age, as well as exam pressure there was surely pressure to be sexually active. Her mind had jumped to Kian, Jessica's university-student boyfriend. 'Far Too Keen', Max called him behind his back, but then no one would ever be good enough for his precious Jessica.

'How's Kian?' she had asked. They hadn't seen him for a couple of weeks because Jessica had been studying in his house. A whizz at maths, he'd been happy to help Jessica out with extra tuition.

'He's fine, Mum,' Jessica had said, sounding bored.

'You didn't happen to see any of your dad's bakery notebooks anywhere, did you?'

'No, why?' Jessica had asked, pausing on the stairs. Her face, as she stared down at Ali, was pinched.

'They seem to be missing from the bakery, all of them.'

'What do you mean, missing?'

'Just that. I can't find his notebooks. They're not in the office cabinet where he usually keeps them.'

'That's very weird,' she'd said as she'd hurried up the stairs, carrying her school bag.

The sooner the exams were over, the better. Ali was walking a fine line between being supportive without being intrusive, trying to make sure Jessica knew she was loved unconditionally without fussing over her too much. Sometimes it was hard to get the balance right.

It was different when Ali had been growing up. She turned in bed yet again and sighed as she thought back. Life had been simpler then, more straightforward, Ali and her mum more like sisters, coping together and supporting each other in the noisy community of life in Larkin Gardens. Ali didn't have quite the same closeness with her own daughter that she'd enjoyed with her mother, even though they sometimes went shopping or to girly movies. Jessica and her three or four close schoolmates led more independent lives, they took it for granted that they would all go to university and had far more confidence and assurance of their place in the world than she'd had at that age.

It was hard to believe she'd only been a little older than Jessica when she'd met Max.

❁

Ali woke later than normal on Tuesday morning, so that she had to rush in order to shower and dress and grab coffee. She had no time for a decent conversation with Tom or Jessica, who both left for their city-centre schools shortly before eight. Tom had just gone, his bike rattling on the gravel outside, when Jessica hurried up the hall, her long blonde hair spilling out from the woollen scarf around her neck, her shoulder bag bulging, her face, Ali noted, already tense.

'I might be late home,' she said.

'Again?' Ali said. 'Oh, Jessica, do you really need more late-night studying?' The words slipped out of her mouth, despite her determination to stay calm around her exam-stressed daughter.

Jessica frowned and rolled her beautiful blue eyes up to heaven. 'I thought we agreed no fuss, Mum.'

'Just so long as you're not overdoing it.'

Ali's words were wasted as Jessica was already a receding blur through the glass of the hall door. It was almost nine o'clock before Ali put on the house alarm, locked the hall door and walked into Booth Street. In the fresh, sunny morning, the missing notebooks seemed less sinister, and during her twenty-minute walk into work, Ali counted her blessings.

When they'd first looked at the ground-floor premises on Booth Street, ten years earlier, the Celtic Tiger had been alive and well but the location had been slightly unglamorous compared to the bling of Grafton Street.

'It's a Dublin 2 address,' Ali had said to Max, hoping her excitement would transfer itself to him and dissolve some of his doubts. 'It's only a stone's throw from Grafton Street. Some of the glitz might just rub off on us.'

He ran his fingers through his thick, dark hair so that it stood up awkwardly. 'Not sure if I want glitz.'

She reached up and tossed his hair further, looking at it with a grin on her face. 'You will if it means customers spending money, securing our children's future.' When the economy started to contract, the glitz had soon faded a little. Nonetheless, when the first-floor premises over the bakery became vacant, right in the middle of the recession, Ali insisted the opportunity of expansion was too good to miss. Business had been slowly picking up in Dublin city centre and the bakery was bang in the middle of one of the hottest new spots in town – the colourful labyrinth of interlinked streets, south of Dame Street, which was becoming known as the Creative Quarter of Dublin.

Ali crossed through the paved streets and turned into Booth Street, grateful that the decision to expand had been the right one, and with hard work was starting to pay off. The morning walk had lightened her heart, and as she stepped into the bakery she told herself there was no reason for her niggly fears that their lives might come crashing down around them.

❁

At Tuesday lunchtime, when Ali was out on the floor helping to clear the tables, a thirty-something woman swept into the bakery and marched purposefully up to the counter. Ali watched as she threw a dazzling smile at Emma.

'Hi there, I'm here for my one-to-one bakery session with Max.'

Emma stared at her, puzzled. 'Sorry, what exactly do you mean?'

'I'm Audrey McMahon,' the woman said. 'I'm booked in with Max for one-thirty.'

Ali blinked. Audrey McMahon was tall, expensively dressed and regal in her bearing. Confidence and control oozed from her perfectly coiffed blonde hair to her killer heels.

'I'm afraid there must be some mistake,' Ali said, moving across to the counter.

Audrey cocked her head to one side and smiled indulgently at Ali as though Ali was slightly thick. 'I'm Audrey McMahon. I won the competition on Facebook,' she said, speaking slowly as though for Ali's benefit. 'I'm looking forward to some individual tuition from the great Max himself. I badly need to up my game in the baking stakes. Is it true Max stands behind you and puts his hands over yours to best show you how to knead the dough? Like the pottery wheel scene in *Ghost*?' She rolled her eyes appreciatively.

A stab of confusion sliced through Ali's chest. She hadn't a clue what Audrey McMahon meant. She laughed nervously.

'I beg your pardon. Do you find it funny?' Audrey asked, her gaze sharpening.

'There must be some mistake,' Ali said, striving for composure. 'Max doesn't hold one-to-one sessions with clients.'

'You're the one who's mistaken,' Audrey smiled sweetly, while her eyes swept disparagingly over Ali. 'It was on Facebook. Last night. A competition for an hour-long individual tuition with Max on whatever area of baking I'd like. Tarts, scones, pastry, breads ...'

Ali forced a smile. 'There's been a little misunderstanding here, I'm afraid.'

By now customers were becoming aware of the altercation, exactly the kind of thing Ali wanted to avoid. Heads were turning in their direction.

'There can't be,' Audrey insisted imperiously. 'I arranged for time off work at the last minute, and at great inconvenience to my staff. Where is Max?'

'Please let me explain, Ms McMahon.' Ali tried to breathe slowly. 'Max doesn't do individual tuition. There was no competition on Facebook.'

Two angry spots came and went in Audrey McMahon's cheeks. 'I want to see the manager.'

'I *am* the manager,' Ali said, without identifying herself as Max's wife.

Audrey McMahon's eyes flicked over her with derision.

Ali wasn't too surprised at her reaction, although it rankled a little. Five feet nothing in her stocking feet, with an open, honest face and the minimum of makeup, Ali had none of the sleek, authoritative assurance that Audrey possessed right down to her toenails.

'For a manager of this establishment, I'm surprised that you can't seem to grasp the essentials.'

Sensing the commotion, Debbie came out of the kitchen and threw Ali a questioning glance. Ali shook her head, as though to say she could handle this.

'I wouldn't mind, but I got a confirmation call this morning,' Audrey said.

'Who called you?' Ali said, hiding her surprise.

'Some woman. I presumed it was the bakery.'

'Perhaps we can discuss this somewhere a little more suitable?' Ali began. 'If I could bring you upstairs to—'

'No, thank you,' Audrey bristled. 'There's nothing to discuss. I don't intend leaving this counter until I get full satisfaction. Where is Max anyway?'

Her narrowed eyes scanned the bakery. 'If the session goes well, he's supposed to be filming it for his television show.'

'What?' Ali couldn't help her surprise.

'You heard me,' Audrey said. 'What are you going to do about it?'

By now the whole bakery was listening intently, all other conversations had frozen. Debbie was standing in the doorway of the kitchen, looking as though she was ready to jump to Ali's defence if necessary. The last thing Ali wanted to do was to involve more people. 'Max isn't here. He's over in London at a convention,' she said smoothly. 'Neither have we been running any competitions recently. The best I can do—'

Audrey raged. 'I entered that competition in good faith. How dare you treat me like this!'

Ali was lost for words. Something hard thudded into her stomach. Max would never have gone off on his own bat to run any kind of competition. *Just like he'd never have taken his notebooks out of the cabinet in her office.*

'Look, Ms McMahon — Audrey — there seems to have been a mix up. If there's anything we can do to compensate your—'

'There certainly has been a mix-up,' Audrey snapped. 'Because you've grossly misunderstood me. I have a very important job in public relations. I have friends in high places and I'll make sure they know about the shabby way I've been treated by this ... hopelessly mismanaged establishment. By the time I'm finished, Max Kennedy's reputation will be in the gutter.'

With a toss of her long blonde hair and an exaggerated swirl of her camel-shaded coat, Audrey McMahon marched out of the bakery, leaving sparks of indignation in her wake, fizzing through the coffee-scented air.

Ali's legs were shaking as she went upstairs to the office and logged on to her laptop. Debbie followed her up, appearing in the doorway, her face creased with worry.

'Are you okay, Ali?' she asked. 'Can I get you a coffee or something?'

'No, I'm fine,' Ali said, bringing up their Facebook account.

'What was that all about?' Debbie asked.

'Search me. It wasn't very nice, whatever it was,' Ali said, feeling a little faint.

'No, it wasn't. She seemed very unpleasant.'

'I think that's rather an understatement.'

'One-to-one session with Max!' Debbie shook her head.

'Can you just imagine,' Ali said dryly.

'Strange,' Debbie said, going across to the window and staring out. 'She seemed very adamant. Still, some people will do anything for a bit of attention. Or a freebie of some kind.'

'I don't think she was just looking for attention,' Ali said, shivering as a funny kind of foreboding unsettled her. She checked the bakery's Facebook page, but it was exactly as it had been that morning, with a few additional likes and comments underneath Ali's post about their lunchtime specials. 'There's nothing on Facebook,' Ali said.

Unfortunately, as the afternoon wore on, it became clear that Booth Street Bakery had fallen victim to some kind of scam.

'This is a disaster,' Ai said, when the third customer had arrived in with the same story as Audrey McMahon.

'Isn't it?' Debbie said. 'They're all claiming they got a message yesterday evening confirming a free one-to-one session with Max and a chance to appear on television with him. They had to give mobile details and they were called with confirmations this morning. I asked the last customer, who was at least not totally unpleasant, to check her mobile, but the number had been withheld. At the time, she'd no reason to be suspicious.'

'Where are they all coming from? I don't understand this at all.'

'Is someone out to cause trouble?' Debbie asked. 'Could your Facebook page have been hacked last night?'

Ali felt a tremor running through her. 'Who would pull such a prank?'

'I'm probably way off the mark here, but if there was someone who's jealous of you and Max, a business rival?' Debbie asked, looking at her closely.

'A rival? Max? That's ridiculous,' Ali said.

'I dunno … look, Ali, it just seems strange,' Debbie said. 'One person might chance their arm, but three? And all spaced out by an hour. Whatever happened, it was planned. I'd even swear those women were also handpicked for their sheer bitchiness.'

Ali rubbed her temples. She felt like telling the super-efficient Debbie to shut up. Every word out of her mouth was reverberating inside her. Debbie might be queen of the kitchen in Max's absence, but Ali looked after the business end. 'If anyone else arrives in with the same story, call me,' she said, fervently hoping that no one would.

There were no more incidents before the bakery closed that evening, but Ali's scalp was tight with tension as she realised that each woman had had an unsettling effect throughout the bakery, the relaxed mood of the afternoon clearly spoiled for everyone. Even the staff didn't know what to make of it all and the sight of some of the floor staff breaking off their conversation as Ali swept down the stairs, or the counter staff glancing uneasily at her as she passed by, weighed on her heart.

Ali was never so glad to see the shutters going down on the front windows.

'What are you going to tell Max?' Emma asked, when she had finished cashing up and they were on their own in the bakery.

'Zilch until I see him,' Ali said. 'He'll be back late tonight and he's going to go mad when he hears.'

'You should contact the Facebook administrators and see if you can find out anything from them.'

'I'll leave that for another day. I don't even want to think about it. I just want to go home and put my feet up for a while.'

'Yes, you look a bit shaken. Will you be okay?'

'I'll be fine,' Ali said staunchly. 'Nothing a glass of vino can't sort out.'

'Did you come across Max's notebook?'

'No. I bet he found it buried somewhere in his bag,' she said, willing it to be true but knowing it was unlikely and that, furthermore, there was no easy answer as to where all the other notebooks might have vanished to.

Rivals? Enemies? She felt sick and decided to get a taxi home.

Five

Tuesday evening

'Are you up for the pub this evening? All the team?' Colin asked, stopping by her desk.

Jo sent her email before swinging around on her office chair and looking up at him. 'Sorry, not tonight. You do realise it's Tuesday?' she said good-humouredly.

'Ah, Jo, what happened to your party spirit?'

Her party spirit had temporarily disappeared because socialising without Finn while he was in this black mood was out of the question. Besides, she had other obligations.

'We need to celebrate,' Colin went on. 'It's Kaz's birthday. And the Health and Beauty Fair was a brilliant success, thanks to your original ideas.'

'It was teamwork,' she said, smiling at the admiration in the earnest twenty-something's face.

'Yes, and you held us all together with your enthusiasm while we were all flapping around in panic. The team can't go out without its innovative leader.'

'Flattery will get you nowhere. Tell you what,' Jo said, making up her mind on the spur of the moment, 'I meant to have a cheese and wine do to mark the success of the fair, but I'll give you a budget for a few drinks for the team instead.'

Colin grinned. 'Nice one. But what'll Dunne say to that?' he asked, referring to the company MD.

Jo shrugged. 'It's my budget. That I've been allocated. If he's a problem with that, tough. Just don't get too drunk.'

'No jäger bombs?'

Jo shook her head. 'I've called a team briefing tomorrow about the launch of a new perfume, and I want lots of fresh ideas.'

'What time?'

'Ten o'clock. On the dot.'

'I'll remind everyone to be in by then.'

At half past five, Jo texted Finn to remind him she'd be a little late, then she slipped on her black woollen coat, cashmere scarf and leather gloves, and took the lift down to the car park where her Audi was parked. She drove out of the south Dublin industrial estate, where Dunne and Conway had a large penthouse office unit, honking the car horn at the half a dozen members of her team heading off to the nearby village pub.

Fifteen minutes later, she pulled into the nursing home car park.

Jo stood in the shadowed porch, giving herself a minute to take a few deep breaths and make the transition from innovative leader to dutiful daughter. She straightened her shoulders, looked up at the arc of light that flooded out from the leaded glass over the door, and pressed the bell, hearing it peal out on the inside. Presently, the door was opened and someone peered out at Jo.

A new assistant. All the staff knew her by now.

'Jo Kennedy to see Mrs Harper?' she said.

The assistant moved back, pulling open the heavy door, and Jo stepped in, across the divide from one part of her life to another, the hallway with the oak parquetry flooring feeling stuffy and overheated after the chilly evening outside. The door thunked closed behind her and the assistant made sure it was securely locked before turning back to Jo.

'You've just missed her tea,' the assistant said, almost as a reproach, as though Jo had timed it on purpose. Jo's eyes flicked to her name badge – Kylie. The name, even before she examined her youthful face, told her that assistants were getting even younger.

'Did she have much to eat?' Jo asked, drawing off her leather gloves and tucking them into her bag. She flicked open the buttons on her coat and loosened her scarf around her neck. She was already in a sweat.

'Most of it. Eventually.'

Which meant someone had painstakingly sat with Veronica Harper, pushing titbits of scrambled egg into her mouth and making sure she took baby sips out of a pink plastic cup with a lid. Such a comedown for her elegant, exacting mother.

'That's great,' Jo said.

She went down the corridor where the oak-floored hallway gave way to a linoleum-covered floor, and Jo's high-heeled shoes made angry chirping sounds as they squeaked on the surface.

In the converted Victorian house, with the annex running along the back, there were two large day rooms for the patients, who sat in chairs grouped around the rooms, some in more advanced stages of dementia than others. To Jo, they all looked like trees in winter. They were there, a solid presence, alive to some form of existence, with stiff, twig-like limbs and gnarled necks, but denuded of their vital force.

Her mother was sitting in a high-backed armchair in the corner near the window that looked out onto a pretty courtyard. In the daytime, it was a pleasant view; now darkness had fallen and pools of garden lamplight illuminated the shrubbery and winter heathers. Veronica had a plaid rug across her lap and knees, and it covered the blue restraining strap that kept her tethered to the chair. She looked as though she hadn't moved since Jo had last called in. Jo bent down and kissed her cheek. She drew up a plastic visitor's chair and sat facing her. Her mother's white hair was like sparse whorls of cotton wool dotted about her scalp. Her face seemed tight, the skin stretched like parchment across fine bones. She lifted her mother's hands, cradling them in her own. The skin felt silky cool, and as soft as velvet.

'Hello, Mother,' Jo said.

Veronica Harper lifted faded blue eyes and they wavered across Jo's face as though she was drunk, her gaze eventually settling on a spot over her forehead. There was no light of recognition in her eyes.

'How are you today?' Jo persisted. 'It's me, Jo.'

Her mother's mouth trembled for a while, before she made an unintelligible sound.

'That's right, yes, it's me, Jo. I'm here to visit you.'

'She can't hear you.'

It took Jo a while to realise that the voice was coming from behind her. Another patient, an elderly woman, was standing behind Jo, supporting herself with a Zimmer frame.

'You're wasting your time,' she went on. 'She can't hear anything.'

'Thank you,' Jo said pleasantly. You don't know that for sure, Jo wanted to say. There's always the chance that she's picking up something. That somewhere in the muzzy depths of her mind, she can hear. That she knows it's me. And that possibility, however remote, was worth the difficult visit.

'You're the only one who comes and talks to her. I seen you here before,' the elderly woman went on. 'Lots of times.'

'Yes, that's right,' Jo said.

After a moment, the woman wandered off and Jo sat for a while, holding her mother's hand, talking quietly about her day, and about Grace and Finn.

Still no response. Her mother's eyes focused vacantly on Jo's chin. Jo had visited religiously since her mother's stroke two years earlier. It had happened around the time of Jo's fortieth birthday. Sometimes she wondered why she bothered. But now more than ever, she'd give anything for Veronica Harper to know she was there. She'd give anything to have a proper reconciliation with her mother and ease the strained relationship they'd had for many years. If her mother broke free from the chains around her mind just long enough to hear Jo and acknowledge her, even a nod or a smile, Jo would see it as a symbol to put the past to rest for once and for all – to get back to the light-hearted girl who had married Finn and reignite the carefree spark they had once shared.

She sat in silence for a while and then she left, feeling slightly guilty that she was able to walk out the door while so many others weren't.

When Jo was eventually released out into the porch, she stood trembling slightly. The cool evening air flowed over her face like silk. She thought of the time she'd met Finn on the beach, when they'd been younger and so much of life was ahead of them, brimming with choices and possibilities.

What would she change if she could go back to that place and time? Or would she change anything? Still, they'd weathered the ups and downs and they could have plenty of good years ahead. She felt a tremendous urge to seize the life they had, to make the best of it and do everything in her power to reconnect with the Jo and Finn who had joked and laughed and fallen in love. She got into her car and put the key into the ignition, but she didn't switch on the engine. Instead she sat in the car park of the nursing home, where brightly lit, uncurtained windows threw oblongs of light onto the shadowy front garden, and you could almost imagine the figures that moved back and forth inside were guests at a party.

And she could imagine she was back there again …

Australia, 1991

'So what are you doing in Australia, Jo?'

When he says her name, he makes it sound sexy and sensual all at once. *Joooh* ... She'd never thought that about herself. Sexy. Sensual. She keeps her face straight and sips her flat white coffee. From where they are sitting on the terrace, she watches the swirl of waves on the beach, sending up foamy spray as they hit the golden strand. The air is warm and redolent with salt, carrying in its drift the muffled roar of the sea and a lilting buzz of laughter and conversation.

She looks at Finn. 'I'm having a blast.'

He sits back in his seat, his grey eyes skimming her face. 'Yeah, right,' he says. 'Saturday nights in fake Irish bars and smart guys telling you to cheer up. Living it up to the max.'

He smiles as if to take any sting out of his words, yet she feels curiously exposed. She tosses her head. 'You left out my fabulous career in BestBuys.'

'Oh, yeah. Can't think of anything more exciting than sending toilet rolls flying down the checkout belt at the speed of light.'

She trails her finger around the rim of her mug. 'I kinda sensed you were going to be hard work.'

'Me? Hard work? In what way?'

She'd spoken without thinking and he looks intrigued, which is just what she doesn't want. The guys she hung around with back home were a pale walkover compared to this potent man with the perceptive eyes and she knows it's going to be hard work resisting the pull she feels towards him. 'You have a smart answer for everything, don't you?'

'Is that why you avoided me in the bar?'

'Did I?'

'Don't look so innocent. After you fixed me with your haughty stare you sent your mate up to get the beer and sat there with your back pointed at me.'

She relaxes into her chair and runs her fingers through her hair. 'Surely you were far too busy to be noticing me.'

'I was looking forward to enjoying more of your ...' he pauses and slants her a smile, 'Irish charm.'

'Another crappy chat-up line,' she sighs.

'Okay so I'm shite at that, but lately I haven't had much practice.'

She searches his face, his honesty surprising her, but his expression is guarded. After a beat she says, 'It shows.' It is her turn to smile, to take any sting out of the words.

'How long have you been in Australia?' he asks, changing the subject.

'Three months. And a month in London before that, so I'm four months out of Ireland.'

'And what part of the old sod are you from?'

'The rolling countryside of Meath.'

'Ah, the Royal county. That explains it.'

'Explains what?'

'The way you walk, as though you own the world. That's why I thought you were a model ... or something like that.'

'As opposed to a brain surgeon.'

'Yeah.'

She thinks about this for a minute. He is way off the mark. But now is not the time to admit that in due accordance with the Harper family tradition, she'd been a Trinity science student until four months ago. 'And where are you from?'

'Galway.'

'Hey, the city of the tribes,' she laughs. 'No surprises you're working in an Irish bar, very tribal.'

'It's not so bad. You meet all sorts. So how old are you? Or is that another shite question?'

'It is. And the answer is just as shite. I'm twenty-one and a bit.'

'So you legged it soon after your big twenty-first celebration.'

'No, I legged it just *before* my big twenty-first celebration.' As in, the morning of the party, but he doesn't need to know that technicality.

'Before? Weren't you looking forward to getting twenty-one kisses? Isn't that what they do at those parties?'

She makes a face. 'What do you take me for? I'd want to be very hard up to look forward to that.'

'Yeah, I'm sure you have hundreds of boyfriends.'

'Thousands.'

'So you won't be able to come to the party with me on Friday night.'

'What party?'

'It's my mate's party.'

She stays silent and, for a moment, there is a flicker of uncertainty in his eyes. 'I'm not trying to lure you off anywhere,' he says. 'He lives around the corner from the bar, you can bring your friend as well.'

'I can't. She has a new boyfriend.'

'So that's why I haven't seen you for a couple of weeks,' he says.

'Who says we would have dropped in to your bar anyway?' she asks in ridiculously exaggerated lofty tones.

He keeps his face perfectly straight as he watches her, yet his eyes smile with amusement.

Then they both burst out laughing.

'More coffee?' He lifts an eyebrow.

'If you're paying.'

'Or if you're not in a hurry, we could go for lunch, and I'd stand you a cold beer after that?'

'I'm not in a hurry. But you need to give me a good reason.'

He gives her a candid look and says, 'You're the first girl I've asked out in a long time.'

Once again, she is struck by his lack of pretence. She finds it refreshing and it warms him to her. 'Asked out?' she jokes. 'Do you think some lunch and a cold beer is a date?'

'It's a pre-date, a test run, to see if we could put up with each other long enough for a proper date. Like my mate's party.'

'Nah, not good enough.' She was enjoying this.

He grins. 'I like the colour of your eyes.'

'I'm sure you can do better than that.'

He looks away, then to her surprise he gazes at her. 'They remind me of the colour of the Irish sea.'

'How?' she challenges.

'Stormy, deep, glittery …'

'You got something right there – stormy.'

'I wasn't finished.'

'Oh?' There is something hypnotic in the way he looks at her and no matter how much she wants to resist him, she's powerless to stop a sudden squeeze in her chest.

'Stormy, deep, glittery, beautiful,' he says.

She sips her coffee too quickly and almost chokes.

'I think me and you would get along quite well,' he says. 'We seem to click.'

'Jeez, I will have to go for a beer with you, even if it's just to get rid of that mad idea,' she says. 'I've never clicked with anyone before in my life.'

She stretches her arms and feels heat on her skin and takes a deep breath; she is suddenly alive to this moment in time, alive to the possibilities that something new and rather startling is happening in the life of Jo Harper.

❀

Lunch was a casual, light-hearted affair, and they enjoyed a few beers afterwards.

But she isn't laughing on Friday night, wondering why she has agreed to an actual date with this guy. Much to Mollie's amusement, it has taken Jo ages to get ready; eventually she puts on her best jeans and a white cotton shirt. She leaves her hair loose around her shoulders and is careful with her makeup. She feels a few moments of panicky shyness when he meets her outside the pub in Coogee and brings her to his mate's apartment, where the party is in full swing. He introduces her around and leads her through the warm squash of people and thumping music, grabbing bottles of chilled beer in the kitchen. They find space between the end of the kitchen worktop and the open balcony door, and she is grateful for the cooling breeze on her flushed cheeks.

'So, Finn,' she says, raising her voice to be heard, 'what brought you to Australia?'

'The chance of working in an Irish bar where I get to meet someone like you.'

'You mean you like women with haughty eyes?'

He smiles and shakes his head. 'Ah, Jo, I saw through your bolshie act straight away.'

'Hey!' she frowns, a little uncomfortably.

'Shh, no worries,' he says. He lifts his head and glances around the room, searching for someone or something, then he looks at her, his eyes purposeful, and says, 'I asked my mate to play a request for us.' He puts his bottle of beer down on the counter top, takes hers out of her suddenly jelly-like fingers and puts it down beside his. The music changes and the opening riff of Neil Young's 'Heart of Gold' floats out across the crowded apartment just as Jo realises what's about to happen.

There is an awkward moment as he hesitates, his mouth close to hers. Then Finn begins to kiss her. It isn't any ordinary kiss though. It is the most slow, sensual kiss she's ever had. He holds her face in his hands as he starts to kiss her lightly, his lips slowly tracing the outline of her face before dropping to her mouth. His fingers thread in her hair as he deepens the kiss, shunting her into the corner with the movement of his hips and long legs until they are locked together, and Jo is clinging to him, eyes closed, kissing him back, all her senses on fire. Long after the final notes fade away, and REM's 'Losing My Religion' comes on, they are still clenched together.

Eventually they draw apart.

'Okay?' he asks, touching her chin.

'Nah, I'm not a bit okay,' she smiles shakily.

❁

'I'm not sure if we do click after all,' he says when he walks her home. 'I think we might need a few more dates.'

'So I still haven't convinced you?' Jo replies. 'I bet you won't bunk off work next week so we can go to a beach for the day,' she challenges. 'That should sort us out for once and for all.'

To her surprise, he grins. 'You're on.'

They both bunk off work the following week. Finn borrows his mate's ancient Renault and they spend the afternoon on a beach south of Sydney. Neither of them has brought swimming togs – Jo feels far too shy to prance around in front of him in her bikini – but they dare each other to run in and out of the waves fully clothed, seeing how far they will go, and they both end up doubled up with laughter and totally saturated and they have to run along the strand to dry off a little before they can get back into the car. Jo feels her heart hammering against her ribs, conscious of her damp T-shirt,

Finn's bronzed limbs and his messy wet hair, and his hand holding hers tightly as they run together by the water's edge.

It couldn't be further from the refined elegance of the house in County Meath and she wants to run on forever.

❁

'So what are your dreams, Jo? Your real dreams, no messing.'

It's later that week and they've had a meal and shared a bottle of wine in a north Sydney beach restaurant on Finn's night off. Darkness has fallen and Jo has pulled on her jacket against the cool of the evening. They sit on a bench along the seafront promenade, the dark sea murmuring in the background. Up closer, the waves are like black soup edged with frills as they break in a shushing noise against the sand. A chain of lights circles the promenade, dispelling the darkness, reminding Jo of cheerful lights at Christmas. Something loosens inside her, but although all her senses feel fluid, she shrinks away from talking about her dreams.

'You tell me yours first,' she says.

Finn sits forward, resting his elbows on his knees. 'Promise you won't laugh, but I want to be an actor.'

'I'm not laughing. But what are you doing pulling pints in a bar, or is it character research? I hope I haven't just been research,' she adds, turning to face him.

'No way. Jesus, Jo, anything but. I came out here to get away from … things. I wasn't expecting you to waltz into the bar with your flashing eyes.'

'What were you getting away from?'

'I made a mess of stuff back home. There was girl trouble … and I fell out with my brother.'

'You have a brother?'

'Yeah, Max. We don't always get on.' He shrugs. 'We never really have. He's popular, good at football, laid back, full of charm.'

'Are you saying you're unpopular, crap at football and totally horrid?'

Finn laughs. 'Umm, we're just different, like chalk and cheese. He's adopted. My mother knew after I was born that they couldn't have more kids, so they decided I needed a little brother. From the time we were old enough to understand, my parents made no secret of the fact that Max was adopted, but even that set us apart …'

'How come?'

'My birth nearly killed my mother.'

'That's not your fault.'

He continues as though she hasn't spoken. 'Whereas Max was found in a Moses basket. On Christmas Eve. Inside the door of the local church, right next the crib. All tucked up against the cold in a little blue bundle. He was two days old and his mother was never traced. She'd left a note in the basket asking her baby to forgive her, but she couldn't look after him and wanted him to go to a good home.'

She smiles. 'That would tug at anyone's heart strings.'

'Yeah, wouldn't it? I had just started school when he arrived on the scene, so I stupidly felt like I was being turfed out to make room for him. School wasn't great either …' He falls silent for so long that Jo is beginning to wonder what pictures he's seeing. Not good ones, she guesses, wondering what happened in school. He straightens up. 'Hey, it's only silly kids' stuff. Funny how it can stick with you. Max is such a bloody charming devil, he makes my parents laugh, always keeps them amused, whereas I …'

'You what?' she prompts softly, finding Finn's honesty totally disarming.

'Next to larger-than-life Max, sort of second best. There was always some kind of competitiveness between us. You'd never guess, but I'm a shy kind of bloke behind the smart-guy exterior,' he says, slanting her a look to see her reaction.

'You must be a brilliant actor so,' Jo says, a little humbled at being taken into his confidence and the way he has shared private feelings with her.

'That's one of the reasons I got the acting bug – I don't have to be just me, it frees me up to be someone else, anyone I want to be.'

'And that's your dream?'

'Yeah, but I messed it up. I might tell you about it sometime … I got the hell out of Ireland for a while, because of the crap, even though it meant giving up a place in drama school.'

She feels even more drawn to him by this admission. She too has left Ireland because of sudden turmoil in her life, even though it meant dropping out of university. But it's still too raw to speak of. 'Did it help, getting away?'

'It has now, because none of it matters anymore.'

'Why not?' she asks.

He lifts his head and looks at her. 'I've met you.'

'Me?' Something thuds into her chest.

'Yes, Jo, there's something about you that makes me feel calm, it's like you click with something inside me.' He curls an arm around her shoulder and kisses her thoroughly. She kisses him back, feeling inextricably linked to him on some level. She feels quietly amazed that she could have this effect on Finn and it, in turn, clicks with something inside her and makes her feel good about herself.

She'd known from the first time she'd seen him that this man with the sensual grey eyes had the power to get under her skin like no one else. She'd had a gut feeling he was going to complicate her life, a life she'd wanted to keep superficial and undemanding. All that falls away from her under the touch of his lips and the way he holds her close. Nothing matters to her either except this – and she lets herself melt into the curve of his arms, absorbing everything about him.

Six

Tuesday night

Max's flight home from Heathrow was delayed. By the time he arrived home, it was almost eleven o'clock and Jessica and Tom were in bed. Ali didn't realise how unsettled she'd been by the incidents in the bakery until she heard the welcome sound of a taxi drawing up outside and his key scraping in the front door. Then he was there, filling the doorway, striding through it. Heedless of her stocking feet on the cold tiles, she fell into his arms before he'd even taken off his coat, the scent of the night still clinging to it, the almost indefinable gloss of being somewhere removed from here, somewhere busy and exciting, clinging to him.

'Hey,' he said, sweeping her off her feet with his hug, 'this is good. I should go to London more often.'

'No, you shouldn't,' she said. 'I missed you.'

He kissed her forehead. 'Missed you too. My bed might have been in a posh hotel but it was awful lonely without you.'

They brought some wine upstairs to their bedroom on the second floor. They sat on the small sofa in the bay window looking out at the dark canal, the rippling surface illuminated here and there with long, shimmering reflections of street lights. Occasional traffic passed by, the noise hushed by the thick double glazing. Ali brought Max up to date on what had happened, the words coming out in a gush, but he gently dismissed her fears.

'Stop worrying, the notebooks have to be somewhere. I bet you ten euro I'll put my hands on them straight away.'

'You better have your money ready,' she said, tucking her feet up under her, leaning back against the cushions.

'They can't have taken a walk by themselves.'

'They have. Besides, you should have saved your stuff onto your laptop or iPad.'

'I'm not arsed with typing up years of notes.'

Ali sipped her wine. 'I'd like to know who was snooping around my office,' she said, voicing something that had been troubling her since Monday morning.

'Don't you keep it locked?'

'Only at night. It's unlocked during the day as I'm in and out so much. Anyone could have popped in, staff or customer. And it doesn't help,' she continued a little edgily, 'that you told the nation all the secrets of your success were tied up in a few old notebooks.'

'Did I?'

'That latest Sunday supplement article, a month ago. You were asked what was the first thing you'd rescue if the bakery went on fire, and why.'

Max shook his head. 'Don't fret, love. I'll find them. As for Facebook, more than likely a few friends had got together and were trying it on with the bakery,' he said. 'It was probably a scam they'd pulled on other businesses before. It happens all the time.'

'You don't think there's anything wrong?' she hesitated, afraid to voice her fears. 'Anyone out to get us?'

Max stared out at the canal, his feet stretched across the space in the bay window. He knocked back some wine and, without looking at her, said, 'Why would you think that?'

'It seems like a kind of vendetta,' Ali said. 'Even Debbie—'

'Debbie what?' He shot her a glance.

'She was asking if I knew of any rivals … or enemies … we might have.' Enemies? Booth Street Bakery? Her and Max? It sounded crazy.

Max laughed. 'Yeah, about half the bakeries and cafés in Dublin.' He reached out his hand and rubbed the back of her neck, gazing at her as though she was the best thing in the world. Then he pulled her close. 'Relax. Don't get spooked about this. I'll talk to Debbie tomorrow and tell her not to be winding you up.'

She dismissed the picture in her head of Max talking to Debbie about winding her up.

'And now for the good news, ta dah.' She watched his face as she told him of the TV5 details, but tonight not even Max seemed overenthusiastic about his glittering opportunity. He finished the last of his wine and said he would think about it tomorrow.

Afterwards in bed, he squeezed her in a tight hug that almost stopped her breath. She closed her eyes as his mouth found hers in a deep, purposeful kiss, his hands caressed her body, and he made slow and tender love to her, as though he couldn't get enough of her. The solidity of his body enfolded her with so much warmth that it softened the unease that had slithered through her veins.

'Love you,' he murmured sleepily, when he dropped a final kiss on her forehead and tucked the duvet around her shoulders.

'Love you back,' she whispered, feeling peaceful and restful for the first time since Monday morning. Whatever was wrong, they would sort it out together.

Seven

Wednesday morning

When Ali woke up the following morning, Max had already left for Booth Street. He and Debbie took it in turns to be in early enough to start the morning's bake, accept the deliveries and turn on the coffee machines. She lay in bed for a moment, thinking how flat and vacant the room seemed without his vital presence.

She was slightly soothed when she inhaled the familiar lemony scent of Max's aftershave lingering in their en-suite, and saw the towels hanging askew on the towel rail, much as he always left them. One of his socks was dangling off the edge of the laundry basket and the toothpaste was uncapped. Normal life had resumed.

Tom came into the kitchen just as she plucked a slice of toast from the toaster, her fingers stinging. She dropped it onto a plate and watched her son go straight to the fridge, her heart softening.

'Uh – whassup?' Tom asked defiantly as he wheeled around with the carton of orange juice in his hand and caught her watching him.

You, Ali wanted to say, and how absolutely gorgeous you are. 'Nothing,' she said.

'Where's Dad?' Tom asked, sloshing orange juice into a glass.

'He went into the bakery early this morning.'

Tom's face dropped. 'I wanted to tell him all about Virgo last night. You see, I just followed the line of the Big Dipper ...'

Ali listened to his chatter without really hearing it. Her heart swelled. Tom was a mixture of childhood need and stark, pre-teenage independence.

'You can talk to him this evening,' she said, hanging around the kitchen after she finished her toast and coffee, cleaning an already-clean counter, doing jobs that didn't need to be done just so she was there in case he needed anything else. After his breakfast, he left for school.

Ali went upstairs and knocked on Jessica's door, surprised her daughter wasn't already up.

'Hey, love – you're late.'

Jessica's voice was almost indistinct. 'I'm not going in today.'

'You're not?'

Ali pushed open the door and went in. Eight years ago, when they'd moved in to this house, Jessica's room had been decorated in all things pink and frilly, a room fit for a princess. By now the fluffy toys and Barbie dolls had long been banished to the attic. The spaces were taken up with clothes and makeup, bags, shoes, school books, and Jessica's laptop and television. The room was a mixture of adolescent student and young, worldly woman. Given Jessica's current touchiness, Ali suddenly felt like an intruder.

Jessica was still in bed, the room dim and shadowy.

'Hey, what's up, love?' Ali asked gently. 'Are you feeling okay?'

'Just a sore throat,' Jessica said in a choked voice. 'I'll be all right.'

Ali made a soothing noise. 'That's too bad. Can I get you anything? Paracetamol?'

'Yeah, thanks.'

❧

As her mother went down the stairs, Jessica turned around in bed and lay on her back, staring at the ceiling. A sore throat had been the first excuse she could think of. Handy enough, because it covered her husky voice and meant she wasn't expected to talk. The reality was, she'd spent half the night crying into her pillow and she hadn't the energy to get out of bed, let alone face her watchful mum and the classmates whose only concern was the exams. Lucky sods.

Mum hadn't a clue what was really wrong with her. Or Dad. Just as well. The last thing she wanted was to blow the family apart. So she let them think she was suffering from exam stress. Maybe she should make more of it. Pretend it was all getting her down in an effort to excuse her pale face and puffy eyes. It was the easiest way to explain her agitation and distress.

Up to three weeks earlier, everything had been perfect, or as near to perfect as could be. She'd revelled in being the beloved daughter of Max and Ali, and even if she sometimes shrugged off her mother's fussing – after all, she was almost eighteen – secretly it gave her a lift. Mum worked hard to help make Booth Street a success, and her dedication was an inspiration, but she was even more devoted to her family, dropping everything with a ready smile if they needed her. She'd no real hobbies or interests of her own, as her whole life and happiness revolved around her family and the bakery.

As for her dad, from the time she was small and he hoisted her easily on his shoulders, he had a warm light in his eyes that was especially reserved for her and her alone. It was a light that she had basked in, all those years from childhood to adulthood. Her big, strong dad had always made her feel so special, and she loved it when she popped into Booth Street unexpectedly and he showed her off proudly to staff and customers.

Oh, Dad! Jessica felt scalding tears slip down her face once more and she turned back into the pillow.

Even thinking of Tom made her cry. Now when their happy family life was under threat, he seemed like the best kind of kid brother you could wish for. He spent a lot of time glued to his telescope, and even if he did wreck her head with his chatter about the sun, moon and stars, at least he never snooped around her bedroom like some of her friends' kid brothers, and he had a kind of cheeky smile that was innocent and cute.

It was funny how you only appreciated the best things in life when you were in danger of losing them.

Jessica closed her eyes but it still ran through her head like a sickening film reel – the night three weeks earlier in a Ballsbridge hotel, and the moment she'd seen him in the foyer. That's when it all had started to go wrong and her privileged and happy life had started to crumble around her.

❀

Ali was glad to be able to do something practical for Jessica, even if it was just bringing her up a tray containing a glass of water and the paracetamol, tea and toast. She sat on the edge of Jessica's bed. A day relaxing in bed would do her daughter all the good in the world.

'It's nice to spoil you a little, even if it's just tea in bed,' she said, not sure where to draw the line between over-fussing and being a mother. It was unusual for Jessica to be in bed like this, and unusual for Ali to have quiet time with her, as Jessica seemed to have been caught up in her studies so much lately. 'If you need me any time today, just call. Or if I can bring you home anything from Booth Street, let me know.'

'Thanks, Mum, I'm just wrecked,' Jessica said in a croaky voice, her face half buried into the pillow.

'You're not too anxious about the mocks, are you?' Ali said, thinking it might be best to err on the side of being a mother.

'Well, er …' Jessica made a funny noise in her throat.

'Sorry I shouldn't be bugging you like this. You don't have to talk,' Ali said, feeling helpless. When the children had been younger, it had been so much easier, easier to cocoon them in love and tell them they were brilliant in their own right, knowing they would absorb the words like a sponge.

'If I fuss I can't help it because you're so important to me, Jessica, and to your dad,' Ali went on, grabbing the seldom-offered chance of a little pep talk with her daughter. She reached out and stroked Jessica's hair. 'It doesn't matter how you do in the exams, darling. Seriously, I mean it. All Dad and I want is for you to be happy with the choices and decisions you make, no matter what they are. You can talk to us about anything, anytime. We don't want to see you fretting, no matter what.'

'I know, Mum, thanks,' Jessica said. 'I'm a bit stressed because I want to do well and after I've done my PhD, I'll be travelling the world, and not getting married until I'm in my thirties. Does that sound okay?'

'Sounds great, but only if that's what you want.'

It sounds better than what I did, Ali thought as she went back downstairs. She'd married the first guy she'd slept with and had Jessica at twenty-four years of age. Motherhood altered you. You lost yourself for a few years. Your life was never just your own. Other people had claims on you and you had responsibilities towards them. Still, she wouldn't have it any other way. She loved them all to bits, Max, Jessica and Tom. Together they were her heart and soul.

Eight

Jo hesitated in the bedroom doorway, looking at her sleeping husband. Finn was lying on his back, his face pale, the duvet crumpled around him. He'd come to bed late, silently turning his back on her in such a deliberate way that she hadn't risked reaching out to give him a cuddle. Then he'd slept fitfully, disturbing her with his tossing and turning. She was tempted to kiss him awake, as she'd often done in the past, when he would usually respond by hauling her back into bed, making her laugh and giggle and catch her breath, sometimes making her late for work.

But given the black mood Finn was in, there was no chance of that happening this morning.

Jo went downstairs quietly so as not to disturb Grace, and let herself out the hall door into the chill of the morning. She reversed her car out of the drive and turned on the radio, heading for the M50 and the offices of Dunne and Conway. Traffic was already building up and, during the twenty minute drive, Jo tried to think about the morning ahead, but it was impossible. She was tired and irritable as she bought coffee in the ground-floor mini-market and took the lift up to the offices and her desk; even the high spirits of her team who were talking about the night before failed to make her smile.

At the ten o'clock meeting, she outlined the timescale for the perfume launch and the briefing supplied by the client, then she left her team in the meeting room, giving them until lunchtime to come up with a few ideas.

'Think outside the box,' she said. 'Nothing is too outlandish to run by me at this stage.'

'Aren't you going to give us some direction?' Kaz asked.

'No,' Jo said. 'I'm giving you all a chance to develop your own visionary skills, without any input from me.'

It was a cop-out because, this morning, she couldn't summon any of her usual enthusiastic guidance and she felt heavy-hearted as she went back to her desk. She missed Finn's love-making and being physically close to him. Throughout their married life, they'd enjoyed good sex. The intimacy and tenderness that they shared in bed had deepened and they both needed it. Up to recently, Finn had still called her his calming force as he cradled her after sex and it never failed to make her feel wonderful. He hadn't so much as touched her in nearly a month, brushing off her advances with a coldness that pained her. She thought back to the early days, when there had been nothing sweeter than those first few times in Finn's rickety bed in his Coogee flat, and they'd often made love until the dawn broke. Was there anything she could do to help bring the magic of those heady days alive again?

Australia, 1991

The first time they make love Finn plays Neil Young, a whole album. It's Sunday afternoon and, from outside, thin beams of sunshine flash through gaps in the light cotton curtains. Although there are far-off noises from the street below, they are in a world of their own.

Jo's heart knocks wildly as Finn eases off her clothes. She has no time to feel shy because he kisses the whole length of her body, from her forehead to her toes, as though every part of her is precious to him. She does the same to him, marvelling at the rock hard power of him. From the way he holds her and touches the curves of her body, she can tell he's had a lot more practice than she has. But none of that matters because when they finally fuse together, she's more than ready for him, and she catches her breath and clings to him as he teases her with slow, deep thrusts, tipping her into a long, beautiful climax. There is something so vulnerable about the way he loses himself in her body, stares into her eyes before he comes and afterwards thanks her so profusely that she feels touched to the core in a way she never has before.

'Calm. Peaceful. At ease,' he murmurs early one morning a couple of weeks later, after they've had their fill of each other. Outside, the hush of approaching dawn is broken only by the sound of birds.

'As in?'

'That's how you make me feel.'

'I can't say the same about you,' she says.

'Why not?'

'You make me feel …' she flips onto her stomach. 'Confused … muddled.'

'What?'

'I didn't expect to meet someone like you who'd get under my skin, someone who makes me feel I can be beautiful.'

'You *are* beautiful. I can't get enough of you.'

'See? That's what I mean. I feel muddled because I didn't expect to meet someone who'd … want me so much.'

'What's wrong with that?'

She shrugs and picks at a thread poking out of the side of her pillow. 'Thing is, I'm confused because I like it. I like the way you want me and need me. It makes me feel beautiful, strong and important.'

'Didn't you ever feel like that before?'

'Nah. I felt … awkward, spiky.' All her defences are down in the aftermath of their love-making and he senses it.

'When?' He turns on his side and pushes her hair back off her face. His eyes are tender.

'Sometimes, when I was growing up.'

'Why did you feel like that?'

She tells him then, about growing up in County Meath, in a house where it was all work and very little play, where her mother ruled the roost with an iron hand, very conscious of her position in the village as the doctor's wife, and very determined to keep up appearances and keep her daughters in check. Jo came along after a gap of five years. Her older sisters, Sasha and Diana, were sweet and biddable, golden-haired and pretty. Jo was the odd one out, dark-haired and plain, the wilful, adventurous child who dared to question everything.

'You are beautiful,' he says. 'Dark and sultry, like the night.'

She tucks that away inside her and tells him about parents who were so used to their docile, sweet-tempered daughters that they didn't know what hit them when she came along. Her older sisters were always top of their class, school prefects, whatever, whereas Jo was bored silly in school and, naturally, felt resentful at being compared unfavourably.

There was war when Jo was caught trying out a cigarette at fourteen, necking a beer at fifteen, and an even more bitter war ensued followed by silence for a week when at sixteen she started hanging around with the wrong crowd and allowed the wrong sort of boy to leave her home after a teenage disco. Even Jo was beginning to wonder if she could do anything right.

'Where was your dad in all this?' Finn asks.

She tells him of the kindly family doctor with the large practice who was always run off his feet. More sympathetic towards her, he had a long talk with her one day, after the wrong boy episode, about making the most of herself and her future.

'So for the sake of peace, I reformed. I knuckled down and did my best to be a model daughter and student,' Jo says. 'I even followed in my sisters' footsteps and got a place in college.'

'Was that what you wanted?'

'Studying science? Nah. I didn't know what I wanted to do with my life. I still don't.'

'How come you legged it before your twenty-first?'

'It wasn't really going to be *my* party. It was mostly arranged by my mother, to show off her newly reformed university daughter to all the important neighbours and family. In my mother's words, there were going to be *people* there,' she says.

'And you couldn't go through with it?'

'No, I couldn't.' She says it so glibly that he shoots her a look, but he stays silent. Just as well. She's not ready yet to talk about what really happened.

❀

A couple of months later, Finn asks Jo to move in with him.

'Move in?' she laughs. 'I hope you're not expecting me to cook and bottle wash.'

'No way. I just need lots of sex. With you. I'll do the cooking.'

'Hmm. I suppose it's worth a try.'

She's never lived with a man before – it's fun and strangely intimate, sharing the shopping, watching him cook, sharing nights together in his bed, getting to know his body with her lips and her fingertips, becoming familiar with the way they move together, watching his eyes darken with desire, and his face as he comes. Becoming familiar with being a couple so that it's not just her looking out for herself, but she has a man with sexy eyes to share the small intimacies of life with, a man with solid limbs who wants and needs her and holds her tight, a man who makes her laugh.

How could it not fill some of her needs? For the first time in her life, Jo feels she fits in somewhere. Ireland and home seem very far away, and she puts it all to the back of her mind, living for the moment with Finn.

They have six months together, working hard and playing hard, spending their free time making the most of everything Australia has to offer – day trips to the mountains and the valleys, a weekend soaking up the vastness of the Great Barrier Reef, a week exploring the primitive beauty of the rainforests, a balloon ride over the Hunter Valley on the cusp of dawn, and long walks together on endless Gold Coast beaches, when they talk about everything, including their hopes and dreams, and Jo agrees with Finn that she needs the kind of job that won't see her chained to a desk all the time. Or a checkout till.

Then they go tandem skydiving, sitting together in a small aircraft in jumpsuits and harness as it climbs to 14,000 feet, along with their instructors, Jo hiding her nerves as best she can amid the jokes and laughter. Finn jumps first, harnessed to the front of his instructor, and her heart thumps as she watches them plunge through the open doorway, then Jo follows, free-falling out into space, shocked at first at the velocity of air that clutches her face and robs her of breath, feeling a surge of adrenaline as the parachute opens and then she is floating above the earth and slowly, very slowly, moving down to a landscape crisscrossed with fields and trees and roads.

Then she sees it on the ground close to the drop zone, a long banner unfurled across the grass: 'Will You Marry Me?' By the time she lands, Finn is there, his harness already removed, and high from excitement and adrenaline, she runs into his arms.

'What's this?' she asks.

'What do you think?'

'I'm shocked, I'm speechless.'

'Did you find the jump exhilarating?'

'Wow, yes. It took my breath away. But all this … *Finn*?'

'I find you even more breathtaking, Jo. I love you and I want to marry you.'

'I love you too, you big romantic softie.' But *marry* him? Living from day to day, in the hot hiatus of Sydney, it was something she hadn't expected.

'Well?' he asks.

She looks into his grey eyes, at the light that is shining there, shining for her, and she says yes. Then she laughs for the sheer joy of it all.

Later that night, they go out for champagne.

'Thing is,' Jo says, picking her words carefully, 'I didn't plan on staying in Australia indefinitely. I always had the idea of going home, eventually.'

'You want to go home for a big white wedding and lots of bridesmaids? That's okay.'

'That's exactly what I don't want,' she says. 'I'm not into that kind of show-offy thing at all.'

'We could get married, here in Sydney … on a beach.'

'Hey, that sounds more like it.'

A whirlwind romance. A beach wedding. Exchanging love vows with Finn by a rippling sea, under a white-blue sky. Enjoyable and fun, and nothing like the smothering, protocol filled, extravagances her mother had foisted on her two sisters. Twice she'd stood, stiff and poky in a voluminous bridesmaid dress, conscious of her mother's critical eyes and the knowing eyes of relations and neighbours comparing her less favourably to her sisters.

There have been occasional letters home, and less frequent phone calls, her sisters furious at first at the way she ran out on her twenty-first birthday party and now just about on speaking terms with her, her parents puzzled and upset, and saying they hope she's happy in a doubtful tone of voice. She has never once explained why she ran. She knows she can never explain.

'There's nothing to stop us from going home,' Finn says. 'Us, together, married.'

'Would you be happy to go back?'

'If I was married to you, yes. I might even chase up that offer of a place I had at drama school.'

'I could go back to college, and do something I enjoy this time.'

The fresh, new possibilities of it all swirl inside her. Getting married to Finn. A fun wedding on their own terms. Returning to Dublin with a new identity, a new life. Mrs Finn Kennedy, secure in her new image, dark-haired and sultry like the night, eyes beautiful like the sea, warmed with his love; a million miles from the Jo Harper who'd run away from home when that stifling, conventional life had turned bitterly sour.

Finn loves her. He wants her. He needs her so much sometimes in bed at night he clings to her like a drowning man might cling to a raft. It makes her feel important and useful. Valuable. It is good to be needed so much, even more special to feel she is the centre of someone's life.

So in that sense she needs him too.

Her family are surprised, to say the least. They know about Finn, and that she's living with him in a cramped bedsit in Coogee. She chooses a call box on a neighbourhood corner in Sydney to break her news, where she can look out through the glass at the graceful arch of the bridge, visible in the distance. She doesn't want to picture her mother picking up the phone in the quiet hallway of their immaculate home, where not a speck of dust is visible to the naked eye and all the floors are smothered with the compulsory Navan carpet, so thick you don't hear even a footfall coming up the stairs …

'I'm not expecting any of you to come out,' Jo says on the phone. 'Finn and I want no fuss whatsoever.' *Finn and I.* She's part of a couple now. She's not awkward and alone any more. A married woman. It's like she has grown a new, glossy skin.

'Jo … it's all such a surprise,' her mother says, very slowly. 'I can't imagine it. You getting married. Are you sure about this?' A note of hesitation in her mother's voice.

'Of course I'm sure.' Jo's voice is hard. 'We love each other.'

'Well if this is what you want and it makes you happy …'

Jo can imagine the raised eyebrows and the sceptical look on her face. 'I'm very happy.'

'It's just—'

'Just what?' *Say you're sorry, say you know why I ran away, that you never meant it to happen.*

Her mother clears her throat, gives a silly little laugh that turns out like a squeal. 'Your father always thought he'd be walking you up the aisle of the local church.'

Her father. Her heart aches. He is the one person she regrets running away from, but it was better than having him see the expression on her face. *What you don't know can't hurt you.*

'I'm not getting married in a church,' she says, wondering how her mother will square that with the neighbours.

'So I gather. As I said, Jo, please yourself, whatever makes you happy …' Veronica Harper says, slowly and carefully, and now she sounds as though she's patronising her.

They send cards and a generous cheque. 'How do you fancy a nice honeymoon?' she says to Finn. 'We're not in a mad rush home, are we?'

She marries Finn on the beach on a gloriously sunny day when life itself is infused with the golden promise of the afternoon. She vows to love him all the days of her life.

The morning they leave Australia, she empties most of the contents out of their suitcases.

'What are you doing?' Finn asks.

'We're leaving our baggage behind – all of it, and we're starting afresh, you and me,' she says, feeling full of a new kind of purpose. Their life together is waiting in front of them, to be lived, a new start, a brand-new beginning for both of them.

'Hey, I like that.'

'I mean it, Finn,' she says, winding her arms around his neck. 'Whatever has happened, whatever has gone before in both our lives is over and done with. We're starting completely afresh. We can do this together and turn our lives around. So whatever we came out here to get away from, it's over.'

Nine

Max hadn't found his notebooks when Ali arrived in to work later that morning. Then at half past one, while Ali was grabbing a sandwich at her desk and making sense of a spreadsheet, Max came up to report that not one but three tables reserved for the prime lunchtime slot hadn't turned up.

'Emma called them, to see what the problem was. Turned out two of them hadn't booked a table in the first place, and the third number wasn't a valid number.'

Ali's head spun. 'Christ!'

'Emma's going through the rest of the bookings for today and calling the customers.'

'Now do you believe me that someone is playing games with you?'

His face was taut with unease. 'I'm beginning to think it's all too much of a coincidence.'

'Max, you haven't done anything to get anyone's back up, have you?'

'No, have you?'

'*Me?* I don't know how you can ask me that,' Ali said. 'Whatever – whoever it is, it's being directed at you.'

'The bakery is both of us, Ali,' he said steadily. 'Everyone knows that.'

Emma arrived in the doorway. 'It's not looking good, folks,' she said, her face clouded. 'Three tables reserved for afternoon tea were hoax reservations. When I called the contact numbers on the reservation, two of them said they'd never even heard of us.'

Ali looked at her, feeling as though she was in the grip of a very bad dream.

Max whistled. 'Sweet Jesus.'

'Do you want me to check tomorrow's bookings?'

'Yes, and Friday's please,' Max said. 'And see if we have any details on when those hoax bookings might have been phoned through,' he called after Emma.

'Who could have ... done all this?' Ali wondered.

'I don't know yet,' Max said, anger giving an edge to his voice.

He was rarely drawn to anger. It was a side of him she seldom saw. Good-natured and genial, Ali was the one who had enough fire for both of them.

'It could have been anyone,' Ali said. 'All they had to do was call and give a fake phone number. God, this feels like intimidation,' she went on, her head in a whirl. 'We might have to call in the police.'

'The police?' Max frowned. 'That's a bit much.'

'It might be unpleasant, but it has to be sorted,' Ali said gloomily. She couldn't begin to imagine the police in their lovely relaxing bakery, their very presence tainting the dream they'd worked so hard for. But someone had already soured their dream.

'We'll see how things go over the next couple of days,' Max said.

❀

In the middle of the afternoon, Ali was coming down the stairs when from the first floor, a customer let out a high-pitched scream. Next moment, the customer was rushing down the stairs, almost shoving Ali against the rail in her haste. Ali looked back up the stairs. The entire first-floor seating area was in uproar. Most of the customers were on their feet, hysterically scattering away from the tables and chairs.

'What's going on?' she called out. The tumult had spread downstairs. Customers had got to their feet and were looking around startled, others bumping into each other in their haste to get away.

'It's a mouse. There are *two* of them,' a woman cried as she rushed downstairs hot on the heels of the first lady.

'A *mouse*?' Ali felt blank at first. A mouse. Loose in the bakery. She didn't know whether to laugh or cry.

Max came out of the kitchen, his face grim. Something about his tense stance alarmed her, even more than the prospect of a mouse running around the bakery.

'Nooooo, there's another one!'

'*Oooooh*! Where?'

There were more cries from the first floor and Ali watched aghast as, in seconds, the space was cleared, with customers rushing for the door and spilling out onto the pavement.

'I know a number you can call,' Debbie said. She was white-faced. 'They offer a prompt response and come in unmarked vans.'

Max glared at her. 'Unmarked vans?' he fumed. 'Great idea, Debbie. Don't you realise the whole neighbourhood knows what's happened here? And if they don't, they soon will.'

It was the first time Ali had ever seen him angry with a member of staff, and Debbie of all people.

'What the hell's going on here?' he said, striding past her up the stairs, where he pulled back tables and chairs. Then he bent down, picked up something off the floor and ran back downstairs, holding them aloft. Two small brown balls of fur.

The few customers remaining on the ground floor made a dash for the door.

'Relax,' he roared. 'It's only a toy mouse.'

'How could it be *only* a toy mouse?' Ali didn't understand.

'See?' He held them out. Up close, it was clear they were toy mice, but they looked so life-like that it was easy to be fooled by them.

Ali let out her breath. 'Jesus, Max, what just happened?'

'I haven't a bloody clue.'

A small muscle flexed just above his jaw. He stared around the empty ground-floor and the circle of customers gathered outside, some of them throwing anxious looks back into the bakery, others laughing and chatting, obviously enjoying the diversion.

'I don't know who the hell is playing games with me,' he said, striding towards the door.

She followed him out to the sunshiny, breezy afternoon and her heart stilled as she watched him face a circle of disgruntled customers as well as the interested bystanders gathering about. Her heart stilled because there was something wrong with Max. She knew by his tense smile, the anxious glitter of eyes and the awkward way he held his body, as if unsure of himself. Something had got to him.

He turned his head and saw her, and just for an instant – so slight she might not have noticed only she'd been studying him – she saw a flash of fear in his face as he looked at her. A small, cold spot formed in the pit of her stomach. She could only remember Max looking like that once before – on the day she'd been rushed into theatre for an emergency section on Tom, when they'd had to prise his fingers from the trolley, his face white as she was pushed through the doors. She dug her nails into the palm of her hand and told herself she had to pretend she hadn't seen that look.

By degrees customers were coaxed back inside, and complimentary snacks were served as well as glasses of Prosecco. Naturally, as Ali discovered later, it was all over Facebook and Twitter, complete with photographs of hysterical customers and accompanied by a range of comments ranging from witty to downright mocking.

Not good.

At four o'clock, she checked the dairy and vegetable orders for the following day and she called them in, then soon after five, before she went home, she had coffee in her office with Max.

'What do you think is going on?' she asked him.

He stirred his coffee absently, and then he leaned back in his chair and stared at his cup as though it was the most fascinating thing in the world. 'I haven't the faintest idea,' he said.

She thought of the streak of fear she'd seen in his face and knew he wasn't telling the truth. She thought of everything that had happened that week and something tight lodged in her chest at the deliberate and hurtful mischievousness of it all. She got up from her desk and put her hand on his shoulder.

'Max?' she asked softly. She half-expected he might put up his hand to cover hers, but he didn't. He stayed perfectly still and stared out the window. 'Is someone trying to rattle you and damage our reputation?'

'For God's sake,' he said irritably. 'How should I know? I'm in the dark as much as you.'

'You'd tell me, wouldn't you, if there was something wrong? Someone with a grudge against you?'

'There's nothing wrong. It's just someone taking the piss and I'm sure it'll be sorted next week.'

'How are you going to sort it? Are you calling in the police?'

'I'll see.'

'You'll *see*?'

'Look, Ali, just leave it with me for now, will you?'

'I'd prefer to know if there's anything going on,' she said as she drew on her coat and snuggled into it, needing the warmth. 'Max, we've worked so hard for everything,' she went on. 'Sometimes I wonder if, between the kids and Booth Street, our lives are almost too good to be true. I want to hold all of us together, so that we're safe and well. I don't want … bad things to happen to us. My greatest fear,' she gave a self-deprecating laugh that sounded more like a sob, 'is that one day, everything we have might be taken away. And I couldn't bear that.'

'There's nothing going on,' he said. 'Someone is just having a joke at my expense. *Our* expense. Whoever it is will soon get fed up.'

He didn't sound sure of himself and that was what drew a fine needle of anxiety up through her stomach more than anything else.

Ten

Wednesday evening

Just as Jo walked up to the front door, Finn opened it. 'I thought you'd be home a little earlier this evening, seeing as we're going out,' he said.

Jo's gut clenched as she stepped across the threshold and out of the cold evening. She'd hoped he might be in a positive frame of mind for once, especially as they would be meeting some of his former colleagues that night. 'I know. Sorry,' she said. 'I got delayed at a meeting.'

The alarm in the house next door was going off, and she knew this would have irritated him. Just last week the same alarm had gone off for several hours, two days in a row, and in an unprecedented moment of anger, Finn had lifted his golf club and threatened to smash the windows if they didn't have the sensors adjusted.

'You could have texted me,' he said. 'You don't have much time to get ready.'

'I'll be quick,' she said. 'I can be all glammed up in less than half an hour.'

He checked his watch. 'I'll book a taxi for thirty minutes.' He was already dressed in his Armani black tux and ice-white shirt, and it was a perfect complement to his dark hair and grey eyes. He reminded her of the Finn she used to know, and so attractive that she caught her breath.

'Thanks. You look great,' she said.

He didn't acknowledge her compliment.

She took off her coat and moved through the hall, catching his masculine fragrance as she passed his taut figure, longing to throw herself into his arms. The television was on in the den, it was tuned to a quiz show and it was far too loud. He had the volume extra high to drown out the noise of the alarm.

'Did you eat?' she asked.

'I did, and so did Grace,' he said.

'Great.'

Thankfully he still enjoyed cooking, as he had in the early Coogee days – the day he didn't cook, she'd know there was something wrong. Up until recently, he put music on while he cooked, upbeat and cheerful, and often he and Grace would end up dancing around the kitchen, colliding and laughing, waving a plethora of kitchen utensils, each trying to be sillier than the other. Tonight, she walked into a sparkling clean kitchen. A silent kitchen. The tea towels were neatly folded and counter tops tidied. All the recyclable rubbish was cleared away.

'Thanks for this,' she said.

His glance flicked over her face, but his eyes were so cold that an icy prickle ran down her spine. What had happened to Finn? He looked so distant it was fearful. Had his sense of identity and purpose been completely defined by his career? Was he secretly terrified of meeting up with his fellow actors that evening? Still, he needed to be out there, showing his face. She felt like weeping and forced a smile. He would need her more than ever to help him come to terms with the way his career had ground to a halt. 'I appreciate what you're doing, it's great, honestly, Finn,' she went on. 'How's Grace today?'

Surely this was a safe topic? Grace was his special girl, the light of his life.

'She's fine. Anytime I saw her today she was messing about with her iPad. So she's almost back to normal. Too busy to talk to me.'

'Maybe it wasn't such a good idea to get one for her,' Jo said, wondering why she felt the urge to placate him. She could cope if he annoyed the hell out of her, she'd put up with it and understand his mood, but she didn't want him being annoyed around Grace.

'Probably not,' he agreed, 'but you were determined.'

She was so not going to be drawn into an argument. 'You know we wanted her to have the same as her friends,' she said calmly. 'We didn't want her feeling the odd one out.'

He stared at her. Then he turned on his heel and strode out of the kitchen. From next door, there was a sudden silence as the alarm was silenced.

Jo gripped the counter top, her fingers clenching painfully around the edge.

'Mum?'

She released her hold of the counter and wheeled around. Grace. Coming into the kitchen, hugging herself with her arms.

At eleven, Grace was so full of a childish beauty that it snagged Jo's heart. Her daughter had no idea how radiantly the bloom of youthful innocence hung around her like an aura, never mind the wonderful promise her life could be. Her hair was a dark auburn shade like her mother's but, unlike Jo's hair, which was a shoulder-length bob, Grace's hair rippled down to her waist. Her face held the rounded contours of childhood, and her flawless ivory skin was so dewy it was almost translucent. Her eyes were a sparkling hazel, the slight shadows underneath testament to her recent illness. Tonight they looked huge and they mirrored the apprehension that seemed to be an integral part of Jo's life at the moment. She was wearing blue jeans and a pale-grey hoodie, the sleeves of which extended beyond her long, slim fingers.

'Grace, darling! How are you feeling?'

'I'm fine,' she said. 'Why were you late?'

'I got delayed at a meeting.'

'Dad kept looking out the front window to see if you were on the way home. He seemed to be annoyed.'

'Don't worry about Dad, I'll sort him out. He just feels a little down at the moment, that's all.'

Grace went over to the press and took out a packet of biscuits, helping herself to one. 'I think he's fed up hanging around the house with me.'

'Darling, you mustn't think that. He's a little annoyed with himself right now, but he's happy to be around for you. His precious princess,' she smiled, using Finn's favourite term for his daughter.

Grace leaned against the counter. 'I don't feel like his princess the way he looks at me sometimes.'

'Grace, darling, your dad's bad mood has nothing to do with you and everything to do with him. He's a bit sore about his job, but he also knows it's just as well he's here at home at the moment.'

'Can I not look after myself?' she asked.

'Neither of us wants you to be on your own all day.'

'I'm eleven, not two.'

Two. There were times when Jo wished Grace was still two years old. Because then Jo had been able to sort out every single one of her little problems and kiss Grace better and tickle her soft tummy and tuck her securely up in bed at night. The older they got, the less power you had, and the less power to smooth their lives. Sometimes Jo was amazed to find herself repeating things to Grace that her mother had said to her when she was growing up, and her ability to appreciate a situation from a different reference point was sometimes often eye-opening.

Jo smiled. 'I know you're not going to get up to mischief, Grace. It's just nice to have some company when you're at home sick, and it sets my mind at rest that Dad is here to keep an eye out for you. That's all.'

'I wish – oh, Mum,' suddenly Grace looked fearful, 'I wish things were back to normal. Me better and Dad in work.'

'So do I, pet. And they will be, in time.' Jo spoke with far more conviction than she felt. 'You're okay with Karen coming in to keep an eye on you tonight?' Karen was her regular babysitter, a student living around the block.

Her mother, Maeve, was a registered childminder who had looked after Grace after school when Finn had been working.

'Karen's fun,' Grace said. 'We'll watch some telly. Can I go back to school next week?'

'Only if the doctor says it's okay,' Jo said.

'I hope she does. At least I'd be normal again.'

All of a sudden it sounded like a forerunner for teenage angst. Not yet, urged Jo silently. *Let me have another couple of years before we start down that bumpy road, especially if she's going to be half as challenging as I was.* Flashes of her own spiky, rebellious personality came back to haunt her. Only now, through the prism of maturity and motherhood, could she recognise the fragile ego that had hidden itself behind her bolshie attitude. The fragile ego that Finn had strengthened with his love.

'Grace …' Jo sighed, 'you can't let your dad's situation get in on you. None of us can. It's unfortunate, but it's not the sum total of our lives. A job is just a job. We have to live and laugh, and keep busy and stay positive.'

'I hope Dad cheers up before he does …'

'Does what?'

Grace looked at her beseechingly, as though she was hoping Jo knew what she meant without putting it into words. All the worries of the world were in her eleven-year-old eyes. Then she said, very quietly, 'Something silly.'

Jo caught Grace to her, annoyed that the atmosphere in the house had got to her, even more annoyed that, at eleven, she was having such anxious thoughts when she should just be thinking about her friends, her school and her swimming and ballet. Grace was shooting up. Which meant that Jo would soon no longer be able to tuck her safely into her chest, under her chin. 'He's not going to do anything silly,' she said, knowing that Grace had been deeply upset before Christmas about a girl in her class whose father had been unable to cope with the burden of his debt and had taken his own life. 'I'll make sure of it,' she said, crossing her fingers and silently sending up a fervent prayer.

She went upstairs to shower and dress; she had barely twenty minutes to get ready. Grace's dark idea that Finn might do 'something silly' made her feel nauseous. Despite his career disappointment, she couldn't understand how the laughing couple they had been on the beach had come to this. The early years of their marriage had been more of a challenge, with ups and downs, good times and bad times.

She'd stuck at an admin job in insurance while she went to college at night, this time studying marketing and advertising, thinking she might find it more of an outlet for her talents. Finn had worked in a bar at night and at weekends while he went to drama school during the day. So for some of those early years, they'd been like ships that passed in the night, living out of a small flat in Rathmines more for the convenience of it all than anything else.

But within five years of returning from Australia, things had started to run around for them: their marriage had settled down, and Finn was making a name for himself both on stage and on television, his initial trickle of work becoming a steady flow. Jo, delighted with her diploma in marketing, started her new career in a big advertising agency in Dublin.

Over the years, they'd both built on their successes, eventually moving from their flat to a house in the suburbs, celebrating each small step forward with adventure weekends away or romantic nights in a plush hotel, even once, Jo recalled fondly, taking a helicopter ride over Ireland to celebrate the millennium. But the highlight of their marriage been the arrival of baby Grace.

So precious to Jo that she would have given her life for this tiny baby.

So precious to Finn that he'd been absolutely terrified of her at first.

'Aren't you going to pick her up?' Jo had asked gently, when Grace's plaintive cry had come from the Perspex hospital cot that first afternoon. Summer sunshine was flooding in through the window of her room, and even though she was still shocked and exhausted after the long, arduous labour, her heart was overflowing with a deep, quiet joy.

'I'm afraid to,' Finn had said. 'In case I don't hold her right.'

Jo had smiled. 'She won't break. I'll show you. You held my hands all right this morning in the labour ward. I'd never have got through it without you by my side.'

He'd kissed her. 'Good. You were never more beautiful to me than you were then.'

Finn had caught his breath as Jo helped him ease the tiny baby into his arms. 'I can't believe she's mine, ours,' he'd said, staring down at the tiny crumpled face. 'She's so perfect, I don't deserve this. I don't deserve her.'

'Yes, of course you do,' she'd said. 'Hey, look, she's even opening her eyes for you.'

Finn had stared at his tiny daughter's unfocused gaze. 'I never thought it was possible to feel this happy.'

She'd leaned over so that their foreheads touched and they'd both looked down at their beautiful baby. 'Neither did I,' she'd said. 'This is our best adventure so far.'

When Grace was five, Finn was cast in *Reprisal*, and he said she was his lucky charm. As his fame grew, he decided they deserved a more desirable address and a new car every year. They got used to spending money, enjoying dining and wining, and holidays twice or three times a year. He'd thought his star was invincible, only it had come crashing down when he'd least expected it. Furthermore, with no sign of any work on the horizon for Finn, their lavish lifestyle would soon be a thing of the past. Jo's hand shook as she sprayed her perfume. Was it any wonder that Finn's black mood was deepening by the day? But not, dear God, deep enough for her to worry about Finn doing something silly.

Eleven

Max switched off the strands of twinkly lights looped up behind the counter area. They were Ali's idea to help brighten the gloom of the long, grey winter and dull days of spring. 'Why have them shining only for Christmas?' she'd said. There was no law that said they couldn't have them on right through until summer.

'I have all the pots and pans done, Max,' Daniel said. 'Will I start on the floors now?'

He jumped. The bakery was closed, Debbie and the staff had left at six o'clock. He'd forgotten Daniel was still here.

'Sure, Daniel, go ahead.'

'I love that picture of Galway,' Daniel said, staring up at the wide tableau of the Claddagh at sunset.

'Ali bought that for me,' Max said. 'But not everyone recognises where it is.'

'I've been to Galway lots of times,' Daniel said.

'Of course,' Max replied. 'Your mum's from there as well. I'd forgotten.'

'I don't think she's ever forgotten her roots,' Daniel said conversationally. 'She sent me over to spend lots of summers with my uncles and cousins. I loved those summers in Galway. I sometimes stayed with my granny too.'

'Mrs Dillon?' Max smiled. 'She used to make the best soda bread in Galway.'

'Yeah, she used to spoil me rotten,' Daniel said.

He was glad when Daniel went to fetch the mops and buckets. He wasn't in the humour for idle conversation tonight. He pretended to be busy checking the dry goods as Daniel swept and cleaned, waiting for him to finish up and leave, wanting to be on his own. Finally, the bakery was put to rights, and Max found himself lingering in the now quiet space, tidying already tidy tables, adjusting chairs and cushions, turning down the main lights so that the bakery was plunged into half-light.

Anything to delay going home, where Ali waited for him, and Tom and Jessica.

As he moved through the bakery, and up to Ali's office, he saw himself reflected in the mirror that hung on the wall above the staircase and he seized on this, as if to reassure himself that this was him, now. It helped to take him away from the image flickering in his mind's eye like a video on an endless repeat: Ali, and the way she'd looked at him earlier that day as she'd asked him if he had ever done anything to get anyone's back up.

Ali. He wouldn't be here now, running this business, making a name for himself, if it wasn't for her.

❁

'It's more than time you set up on your own, Max,' she'd said to him, as they lay together in bed one night. They were living in their first home in Harold's Cross, and Jessica was asleep in the cot beside them. Max had his arm angled around Ali's shoulders and his hand was sifting through her hair. She said, in that soft but firm voice that stole into all the crevices of his heart, 'You have the talent and skill, but most of all the personality.'

'Personality?'

'Yeah,' she said. 'You're an affectionate and friendly kind of person.'

'You make me sound like a puppy dog.'

'Nah. You're more like a big teddy bear. Protective of me and Jessica. Strong, but friendly. People warm to you and that's half the battle. They *like* you. And you're good.'

'But am I good enough?'

'Well you've already won about half a dozen awards. How much convincing do you need?'

'I love what I do, but I'm not sure I'd be able for the other half of that battle. The number crunching. The hiring and the firing. I don't have the mentality.'

She wiggled around in bed, disappearing under the duvet until she was lying on her stomach and then her head with its riot of fluffy hair popped up at his shoulder. 'No, you don't, and that's why people like you. You have great rapport. You're sympathetic. And kind. People would love working for you. But I could be your manager. I was half thinking …' her voice was softer than usual.

'Half thinking what?'

'If we have another baby, I could give up my job in Thornton's? And work for us? Taking care of the business end?' Her voice came out in a rush, as though her ideas were running ahead of her, but knowing Ali, she'd already thought it all through. 'Why should you be making a fortune for someone else,' she said, her voice gently persuasive, 'when we could make one together?'

'I'm not sure … I don't think you've any idea of the work involved, the long hours and crazy sacrifices, the stress of it all. You'd sometimes need to be a psychologist to keep both the staff and the customers happy. You know me, I'm all for a quiet, easy life.'

'You only get one chance at life, Max. Do you want it to be quiet and boring? Or have you the balls to grab it in both hands and make it exciting and fulfilling?'

'How come you're like this? So fearless. Where did you get it from?'

'I got it from my mum,' Ali said, her eyes soft. 'We had hard times when my da went off and left us. It's not something I like to talk about but it made us stronger. Mum always told me I could do anything I wanted, if I was determined enough and worked for it.'

'Sorry I never got to meet your mum,' he said.

'So am I,' Ali sounded wistful.

Now, years later, thanks to Ali's staunch commitment, sacrifices, her boundless energy and hard work, their business had flourished and thrived, and he was doing what he loved, and getting paid quite nicely, and here they were today, happy and successful.

Mostly.

'Have you ever done anything to get anyone's back up?' The words echoed in his head and Ali's face swam in his vision. Her perplexed yet totally trusting face, childlike in its absolute wide-eyed confidence, as though she didn't, for one moment, believe that he might have. Gotten someone's back up.

Max halted on the staircase, the bakery around him full of silence and secrets, and he stared at his face in the shadowy mirror, at his traitorous eyes, the image vanishing as he reached into the deep, dark part of himself and saw instead the silhouette of a woman against a New York City night-time skyline.

New York, 11 September 2001

She snatches her mouth away from his but stays in the circle of his arms. 'We shouldn't,' she says.

'I know,' he says, resting his forehead against hers. Despite the madness of this moment, he revels in the hot current radiating between them. It gives him heat, energy and, most of all, blessed, beautiful life. He has never been so glad to be alive, and it is intoxicating to hold her wonderful warmth in his arms.

'I mean it,' she whispers. 'This is insane. But I can't help it. We're here. We're okay.' She leans in closer to him, as if she needs to breathe in every inch of him.

'Tonight is … crazy …' he hesitates. He tightens his grip around her waist and even through her clothes she is hot to his touch. 'It's different … a time apart. Isn't it? And after today …'

He closes his eyes, freshly assaulted by the surreal horror of that day.

One minute he'd been glorying in the bright-blue sky of the perfect morning from his top-floor, mid-town Manhattan hotel room. He'd turned around to get his notes ready for the first day of the bakery demonstrations at the Irish Food Festival in the Rockefeller Center. When he'd turned back to the window, he'd been transfixed with horror at the sight of a towering pall of dark-grey smoke sullying the New York skyline.

He'd switched on the television, thinking there had been an accident, but the news reports told him otherwise. An ordinary morning had turned into something horrific. It had filled him with a mounting terror. He was lucky to be able to phone home – later most of the circuits were disconnected.

Then he'd gone looking for her. Out into streets covered in white dust, where the bright-blue sky had turned dark, with nothing but wailing sirens to break the surreal silence of dishevelled people moving as if in a horror movie. He'd walked, the air so thick with swirling dust that it was difficult to breathe, pungent with the smell of burning metal, and resonating with panic, disbelief and outrage.

They had joked, a month or so earlier, about being in New York at the same time, although their visits overlapped by just one day, and their hotels were blocks apart. That was as far as it had gone, a joke, a chance remark, neither of them expecting to see the other – but it had become imperative for him to make sure she was safe.

He'd reached her hotel and waited, unable to grip the width and scale of the atrocity. His head had pounded as time went by and there was no sign of her. In the hotel lobby, everyone had gathered around the television screen, trembling and crying as the full horror of it all had unfolded and, before his disbelieving eyes, as the second tower had collapsed. Something inside him had cried out at the loss of it all; life, love, mothers, fathers, sons and daughters.

Then she had walked through the lobby, her movements stiff, her dark clothes covered in white residue, her face numb. He'd stood up and called her name. She'd turned and stared at him as though she'd never seen him before, and she'd walked into his arms like an automaton, too stunned to cry. His heart had contracted when he'd caught the scent of burning in her hair.

She'd gripped his hands as they'd sat with others and watched the television, their knuckles white and fingers interlocked. More and more they had become enmeshed together in the day, clinging to each other like survivors after a shipwreck. He'd waited while she showered and changed and washed the dust and scent of burning out of her hair. They'd watched more television and, later that evening, had ventured into the restaurant but it was eerily quiet and no one was eating very much. She'd asked him to take her back to her hotel room and, looking at her haunted face, the pained distress in her beautiful eyes, how could he not?

A drink from the minibar had been followed by another. And then he hadn't been able to face trudging back through sad, sombre streets to the cold emptiness of his hotel room. Couldn't find it in himself, either, to leave her to face the nightmares she would surely have that night.

He shivers. He opens his eyes and brings himself back to the utter craziness of being in this woman's arms. The awful day is almost over but never to be forgotten, the sky is dark so they can't see the smoke. He sees the twinkle of intermittent lights, and he marvels that he could well believe nothing is wrong. As though nothing terrible has happened and close to three thousand people haven't been pulverised into microscopic dust in a morning when the sun shone with so much hope and optimism. The sheer fragility of life slams freshly into his head, leaving him in shocked awe at how swiftly and irrevocably the threads of human existence can snap. And in shock at how being in the wrong place at the wrong time can be lucky for some and horrendously unlucky for others.

Only for her taxi being delayed and getting caught in traffic, she would have been in the World Trade Center herself.

'Yes,' she whispers, 'tonight is different. I need you like I've never needed anyone before.'

Surely the night wasn't different enough to take this foolhardy risk? She stands very still, glowing with life and warmth. The few inches of space between them are humming with expectation. There is still time to call a halt, but even as this thought forms, it is too late. Her hand traces the side of his face, from his forehead to his chin. Her head is tilted, her mouth inches from his.

He dips his head and kisses her. Slowly this time, deeper, cradling her face softly and gently. She kisses him back as though she never wants to stop. His fingers brush against her skin as he slowly unpicks the buttons on her white silk shirt. He lifts the silver locket hanging around her neck, staring at it for long moments. He gently replaces it, his fingertips touching the swell of her breasts above her lacy bra and sending shock waves up along his arm. He presses his face to her skin, and she feels soft and warm and alive.

He never intended to cheat on Ali. She trusts him with her whole life. But here, now, it doesn't feel like cheating. He is adrift from reality. Neither of them has lived through a day like this before. At this moment, all that matters beyond the horror of the day is that they are alive and well.

'I need you too,' he murmurs, sliding his hand in under her shirt. 'You being here is the only thing that's holding me together. I need your warmth, your *alive*-ness. Does that make sense?'

'Perfect sense,' she says. Her beautiful eyes look at him imploringly and in that cry for help lies his downfall.

She reaches around the back of her neck for the clasp of her locket. She releases the catch, letting it slip away from her neck, and he sees it in the palm of her hand before she puts it on the small bedside table where the chain gleams like a silvery snake coiled around the shape of a heart. Then she leans into him, pressing her body against his as tightly as she can.

'Just this. One night,' he murmurs.

'Yes.'

'We'll never speak of this again.'

'Speak of what?'

She crosses the room to close the drapes and switch on the lamp.

'Leave them,' he says in a thick voice he doesn't recognise. Her hotel room is up high enough to be safe from prying eyes and the bedroom is shadowy save for night-time city lights framed by the wall-to-wall window. He wants to see this, to remind him that he's in a different place, a different country, caught up in a sliver of time apart from normal life. One that will never be repeated.

They come together in the middle of the room, sliding out of their clothes before they collapse onto soft linen sheets. She leans over him and looks at his face in the semi-darkness, and then she touches her mouth to his. As his arms go around her, he knows there is no stopping this: he feels her touch on his body, breathes in the scent of her skin, tangles his limbs with hers; their mouths lock together, then a sudden pause, a moment where they catch their breath and stare at each other, and everything hangs in the balance; next, he is inside her, hearing the sound of her short, sharp gasps against his ear, and her involuntary groans of pleasure.

Now, years later, it just takes an image, a sound, or a scent – a plume of smoke in the air, the wail of a siren, a scent of burning metal – to make him pause and slow his breath and remember almost three thousand people whose lives were cruelly cut short on that faraway September morning. To remember what he had done.

Sometimes, in restless dreams, he sees the silhouette of a woman against a New York night-time skyline and something fearful scuttles across the floor of his conscience in the dead of the night. Occasionally, when he finds himself recalling that night, in an idle nanosecond between one busy moment and the next, something plummets down to the base of his conscience and he is held in a vice-like grip of terror lest fate exact some kind of cruel retribution, or put a stop to the happiness and contentment he knows he doesn't deserve.

But mostly the memory of the night he spent in her arms is hidden beneath a mountain of useless regret, the time and space between then and now lending it the merciful delusion that it had never happened.

This evening, as that long-ago night fades away and the dimly lit bakery takes shape around him, he stares at himself in the mirror, thinking of everything that has happened that week, and he wonders why it fills him with dread.

Twelve

Wednesday night

In the Gresham Hotel, the elite of the Irish celebrity world plus a golden handful of American movie moguls were gathered at the reception to celebrate the European premiere of the Oscar-nominated movie *Independence*.

Finn Kennedy threw back a swift gulp of champagne and smiled down into the upturned face and heavily mascaraed eyes of the twenty-something wannabe starlet.

'Come on, spill the beans,' she wheedled. 'What's coming up next in *Reprisal*? I won't tell, honest!'

'I'd have to kill you if I told you,' he said. 'All the crew and cast are under a strict oath not to reveal any of the plot lines.'

'Yeah, right,' she smiled, clinking her glass to his. 'Don't they usually let something leak out, to whet our appetites, like?'

'Like what?' he asked, on guard for a moment, wondering if by chance she'd heard a rumour of his demise.

'I heard that things really hot up between Jimmy and Lorna, and they're found in bed together.'

Relief trickled through his veins. She didn't know. To her, he was still *Reprisal*'s Larry Boland.

He still couldn't believe what had happened, although it had been over four months ago now. He felt as though he was dreaming when he recalled the grey day last October that had effectively ended his career. It was just another day's work for the crew, but a milestone day for him in the worst way possible. The car picked him up and brought him out to the location in a quiet suburban housing estate. It was a wet, drizzly day and there were a few hangers-on, housewives mostly, with the kids dropped off in school, sensing the buzz created by the crew, dressed up to the nines in case there was a remote chance of a walk-on part. They had had a couple of rehearsals in a damp back garden, Finn hating the way he had to throw himself on the ground in front of a masked gunman, hating the fact that, when they went outside and broke for tea and coffee and some of the residents hanging around by the van asked for autographs and took photos of him with their mobile phones, they were unaware of what was being filmed in the back garden.

He kept hoping the directors and script editors would change their minds, right up to the end, right up to the final take, when his last moments in the crime drama were of him lying face down in a patch of wet, bloodied grass. Six years of fame and recognition and a very decent pay cheque was over in minutes, in the most ignominious way. The fame and recognition synonymous with his character of Larry would ensure that he was typecast to the extent that it would be difficult if not impossible to find similar work again in Irish televisions circles. Even now, he was stupid enough to think that if rumour hasn't yet reached the general masses about his character's on-screen death, maybe, just maybe, the producers and directors would change their minds.

And pigs might fly.

The current season, where he was due to get his comeuppance in the final episode, had just begun to air. They'd already begun to shoot the next season, and his contract hadn't been renewed. Why had they been so set on getting rid of him? He was a bankable actor, wasn't he? One of the main stars – if not *the* star – of the show. The programme drew major audience figures every week, partly thanks to his gritty exploits and brooding, on-screen presence. Still, the final episode of the season wasn't due to be aired for another ten weeks. Technically, he was still part and parcel of it all.

From across the reception room, Jo's eyes sought him out as she checked to see if he needed rescuing, in case – Jesus Christ, it rankled – he couldn't hold his own in this star-studded VIP reception and needed her support.

Not so long ago, he'd loved the way she did this – checking with a look or a gesture to make sure he was happy, that he wasn't bored or needed extricating from an over-eager fan. Her lovely eyes had always eased something inside him, a lack of self-assurance that seemed to need a validation of sorts. Tonight, her searching look seemed like a gesture of compassion, the look you'd give to a sad case, and he couldn't help wondering if that was the way she'd looked at him all along but he was only seeing it now thanks to the way his life had crash-landed around him.

He raised his champagne glass so that he was staring at Jo over the rim. Her face reddened slightly and she turned away to join a group chatting to an elderly gentleman. She looked beautiful. Her dark hair was coiled in smooth silky loops at the back of her head, the elegant slope of her bare shoulders rising above the bodice of her black evening gown as soft as velvet. He wanted to slide down the zip of that dress, watching the way the dark material would cleave apart, revealing the delicate indent of her spine, his fingers grazing that skin as he lowered the zip, down to the cleft of her curvy buttocks. He wanted to release her hair and allow it to fall freely so that he could bury his face in it, inhaling her delicate fragrance, while his hands pushed her dress away and she laughed softly and twisted around in his arms and raised her face to his …

Just the way she used to when he'd reach for her. He realised with a sudden jolt that in spite of his world caving in, he still lusted after her.

He tried to focus on the wannabe in front of him, who was no doubt hankering after an opportunity to network, just as he should be networking with Steven Spielberg. The mogul himself was holding court further down the room, chatting to Bono, and there was no getting near him, anymore than he could get near Colin Farrell. The *Reprisal* producers were here, but in the fickle and competitive world of acting he was no longer flavour of the month. He'd talked to people in Belfast and London, but those talks had been fruitless as there were no openings there for him either.

Why wasn't he standing where Colin Farrell now stood? Where had it been ordained that Finn Kennedy's acting career would be limited to Irish soap opera dramas and occasional voiceovers? That he wouldn't cut it on the international stage? Yet he'd always felt, deep down somewhere, that he wasn't really good enough, hadn't he?

Now he knew for sure.

'You could be Colin Farrell's older brother,' she said.

He smiled his most disingenuous Larry Boland smile. The one that seemed friendly enough until you looked into his eyes. '*Older* brother? You don't say …'

She looked uncomfortable. 'Well, just a wee bit older,' she qualified.

Like more than ten years, he admitted to himself, watching the throng gathered around the actor, who was tipped, they said, for Oscar glory for his role in this film.

'Oh my God, there's *Barry*,' she squealed, her body so animated that the swell of her boobs shifted and bounced where they spilled out over her low-cut top. She was gone like a light, zoning in on the young actor who was barely out of his teens and barely out of drama school. In no time, Barry was surrounded by a gaggle of adoring female fans.

Barry. His on-screen son. Young, keen, cherub-faced, yet vicious and cruel. Poised to take over the drug cartel as soon as his father was knocked off. Even Finn heard the closely guarded rumours that, in the next season, it transpires that Barry put out the hit on his own father. A plot line guaranteed to put the ratings through the roof. So what if it came at the expense of Finn's career?

Finn's fingers tightened around the stem of his champagne flute as he watched the young actor being borne through the crowd towards Spielberg himself by one of the *Reprisal* directors. He knocked back his drink and grabbed another glass off a circulating waiter.

'Are you okay?' Jo's face appeared in front of him.

From the first time he'd met her all those years ago, in the crowded bar in Coogee, when she'd flounced up to the bar full of false nonchalance, he'd been intrigued by Jo. He'd seen right through her thin veneer of brashness that first night when she'd opened her eyes during the last notes of 'Heart of Gold' and stared at him, totally unguarded. She'd covered over all the stagnant places of his life with her sparky eyes and fiery attitude and was the most beautiful woman he'd ever seen. He thought he'd been in love before, but Jo Harper had stolen his heart and soul like no other woman ever had.

Marriage to Jo had been everything he'd wished for. They'd been there for each other during the early years while they adjusted to life back in Dublin, Jo encouraging him with her unshakeable belief in his talent, and he shoring up Jo's insecurities with her family. While Jo had developed her career, he'd waited for his great break, doing stage and television bit parts and voiceovers, working on and off in pubs to supplement his income. When he started to make a name for himself, he'd been relieved to vindicate her support in him and was very proud of his new-found stardom.

Now all of that was gone, everything had changed and, sometimes lately, her solicitous look almost unhinged him. He wanted to tell her to fuck off. He wanted to tell her lots of things, but this was not the time or place.

'I'm great,' he said. 'Good night, isn't it?'

Her face cleared. With an almost imperceptible glance at the level of drink in his glass, she said, 'I think we're moving into the Savoy in a minute, so get ready for the red carpet.'

'I'm as ready as I'll ever be,' he said. Or, rather, as near as he would ever get, treading a carpet laid for other big noises. But not for him. He was always going to be the runner-up.

His eyes scanned the room. He finished his champagne and drew Jo close to him, putting his arm around her shoulder, squeezing her close. At first, she was a little startled at his proprietorial touch – he knew it had been weeks since he'd reached for her in bed, and God he missed it so much – but she smiled nonetheless. He smiled back at her, as though he was perfectly happy and his life hadn't started to drop into a deep, dark crevasse.

There were times when it was useful being an actor, adopting a role, sliding into a persona, putting on the performance of your life. This was one of them. He hoped he could give as good a performance next Saturday night when, knowing what he now knew, he would really be put to the test.

He'd been put to the test before, only he'd failed abysmally. It was a snapshot of time in his life that very occasionally drifted back into his bad dreams just when he least expected it ...

Galway, December 1989

The minute Finn sees the silver locket gleaming in its bed of white satin in the brightly lit window of a jeweller's shop on Quay Street, he knows it's perfect. Excitement sends his heartbeat tripping despite the greyness of the dull, early December evening.

He doesn't hesitate at all, pushing open the shop door, the tinkling chime sounding like a welcome to him, a sign that he is doing the right thing. He walks towards the counter, sudden alarm making him search for his wallet. He opens it and checks it, relieved he has enough cash on him to secure a deposit. He doesn't own a credit card and it's two more days to pay day at the cash and carry where he works, but he'll be due more overtime given the extra hours he's putting in during the pre-Christmas rush. He puts down a deposit, tucking the receipt very carefully into the slot of the wallet reserved for twenty-pound notes and, as he walks out of the shop, the bell tinkling again on his opening of the door, he works out how much he'll need to pay off each week so he'll have it in good time for Christmas.

He wants to give Debbie Dillon, the love of his life, something really special.

He's going to ask her to marry him, and he hopes she'll say yes, and that she'll be happy with all his grand plans for them both. He's twenty-five years of age and he has his hopes and dreams for their future together all mapped out. If things go well, they could get engaged for her birthday in March, and after that, the sky will be the limit.

He's known Debbie since he was a shy, unsure sixteen-year-old, hanging back at the youth club dances, watching her from afar. It took him a year to pluck up the courage to ask her to dance, and when she allowed him to walk her home that night and agreed to go to the movies, he strolled back home past Galway Cathedral, looking up at the spire in the shadowy night, feeling he could soar to the top of it.

The world was an even better place the summer he was twenty and Debbie planned a weekend away for both of them in a seaside hotel in Sligo, pretending to her family she was going to visit an old school friend. He woke early, after their first night together. He looked out the window at the breadth of the sea and the soft grey horizon and recalled how she'd fallen into his arms, a bundle of soft, silky skin and unbearable tenderness, and he felt invincible.

Since then, they've been going steady together, Debbie's warm brown eyes becoming his touchstone, their occasional differences easily sorted. She makes him feel special and sexy, and she knows there is a lot more to Finn Kennedy than being a forklift driver in a cash and carry warehouse. Finn has big dreams of the stage and screen and Debbie is fully behind him, encouraging his involvement in local amateur dramatics, sitting proudly in the front row of Galway theatres as he gradually progresses from the supporting cast to lead roles.

He knows Debbie's brothers don't really think he's good enough for their precious sister. During his school days, they had played with the same GAA club, not that Finn was much good at the game, in fact he was so hopeless at tackling the ball that he was usually relegated to the sidelines and in the end he gave it up.

When he first started to call for Debbie, her big-framed brothers looked him up and down suspiciously, which is why he's always preferred to meet her after work. Debbie's Mum, Mrs Dillon, likes and approves of him. She always has a smile and some buttered soda bread ready for him. Although calling to the cake shop means he sometimes bumps into Max and it annoys him to be reminded that his brother spends more time hanging around the same space as Debbie than he does. Trust Max to start work in the very cake shop that Debbie's mother owns, where Debbie also works. Max also gets on better with Debbie's brothers, partly because he's fearless on the GAA pitch.

Once or twice, Finn had asked Debbie what she thought of Max, but she'd laughed dismissively. 'He's like my little brother,' she'd said. 'A bit of a nuisance at times, other times he reminds me of a big, friendly bear.'

Soon, though, if his plans work out, Finn won't have to concern himself anymore with Debbie's brothers or Max. When he gets home on that dull December evening, he puts the receipt for the silver locket away carefully.

But the next night he sees her, Debbie says she won't be around for Christmas.

'We're going to Dublin, to my aunt,' she tells him.

'What, all of you?'

'Yes, me and Mum and my two brothers. We'll be gone for a week. From the day before Christmas Eve ...'

'That's mad,' he says, disappointment crashing through him. 'Isn't it your busiest time in the shop? I thought Max was working flat out?'

'Yeah, we all are, for now,' she says lightly, 'but we'll be winding down by then and all the Christmas orders will have been collected. We're packing up the car and heading off at the crack of dawn on Saturday, before the worst of the traffic.'

'And when am I supposed to give you your present? I'm doing a long shift on Friday night to make sure the warehouse is cleared before Christmas Eve.'

'Tell you what,' she says, leaning into him and smiling at him with her big brown eyes. 'Leave it until afterwards. How about New Year's Eve? I'll be back by then, and we'll celebrate together and say good riddance to the horrible eighties and hello to the nineties.'

New Year's Eve. The night Galway, Ireland and the world were going to rid themselves of the miserable grey cloak of the eighties and turn their faces to the oncoming decade of the nineties in search of some kind of hope. It would be the perfect night to talk seriously to Debbie about his hopes and dreams and what he has been planning and saving for these past few months.

He's impatient for Christmas to be over and done with, for her to return from Dublin. Then on New Year's Eve he is suddenly stricken with nerves. Even though it starts to rain and the scent of thunder is heavy in the air and the silver locket in its satiny bed is burning a hole in his pocket, he stops for a moment on the bridge looking down at the dark silk of the River Corrib, the running surface glittering here and there with reflections of streetlights, and he takes a few steadying breaths. Then he turns up his collar and hurries towards his future ...

Thirteen

Friday evening

'You've opened my post,' Jo said, picking up the ripped envelope off the hall table.

Finn shrugged. 'It's just a phone bill. I didn't think it was a state secret.'

'It isn't,' she said shortly. 'But it's *my* bill.'

'That you're well able to pay with your salary.'

'So?' She faced him, trembling a little. Was he about to talk? Was this the opening she needed? They had to sit down and discuss their financial situation sooner or later. If Finn didn't get work in the next three months, it would be difficult to keep up the repayments on his top-of-the-range BMW let alone their considerable mortgage. 'I'm happy to pay as many bills as I can with my salary,' she said. 'Have you a problem with that?'

He didn't answer her. Once again, he'd been skulking around in the hallway waiting for her to come home. She'd been later than normal after another futile and frustrating visit to the nursing home.

A flash of irritation rose inside her. 'Aren't you even going to ask how my mother is? She's stuck in that home with lots of other pitiable souls who can't fend for themselves any more. They're clean and well cared for but have little quality of life. We don't know how well off we are in comparison.'

'Jesus, Jo,' he laughed, 'I never thought you'd play the sympathy card where your mother is concerned. You must be getting soft in the head.'

She took a deep breath and put her hand on his arm. 'We have to talk,' she said, as reasonably as she could. 'I know you're in a bad place, and it's very unfortunate and difficult, but can't you see it doesn't define your life? You have so much, Finn, and we could be a lot worse off. There are good things in your life, if you'd just appreciate them a bit more.'

His eyes glittered, as if spoiling for a fight. He shrugged off her hand and his body tensed as though he was squaring up to her. 'Name some.'

She stared at him. He'd had bad moments before, when a much-coveted role went to someone else, but she'd always been able to cheer him up. She'd never seen him with his anger and frustration barely concealed below the surface. She could have pointed out that he had her and Grace, his two best supporters; that in his late forties he was in perfectly rude health, and had matured so that he had a certain stature, a gravitas that was very attractive. He had so much to be thankful for.

'Oh, for God's sake, stop feeling sorry for yourself,' she snapped, her unease making her respond rashly. As she went to move down the hall, he caught her by the arm.

'Sorry for myself? Is that what you think?'

'Let go of me,' she hissed, knowing she shouldn't have started this, with Grace somewhere in the house. Most likely in her room, sensing her father's bad mood. He let go of her so abruptly that she was unsteady on her feet for a moment.

She hung her coat in the cloakroom and went down to the kitchen, leaving him standing outside the den. She felt like she was walking along a gangplank over a deep ravine.

'And by the way,' his voice followed her, 'don't forget about Max and Ali coming over for a meal tomorrow night.'

'They're definitely coming?'

'Yes.'

'Well then, that's great.'

'You're pleased?'

'Why shouldn't I be?'

'It'll just be the four of us as Grace will be at a sleepover with her friend.'

'Yes, Amy's mother has already talked to me about that.'

'We have to be nice to Ali and Max because they're not having such a good week, from what I gather. Some problems in the bakery.'

'Of course I'll be nice to them. It'll be good to have some company.' She spoke evenly, knowing she'd need a stiff drink or two, considering the way Finn felt about his brother. Despite Finn's success through the years, Jo knew a small part of him still believed, to this day, that they were in some kind of competition with each other. It had coloured all his snippets of news:

'Max is setting up on his own – the Booth Street Bakery, what kind of a name is that? And it's on the wrong side of Grafton Street. Hope he doesn't live to regret it.'

Then later: *'Would you believe they're extending the bakery? Must be mad in this economy, more fool him. Then again, things have always had a habit of coming up roses for him. Even Debbie Dillon is back on the scene.'*

She hadn't commented at first, because her heart had given an unexpected lurch. She'd known exactly who Debbie Dillon was.

'Does that bother you?' she'd asked very casually.

'Nah,' he'd shrugged, smiling at her. *'Ancient history.'*

And just a month ago, coming at the worst time possible, as if Finn wasn't embittered enough about his television career, *'Max has his mugshot in the paper again. The jammy bastard. There's talk of him getting his own telly programme.'*

His voice had been slightly slurred, as though he'd needed the benefit of a drink to tell her, but that hadn't softened the caustic edge to his voice.

Even though she wasn't hungry, Jo forced herself to eat the chicken casserole that Finn had cooked. Things were bad enough, but the day he stopped preparing food would be a very bad day indeed. She thought back to the day she'd married Finn, when she'd hoped that, with lots of love and affection, she could help him to leave his baggage behind – and she had, mostly. She remembered how even before they arrived back in Dublin, when they were still on honeymoon in Singapore, she got the first inkling about how deep his insecurities ran.

Singapore, 1992

They spend the afternoon in the Botanic Gardens, Jo taking lots of photos of the Orchid Gardens.

Photographs of our honeymoon. The whole idea of being on honeymoon feels weird. Yet why should it feel more bizarre than a wedding? She finds herself taking sneak peeks at Finn as a stranger might look at him, viewing this man she'd chosen to share her life with from a fresh perspective, watching the way he moves around and throws her glances with his darkly lashed eyes, feeling the touch of his hand on the nape of her neck.

Wondering, funnily enough, what her parents and sisters might think. Or if, the gossamer thought hovers, in getting married to Finn she had pulled the ultimate rebellious stunt. Later, they are in bed together in the warm, languorous early evening, making love before they shower and dress and go out for drinks and a meal.

'I love you, love you, love you,' Finn says, leaning on his elbow, his dark-grey eyes flooded with desire.

'I love hearing you say that,' she sighs, absorbing the words, feeling warm under his gaze. This is it, why she's married him. It has nothing to do with rebellion. He kisses her neck. 'I'll always love you. You're almost too good to be true.'

Too good to be true. No one had ever told Jo Harper that.

He touches the most sensitive part of her. They'd made love twice already, yet she was ready to come again. Which she does, her hands reaching back over her head and grabbing on to the bedrail as he brings her to another shattering climax, pressing his mouth to hers and kissing her deeply as she comes.

'I love it when you're like this,' he says. 'Wild and passionate and abandoned. I love how I'm making you feel.'

'So do I,' she says, her breath heaving. 'It makes me feel beautiful and loved.' Jo Kennedy, all grown up, a woman in her own right who can give pleasure to a man and receive it from him.

They lie quietly for a while, Jo slowly floating back down off the whirl of pleasure when he says, 'We should be home just in time for my brother's wedding.'

'I didn't know Max was getting married.'

'I didn't tell you,' Finn says. 'I was going to surprise you the way I'm going to surprise them, but then I realised it wouldn't be fair on you, that you'd need to get something to wear.'

She laughs, thinking she has surely misinterpreted what he's just said. 'What do you mean you're going to surprise them?'

He turns towards her and strokes her face. 'They don't know we're coming home. Neither do they know about you, about us.'

She feels hot and cold. 'What do you mean?'

'I never told them we got married. It'll be a surprise.'

'I thought … surely you told them? Didn't you say they weren't coming out for the wedding?' She leans back so that she can look at his face. He's smiling at her as though everything is perfectly normal.

'I didn't ask them. I knew Max and our parents wouldn't come out, or his girlfriend, Ali, so what was the point? I thought it would be a bit of fun to turn up on their wedding day, right out of the blue, and join in the celebrations. So it'll be a double celebration.'

There is a beat of silence, broken by a door banging and the noisy squeal of a child, somewhere out on the hotel corridor. Any excitement she had felt a few moments ago has drained away. 'Could you start again, Finn? At the beginning. How long have you known about Max's wedding?'

'Oh, about three, four months.'

'And you didn't tell me, all this time.'

'No, because I didn't want anything to take away from our wedding.'

'But how could it have?' she says, trying to grapple with the essentials of what he is saying. 'Our wedding was all about you and me. And it was exactly what *we* wanted.'

'Yeah, you're right. Max's will be one of those conservative affairs, the kind you hate, with the bride in a frilly white dress and a bridesmaid or two glued into a frothy meringue, Max buttoned up in a badly fitting rental suit, and a three-tier cake with all the trimmings.'

'Then why do you think it'll be a good idea for us to join the celebration?' she asks, thinking there is something deeper here that she doesn't fully understand.

'Not join in, as such, and we could skip the church part, but I can just picture us turning up at the hotel, the alternative and very trendy Mr and Mrs Kennedy. Newly married, surprise, surprise, and all the way home from Australia.'

They'd cause a major sensation, Jo realises, falling back against the pillow. She's okay with that, in general major sensations are fine. But not in this case. They would take some, if not all, of the spotlight away from Max and his new wife. And on their wedding day. She doesn't know them, hasn't yet met them, but they are Finn's family and, whatever about her own family, this is a new beginning for her, a chance to start afresh, and she doesn't want to kick off on the wrong foot. It's supposed to be a new beginning for both of them, isn't it? It concerns her that Finn hasn't let go of all his baggage.

She asks, very gently, as she pushes a lock of his hair off his forehead, 'I hope you didn't marry me just because your brother was getting married.'

The thought is slipping through the back of her head like a grey shadow, but even if it dents the perfect image she has in her heart of their wedding day, she needs to know the truth.

'Christ, no,' Finn says. His hand caresses the side of her face. 'Jo, I was gone, demolished, the first time your haughty green eyes bored into mine.'

'Good,' she says. 'Cos if you think I'm living in the shadow of your brother, you can forget it. We're *us*, Finn and Jo, forever.'

'I like the sound of that.'

Finn and Jo, forever. She likes the sound of it too as she nuzzles into him. Then she asks him softly, 'Finn, what exactly happened with your brother?'

He shifts slightly away from her. 'It's not something I'm very proud of.'

She raises herself on her elbows, moves in closer to him and says, 'You can tell me …'

❀

She talks him out of his idea to crash Max's wedding. Somewhere between Singapore and Amsterdam and flying back to a cold breezy Dublin, where they stay in a city-centre hotel for a few nights before they find a flat to rent, she coaxes him around to her way of thinking.

'Why piggy back on their celebration?' she says ultra-casually. 'Why not have one of our own, and put our stamp on it, the mark of Finn and Jo? Surely we deserve to do something of our own, something unique?'

'Yeah, you're right. What do you suggest?'

'Let them know you're home. Invite them out for a meal. Then you can introduce me and we'll break the news about our wedding and show them photos of our amazing day. And we can tell Max and Ali we're delighted to be home in time for their special day.'

'Ah, Jo, this is one of the reasons I married you. You save me from myself and believe in me.'

'Course I believe in you, Finn Kennedy. I wouldn't have married you otherwise.' She leans over and kisses him. She loves this grey-eyed man who can make her laugh, who can stand up to her false bravado but who's not afraid to let her see into the depths of his fragile heart with his disarming honesty. To hell with his brother. From the sound of it, and despite what went wrong in Galway, there is nothing spectacular about Max that should make Finn feel second best.

Fourteen

Saturday evening

By Saturday evening, Ali felt as weak as a rag doll. The hectic day in the bakery had, thankfully, gone by without any incidents. She hadn't realised how tightly she'd been holding her breath and clenching her facial muscles until she was getting ready for Finn and Jo's. She'd been undecided about what to wear and in the end settled for a blue lace Monsoon dress with her silver sandals. Max was wearing his black Levi jeans and black shirt.

'I'm glad that day is over,' she said to him, leaning into the mirror to deepen her eye shadow.

Although their problems wouldn't be over as long as Max's books were missing. Or until they got to the bottom of the strange things that had happened that week. A fresh wave of anxiety washed over her. 'Never mind the day, I'm glad that week is over,' she went on. She glanced up and caught Max staring at her. He looked like he wasn't really seeing her, but that he was looking through her and beyond her at something only he could see.

'Hey,' she said, waving her hand. 'It's me.'

He blinked. His face looked guarded in that instant as he came back from wherever he'd been. She remembered the way he'd looked at her on Wednesday, outside the bakery in the blowy afternoon, as though he'd been afraid of something.

She had to ignore it.

'And now we have tonight to look forward to,' she said. 'I know we'd both rather put our feet up and open a bottle of wine, and it's bad timing in a way, coming on top of a difficult week, but—' she tried to think of something positive to say – 'he is your brother after all and we hardly see them, as much our fault as theirs, we're all so busy we have no time to be sociable …' But all this died on her lips.

He was staring into space again. He didn't look a bit like the Max she knew, the kind, good-natured, easy-going guy, who wasn't so easy-going when he reached for her in bed, as she brought out his hungry, passionate side. He looked like somebody different, somebody extremely troubled. The walls of the bedroom closed around her. She put a smile on her face. 'I hope you're not having second thoughts. It's a bit late to back out now.'

He blinked. He was so transparent that she could see him pulling himself together, bit by bit. 'I'm not backing out. I'd never hear the end of it.'

'I wonder what Finn has in mind – can't remember the last time we were asked to dinner.' She tousled her blonde hair, fluffing it up with some styling gel. 'He must be feeling guilty that he's ignored us for so long, or what's the betting he wants to talk about his massive ratings and Twitter following.'

'I'm not sure about that,' Max said. 'I've heard rumours that the next season has started shooting and he hasn't been seen out on location. That he might have been bumped off. But don't say a word tonight.'

'Oh, great,' Ali said. 'Thanks for telling me. I feel *soooo* relaxed.' She sprayed one more of her Jo Malone Blackberry and Bay, narrowly avoiding her eyes.

❄

'Don't forget, there's a lasagne in the oven,' Mum said.

'As if I'd forget, ha ha,' Tom chucked as though Mum had cracked a brilliant joke.

Jessica forced a smile and threw a cushion at him. 'It's not all for you, Tom.'

'It's nice to see you two watching the telly together,' Mum said wistfully. She patted her hair and looked like she'd rather be sitting on the sofa with them, eating popcorn and watching a rerun of Harry Potter instead of going out. 'And I'm glad you're taking a break, Jessica,' she said, oblivious to the knife she was twisting. 'You must have been in your room all day.'

'I'll be going back up after this,' Jessica said, pretending to be engrossed in the movie. She'd had to come downstairs because the walls of her bedroom had been closing in on her and she'd thought she was going to go mad. She didn't know how much longer she could keep this up, pretending nothing was wrong with her other than her exams. Sometimes she felt sick right down to her toes, as though she was going to vomit on the spot; other times she just felt scared shitless, not knowing what might happen. This evening, it was like she'd just slammed into a wall of prickling anxiety and she'd had to get out of her room, even if it meant facing her family, in particular her parents all dressed up for a night at Finn and Jo's. She tried to make out she was glued to the screen, but she couldn't help glancing at them as they said their goodbyes and got ready to leave.

They looked good together, her mum and dad. Even her friends thought her parents were cool. Mum seemed more like thirty-two than forty-two, with her soft blonde hair and innocent kind of face. If she knew what was going on, she'd look more like sixty years of age. And Dad ...

God.

'Goodnight, Princess,' he said to her, jingling his car keys. 'Don't work too hard.'

'I won't,' she said, disguising the sudden lump in her throat with a little cough as she felt despair sweep over her again.

'Come on, Ali, time to face the music,' her dad joked as he tipped her mother on the shoulder.

Jessica held her breath until she heard the hall door closing after them and she made a half-hearted attempt to watch the movie. Not that she could relax. Anything but. It was getting harder and harder to stay silent. And next to impossible to put on a face. But it had to be done, she told herself firmly. Otherwise their happy family life would be ruined.

❖

Ali felt even more on guard when Finn greeted them warmly, throwing back the hall door with effusive ceremony. Jo fluttered around in the marbled hallway with the sweeping staircase as she welcomed them. Their beautiful and spacious home was straight out of a *Better Homes* catalogue and a far cry from Ali and Max's cosy, lived-in townhouse.

Jo seemed slightly too nervy for Ali's liking. Looking at her – she was elegantly chic in a cream cashmere jumper and long navy skirt, with stiletto pumps – Ali was struck by the transformation into stylish woman from the laughing girl with lots of attitude that she'd first met just before her own wedding. Years of marriage to Finn had softened her spikiness, so that she glowed. To judge by the media, he had plenty of women falling all over him with his TV role, but he just laughed it off, saying he was madly in love with his wife.

Then again, they'd all changed over the years. Looking at Finn and Jo now, and their fabulous home, it was hard to believe that they'd come home from Australia, jobless and virtually penniless, starting their married life in a shabby two-roomed flat. Like Ali and Max, they had worked very hard to get where they were today. Still, she thought, there had been a crackling excitement, an energy and optimism about those early years that seemed to have faded.

Tonight, Finn seemed to be trying too hard to be an urbane and smooth host. He was wearing a beautiful suit, almost overdressed for the occasion. The long dining table was flawlessly set, with cutlery, glasses and napkins arranged to such precision that Ali found it daunting. The curtains were closed against the dark evening and candlelight flickered welcomingly.

'Wow, some table,' Ali said, clutching her gin and tonic, managing to prevent a comment on how long it must have taken him to set it.

'This is a practice run at *Come Dine with Me*,' Finn said. 'I hope you're up for it.'

'We're up for everything, aren't we, Max?' Ali said, hating the way she was watching every word that came out of her mouth.

Max gave her a tight grin and changed the subject to the Irish rugby team.

The food was delicious; Finn cooked the beef to perfection, as well as crisp vegetables and lightly roasted potatoes.

'You have Finn to thank for all this,' Jo said, when Ali made murmurs of appreciation.

Once again, Ali had to remind herself to hold her tongue on the time and effort that must have been involved in the cooking. Finn seemed to be watching them closely as they ate, proffering extra vegetables before they were ready for them, hovering with the wine even though Max was only having a small glass because he was driving. When their plates were cleared, Ali beamed her brightest smile as Finn sloshed yet more wine into her glass, putting up her hand to call a halt.

'That's plenty, Finn, ta very much. Look after yourself.'

Finn adjusted the kitchen towel slung over his shoulder as though he was making a statement. 'I'm chief cook and bottle washer tonight so I'm taking it very easy. It's only cheap and cheerful Aldi, so there's lots more.' He nodded in the direction of the sideboard where another bottle of rioja was uncorked.

'Maybe Jo?' Ali smiled across the table at her sister-in-law.

'Just a small top-up for me,' Jo said.

'That's all you're getting,' Finn said, trying and failing to sound funny.

Max put his hand over his glass as Finn moved down the table. 'No thanks, I'm driving.'

'Spoil sport. You should have let me collect you and got a taxi home,' Finn said.

'Thanks, but I want to keep a clear head. I've a busy week coming up getting ready for a food exhibition in France, so I need to be on the ball,' he said.

There was a tense pause. Ali felt the mood shifting and wondered why Max had drawn attention to the fact that he had a busy and successful job, when they had both agreed to keep the conversation low key and safe. Safe from any awkward subjects. Like the success of Max's job. He'd already joked about the mouse incident in the bakery, but in a very self-deprecating way, making it sound much funnier than it had been. And it was Jo who had raised that subject, saying that Grace had seen it on Facebook.

'A food exhibition?' Finn said. 'Sounds very important. And it's a helluva long way from penny buns in the cake shop in Galway.'

'All our lives have come a long way since then,' Max said evenly.

'Have they, really? Do you remember those good old days, Max?'

'I don't look back. I never have.'

Ali gulped more wine, feeling there was a subtext that she wasn't aware of. She watched the way Finn gazed steadily at Max from across the table. 'I wouldn't say you want to. Look back.'

'I wouldn't say you want to either,' Max said. 'I far prefer to live in the present.'

'Oh yes, it's much easier to move through your days without any baggage. Still, it must be a blast from the past working with Debbie Dillon again. Especially in the heat of a kitchen.'

'I didn't think that bothered you,' Max said.

'There are some things you don't forget,' Finn said.

Ali almost choked on her wine.

'We're lucky to have Debbie, aren't we, Ali?' Max said pleasantly. 'She's good at her job and my kitchen is an oasis of calm. We're busy, but we're careful with our menu planning and it's always in our control.'

Finn smiled thinly. 'Would you say that life, like history, has a habit of repeating itself?'

Max shrugged. 'I hope not. It was hard to see the shop in Galway closing down but there's no comparison between it and Booth Street Bakery.'

'Certainly not if you're off to fancy food exhibitions,' Finn said. 'But that's not what I meant about history repeating itself.'

'Food fairs and exhibitions are part of the job nowadays,' Max said, disregarding Finn's final comment. 'To stay in the game you have to keep on upskilling, network with other industry experts, share best practice …'

Too much information, Max, Ali felt like saying. Least said in this case and no need to remind your brother that you're staying on top of your game. And what the hell has Debbie Dillon got to do with anything?

'I bet gold circle lounges, quaffing champagne and business class to Paris is real hard work.' Finn raised an eyebrow as though he'd made a very good joke, but was unable to disguise the flicker of hostility in his eyes.

'Not quite,' Max said evenly. 'It's Bordeaux and economy.'

'No wonder I can't tempt you with any wine,' Finn said. 'You'll be tasting the finest next week.' Finn picked up the bottle of wine again. 'It's the best of Aldi, seriously. Not that you guys would ever have to lower yourselves to—'

Ali butted in, 'Shop in Aldi? We do shop there, Finn. More often than you'd think.' She could have bitten her tongue, realising too late how patronising she sounded. She met Max's eyes across the table and without saying anything, his warm smile told her she was fine, it was okay. But it wasn't all okay, she felt very much on edge. She pulled a face in return. He raised his eyebrows questioningly, as though there was nothing for her to feel uneasy about.

Finn held up the bottle of wine and examined the label as though it was an expensive burgundy. 'It doesn't seem that long since we were all running up astronomical wine bills and boasting about our collections of chateau this and that,' he went on, as though she hadn't spoken. 'Now it's all about cheap and cheerful. The cheaper the better. Apart from yourselves,' he broke off to glance at the bottle of Moët that Max had brought.

Jo glanced across the table at Ali nervously, as if to apologise for her husband's thinly veiled envy.

Finn must have caught the expression in Jo's eyes, because he smiled at her and said, 'Hey, relax! Don't mind me prattling on. We're family, aren't we? No secrets between us, eh, Max?'

'Absolutely none,' Max replied, rather too quickly.

In the brief silence that dropped around the table, Ali felt a prickle at the back of her neck. 'Speaking of family . . .' she turned to Jo. 'How's Grace? I'm sorry we missed her tonight.'

Jo's face lit up. 'She was sorry too when she heard you were coming, but she'd already been invited to *The Lion King* with Amy, her best friend, and her parents, and she's staying with them overnight as it's Amy's birthday tomorrow.'

'And how is she feeling now?'

'A lot better, thankfully,' Jo said. 'I've been up to my tonsils in work these past few weeks so it was great that Finn was around to keep an eye out for her.'

Ali watched Jo's eyes widen, as though she'd said the wrong thing in letting it slip that Finn had spare time on his hands and it fed her tension further. 'She's getting very grown up,' Ali said swiftly. 'She looked really beautiful when we saw her at Christmas.'

'Thanks Ali, she's at a lovely age now, with a couple more years left, I hope, before we come to the watching-our-step-with-her phase. Then beyond that the boyfriends, alcohol, you know the story.'

'Yes, I do,' Ali smiled. 'I'm the same with Tom, but I think boys are a little behind the girls when it comes to the teenage years. Tom is very quiet, a bit of a nerd at times, and not like either of us. Sometimes I worry about him out there in the big bad world, whereas Jessica is well able to fend for herself. We're very proud of her, aren't we, Max?' Too late, she regretted the smug tone in her voice.

'Absolutely, as we are of Tom,' Max said, sounding to Ali's ears even more smug.

'It must be wonderful to be so proud of your kids,' Finn said smoothly.

'We've always talked to them,' Ali said. 'You need to keep the lines of communication open at all times, know their friends and where they are.'

'Sounds like you have it all under control, Ali,' Finn said. 'It must be a very good feeling.'

It was the mocking tone in his voice that unsettled her. She stared at him. 'Our children mean the world to me and Max, so, yes, it is a good feeling. We've put a lot of effort in, both of us. I'm sure you're the same with Grace.'

'There you are, Jo,' Finn said, 'the secret formula for guiding Grace through the dangerous years of boys and alcohol. Good communication. No secrets. What do you think?'

'To judge by what I'm seeing already, I think Grace will be able to fend for herself,' Jo said.

Her smile, Ali thought, didn't quite reach her eyes. 'I suppose we can just hope they all turn out like decent human beings,' she said, gabbling along as she felt she was on a safe topic. 'Kind-natured and confident, not afraid to explore outside of their comfort zones and grab life. So far so good, and Jessica has come through the worst of it. She's confident and outgoing, and she's not afraid of hard work. She's at home tonight, glued to her books.'

'Jessica sounds a bit like you, Ali,' Finn said. 'Dependable. Trustworthy. Who do you think Grace will turn out like?'

'Jo, I guess,' Ali said, wondering if she should have said Finn as a sop to his ego.

'Not me, so,' he laughed. 'I don't know whether I'm glad or sorry that we didn't have a sister or brother for Grace,' he went on. 'She's never had to put up with any comparisons or competition, or have anyone messing about with her things ...'

'You mean like the way I messed with your things?' Max asked.

Finn laughed. 'You said it, Max. I could never have anything with you around. No matter what I had you wanted it and invariably you got it. We used to kill each other.'

'Did we?' Max stared at him coldly. 'I thought it was mostly you killing me.'

You could cut the tension with a knife, Ali thought. What was wrong with Max? He'd never talked to Finn like that before. She wished she was relaxing on the sofa at home. *Anywhere but here.*

'Okay, you guys,' Jo said, flapping her hand, 'let's leave the trip down memory lane alone for a while. It's time for dessert.'

'I'll sort that out,' Finn said, getting to his feet and moving around the table, carefully clearing their plates and cutlery. 'You can chat about our futures, and plan where we'll be in ten years' time.'

The conversation moved on to the wider family, the cousins in Galway, the mates Max kept up with who were now living in Dublin, the holidays they had arranged for the summer.

'We're spending a week in France,' Ali said. 'It could be our last year with Jessica. She'll be in college next year and no doubt keen to spread her wings on a J1 to America.'

Finn reappeared with plates of tiramisu and they were just halfway through them when Jo's mobile rang. She picked it up from the sideboard and went out into the hall, returning shortly afterwards, her face a little pale.

'Sorry folks, I'm going to have to leave, that was the nursing home. Mum's being rushed to Vincent's Hospital. Again. I'm afraid I have to cut short our evening and love you and leave you. So if we were having a *Come Dine with Me* challenge, I'm down points already.' She made a joke of it, but Ali could see by her eyes that she was troubled.

'Oh dear, is your mum bad again?' Ali asked.

'Yep, another turn,' Jo shook her head. 'Another long night of waiting and watching, and counting her breaths in a noisy corridor, or if Mum's very lucky, a cramped hospital cubicle.' She scrolled through her phone. 'I'll call a taxi.'

'No need for a taxi, Jo, we were going to be leaving shortly so we can drop you,' Max offered.

'We can't have that, you're our guests,' Finn said, flicking a look at Max as though to say that he didn't want to be under any obligation to him. 'Besides, you can't cut the party short. We were only getting started. I'll drive you in, Jo. I wasn't drinking. I'll be back to you guys in no time and you can sample all the wine you like while I'm gone.'

'It's not that much out of our way,' Max insisted, rising to his feet. 'There's no point in dragging you out, Finn. We didn't intend staying late anyhow.'

'Of course, you guys need to be on top of things in your perfect little empire,' Finn said. 'I hope you don't spoil the kids' free night by arriving home too early.'

In the scramble to get coats, scarves and gloves, say goodbye to Finn and organise themselves in Max's Voyager, Ali bit her tongue and pretended she didn't hear Finn's last remark.

'Sorry about this, folks,' Jo smiled ruefully, as Max headed for the bypass. 'Mum's eighty-one and a bit senile, and along with her stroke anything could happen at any time.'

'It's hard when you're the only one around, Jo,' Ali said, her voice soft with empathy, remembering when her mother had passed on and she'd no siblings to share the burden with.

'Yeah, it's not as if Sasha and Diana are just down the road and can jump into the car.'

'Do you think your sisters will ever come home?'

'Not now. Sasha has said they'll never leave New York, the kids love it, her husband has a big job on Wall Street and she lectures in the university. Diana and her husband are far too busy enjoying the lifestyle and her research career in Paris and their daughters are bilingual. Funny how they ended up living abroad and I came home and stayed.'

They dropped Jo outside the entrance to the hospital, both of them getting out of the car to hug her in the cold night air.

'Will you be okay?' Ali asked. 'Do you want me to go in with you?'

Jo shook her head. 'No, you're fine, thanks, chances are they'll only allow one person in.'

It was only as Max and Ali headed towards the city centre and the canal that Ali finally exploded.

Fifteen

'What was all that about?' Ali fumed.

'All what about?'

'I don't know what kind of mood your brother was in tonight, but remind me not to visit him for a long time. What was all that stuff about Debbie?'

'Debbie?'

She glanced at him, but Max's face was blank. 'You and Debbie and the heat of the kitchen,' she said angrily, realising how ridiculous she sounded.

'Don't be minding Finn. He was just stirring.'

'What's she got to do with him, though?'

'He used to go with Debbie.'

'What? How come I didn't know?'

'It was years ago, Ali.'

'And you never told me?'

'Like I said, it was a long time ago. I'd almost forgotten.'

'Well he hasn't. Then there was all that crap about you and him, growing up.'

'That's exactly what it was, crap.'

'Did you really kill each other?'

'Nah.'

'Then why did you get annoyed with him?'

Max sighed. 'There were just … squabbles.'

'Squabbles? It sounded like more than just squabbles to me.'

'Ali, if the rumours I heard are right, I'd guess Finn is going through the horrors at the moment with his career. I know how much that meant to him. So he's bound to be feeling upset. I tried not to rise to the bait.'

'That doesn't give him the right to take it out on us. And then there was that smart remark about the kids and a free house.'

'It's all ahead of him, you see. He's probably petrified of something happening to Grace.'

Ali plucked her mobile out of her bag. 'Will I let them know we're on the way home?'

Max took his eyes off the traffic in front long enough to shoot her an amused glance. 'No, hey, let's just surprise them.'

'So long as it's not too much of a surprise.'

'We might surprise Tom, who's invited all his mates around and someone's older brother got them a couple of slabs of beer from Finn's beloved Aldi. They put it out on Facebook and there are now a horde of eleven-year-old pre-hormonal teenagers tramping around our house, wrecking everything in sight.'

'That sounds spot on,' Ali laughed. Their son was almost nerd-like in his absorption with his beloved astronomy, and she doubted if he'd even recognise a can of beer.

'It's good to hear you laugh,' Max said.

They drove through Rathgar village, the roads quiet at this hour, shops closed and shuttered, welcoming lights from houses pressing against blinds and curtains, streetlights flowing by the windscreen. She felt cocooned with Max in the warmth of the car, the radio on low and tuned to a music station playing a Robbie Williams love song.

Max said, 'Anything else on your mind?'

'Apart from Tom and his Facebook friends running riot around our house?'

'It does happen, you know.'

'Yes, but not to us. And not Tom, for God's sake.'

'You were the one who asked.'

'And what about Jessica?'

Max smiled. 'What's the betting our darling daughter will be having her schoolmates around for a hair and makeup session? We might find the bathroom in a terrible mess because she thought she'd have time to tidy it before we got home.'

'I hope so,' Ali said. 'She's been working far too hard lately.'

'Hey, you're not really worried, are you? Our kids are fine, we'd hardly have left them to their own devices otherwise. Or do you know something I don't?'

'No, it's just that it's been an unsettling kind of week.'

She didn't want to spoil their mellow mood by talking about Booth Street. They were coming onto the canal now, orange street lights casting long wavering reflections on the surface of the inky black water, a cluster of ice-white swans gathered by the reeds at the far bank of the canal. A sight she'd never tire of. She had a sense of it being home, their world, their place. The special place and time in the hugeness of the universe, inhabited by Max, her and the kids.

As Max spun the wheel of the car and turned off the canal and around into the quiet, shadowed avenue, Ali thought of anxious Jo hovering about a brightly lit hospital, and dark-eyed Finn tidying up everything after their meal. The garden gates were open, so Max drove straight into the driveway, activating the garage door and parking the Voyager neatly, leaving room for Tom to take out his bicycle.

Ali went into the house through the connecting door as he locked the garage. She blinked in the bright light of the kitchen, momentarily disorientated. She inhaled lingering traces of the lemon-scented disinfectant she'd used on the worktops earlier that evening. There was a low hum coming from the refrigerator and some papers in a neat pile waiting to go into the green bin.

She went through the kitchen, shrugging out of her coat and hanging it in the cloakroom. She kicked off her high heels, and lifting them in one hand along with her bag, she went up the stairs. Everything was quiet, with so sign of Tom or Jessica.

'Tom? Jessica?'

She paused on the landing, thinking her children were too engrossed in either their tablets or computers or televisions to pay her any attention, and was about to go up the staircase leading to her and Max's top-floor bedroom when Tom appeared at the door of his room.

'Hi, Mum.'

'I thought you were all having an early night,' she said in a jokey tone of voice.

'No, Jessica's gone out.'

'Out? Where?' she asked, casting her mind back, trying to remember what, if anything, Jessica had said about that night. Ali couldn't recall anything beyond the impression she'd had that Jessica had planned to stay in and study for her mock exams.

'Yeah, about ten minutes ago.'

Deep in her gut, a flicker of unease. 'You mean she only went out ten minutes ago?'

'Yeah.'

'But it's half past ten,' Ali said. 'Where is she off to at this hour? Did we run out of milk?' she went on, telling herself that Jessica might just have popped to a nearby convenience store. *Hoping* that Jessica had just popped out for milk. And how come she had left Tom on his own? He was only eleven years of age. She wanted her daughter safe, here, under their roof. Where she should be.

Tom shrugged. 'I dunno, she knocked and said she was off out.'

'So you didn't actually see her.'

'Nah.' He grinned. 'I was busy searching for Jupiter in Taurus. You should see—'

'Did she say where?' Ali interrupted him.

'Joking? Uh? Didn't dare ask.'

Ali pushed open Jessica's bedroom door, half hoping her daughter might have returned without bothering to tell Tom, but the room was in darkness and a sliver of unease darted around her tummy. It was unusual for Jessica to decide to go out after ten on a Saturday night. Unusual too that she hadn't even texted Ali to let her know.

'What are you all up to?' Max said, his head appearing through the banister rails as he came up the stairs.

'I'm trying to work out where Jessica's gone,' Ali said, momentarily reassured by his presence as he joined them on the landing. After all the years they'd been together, there was something protective about Max that always made her feel safe.

'Hi, son,' Max said, throwing him a high five. 'Why, where's Jess?'

'That's the thing,' Ali said slowly. 'I don't know.'

'You don't *know*?'

'She went out without texting me.'

'She must be with Far Too Keen,' Max said easily. 'A last-minute party, and she didn't want to tell you in case you said she couldn't go.'

'Too right, I would have, especially with her mocks next week,' Ali said, unable to shake off her feelings of unease and wishing she could be as calm as Max.

'You needn't think I'll be telling you every last thing about *my* social life,' Tom volunteered.

'Hey, is this an insurrection?' Max bantered. 'And what could you be getting up to?'

Tom went red and grinned shyly at his father. 'Don't forget, this time next week we'll be getting set for the park, okay?'

'Okay,' Max said. 'We can't miss that.'

'What's that?' Ali asked.

'We're all going to the Phoenix Park next Saturday night if the sky is clear,' Tom said, his face bright with excitement.

'All of us?'

'Yeah, Dad agreed. There's going to be a meteor shower and you might be able to see the meteors every three minutes. It's the best chance in years. But you need to go somewhere dark away from the pollution of the city lights.'

Later, Ali remembered how she took a snapshot of that moment in her head, all her senses filling up as she watched them – her husband and son. Tom, the happy, chatty young boy with so much future promise wrapped up in his eleven-year-old face; Max, his pride in him somehow making him appear larger and more magnanimous a person. It was funny what having children could do for you – they knocked the edges off you, made you more responsible, drove you mad, gave you lots of sleepless nights, but brought a huge richness to your life.

The moment vanished like a burst bubble, as she left them chatting about an upcoming Six Nations match and went on upstairs to their bedroom, dropping her silvery shoes and bag on a chair and going across to the window. She stared out at the lights of occasional traffic passing up and down against the backdrop of the dark canal and wondered where her daughter was, hoping she was happy, trusting she was safe, wondering why she hadn't texted or called to say where she was going. Ali called her mobile, but it went to voicemail, and she was unable to stop a prickle of annoyance from solidifying inside her, like a thin prism pulsing from the top of her head down to her toes.

Restless and uneasy, she went back downstairs, trying Jessica's mobile again and again.

'I'm not going to bed until she comes home,' she said to Max when he joined her in the sitting room.

'Have you heard from her yet?' Max said, frowning.

'No.' Her voice was flat.

'That's not like Jessica.' He went to the window, pulled aside the blind, and looked out.

'Staring out the window will hardly bring her home,' Ali said irritably.

'You're right,' he said, turning around from the window. 'You look exhausted,' he went on. 'Sitting down here won't bring her home any quicker. Why don't we go upstairs and lie in bed while we wait for her.'

'Okay,' she said grudgingly. 'Not that I'll sleep.'

'Neither will I. We'll stay awake together.'

Still, she dropped into a fitful slumber, one ear open waiting for Jessica's key to turn in the lock and the sound of her light footsteps on the stairs. Then, from the hall below, the doorbell rang, the shrill tone piercing the shadowy calm of the stairwells and passageways in the night-time house.

'Jessica must have forgotten her key,' she said quietly as Max clicked on the lamp and rolled out of bed. He pulled on his jeans and padded barefoot out of the room. Ali picked up her mobile and checked the time. It was just after midnight. She waited quietly in the dimly lit bedroom, her annoyance with Jessica far, far outweighed by the wave of relief that she was home. She was vaguely aware of Max's low tones echoing up the stairs in the calm hush. She listened for Jessica's light voice, a trace of her laughter, an apology for having forgotten her key. It seemed to be a long time coming. Instead, she heard a man's voice. There was a pause. The house was suddenly deathly quiet and she felt a chill run through her.

Then Max appeared in the bedroom doorway, his face set and still.

He began to talk, but through the jumble of words he was saying, she only heard two.

Jessica … accident …

PART TWO

Afterwards ...

Sixteen

It had started on the spur of the moment. Unintentional. Then he realised he had valuable ammunition to get back at Max. To make him pay for what he'd robbed. Stolen, then. Without a qualm.

Max was the kind of person who sailed through life, and just about everything turned up smelling of roses for him. He was always so bloody cheerful, it could irritate you, and he even walked around like a prince – purposeful, steadfast, carrying his broad height with such confident ease that you could imagine a crown on top of his head. It was enough to make you feel sick, let alone downright envious.

Then there was Ali and Max together – almost a force of nature.

There was something about loved-up couples that could put your teeth on edge. But these didn't. They weren't smug or blatant, they were – and there was no other word for it – just bloody nice. Even though they sometimes joked and slagged each other off, you could see that behind that they were good and kind to each other, and had respect for each other. You knew this immediately by the way they looked at each other as though they each thought the other was the most important person in the world. Even the way they listened and spoke to each other, and moved around each other as though they were enclosed in a private space of their own.

Of course it was easy for them, because they had no worries, no *real* problems; their lives were not only smooth and plain sailing, but extremely successful. Together they had defied the odds, and at a time when so many businesses were going bust, theirs, naturally, was booming.

Proof, if you needed any more, that whatever Max Kennedy wanted, he got, without putting in too much effort. Even if it rightly belonged to someone else.

So, yes, it had been a bit of a joke to start off, to give Max a taste of what it was like when life threw a spanner in the works. When something was taken away from him.

Karma.

Only it hadn't quite gone to plan. Because it had suddenly spiralled out of control with rather crappy consequences. Drastic consequences, more like, borne out by the revolving blue lights of the ambulance and the police cars, which lit up the countryside for miles around. After a while, the ambulance moved off, siren screaming as it accelerated down the laneway and took the road towards the hospital.

Jesus. This wasn't supposed to have happened.

Seventeen

The nurse said they would be bringing Jessica up to theatre, but they might be able to see her before she went in, just for a minute.

Jessica wasn't theirs anymore. She belonged to others, and her life was totally in the hands of these faceless people whom Ali had never met. The heart had been ripped out of their family and it lay broken and battered on an anonymous bed somewhere in the bowels of this cavernous hospital.

The nurse had a young face, not much older than Jessica's. It swam in front of Ali at the same time as she felt a plastic cup of water being pushed into her hand. Max saw that she had no grip, so he placed his hand over hers and guided the cup to her lips. Ali's mouth gagged on the plastic rim when she caught the faint scent of disinfectant. The nurse said something to Max before walking away.

Her thoughts flew off on a wild tangent. There were giant-sized vending machines in the waiting area close to the Intensive Care Unit and the hospital theatres. She wondered if their oversize indicated how long people were likely to be hanging around here. They offered a selection of water, stilled, sparkling, flavoured, in addition to soft drinks, crisps and chocolate. In the short time they had been waiting, Ali had already stared at the items so much that she could recite every brand available. She needed to focus on something other than the black nightmare engulfing their family like a dark tsunami.

'She'll be fine,' Max said.

'How do you know?' she asked, her voice hoarse as she grappled with words, unable to comprehend this monstrous thing that had crash-landed into their lives.

'She's our daughter, she's *Jessica*. She'll pull through.'

Questions raced through her head. How would he know? How would any of them know anything anymore? They hadn't even known where their daughter had been that night. But she stayed silent, partly from shock and because … because the alternative was unthinkable.

A large family occupied half the waiting area, spreading themselves and a jumble of coats and bags around a circular arrangement of plastic chairs. They ranged in age from seventy-something to seventeen. They passed around tinfoil-wrapped sandwiches and packs of biscuits as though they were sitting in the park having a picnic. Their subdued glances and anxious faces told her otherwise. She wondered how long they had been waiting. Every so often, they came and went through the doors into ICU. They were allowed in two by two, and it made her think of animals going into the Ark.

Tom was standing over by the window, staring out at the other wing of the hospital, and she looked beyond his thin and achingly vulnerable frame across a landscaped passageway where that past of the building was rising up, like a cruise ship with its serried rows of lights blazing cheerfully into the darkness, belying the distress and discomfort going on behind those windows.

The busyness of the hospital in the middle of the night had thrown Ali at first.

The police had offered to bring them in to the hospital, but Max had refused, saying he'd drive his family in. The police had then said they were just there to break the news, they'd been on patrol in the area and that other officers would meet them at the hospital, the team who would be looking after the investigation.

It had been unreal, throwing on some clothes, her fingers fumbling with the zip of her jeans, scrambling into the faux fur coat she'd just worn that evening. It had been unreal driving through dark, deserted night-time streets into the hospital, streets where traffic lights still glowed in sequence despite the near empty roads, telling Ali that somewhere outside of herself, life was still going on as normal. The brightly lit hospital had resembled a huge department store on the first morning of the post-Christmas sales; an overcrowded A+ E department, manic, noisy, and full of frenetic activity, people everywhere, staff rushing around like headless chickens. A whole busy industry rising up in the middle of ghostly, silent streets. She'd stood quietly beside Max, clutching his arm as he spoke to different policemen, to the nurses and a white-coated consultant, but beyond a few words she was afraid to heed – multiple injuries, traumas, fractures – most of what was said swam over her head. After a while, Max had gone behind a curtain and had come out with his face as white as the consultant's coat. He told Ali she could see Jessica very shortly, and then he'd ushered her down a long corridor to this waiting area, his other arm looping around Tom's shoulders, securing the three of them together.

A middle-aged couple, sitting close to Ali, were reading the newspaper, sharing sections of it between them. It reminded her of the way she and Max sometimes shared the paper on a lazy Sunday morning, the one day they could be lazy because the bakery wasn't open. The perfect pearl of memory already seemed like a distant life. She gathered from their conversation that the woman's father had had a heart attack. He was in his late seventies.

She felt a flash of irrational anger. Late seventies was okay, late seventies was fine. Even brilliant. You've had a life by then. Not like Jessica. Seventeen going on eighteen. Jessica couldn't possibly be here or belong to this place. A mistake had been made. Could they please go home now?

Max squeezed her shoulders. 'They're ready for Jessica now, in theatre. We can see her for a minute.'

Ali looked up to see the nurse beckoning, a clipboard held in front of her chest like a plate of armour. Ali had a vague recollection of Max's taut face as he scribbled something on several sheets of paper; his signature, as he signed away permission for the priceless gift that was his daughter's life and put her in the hands of faceless consultants. People who up to now hadn't a clue about the warm, vivacious Jessica, how her eyes crinkled when her lovely face broke into a smile, the sound of her laughter echoing up the stairs, the way she wrapped her scarf around her neck as she hurried out the door, the fun way she danced at a party ...

Ali didn't want to move. She would have given everything she had for it not to have been this Saturday night, but an ordinary night during the week, like thousands they'd had before: at home in her bed, Max sleeping beside her, Tom and Jessica safely tucked up in their bedrooms, his telescope angled in front of the window, their school bags and Tom's rugby kit ready in the hall for school. The sound of occasional traffic going by outside. Max rising early in the pre-dawn light and kissing her forehead. Turning over in the marshmallowy comfort of her bed for another blissful hour.

Precious jewels of ordinary life.

Her back was stiff as she got to her feet. Her legs were like jelly. Her stomach had turned to water. She wasn't sure how to move or where to put her hands, or where to look or how to hold her face in this nightmarish reality. Sparks of panic chased each other around her head. Deep down inside, she was screaming at the top of her lungs. She sensed the couple beside her putting down their newspapers and watching her struggle to put one step in front of the other, vicariously absorbing this mini-drama.

She was amazed at how vicious she felt towards them.

Outside the waiting area, farther down the corridor, there was a rattling sound as a lift door opened. A mist formed in front of her eyes. She heard the clatter of wheels rolling across the entrance to the lift and a bed flowed out, surrounded by people who were wearing loose, blue pyjamas and matching head gear. A forest of drips and tubes snaked around the bed.

'Just two seconds now,' the nurse said, beckoning them forward as the bed was rushed up the corridor.

In the middle of the sea of frightening apparatus, and half-covered by an oxygen mask, Ali caught a glimpse of a small putty-coloured face, dark with bruising along one side, a gash on her forehead. The face was rimmed with a silvery hat, like a plastic shower cap.

She felt momentary relief. It wasn't Jessica. It didn't look a bit like her. A mistake had been made. But when she saw Max kissing the inside of his fingers and placing them on the forehead, she felt she was being sliced in two by a meat cleaver. She wanted to clutch herself with the pain of it but instead she clutched at the rail around the bed. The doors to the theatre lobby opened and Max had to lift off her fingers as the bed was hurried through. The nurse with the clipboard followed the speedy cavalcade and the doors made a soft sucking sound as they closed. Standing in the corridor, every cell in Ali's body felt raw and wounded, as though someone had ripped a giant sticking plaster off her entire body.

When they trudged back to the waiting area, the middle-aged couple looked up with a mixture of sympathy and expectancy. Ali glared at both of them until they looked away. No way was she getting involved in a what-are-you-here-for, oh-how-dreadful, but-the-staff-are-saints type of conversation. Tom went over to the vending machine, looking particularly forlorn as he returned with a bottle of Lucozade.

Max said, 'Jessica will be hours. Do you want to go home for a while?'

'How can you even ask that question?' she choked on the words. 'I'm not going anywhere.'

'I'm just trying to help. You look exhausted. Sitting around here is not going to make any difference to Jessica. She's in the best hands possible. They're optimistic she'll pull through.'

She wondered how he knew this and remembered that he'd talked to the nurses and the consultants and the police who were waiting in the hospital.

One ring of the doorbell. That's all it had taken for their world to cave in. Their daughter, the victim of an apparent hit and run. Up a laneway at the foot of the mountains. They'd found her bag several yards away with her student card in it. There had been no sign of her mobile.

She closed her eyes and tilted her head back against the wall above her chair. What had Jessica been doing there in the first place? How come she, her mother, hadn't known she was there? Or sensed the moment her daughter had been hit?

Someone tipped her on the arm and she opened her eyes.

Max said, 'Would you like a sandwich?'

She felt a rush of anger that he could be asking something so banal at a time like this. Then she realised that one of the young guys from the large family group had come over to them and was holding out a tin-foil packet containing a selection of sandwiches.

'Here, miss, we made far too many,' he said. He looked like the kind of young guy she'd be suspicious of, the kind she'd cross the street to avoid on a dark evening, with his black jeans and navy hoodie. Now their lives intersected and they were united in the sheer, unrelenting anxiety of an ICU waiting room. She thought he was the better one, able to reach out to someone else in spite of his problems, while she was totally unable to communicate on any level.

She shook her head, wondering if she'd ever feel like eating food again.

The young guy proffered the tin-foil-wrapped sandwiches to Tom, who looked at his mother before refusing them. It was the first time Tom had refused food since he'd been eighteen months old and having a bad time with his back teeth. Ali thought that if Max helped himself to a sandwich, she'd never talk to him again.

He didn't. The young guy walked off, seemingly unperturbed by their lack of interest. Two of his family group came slowly out of ICU, an elderly man not attempting to hold back his tears but letting them run freely down his aged, shrunken face. It smote Ali's heart. This was a place full of bad news and sadness. Nights when Ali sat watching a movie with Max or sipped wine in their bay window or checked on the kids before they went to bed, drama after drama had been unfolding along this corridor. One of the young lads, a grandson, Ali thought, jumped out of his chair and offered it to the elderly man. He was helped into the seat and offered tissues. A woman leaned over and hugged him, and patted his hand.

Ali stared blankly into space.

Multiple injuries. She couldn't bear to think what that meant.

Max curled his arm around her and took her hand, drawing it towards him and interlacing his fingers with hers. She was glad of his firm grip. She huddled into her faux-fur coat, rested her head on his shoulder and closed her eyes.

She lost count of time.

Eighteen

'Here we go,' Max said.

Ali opened her eyes. The nurse with the clipboard was walking briskly towards them, her feet making no sound on the floor. 'Mr and Mrs Kennedy?'

They nodded. Tom loped across, the nurse pulled out a chair and they huddled towards her, anxious for precious titbits of information. To the nurse, it was just another night in the busy hospital. To Ali, every word out of the nurse's mouth had become the whole meaning of her life.

'I'm Cathy. I'll be keeping you updated on Jessica's progress in surgery,' she said, her tone respectful and empathetic. 'She's very lucky that we have a great team looking after her. I can assure you she's in the best of hands.'

Max nodded. Ali stayed still. She didn't agree. In the best hands would mean that Jessica was at home, with her parents and brother, slagging Tom over his latest stargazing, watching television, eating pizza, coming downstairs after a shower, her hair swathed in a towel, her face all shiny; at home where she was loved, not here in this ghastly nightmare where she was a patient and all her vitality was reduced to papers on a clipboard.

'As you know, your daughter has suffered a range of blunt-force trauma injuries, consistent with being knocked down by a car,' Cathy said slowly, checking her notes. 'We're not quite sure yet of the extent of her internal injuries, but we have managed to stem the internal bleeding. She's actually lucky to be alive, and she was found in good time,' the nurse finished up in a sympathetic voice.

'She will pull through, won't she?' Max asked the question Ali was afraid to even formulate in her head, let alone say out loud.

'Her vital signs are good, and the fact that she's survived to this stage is a positive indicator.'

'How long will she be … in theatre?' Max asked in an ultra-soft voice, which told Ali he couldn't bear the image of his daughter in a hospital theatre.

'It's difficult to say, but it could be four or five hours. Then post-surgery, we'll need to make sure she's stable before we can move her to ICU, where we'll also need a suitable bed, and that could take another couple of hours. So even if all goes well, you won't get to see your daughter for at least another six or seven hours. I'm just letting you know what kind of time frame to expect. But I can assure you she's in good hands and everything possible is being done. I'll pop out again in another couple of hours.'

Ali stared at the nurse. Her words were jumbling together in her head, like lotto balls spinning and colliding mindlessly in the Perspex drum. She was unable to comprehend that they would be working on Jessica's battered body for so long, that it would be another couple of hours before they had an update, let alone having to wait hours upon hours before they could see her again. She couldn't bear it. She opened her mouth to object but no words came out.

'Thank you,' Max said. 'You've been very helpful.'

Cathy smiled, got to her feet and turned to leave. Ali wanted to call her back, to sniff at her uniform in case it held a trace of Jessica's scent. How come she was allowed to see Jessica while Ali had to wait helplessly outside? *I am her mother, for God's sake.*

Max had cradled Ali's shoulders and kissed her forehead while Jessica was being born. And she'd been glad of that because she'd been scared.

She wondered how scared Jessica had been earlier that evening. Why hadn't she known, on instinct, that her daughter had been in trouble?

'Excuse me,' she said, speaking over a huge lump in her throat.

Cathy turned and looked at her sympathetically.

'Tell her …' Ali began, then paused. She drew breath from somewhere. 'Tell Jessica we love her. Very much.'

'I will, of course.'

Then she disappeared.

'Okay?' Max asked.

'I need to go to the bathroom,' Ali said.

'Out onto the corridor and down to the right,' he said. 'Will I walk out with you?'

'No, I'll be fine.'

She needed a few moments alone. Time to connect with her scattered self, to regroup all her spinning senses and find some ground in the new shape her life had taken. She felt as though she were taking baby steps with unfamiliar limbs as she headed out onto the corridor, and she almost baulked as she recalled Jessica being whooshed by, criss-crossed with drips and tubes, and surrounded by strangers.

The ladies was functional and cold, the air redolent with cheap disinfectant. The two cubicles were empty and a tap was dripping. She looked at her face in the mirror and didn't recognise the woman with the hard, pained eyes staring back at her. She touched her face as if to make sure it was still there and she felt cool fingers on her cheek.

A head trauma. Did that mean they'd have to shave off Jessica's hair? Could they be doing that now? Or were they sawing at the jagged bits of her shattered leg? She recalled the way baby Jessica had continued to curl both her legs into a foetal position for weeks after she'd been born, and the silky perfection of those legs as Ali ran her fingers up and down. She clutched the basin and leaned forward, opening her mouth as wide as it would go in a long, silent scream. When she had expelled all the air, there was a long moment of emptiness, and she felt she could simply expire.

There'd been a moment's silence after Jessica was born, and then she'd drawn her first breath and begun to cry that high-pitched, quavering new-born cry, a sound that echoed around the delivery ward and filled Ali and Max with joy.

Ali stood in limbo for a moment, not wanting to breathe, and then her lungs automatically drew in air, gulping for oxygen, and she could still hear that cry in her ears as she splashed her face with cold water and rinsed her hands.

She hadn't heard Jessica cry earlier that evening. She'd stood at her bedroom window, annoyance mixed with disappointment that her daughter had slipped out of the house without telling them. But she hadn't sensed her cry for help.

When she went back to the waiting area, she saw the police talking to Max.

Nineteen

Jessica wasn't theirs any more. She belonged to the faceless people behind the closed doors, and now she belonged to the young guys wearing garda uniforms, whom she had never met in her life and who looked as though they were barely out of training school.

They introduced themselves as Paul and David. They were attached to the area where Jessica had been found. They were not much older than Jessica, but if this was their regular Saturday night stint, they were way ahead of her in terms of appreciating the finer and not so finer details of the great underbelly of the city's weekend nightlife. They didn't look all that fazed by the enormity of Jessica's serious condition, and while they were respectful enough, their intrusive questions were routinely uttered as though they were discussing the weather forecast. At least that's how it seemed to Ali's raw heart. She was grateful that Max was able to answer them.

They were all sitting in a small room at the end of a corridor, containing a shabby table and some mismatched chairs. A couple of dog-eared posters were staring down from the wall, proclaiming stark reminders about the importance of regular hand washing. Ali shivered as she looked around and wondered if this was the room where people were brought to hear sad pronouncements about their loved ones. If so, it was intolerable. She would fling the furniture around this room if she was brought here for bad news.

'So you're not sure exactly where Jessica was going tonight?' Paul said. He was asking most of the questions, David was writing the answers down in a notebook.

Ali bit her lip. The question was asked in perfectly neutral tones, but she felt censure of some kind. How come she didn't know where her daughter was going, late on a Saturday night?

Max glanced at her reassuringly and looked back at the young guard.

'No, my wife and I were out and when we came home, she had already left.'

'What time was this? It's really important,' Paul said, softening his voice a little, 'that we know the time as accurately as possible.'

Max looked at Ali. 'We were home after half past ten. Ten forty, I guess.'

'Jessica went out at about twenty-five past ten,' Tom said, his face red.

'Did you see her leave?'

'No, she just knocked on my bedroom door and said she was off.' Tom's face crumpled. Ali wondered what agony he was going through, knowing he was the last person to talk to Jessica before she left.

'We thought …' Max faltered. 'We thought she had gone out to a last-minute party or was with her boyfriend …'

For the first time since the doorbell rang, Max broke down. He leaned forward and covered his face with his hands. In the thick silence of the room, Ali heard him struggling to breathe.

Nobody said anything for a moment. David put down his pen and looked at them sympathetically. 'We know this is difficult,' he said, 'but our purpose in all of this is to apprehend whoever knocked Jessica down as soon as possible. It appears she has been the victim of a hit and run. The area where she was found has been closed off for forensic examination, which will commence at first light. Any and all information you can give us will be a big help. Especially the timing of the events. We'll be talking to Jessica herself, obviously, as soon as the doctors think she is fit for questioning, but that could take a few days and, in the meantime, we need to gather as much information as we can.'

Max straightened up and Ali could sense him pulling himself together enough to shoulder whatever weight he had to. 'My wife and I will give you whatever help you need. I want to find the bastard who did this—'

'Max.' Ali's hand reached out for his.

By the time they were finished with their routine questions, a lot of Jessica's young, promising life had been reduced to the pages of a spiral notebook; the names of her closest friends, her school, her usual haunts.

'That seems to be most of the details,' David said.

No, it's not, Ali wanted to protest. This isn't Jessica. You can't capture the essence of our amazing daughter just like that.

'Except her friends' mobile numbers,' David looked at them expectantly, his biro poised.

'We don't have her friend's mobile numbers,' Max said, the strain of it all evident in his cracked voice. 'I don't know why that is.'

Because we trusted her. Ali bit her lip. *We didn't feel the need to be cross-checking anything.*

'Not even Far Too Keen's,' Max said.

'Sorry? Who?' David looked puzzled as he checked his notes.

Max shook his head. Again, he couldn't speak for a moment. Ali was filled with a rush of love for him. 'That's our pet name for Jessica's boyfriend,' she said, finding her voice. 'Kian Costello. We've already given you his name.'

'So you have,' David said, glancing shrewdly at Max. 'Is there any particular reason you call him that?'

Ali had the sense that no matter how pleasant the police were, every word they said was up for analysis. Max was unable to answer. She pressed her nails into the palm of her hand and said, her voice quavery, 'Jessica is very precious to us. She is equally precious to her boyfriend, who seems to be particularly keen on her. That's our pet name for him.' She couldn't help lifting her chin as she stared at David. It was a personal sliver of family life, joked and laughed about in the good times, now laid bare for any kind of interpretation and it had no place in this dilapidated room.

The guard seemed satisfied. He glanced at Max a little more deferentially. Ali tried to breathe evenly. It wouldn't be until he had a daughter of his own that he would have an iota of a clue of what Max was going through right now.

'We just need Jessica's mobile number,' Paul said. 'Her phone could yet be found near the scene, but we might be able to obtain some helpful details without it.'

'She was on the phone before she left,' Tom suddenly said. His face reddened further when everyone turned to look at him.

Max smiled at him as though he was trying to convey some support through his eyes. 'What happened, son?'

'I heard her talking to someone,' Tom said. 'When I was coming back up the stairs and passed by her bedroom.'

'How did she sound? Have you any idea who that was?' Paul asked.

Tom shook his head. 'I just heard her voice. Normal, like. I don't know what she was saying. The television was on in my room and my bedroom door was open, so that was louder.'

'I think it's possible that Jessica went out to meet whoever she was speaking to,' Paul said. 'Or at least she might have told them where she was going. We should be able to get some call details from her network provider.'

He sounded sure of himself, Ali thought. In her mind's eye, she flicked through images of Jessica's friends, who mostly comprised her schoolmates. She had come up through secondary school with two or three close friends, Mia, Sophie and Rachel. They shared birthday parties and exam stress, and together they found their feet in the exciting world of adolescence. Now they were young women, well educated, with the world at their feet. And best of friends, *good* friends, always there for each other. She thought of Kian, academic and responsible, a little shy perhaps but crazy about Jessica.

'It doesn't make sense,' she blurted, not realising she had spoken aloud until Max looked at her.

'What doesn't make sense?' Paul asked.

'All this …' she waved her hand ineffectually. 'How come Jessica was all alone? There's no way she'd go off on her own … even if she fell out with someone, her friends always made a point of sticking together until they were all safely home. They wouldn't take any foolish chances. And Kian would hardly abandon her. I don't understand how …'

Max tightened his hold of her hand and she realised he had already been torturing himself with this.

Paul gave her a long, steady look, tinged with sympathy. As though he had seen and heard all this before; parents who thought they knew where their children were and what they were up to, when they didn't know anything at all. Ali stared back at him. She wanted to shout that Jessica was not like that. She was the gorgeous, wonderful daughter of Ali and Max, responsible and kind, and they trusted her implicitly.

'I think we have enough information to begin making enquiries,' Paul said. 'I expect it'll be tomorrow before any progress is made.'

David flipped through the pages of his notebook, checking his synopsis of Jessica's life before closing it. 'Yup. That's all fine.'

'Another thing,' Paul said, 'we'll hold back from releasing any details to the press for now. It'll give you a chance to talk to your families. We'll be asking members of the public for any information, and looking for witnesses, so we'll be issuing a statement along with that, but we'll inform you of that first.'

'How optimistic are you that you'll find the … culprit?' Max asked, choking over the word as though it should never be synonymous with his darling Jessica.

'We won't leave any stone unturned in our efforts to apprehend whoever was responsible,' Paul said. 'Someone, somewhere must know that they have knocked a pedestrian down. However, there is also the possibility that it was a drunk driver, someone so far out of it that they might not have noticed his or her actions. We'll be checking all the taxi cabs that could have been in the area at the time. And we'll be able to get more information when we receive the full report of Jessica's injuries. It should help indicate the speed of the vehicle and the point of impact, which could have a bearing as to whether the driver is aware of what happened or not.'

Ali felt sick. She had to breathe slowly so that she wouldn't gag. She couldn't rid her mind of the heart-rending image of Jessica being hurled into the air on a dark, lonely laneway, thanks to a split-second, senseless point of impact.

'The couple who found her ...' she said, trying to recall details the police had told them, 'had they any idea of how long Jessica was lying there?'

She knew straightaway that was a stupid question.

David looked at his notes. 'They are a married couple who live up at the top of that lane and were out on a late-night walk with their dog. There's no way of knowing how long she'd been there until we have the consultant's full report, which might give some indication.'

'You've been most helpful,' Paul said. 'I know this is difficult but our job is to help you and Jessica. I'm sure we'll be talking to you soon.'

'Hope it all goes okay for you guys,' David said. 'The hospital will be keeping us updated on her progress.'

At first Ali thought it was caring of them to want to know Jessica's progress. Then something cold ran down her spine when she realised that if Jessica didn't pull through, it would change the whole course of the investigation. But that wasn't going to happen. It just can't happen, she told herself, as they left the room and watched the guards stride off down the corridor.

They returned to the waiting area. Most of the family group had gone, with just a couple of teenage boys left behind, sitting hunched forward among the detritus of bags, coats and empty bottles of water and soft drinks. There was something about their abject figures that caught at her throat.

Other people had come into the waiting area. They looked dazed and freshly shell-shocked, awkward and ill at ease. Ali must have looked like that when she first arrived, which seemed to her a long time ago but in fact was barely two hours.

Then the family group arrived back en masse. Most of them had tears running down their faces and some were openly sobbing, heedless to whoever was watching them. They pulled on coats and jackets, picked up bags and gathered whatever was left of their food. Some of them hugged each other before they drifted off in twos and threes. Soon they were all gone, the seats they had occupied vacant, the whole space suddenly empty, as though they had never been. 'I'm gonna stretch my legs,' Tom said.

Max made to get up, but Ali stalled him. 'Leave him for now,' she said, knowing how much Tom needed some space.

'I need to call Finn and Jo,' Max said. 'And Debbie. But I'll leave it until later. No sense in calling them at four in the morning.'

'Yes,' she said. 'Besides, it's better to wait until Jessica is out of theatre and we have something definite to tell them. Something that's more positive, hopefully. And anyway, we don't know what's happening with Jo and her mother. You didn't hear anything from Finn?'

'I'd forgotten about that.' Max checked his mobile. 'Nah, nothing.'

'Pity we all weren't in the same hospital. At least we could have kept each other company and they're the only people I feel I could talk to right now.'

'Even Finn?'

Ali thought for a minute of the family that had just left the waiting area, and the way they had all come together in a show of love and support that fizzed between them, despite the fact that such a diverse group would surely have their differences. 'Yeah, well it's at times like these that family means everything, isn't it? And I don't have much of a family, do I?'

'Come here.' Max looped his arm around her, tucking her into him. She rested her head in the warm spot between his shoulder and his neck as though it was made for her. They got as comfortable as they could on the plastic chairs.

And waited.

Twenty

Jo pulled up the collar of her cashmere coat as she walked through the automatic doors and out into the chill of a brand-new morning. After the fusty atmosphere of the cramped melee of the A&E, the fresh air stung her face like cold spikes. She gulped it in, ridding herself of the staleness she sensed clinging invisibly to her like a second skin. The navy sky to the east was beginning to separate into bands of lighter blue with the approach of morning. In the distant northern sky, she saw the glimmer of aeroplane lights as it banked into the heavens having taken off from Dublin airport.

She wished she was on it. With Grace and Finn. Going somewhere new. Somewhere they could begin all over again. Somewhere Finn could learn to get over his huge disappointment before it really damaged their marriage, and they could try to be that couple on the beach in the wedding photo. But she couldn't go anywhere just yet.

Her mother's condition had stabilised. Jo knew that while there was any kind of life, there was hope. When Veronica Harper drew her last breath, that would be it, and no power on earth would bring her back again. There would be no possibility of any kind of reconciliation, no opportunity to make some kind of peace between them.

'We'll be sending your mother back to the nursing home later this morning,' the doctor with the tired face had said. Then she'd hesitated before continuing, 'Every time your mother has a turn, a mini-stroke, she's fading more and more. It might be advisable to put your family on the alert, because the next time could well be the last.'

It was the third time since Christmas that Veronica had been close to death's door. 'Thanks for letting me know,' Jo had said.

Jo walked past knots of people straggled together by the wall outside the A&E. She slowed her pace as an ambulance hurtled up and passed her, sirens screaming. From behind, she heard the siren abruptly silenced in mid-shriek. Then the clatter of doors being opened echoed across the still morning air. She kept on walking towards the idling cluster of taxis, and she rapped on the window of the first one, disturbing the driver who had been texting on his mobile. He nodded his head and put down his phone, and Jo opened the back door and sank into the seat.

❁

At home, the house was quiet, Finn still in bed. Despite her exhaustion, she didn't want to go to bed to snatch a few hours' sleep just yet. She hadn't spoken to Finn since last night. She had texted him twice to update him on Veronica's condition, and he had replied to wish her well. There had been no point in him coming in, as patients in the A&E were only allowed to have one visitor apiece.

In the calm of the kitchen, she popped some bread in the toaster and made a mug of tea, her hands cupped around the warmth of the mug, making her realise how cold she was. She spread a little butter on her toast and took a bite of it, the taste surprisingly delicious and comforting.

The doctor had said to put her family on the alert. She had a good mind not to bother. Why should she? Why not leave Diana and Sasha in the dark?

Just like she had been.

1992

'Oh it's you, you little bitch,' Diana hisses down the phone.

In the public phone kiosk on a busy road in Rathmines, Jo automatically holds the receiver away from her ear for a moment, as if to let the venom in Diana's voice dissipate into the air.

It's Tuesday evening, a week since she and Finn had arrived home from their honeymoon. They had met Max and Ali last week and were guests at their wedding at the weekend, and something about the warmth of the day, the laughter and happiness and exchange of vows in the company of their small families and a group of friends, had touched Jo in a way she hadn't expected. So much so, that she wants to see her own family and introduce Finn to them. She'd expected her father to answer the phone, home from his surgery, with her mother out at her church meeting, but instead her sister Diana has answered. Jo hadn't expected the warmest of welcomes, but neither had she expected the degree of animosity in Diana's voice.

'How dare you!' Diana's voice shakes.

'How dare I what?' Jo counters back.

'Waltz back into our lives as though everything is fine, and you're probably expecting the fatted calf to be laid out for you too – you and your fancy man. Well that's not going to happen.'

'He's not my fancy man, he's my husband,' Jo says. 'And his name is Finn.'

'As far as we're concerned you and Finn can take yourselves right back to where you came from. You're not wanted here.'

Jo feels stung. 'I'm not having this conversation with you, Diana. Can I speak to Dad?'

'No, you can't.'

'Is this because I got married? I thought they were okay with it, Mum and Dad.'

'Well you thought wrong. They weren't.'

Jo feels incensed. She counts to ten and stares at the graffiti inside the phone kiosk. Names and phone numbers. Declarations of love. Meaningless scribbles. 'You mean they wanted me to go along with the whole white, frilly extravaganza, to show off to the family and neighbours,' she laughs self-deprecatingly. 'Not that I ever thought they'd want to show plain Jo Harper off.'

'Give over, Jo,' Diana's voice hardens. 'They knew that wasn't your style.'

'Oh really?'

'For God's sake, Jo, Mum and Dad always loved you. They couldn't understand why you didn't come home for your wedding. Or why you ran away in the first place, thumbing your nose at your lovely birthday party. You've no idea what Sasha and I have had to listen to from Mum. She was terribly upset.'

Jo can never explain to her sister and her heart races for a moment at the unfairness of it. She tells herself that it is all behind her, left on the other side of the world. Finn is the centre of her life now. Jo Kennedy, with Finn by her side, has made a fresh start.

'Then she was all up in arms about why you got married in such a hurry.'

'I'm not pregnant,' Jo bristles.

'That wouldn't have mattered,' Diana says, her voice subdued.

'Oh yeah? You're kidding me.'

'They thought it was another of your rebellious stunts.'

'Didn't they trust my decision?'

'Jo, you got married. To someone you'd only known six months.'

'No, it was nearly a year.'

'They were worried about you and they missed you,' Diana says in a funny voice. As though she was holding back tears. 'They were afraid you were never going to come home.'

'That's not what I heard. I was told to please myself, as though it didn't matter to anyone.'

'Well of course they told you to please yourself. Mum and Dad would never have expected you to suit them and go against your own dreams, your *principles*,' Diana mocked, using one of Jo's favourite teenage phrases.

'I'm more mature now,' Jo says.

For a moment, there is a silence. Then Diana speaks, her voice cracking. 'It's a bit too late for that, because Dad—'.

'Dad what?' Something stills inside Jo.

'Dad's gone.' There is the sound of crying at the other end of the phone.

'What do you mean "gone"?' Jo grips the phone painfully. It couldn't be. *Noooo*. Not Dad. He is only what – early sixties? And then the words come, implacable, merciless and, oh, so final.

'He's dead,' Diana says, her voice muffled. 'He had a heart attack, on your wedding day. He died a few days later.'

'*What?*' Blood rushes to Jo's head and turns to water in her veins. Somewhere inside her everything is falling down. She grabs the shelf that was there to hold a missing phone book and holds on tight. Otherwise she would have crashed to the floor.

'You heard me.' Diana is crying noisily now. 'And it was your fault.'

'Why didn't you tell me? *Why didn't you tell me?*' she screams, ignoring the other horrific words for now.

A middle-aged woman passing by with a shopping bag looks in at her sharply. Two kids going by stick out their tongues and press their faces against the glass, contorting their images. The kind of thing Jo used to do at the kitchen window.

'How could we tell you when we didn't know where you were? We sent a message through to your address in Sydney but you were gone. You could have been anywhere.'

'I was on my *honeymoon*,' Jo cries. 'I was on my way home. Why didn't you try harder to find me?'

'We hadn't a clue where to start. Anyway, do you think we wanted to look at your face, Sasha and I?' Diana says, in a smothered voice. 'After what you caused? I'm here with Mum now. She's too upset to be left on her own. And she's far too upset to talk to you.'

Jo drops the phone. She can't see in front of her with the tears coursing down her face. She gropes her way out of the phone kiosk. Then she starts to hurry, trying to outrun the feeling that something inside her has died. She doesn't care what people think of the mad girl tearing up the main street in Rathmines, dodging pedestrians and litter bins and lampposts. She keeps running until she reaches the entrance to the house where she and Finn have set up home in a two-roomed flat. She has to stop and catch her breath in the hallway before she goes up two flights of stairs and her heart is beating as if it will fly out of her chest.

When she bursts into the flat, Finn is sitting at the table, the newspaper open in front of him at the situations vacant page, and he is circling possible jobs with a red biro.

'Hi, Jo, what did they—' Finn's voice breaks off as he sees her face and jumps to his feet. 'Hey – what's up?'

'Oh, Finn! Everything! Everything is wrong,' she cries, half-weeping, half-gasping as she falls into his arms.

She tells him when she is able to talk, to put the words together. She has no problem recalling every word Diana has uttered, because they are permanently engraved on her heart and soul. But she holds back a couple of things, like the way Diana blames her for her father's death, and the way she said Jo's wedding had been a rebellious stunt. She could imagine Finn's reaction to those inflammatory words. Besides, they aren't true. She loves Finn. And he loves her. Almost feverishly, she thinks, almost too much, recalling the possessive, impassioned way he made love to her on the night of Max's wedding.

'I'm here,' Finn murmurs, hugging her close, pushing her hair back gently from her wet face. 'I'll always be here for you, I promise. You're not on your own, Jo. We'll face whatever you have to face together.'

Right then, she doesn't care if she never sees her sisters again. Or her mum. But she does, of course. Early the following week Finn encourages her to call home. 'You need to talk to your mother at a time like this,' he says. 'You need to be around your family.'

Jo freezes. She's on the brink of telling him the part her mother played in sending her running to Australia but she hesitates. What's the point? It doesn't matter anymore.

The minute she hears Jo's voice, her mother breaks down on the phone.

'You don't have to talk to me if you don't want to,' Jo says.

'Of course I want to talk to you,' her mother says. 'I want to see you. And your new husband. I want to make sure you're happy.'

'I am. We are,' she says.

❁

She brings Finn home the following Sunday and his jaw drops as they turn into a long driveway leading to a spacious house in County Meath.

'You never said ...'

'Never said what?' she asks with a touch of belligerence.

'Doesn't matter,' he says, giving her a warm glance as he squeezes her hand, and she knows he understands her sharpness is just a cloak to hide her anxiety. He loves her and it is enough to calm her a little. Especially when she walks inside. Her mother could be wearing a mask because her face looks so different. As though it's a fragile shell, with all the imperious life sucked out of it. Her eyes are dull pebbles. Jo doesn't ask if her mother blames her for her father's death. Her mother doesn't ask why she left home so abruptly, but the awkward questions are darting silently around the air between them. Her sisters arrive along with their husbands, and on the surface it is all very polite and gracious;, they welcome Finn with their usual good manners, they all shed a few tears as they talk of Jo's father and his sudden death. Only for Finn by her side, supporting her with a loving look or an affectionate gesture, Jo knows she would have fallen apart.

Afterwards, over tea and sandwiches, they talk about the wedding as though it was a strange party that happened on a far-off planet and it is all very delicate. To her face, no one has the temerity to mention her father's death in the context of her wedding, not even her sisters; it was as though there was a complicity between them and Diana's angry phone call had never taken place.

But the link is there; she sees it in her sisters' red-rimmed eyes as she catches their glances sliding away from her, she sees it in her mother's empty face as she stares into the middle distance over Jo's head. And she sees it in her own heart, embedded like a cold, hard pellet.

Even when her father's death is overlaid and softened with the normal family rituals that play out over the passage of time and the change of seasons from one year to the next, when grandchildren arrive into their lives, bringing joy and happiness to the family, it stays in the lining of Jo's heart and refuses to dissolve.

Because there is no grandfather around to share the joys.

Twenty One

Max's phone buzzed, and Ali sensed the ripple of interest that flowed around the waiting area.

Jessica's nurse had come out at six o'clock to say the surgery was still proceeding according to plan, which told them nothing really. Since then, Max and Ali, along with Tom and everyone else, had been sitting, mostly in silence, as staff came and went through the doors into ICU, largely ignoring the disparate group waiting hungrily for a morsel of news of any kind. Outside the sky was beginning to lighten, but inside, the air seemed heavy with a dull fatigue.

Max squeezed Ali's hand as he got up and went out into the corridor, where she knew there would be less chance of the whole waiting area overhearing him.

Minutes later, he motioned Ali to join him.

'The police have traced Jessica's mobile.'

'Already? Where?'

A muscle flexed in his cheek. She was sure his face had become thinner in the few hours since the doorbell rang.

'That's the funny thing,' he said slowly. 'Initial traces show it to be just south of the city centre. The general area where we live. There's a chance she might have left it at home.'

'But I called it last night and didn't hear it ringing. Anyway, Jessica would never go anywhere without it.'

'I know. They asked if I could check our house as soon as possible. Just in case.'

She stared at him.

'At this hour of the morning, I could be there and back in no time.'

'Don't leave me, please.'

He pulled her close. She sensed his exhaustion. It was like some kind of static in his chest as she leaned into him. She thought of their wedding photo, the one that the children sometimes made fun of, where she was snuggled into Max's chest, her arms around his waist, his arms tightly enfolding her. A chink of pale yellow light, like a pencil beam, slanted across the ceiling of the corridor, over their heads. The sun was coming up. It would be lighting up the narrow laneway where Jessica was knocked down. The police would be looking for any kind of clue that would help find out what happened to their daughter. She pictured them sifting painstakingly through undergrowth and bushes, poking behind each and every clump of earth and stony pebble.

Jessica's phone could be very useful.

She pushed herself away from Max.

'Go on. Go home and see if it's there.'

'Are you sure?'

'From what the nurse said earlier, nothing's going to happen for at least a couple of hours. Just drive safely. Do you want Tom to go with you?'

'I'd rather he stayed with you. The police said to let them know when I'm on the way as they'll meet me there. To save time. Can I bring you back anything?'

'Just yourself.'

He kissed her. 'Call me if there's any news. I'll turn around and come straight back.'

It took a big effort to smile, her face was so stiff with tension. 'You won't be long.'

When she saw him loping down the corridor, with long, brisk strides, part of her heart went with him. She wondered if this was how women felt down through the ages when their men went off to war.

❁

Max forgot to pay his car parking fee and had to turn on the hazard lights, jump out at the barrier, and rush back inside, rummaging for his ticket. He eventually fished it out of the back pocket of his jeans, and fed in a twenty-euro note. He grabbed his change, and was halfway back to the car when he realised he had left the ticket in the machine. He raced back and, luckily, his ticket was still poking out of the slot. He hurried to the car, pressing the unlock button on his key, only to find he had left the door open in his haste to get to the pay machine.

It was, he thought, the mundane things that had the power to reduce you to tears of frustration.

When he reached the canal, the glare of low-morning sunshine caused him to pull down his visor. How could it look so cheerful, he scowled, considering what had happened? He wanted to pretend, for a few precious moments, to be an ordinary man on an ordinary Sunday morning, out for a drive along the canal, without the nightmare that was stalking them all. He saw the gleam of a Luas tram halted up on Charlemont Bridge, with a scatter of passengers sitting inside and the movement of others as they passed down the carriage, and he asked himself how things could look so normal. In a corner of his mind, somewhere that wasn't fogged up by anxiety and shock, he realised that he probably appeared normal enough to everyone else and maybe some the passengers on the Luas were looking down at him driving along in the sunny morning and were envying him his big MPV with the Booth Street Bakery logo on the side.

There was a squad car outside the house, preventing him from parking in the garden, so he pulled in behind it and leaped out. Paul and David got out of the car.

'Hello again,' he said, feeling unaccountably jittery.

'Good morning, Mr Kennedy. Thanks for being so prompt.' The blend of careful and sympathetic politeness softened the resolute look in their eyes.

They followed him up the path and he wondered with a jolt if he was some kind of a suspect. He didn't particularly care. He fumbled with the key in the lock, temporarily forgot the alarm code and had to take a deep breath and clear his mind before he was able to key it in. He moved down the hall, quietly amazed to find everything standing more or less the same as it had been the previous night. Surely what had happened would have left a mark somewhere?

'I'll check her bedroom first,' he said.

'If you do see it, call us. Don't touch it,' Paul advised.

Max took the stairs two at a time, pulling out his mobile to call Jessica's number, just in case, but it went to voicemail again. Jessica's bedroom was in darkness, the blinds and curtains still closed. He drew back the curtains and looked around helplessly, unable to pick out anything at first in the clutter on her bedside table and dressing table. Then as he moved across to her desk, he saw it, sitting there. He froze, wanting to pick it up. Instead he went back to the top of the staircase and called the police.

'It's up here,' he told them.

Paul dropped the mobile into a clear plastic bag, sealing it shut. 'Great stuff, we'll get this checked out.'

Max felt as he had in the early hours of the morning when he'd signed away permission for the doctors to open Jessica up. Dislocated. Sad. And unable to get a grip on the deep river of distress and anger that coursed through his veins.

'How soon will you have any information from it?' he asked, walking downstairs after Paul.

'Later today, hopefully,' Paul said. 'We'll call you. We'll check Jessica's contacts for phone numbers against the names of her friends that you gave us and we'll talk to them too.'

They marched out the door and Max was left alone. The hallway was the emptiest place in the world. He went back upstairs to Jessica's room and looked around at the familiarity of her things: the cluttered surfaces, her desk with the laptop closed, messy with an assortment of books, papers and her iPad. Her bed was strewn with clothes, as though she'd had trouble deciding what to wear – because her outfit was important to her, his thoughts ran on, causing his heart to clench unbearably.

He thought of his beautiful daughter in happier times – the baby warmth of her fitting into the palm of his hand, the once-upon-a-time way she used to launch herself into his arms, snuggling beside him to watch Christmas television, chasing kites together on a windy beach with her hair flying in the wind – her sweet, all-too-brief childhood reduced to a series of snapshots in his head, where by degrees Jessica's all-important dad was relegated to the periphery of her adolescent life, his omnipotence and power waning year by year.

He wanted to throw himself down in the middle of her clothes on top of the bed and bury himself there forever. But he didn't have the luxury of that right now, or the ordinary luxury of his daughter at home, sleeping in on a Sunday, much as usual, trailing downstairs in her dressing gown with her face so like Ali's, suddenly childlike, free of her usual makeup.

'Hi, Daddy, any chance of your delish blueberry pancakes for breakfast?'

He felt his mouth convulse and he pushed his hand against it.

Oh, God, stop this nightmare, please.

Twenty-Two

'Mr and Mrs Kennedy? Would you come this way please?'

Ali looked up at Cathy and struggled to her feet. She felt the eyes of the entire waiting room occupants upon her as she clutched Max's hand and nodded reassuringly at Tom. Cathy had come out twenty minutes earlier to say that Jessica would soon be out of theatre and that Mr Boland, the lead consultant, would talk to them. She gave no indication of how Jessica was other than she was holding her own. They were back in the small, shabby room, joined this time by a white-coated Mr Boland, who told them he was in charge of the team of doctors and surgeons looking after Jessica.

'Jessica is stable for now,' Mr Boland said. 'I don't need to tell you that she has been through a tremendous ordeal.'

He spoke, Ali realised with a rush of gratitude, as though he personally knew Jessica, that she wasn't just another Saturday-night statistic or notch on his surgery belt. He was in his mid-fifties and he looked very capable and in control, even though he had spent hours in theatre.

'She had lost a considerable amount of blood from internal haemorrhaging by the time we got her into theatre. Stopping that was our first priority. The bleeding was coming from a damaged spleen, on account of two broken ribs.'

He spoke very slowly, as though he knew it would be difficult for Ali, Max and Tom to take all this in.

'Does that mean—' Max said. Then he shook his head. 'Sorry. Go ahead.'

'We have repaired the spleen as best we could, but only time will tell if it heals completely or needs to be removed.'

'Oh, gosh.' Ali bit her lip.

'Don't worry about that yet. People can survive quite well without a spleen. If it comes to that. We've a few more hurdles to cross. Jessica also sustained a pelvic fracture, which caused bleeding to tissues and muscles in that area.'

Ali couldn't stop herself from crying out. Max held her hand. Tom – bless him – touched her on the arm.

'We have stabilised it and without going into details we are confident that, in time, Jessica will make a good recovery as regards those injuries. The orthopaedic surgeon has done some work on her leg, but further surgery will be required. Overall, it's a question of time being needed to allow these injuries to heal; we're looking at several weeks, but they should heal well, with the right care and attention. And there will be some physiotherapy required further down the road.' He paused.

'Anything else?' Max asked.

The consultant gave him a steady look. 'While Jessica pulled through the surgery, and we're positive for her recovery, she is in a mild coma, and that's due to a small amount of swelling on her brain.'

'What does that mean?' Max asked.

'I can't say exactly.' Mr Boland was deferential. 'When the brain is bruised, following a knock, it swells. You could say it's gone into self-defence mode, fully functioning, but in its slowest stage of alertness, which has resulted in concussion. It's a temporary condition, and thankfully it's only mild swelling and not a bleed, but her coma could last several hours or a few days. From scans, we're confident that there hasn't been any damage to the brain stem.'

'How confident?' Ali's voice was strangled. It was too much to take in.

Tiredness and anxiety had seeped into the marrow of her bones so that she felt she was moving around in a big black pall.

'Very. You can see her as soon as she's been settled in ICU, but that will take a couple of hours.'

❁

Ali was in more need than ever of Max's strong support and the feel of his arm around her as he had to hold her up when they finally got in to see Jessica. Her pale, still daughter was like a stranger in the hospital bed, the outline of a cage under the blanket reminding Ali forcibly of her shattered limbs, a battery of machines keeping her alive. Cathy had handed her over to the care of Monica, another nurse, who would be looking after her vital signs for the next twelve hours.

In other words, she would be in charge of Jessica's life.

'She'll be fine,' Monica smiled, adjusting a few buttons on the big monitor beside Jessica's bed. 'She's a fighter.'

How do you know? Ali wanted to ask. You've only just met her. You don't know my daughter at all. Questions ran through her head in a seamless loop, because she was reduced to a fearful silence by the enormity of all this. *Was Jessica okay? Did she feel anything? Did she remember anything about what happened?* As she sank down on yet another plastic chair beside the bed that contained her comatose daughter – and within touching distance of her face – she realised she was totally drained.

Two hours later, she finally allowed Max to bring her home.

'We'll be back soon, Jessica,' she said to her daughter, knowing she probably couldn't hear her, feeling foolish and stupid with tiredness.

'If there's any change, we'll call you,' Monica said, giving them the direct line to ICU, telling them they could call through at any time.

Ali was silent as they left the hospital, Max's arm around her shoulders, Tom loping along beside them. She had forgotten it was a Sunday until she noticed that the traffic was quieter than normal and children were out walking with their parents. She was glad she was too exhausted to feel anything as they arrived home to a house that would be minus Jessica but still echoed with her laughter, and Ali saw the shadow of her smile in the hallway, in the kitchen, and she deliberately looked away as she passed by Jessica's room and went on up the next flight of stairs. She heard Max talking to Tom, their voices low and considerate, and their bedroom was cool and dim, the curtains still drawn from the night before. It all seemed different, and then she realised that she was the one who had changed because life as they knew it had vanished in an instant. She was still wearing her coat as she flopped down on top of the bed like a rag doll. When Max joined her, he took off her shoes and removed her coat and he covered her with the patchwork throw before falling into bed himself, and she rolled over close to him and burrowed into the comforting heat of his chest.

They were disturbed a couple of hours later by Max's mobile and at first Ali didn't know where she was; her mouth was stiff and tasted stale, her head was pounding. Light was pressing around the edges of the curtains as though it was the middle of the afternoon. There was a catch across her chest and she couldn't understand it for a minute, and then she knew it was a mixture of crippling tiredness and sickening dread, and everything rushed back, taking her breath away.

She watched Max's face as he listened to what was being said, his expression giving nothing away. He put down the phone and looked into space.

'That was the police,' he began slowly. 'They found no activity on Jessica's phone for last night. No outgoing calls, no texts. Nothing since ...' his voice trailed away.

'Since when?' Ali asked, her heart beginning a slow thump.

'Since Saturday morning.'

Ali fell back against the pillows. 'You're joking. There must be more ...'

'They're going to check all her recent calls and texts to see if they can find out who she's been talking to in the past week or so. Her phone was out of charge, that's why you didn't hear it ringing last night.'

'But Tom heard her. Talking. Before she went out.'

'I know. They were wondering … the police …'

'Yes?'

'If she had another mobile. They asked me twice.'

'Jessica?' Ali's voice was a whisper.

'I told them no. They didn't sound as though they believed me though. But she could have, couldn't she?' He turned and looked at Ali, his face sad and puzzled.

'What are you saying?'

'She could have had another mobile that we knew nothing about.'

'Ah, no, Max. No way.'

'One that she brought with her last night, one that hasn't yet been found.'

'But why would she keep that a secret? From us?'

Max rubbed his face. 'I don't know. I just don't know anything at all anymore.'

'What's happening?' Ali sat up beside him. 'I'm scared, but I don't know what I'm scared about. It's like something inside me is bubbling up with dread.'

He pulled her to him so that her face was tucked into the nook of his neck. She silently absorbed the scent and feel of him. 'It's natural to feel like that. We've both had a shock. We've been up all night.'

He picked up his mobile in his free hand and called the direct line to ICU. 'There's no change in Jessica,' he said. 'She's stable for now. We can go in any time.'

'Good. Did the police have anything else to say?'

'Only that they're contacting Jessica's friends to find out if they know where she was last night.'

'How can they do that when we can't?'

'They have her mobile, remember? With all her numbers. We gave them her friends' names last night.'

'I would have preferred her friends to hear the news from us.'

'I'm sure they'll be on to us as soon as the police contact them.'

'She must have been with one of them,' Ali said. 'She was hardly on that laneway all by herself.'

'The laneway where Jessica was found was near Johnny Fox's pub.'

Ali didn't bother asking how he knew. Most of what the police had said last night had gone over her head.

'We're forgetting something in all this. Where was Kian?'

'He couldn't have been with her,' Max said. 'He'd never leave her on her own, no matter what, even if they'd had a row. He'd always make sure she got home all right. Otherwise ...'

'Otherwise what?'

'If I thought he'd endangered Jessica in any way, or hurt even a hair on her head, I'd kill him with my bare hands.'

Max tightened his arm around Ali.

'I couldn't face this on my own,' she said, leaning into his chest.

'You don't have to. But what happened to my go-getting, can-do warrior?'

Ali gulped. 'I guess she's not so invincible when it comes to the people she loves. When I looked at Jessica on that trolley as they rushed her into theatre, I could actually feel my heart breaking in two, as though it was physical.'

He was silent for a while. Then he said, 'No one could be invincible in that situation. I thought I was going to have a meltdown too.'

'We all need to be strong for each other. And we need to work out how we're going to get through the next few days, so that one of us is there for Jessica when she wakes up. As well as keeping the bakery ticking over.'

Max smiled. 'That's more like my practical Ali, but we can only take this one day at a time. And we need to be ready for whatever the police might find as well.'

Ali shivered as fresh anxiety shot through her. 'Sometimes I feel so overwhelmed with Jessica being in ICU that I forget someone actually put her there. Oh God, Max, to think that someone is going around today knowing they knocked her down. Who could be so cruel? So criminal?'

Max sifted his fingers through her hair in a comforting gesture. 'Let the police concern themselves with that. That's their business. We just need to concentrate on Jessica. And I have to call Finn and then Debbie, and let them know.'

'Okay,' Ali said, disentangling herself from her husband. 'I'm going to have a shower and get a change of clothes, then organise some food before we go back to the hospital.'

❁

They were sitting at the kitchen table, Ali forcing herself to eat a sandwich, when the doorbell chimed and she froze. She already knew she would never hear the doorbell again without a stab of anxiety cutting her stomach.

'Relax, I'll get it,' Max said, squeezing her shoulder as he passed her seat. 'It's either Mia or Kian, both of them phoned while you were in the shower to see if it was okay to come around.'

Ali tensed when she heard the voices in the hall and presently Max came down into the kitchen followed by Kian.

Ali jumped to her feet. 'Kian! Have you—'

'The police have already been talking to Kian,' Max said, looking at her gravely. 'You need to hear what he has to say.'

'Do you know what happened?' Ali asked, hoping he could offer some explanation.

Kian stood awkwardly in the kitchen and dashed her hopes with his first words. 'I don't, Ali,' he said, his eyes haunted. 'I can't believe what has happened to Jessica, but we haven't … thing is …' He couldn't continue.

Then Max said, his voice devoid of any feeling, 'Kian tells me that he and Jessica split up about three weeks ago.'

'*What?*' Ali grasped the table to stop herself from pitching forward. 'That can't be.'

Twenty Three

Ali's mother had once told her that the human spirit is incredibly strong. That until people are put to the test, they have no idea how much they can cope with, or how strong and resilient they can be. 'Sometimes strength can come from nowhere,' she'd said, 'out of the blue, when you least expect it.' Ali guessed that her mother was making reference to the time her dad had gone off to England, leaving them all alone. But it wasn't until now that she had some inkling of what her mother had meant, because as she stared at Kian, she marvelled that she was still breathing after the bombshell he'd dropped.

Kian looked unhappy. 'We weren't getting on ... there were a few rows and we split just over three weeks ago.'

'Sorry, I don't get this,' Ali said, shaking her head. 'You and Jessica? But she—'

She looked wildly around the kitchen.

Something in Max's eyes prevented her from speaking further, stopped her from blurting out that not only had Jessica not told them about the split, but she'd been making out that they were still together. There had to be more to this. Where had Jessica been going the evenings she said she'd been with Kian? What had she been hiding?

Now that Ali thought about it, Kian hadn't called to the house in a while. Ali had commented on it, but Jessica had laughed dismissively and mumbled something about his exams, as though that explained it.

Not once had it entered Ali's head to doubt her words.

'Did you call it off?' she asked him.

'I did,' he said, unhappiness clouding his face. 'Thing is, Ali, we had sort of out-grown each other. We had been drifting apart anyway … there were silly little rows over nothing …'

Ali was silent. She glanced at Max. He was looking at Kian as though he wanted to tear him apart limb from limb.

'How is she?' Kian asked.

'She's stable for now, but that's all we know.' Ali was curt. If they hadn't split, it was likely they would have been together last night, sitting in safely, either studying or watching a DVD. And Jessica wouldn't have been wandering around lonely laneways that led to her lying in Intensive Care.

He shifted from one foot to the other, his face a mask of awkwardness, clearly out of his comfort zone. 'I don't suppose I could see her?'

'No,' Max snapped. 'Only close family are allowed in to ICU.'

Ali wanted to tell him that he gave up any rights to be near Jessica when he called it off. Anger rose inside her at the thought of him rejecting her beautiful daughter, and she wanted to hit out at him in some way. She felt actual rage that he was standing there in front of her, in perfect health, while Jessica was lying torn and bleeding in a hospital bed. She came very close to understanding how some people could lash out physically at others, in certain pressurised situations.

In a tone of voice that implied the conversation was at an end, Max said, 'We'll let you know how she is.'

'Thanks, I'd be glad of that,' Kian said. 'It's serious, isn't it?'

'Very,' Max said. 'Someone almost killed our daughter, I'd say that's as serious as you can get. The police have said they will leave no stone unturned in their efforts to catch whoever is responsible. So if there is anything at all you know ...'

'I wish—' Kian shook his head as he moved out into the hall, shoulders slumped. Ali could only guess what he'd been about to say.

'You'd better give me your mobile number so I can keep you updated,' Max said, picking up his phone. 'Take mine as well,' he said. 'If you think of anything at all, call me immediately, day or night.'

As soon as he closed the hall door, he turned to Ali. 'Do you believe him?'

'Why, don't you?'

'Surely to God Jessica wouldn't have lied to us about her whereabouts the past couple of weeks. How often did she say she was seeing Kian?'

Ali struggled to think, her thoughts going around in circles just out of reach of her brain so that she couldn't even catch the tail end of them. 'At least once or twice a week. I can't remember, I just took it for granted ...'

'How do we know they didn't just have a row last night, maybe in Johnny Fox's, and he left her to make her own way home?' Max said. 'She could have met up with him to try and make it up ... that's why she went running out after ten o'clock.'

Ali sighed. 'I don't know ...'

'Yes, but why did Jessica keep that from us? Her friends must have known ...' he said, his jawline suddenly tight as if realising that his precious daughter's friends were privy to more about her life than he was.

'I'm sure we'll find out the answer to that soon.'

Ten minutes later, as they were getting ready to go back to the hospital, Mia and Sophie, Jessica's two closest friends, arrived, and they practically fell into Ali's hall, crying and distraught, throwing themselves into her arms. They were followed by Mia's mother Carol, who had brought them in her car. She looked as though she had just glided out of the pages of a fashion magazine having spent the morning pampering herself, and Ali wondered if she would ever again have the energy and inclination to spend time on her hair, makeup and clothes.

Max ushered them down into the kitchen, where they hovered, both of her friends holding a bunch of tissues against their tear-stained faces.

'Oh God, it is true?'

'Not Jessica! I can't believe it!'

'I couldn't even talk to the police when they called. I was so shocked,' Mia said.

'We won't take up too much of your time,' Carol said. 'The girls just needed to see you, to find out how Jessica is. I'm sure you have a lot on your mind.'

'We have,' Max said. 'Were either of you talking to her yesterday?' He asked the question as though he wasn't too anxious, as though they, her parents, knew exactly what Jessica had been up to.

Ali wondered if there was any point – surely the police would have dropped the information that they are all in the dark as to how Jessica met with her accident.

'She called me yesterday morning about our science homework,' Mia said. 'I wasn't talking to her after that.'

'I haven't talked to her since school on Friday. Oh God, I can't believe I won't be seeing her in school tomorrow.' Sophie broke into fresh tears.

'How did she seem on Friday?' Ali asked, struggling to hold herself together in the face of this display of emotion. She caught Max's eye, hoping he would understand she didn't want to mention Kian, but just needed to see if Jessica's friends knew anything.

Sophie shrugged. 'Much the same. Very preoccupied with our mocks coming up, but the whole class is stressed out. None of us feel we've studied enough.'

'So she didn't seem to be having any problems, say at school?' Max asked evenly.

It was Mia's turn to shrug. 'Not particularly. Apart from the fact we're all up to ninety with the mocks, and Jessica is as anxious as we are, but that's all. Until now. Oh God, I don't know how I can even look at an exam paper, with Jessica in Intensive Care.'

'If we feel like this, Kian must be in bits,' Sophie said. The friends hugged each other again, as if offering comfort at the thoughts of Kian's heartache.

'Yes, you've just missed him,' Ali said, catching Max's eye again.

'It's funny, though,' Mia paused. 'We thought she was with him last night.'

'Yeah,' Sophie agreed. 'Rachel was having a birthday bash at home, and she said she couldn't come.'

'And what makes you think she wasn't with him?' Max asked.

Mia looked totally surprised at the question. 'There's no way Jessica would have been in an accident like that if Kian had been with her. He always looked after her and wouldn't let her out of his sight.'

'And the police said she was near Johnny Fox's. That's way off our usual scene.'

Sophie and Mia now looked at Ali and Max as though expecting some kind of explanation. Ali wanted to slide through the ground. Max came to her rescue.

'Yes, well, we can't comment on anything while the police are investigating,' Max said smoothly as though they knew exactly why Jessica was so far from home, and who she might have been with.

Jessica's friends made understanding noises, but Carol darted Ali a sympathetic look as though she wasn't fooled and Ali suddenly hated her for standing there, all glammed up in her smooth blonde hair, white jeans and pink top, car keys dangling from her manicured hand, as though it was a normal enough Sunday for her. Which of course it was. *Her* daughter wasn't lying smashed up in hospital.

Ali forgot for a moment that she had had hundreds of such Sundays, afternoons that slipped past almost unnoticed and unacknowledged, taken totally for granted, Sundays when her main concern was synchronising the dinner, or getting to Dundrum Town Centre before the car park was jammed.

Jessica's friends left – Max took their mobile numbers and gave them his. Then he and Ali got ready to head back to the hospital.

The landline pealed and Ali jumped. Max answered it, and Ali gathered from his side of the conversation and the way he was looking at her that it was Linda on the phone. Tom had told his best friend Kevin about Jessica's accident and she was offering to take Tom and keep him overnight if it was a help. Max put her on speakerphone.

'He and Kevin can talk about superclusters and the cosmos,' Linda said. 'Better than having him hanging around the hospital, especially if you're going to be late, but only if he wants to and it suits you.'

'Linda. Thanks, old friends are definitely best,' Ali said. 'I'll see what Tom says.'

Tom was torn in two. He came downstairs, his face pale, with dark rings under his eyes.

'You might as well stay with Kevin,' Ali encouraged gently. 'We can only get into Jessica two at a time and there's no point in you hanging around the waiting area for hours.'

He looked slightly scared. 'I dunno – at least I'd be there if—'

'Nothing's going to happen,' Max said, sounding reassuring even to Ali's ears. 'It's going to take time for Jessica to come round. And after that, it'll take her longer to recover. So your help will be needed in keeping her amused when she gets home, making her cups of tea and letting her in charge of the remote control,' he went on, attempting a joke.

When she gets home … Ali told herself. Not *if*. There was a faint smile on Tom's face and she felt thankful to Max.

'Yeah, I get the idea,' Tom said.

'Look on it as payback for shirking your hospital duty for now.' Max suddenly caught him, looping his arm around Tom's shoulders and pulling him close in an awkward hug.

Tom looked embarrassed but pleased.

'Isn't that right, Ali?' Max said, smiling at her and catching her with his other arm.

'Oh yes, absolutely,' she said, feeling a tiny glow in her heart in spite of everything. They were together in this. All three of them. Outside, it was a perfect Sunday afternoon at the start of March, the sky a milky blue, a pale sun shining through a slight haze. The air tasted crisp and fresh on her tongue, like a semi-sweet apple. Ali didn't remember them having such a lovely afternoon since Christmas, or maybe there had been and she just hadn't noticed how beautiful it was. In the garden next door, clumps of daffodils were a bright splash of colour dancing in the slight breeze. They looked so vibrant and alive, her heart lifted.

Everything will be fine, she told herself as Max looked back through the rear window while he reversed out of the driveway. They dropped Tom to Linda's, and when she saw her son standing on the pavement, watching them depart, nightmare feelings of dread clutched at her heart again. She never wanted to let her children out of her sight ever again.

'Have you talked to Debbie? Or Finn?' she asked as they swung around by the canal.

'No,' he said, 'I forgot. I'll need Debbie to open up in the morning and look after things ...' He let the sentence trail away, because, Ali realised, he wasn't sure how long this nightmare was going to last.

'You'd better call them before we go in,' she said.

'Yes, boss.' He threw her a quick glance, his blue eyes warm.

Ali felt her nerves tautening as they turned into the hospital car park, and as Max slid into a vacant spot and cut the engine she was suddenly nauseous with anxiety at the thoughts of Jessica inside, fighting for her life.

'Max ... I ...'

'Yes?'

'I don't think I can do this.' Her voice came out thin and wavery.

'You can. We all can. We have to. We must.'

She tried to take a few deep breaths, but her breath fluttered in her throat. 'I'm afraid.'

'Afraid of what?'

'Of what Jessica will be like. Looking at her. Of what will happen to her. It terrifies me.'

Max pulled her close against his jacket. 'Hey, where's my bright little warrior when I need her? I'm frightened too. It's just all so crazy. But of course you can do it. We'll help each other. We'll get through this together.'

Ali leaned into him for a while, absorbing all of him, breathing in his scent, filling her senses with his reassuring presence. Then she pulled back and stared at him. Suddenly he caught her face between his hands and gave her a long, slow kiss.

It meant more to her than anything else right then, it was something warm, lovely and soothing between the two of them in the middle of this craziness, this nightmare. Afterwards he touched her face gently and she smiled a shaky smile as he wiped away the tear that had started to trail down the side of her nose.

'Feeling any better?'

'A bit.'

'Good. That's more like my brave little warrior.' He kissed her forehead and squeezed her arm and it gave Ali the strength to keep her chin up as she walked to the hospital entrance hand in hand with him, the courage to step out of the beautiful afternoon and be sucked through revolving doors into the flat air and harsh fluorescent lighting of the hospital.

They walked past the shop and reception desk and a ground-floor cafeteria, and knots of people gathered, laughing and chatting. They reached the waiting area outside the ICU. Already Ali felt a suffocation of sorts and a moment of abandonment as Max found a quiet spot away from the waiting area and took out his phone to make his calls.

Ali rang the bell and was allowed into the unit where Jessica was lying still and comatose, exactly as she had left her earlier that day, freshly shocking Ali at the thought of the rest of her life in the hands of these strange machines, flashing with lights and buttons and zigzag lines. There was a new young nurse, Joanna, in charge of her daughter and Ali envied the ease with which she moved around the various machines. She wanted to grab her daughter's file away from her and look through it. She realised that this small corner of the vast hospital was becoming far too familiar to her; she didn't want that. She didn't want Jessica to be here, she wanted her to be hanging out with her schoolmates, or messing around with her iPad instead of studying, or wafting into the kitchen in her tracksuit, sniffing the aroma of roast beef, telling Ali she was starving and picking off a small slice of meat from the joint Ali is carving for the dinner. Only last Sunday . . .

'Is your husband with you?' the nurse asked, her voice light, her expression carefully bland as she picked up a note stuck to the cover of Jessica's file.

Everything vital about her daughter was contained in that cheap brown folder. Lots of stuff that Ali didn't know about or couldn't begin to comprehend.

'He's outside making a couple of calls,' Ali said. 'He'll be in shortly. Is there a problem?'

Her thin voice echoed in her own ears. 'Is there a problem?' What kind of half-arsed question was that? And why was she being so polite when she wanted to scream the place down?

'No, we hope to bring Jessica down for a scan soon.'

'To find out what?'

'It's just routine,' the nurse said.

No way was this routine, Ali silently screamed. This was a nightmare. She wished Max would hurry up. Without him, she didn't feel remotely like a 'brave little warrior' or a go-getter. Without him by her side, she was shrunken. She slumped in her seat, wanting to cry again, only her throat was far too tight for that luxury. She waited by the side of Jessica's bed, feeling more helpless and ineffectual than she ever had felt in her whole life, and when she glanced up and saw Max coming up the ward, she couldn't help jumping to her feet and rushing into his arms.

'Did you make your calls all right?'

Max's face was grey. 'I did. Finn was shocked – funny, we were only with them last night and he was joking about us going home early to the kids, remember?'

'Was that just last night? It seems like last year ...' She swallowed hard.

'And Debbie was very upset as well. She said she'll keep the show on the road. We're just to concentrate on Jessica. Debs is so competent, Ali, probably better skilled than I am, we're very lucky to have her.'

Debs.

Ali willed herself to believe they were lucky to have Debbie on board for now. She had far more important things to worry about than Debbie Dillon and the silly insecurities the other woman had always raised and that were even now, thanks to Finn's comments the previous evening, niggling away at another level beneath the nightmare she was in.

Galway, August 2001

The closer they get to Galway, the more tense Max's face becomes.

'Hey there, are you okay?' Ali puts her hand on his jean-clad thigh. A sudden wave of lust ripples inside her at the drum-tight feel of it. Nine years married, and Max still has the power to excite her. Nine years married on top of her thirtieth birthday earlier in the year, and the young girl Max had met in Nolan's has been transformed, and thanks to years of living and loving with Max, she feels a lot more radiant, confident and happy.

He continues to look straight ahead, his eyes on the road, but she can see a muscle flexing in the side of his cheek and there's something in the tilt of his chin that suggests he's on the alert.

'I'm fine, why?'

'It's just – well you haven't said anything for the past twenty minutes.'

'Jessica is asleep.'

Jessica asleep in the car never prevented him from talking to her before, their conversation conducted in hushed tones.

Ali looks out at the countryside sliding by the window, the hedgerows laced with cow parsley, the low stone walls, and beyond them the vista of green patchwork fields, rolling away to blue-grey hills in the distance. It has been a summer of intermittent sunshine and wet, grey days and it is reflected in the green abundance of the fields and the trees bordering the road, which are heavy with thick foliage. She wonders if Max is regretting his sudden decision to attend the funeral of Mrs Dillon, his first employer, and take a trip down memory lane at the same time. They haven't been to Galway in five years, Max's parents dying within a year of each other, soon after Jessica's birth, his little daughter the lifeline that Max clung to along with Ali. When he heard of Mrs Dillon's death through some of his old Galway mates, he thought it would be a good idea to attend the funeral on the Friday and spend the rest of the weekend in Galway, showing six-year-old Jessica the city in which he'd grown up.

'Will Finn be here?' she asks.

'No.' His answer is terse.

She knows there's not much love lost between Max and his brother, and it bothers her. She'd expected them to be closer, and she made efforts to always include Finn and his wife Jo in invitations. Only the previous week they'd had friends in for drinks, including Linda, Ali's close friend from Thornton's, along with her husband, and a couple of old school mates from Galway who were now living in Dublin that Max kept in casual contact with. Finn and Jo had been invited and they'd come along, but it saddened her to see that Max got on better with his friends than with his brother.

Although sometimes she doesn't know what to make of Finn, and the quiet intensity of his dark, observing eyes. From the way he looks at Jo, he is mad about her. From the way he looks at Max, it seems he is sometimes dismissive of him. Sometimes she doesn't know who the real Finn is, or how much of a part he is acting. His career is doing quite well, with regular appearances on a long-running Irish soap opera and a couple of low-budget, home-grown movies. Although he was hotly tipped for the big time in an article Ali had read the previous year, that hasn't happened yet.

'You don't have to come to the church with me,' Max says finally as they near the outskirts of Galway. 'You and Jessica can splash around in the hotel pool, or go shopping or something . . .'

She wonders if he has been turning this over in his mind. 'Of course we'll go with you,' she says.

They are barely in time for the service as Max takes a wrong turn in the one-way traffic system, so they slip in at the back of the church. Afterwards, Ali brings Jessica across the road to the shops, returning to the churchyard in time to see Max hugging a tall, curvy brunette. She watches them together as she draws near, noting the way they seem to be comfortable and familiar with each other, seeing the way the tall woman draws back and laughs at something Max has said, as though they are sharing a joke.

Jessica stops to pick up some daisies from the grass verge and a gut feeling impulses Ali to join Max and slide her hand through his arm in a possessive gesture. There is something in the other woman's eyes as they sweep Ali with a head-to-toe glance, followed by the affectionate and relaxed way she is looking at Max, that puts Ali on guard.

And that is how she meets Debbie Dillon.

She is glad when Jessica skips up to them and presents Ali with a bunch of daisies and Max sweeps his daughter up into his arms. At six years of age, Jessica is innocent and adorable in her white broderie anglaise dress, her hair a bright fluffy halo around her head. Debbie points out her son Daniel, who is a grave little figure quietly watching them from where he sits on the steps of the church with some of her nephews. She beckons him over to say hello, but he doesn't move. 'He's shy,' Debbie laughs.

Then they mingle with the crowd, Ali feeling oddly vulnerable when she catches Debbie's glance resting on her now and then. In the cemetery, Ali keeps Jessica at the back of the crowd, and she is relieved when Max says his goodbyes after that and refuses Debbie's invitation to join the family in a hotel for food.

'So how long have you known Debbie?' she asks when they are driving out to Salthill for lunch.

'Debbie?' He gives a careless laugh and it makes Ali wince. 'Forever, I suppose. I went to school with her brother. Then we trained together in cookery school and she got me my first job in her mother's shop.'

Forever. Old friends, going back years by the sound of it. Working together in the pressure pot of a small bakery. She is amazed at the way her stomach gives a lurch.

'I haven't seen her in years,' he says. 'Since the shop closed. I came to Dublin and she went to Liverpool, where she still lives.'

'Is she married?'

'She was. It broke up. At least she has Daniel. And she's working in the kitchens in a big hotel.'

He sounds a lot more cheerful that he did when they were driving to Galway the previous evening.

'So was it good to catch up with her?'

'Absolutely. It was all a bit messy when her mother's shop closed. So I was glad that we've all moved on. As well as that, I owe her for helping me with my career.'

There is an odd note in Max's tone of voice that tells her there is more, there is some kind of history there, but she feels too awkward to push it. Just as well, she decides, that Debbie Dillon lives in Liverpool, safely away on the other side of the Irish Sea.

2010

Ali is walking by the counter at Booth Street on a Wednesday afternoon when Max comes back from a meeting with one of his dairy suppliers and he sweeps a dark-haired woman through the door, saying, 'Guess who I found?'

She recognises Debbie immediately and the triumphant note in Max's voice raises the flesh on her arms, like goosebumps.

'This has to be serendipity,' Max says, when he has shown Debbie around and the three of them sit down for coffee. 'We're looking at expanding and it would mean hiring more staff . . . See, Debbie, Ali has plans to move upwards and double our seating area. Thanks to the recession, the first floor is up for sale at a knockdown price . . . you could be just the person we need.'

He'd bumped into her just around the corner, he'd told Ali later. Debbie had known he had a bakery in the area and had planned to pop in and say hello. Her job in Liverpool had folded, as the hotel had closed, and Daniel was nineteen now and had taken off to backpack around the world. It seemed like a good opportunity to come back to Ireland. She was amazed, though, that Max offered her a job. It had to be fate.

'I'm glad I can help Debbie out,' Max says later to Ali. 'Her life hasn't been easy and a lot of my success is based on her mother's traditional recipes.'

'I didn't know that.'

'So I guess I owe her.'

Ali doesn't know what to think, and can't pinpoint why Debbie makes her feel a little uneasy. But she does know by now that Max is a soft-hearted and generous person, happy to help, wanting to do his best, even by his old friends. Besides, she thinks very firmly as she curls into his arms, if he'd been interested in Debbie, he'd had his chance all those years ago.

Twenty-Four

At first Jo didn't understand what Finn was trying to say.

He was standing at the end of the bed, running his hands agitatedly through his hair, and the words stumbling out of his mouth were like boulders thudding into her chest because they were all about Max and Ali's daughter Jessica having some kind of accident.

In between the waves of noise roaring in her ears, she grasped some of his words – a serious accident ... Jessica in a coma in Intensive Care after hours of surgery. She was expected to pull through but she was badly injured. He could have been speaking in a foreign language, such was her difficulty with taking it in. She pushed back the duvet and sat up, suddenly dizzy, realising she was still wearing the jumper she had on the previous night.

Like some kind of shield preventing the shock of Finn's words getting through to her, pieces of the night before slammed into her head – the meal with Max and Ali, the call from the hospital, hanging around A&E for most of the night, lucky that her mother was on a trolley behind a flimsy curtain, then she'd come home, sipping coffee, feeling so full of pent-up frustration that she'd put on a wash and ironed some clothes. When Finn had come down for breakfast, she'd cooked bacon and eggs for them both. He'd said he was going to work on his book that morning before collecting

Grace from her friend's house, and then she'd come upstairs and fallen into bed.

Now this. This unbelievable, awful catastrophe.

'Max said he'll keep me updated,' Finn said, pacing the floor between the end of the bed and the wardrobe like a restless puma. 'I had to wake you … I thought you'd want to know, especially as Ali and Max were only here last night. I can't believe it.'

She stared at him. She couldn't believe it either. 'Could you tell me that again?'

He told her again, repeating what Max had said on the phone, and she was sorry she had to ask, as his words weren't any easier to take second time round.

'Where's Grace?' she asked, her mind flying off on a tangent.

'She's in her room.'

She closed her eyes with the sheer relief of having her daughter safe in her room. She couldn't begin to imagine what Max and Ali were going through. 'What time is it?'

'Just after three. I can't believe Max took so long to call me,' he said, turning to face the mirrored wardrobe so that from where she was sitting, she could see his reflection staring at her. His face was tense and unhappy. He raked his fingers through his hair. 'You'd think he'd have let me know immediately. You'd think he might have wanted my support.'

'For God's sake, Finn,' she said. 'Max is probably beside himself with worry. And if you spent any time in a hospital emergency unit, you'd know what it's like. Mostly you can't use your phone. And you've just told me Jessica was in theatre for hours. Poor kid. What would have been the point in disturbing you in the middle of the night? Max was probably waiting until he had something definite to tell you.'

She got out of bed and saw herself in the wardrobe mirror, a white-faced woman with messy hair in a thin cashmere jumper, black lace panties and long pale legs.

'Sorry,' he said, halting her in her tracks. 'I'm just really upset.'

'*You're* upset? Not half as upset, I'd say, as Max and Ali right now.'

'They must be going through hell. I wish there was something I could do …'

Jo shivered. 'Do you think we should go to the hospital? Is there anything we can do, apart from feeling helpless?'

'I asked, but Max said not to visit, just yet. He'll let us know if there's anything he needs. It's a waiting game for them.'

'Then we'll just have to wait as well. Sounds like they have more than enough to worry about without us being in the way.'

'You don't expect something like this to happen to Max and Ali, of all people. I wish I didn't feel so helpless …' He threw out his hands futilely and looked lost for a moment.

It was a look that snagged at Jo's heart. 'I know,' she said.

As she had half-expected, he'd been tense during dinner the previous night, but today all that irritation had melted away. For the first time in weeks, he seemed softer, more vulnerable, defenceless even, and she wondered if this was her chance to heal the rift between them and wrap him in her arms as tightly as she could. She walked towards him and reached out her hand in a comforting gesture, felt herself lean towards him, felt her breath quicken in her throat, her lips parting. For a long, electric moment Finn stared at her, longing in his grey eyes, then he blinked and the look vanished, the moment was gone.

'No, Jo,' he murmured, so softly she barely heard it. He turned on his heel and left the room.

Jo's legs were trembling as she went into the en-suite. She stepped into the shower cubicle and tilted her face to the soft waterfall drizzle. She picked up a Molton Brown shower gel and slathered it all over her body. Only then did she allow herself the luxury of tears. What would it take to connect with Finn again, to break down the wall he had put between them and set their marriage to rights? They'd overcome setbacks before, hadn't they?

'Finn and Jo, forever', she'd said to him on their honeymoon in a blaze of optimism, little realising the challenges their impetuous marriage would face when they returned to Dublin.

It had been one thing to brave her family, but it had been something else to come face to face with Max and Ali.

1992

What do you do when the rug is swept from under your marriage by the very man your brand-new husband regards as his biggest rival? When you're fresh from your honeymoon and you've all arranged to meet up, but your husband takes ages to get ready, changes his mind several times about what's best to wear, and then takes off his Wrangler jeans and blue-checked shirt and makes last-minute love, but his thinly veiled anxiety transmits itself to you so that you're also on edge at the thoughts of meeting his brother?

The restaurant in Dawson Street is half-full. U2 are on in the background, singing something about one love. They are waiting a few minutes, Finn fidgeting with the condiments and checking his watch impatiently several times. She wants to tell him to relax, to stay cool, but knows by his face that there is little point in agitating him further. His face is tight with tension and she has never seen him quite so wound up before.

She is ready to dislike his brother on sight, to have to put up with him for Finn's sake. She has already pictured a thin-faced, mean-spirited guy, with no personality or sense of humour. Someone who overshadowed Finn's life like her sisters had hers.

Then there is a flurry. A tall, broad-shouldered guy wearing a denim shirt and blue jeans is walking purposefully towards them, leading a slender, petite girl by the hand, her high heels clicking on the tiled floor.

Finn throws Jo a final glance, apprehension evident in his eyes. She meets his gaze, smiling in reassurance.

Then, the introductions. 'Jo, meet Max.'

Three words are all it takes for her preconceived notions to dissolve. In a blur, she shakes hands and exchanges welcoming hugs with the couple. When they are all seated, she looks across the table to the well-built guy with the dark, floppy hair. His face is boyish, making him look far younger than Finn. He has an open and honest face, telling you that what you see is what you get.

She tells herself Finn's last-minute nerves are to blame for her heightened emotions. She tells herself that he had planted a seed in her brain, putting his brother on a pedestal. Because she finds it hard to take her eyes off Max – the way his dark brown hair falls across his forehead, his young yet sensitive face, the dimple in the cleft of his chin, the warm eyes full of amusement, his long fingers as he tears some bread or lifts the bottle of wine, the warm way he looks at Ali. The whole, alive feeling of being in his company, as though something inside you has been switched on. The speculative glances he throws at her, as though he can't figure out what she's doing with Finn.

She can see why Finn would feel subdued in the face of Max Kennedy, she understands the way Max might put a dent in her husband's self-esteem, because she has never known anyone who is quite as comfortable in his own skin, or who possesses a relaxed, easy-going charm in such spades.

She tries to talk to Ali. Max's fiancé is a little younger than she is, and her face is glowing with happiness. She has shoulder-length, curly blonde hair and is wearing a yellow blouse with puffed sleeves, and a gold T-bar chain around her neck. She seems so bubbly and colourful, so full of joie de vivre that Jo feels dull in her black-and-white-striped blouse. She makes Jo think of a cheerful daisy, except there is nothing particularly fragile about her, but rather she gives the impression of being quietly confident.

Well naturally, she would be, with someone like Max wrapping his big strong arms around her and making love to her. And going to marry her the following week, in a wedding ceremony with seventy-five guests and all the trimmings.

Together they seem so sure of each other and what they are about that Jo feels a sharp jolt of resentment running through her veins.

'So you pair got hitched in Australia,' Max says. His gaze rests softly on Jo as though to ask: Is that really true? You're married to my brother? She has the sensation of something falling down inside her and tells herself he probably looks at everyone like that when he talks to them, making them feel as though they're the only person in the world at that moment. She'd heard of people like that, charismatic they called them, only she'd never actually met someone quite like Max before.

'Yes, we did,' Finn says, a smug tone in his voice. 'And here's the proof.' He lifts Jo's left hand and shows off her wedding ring.

She doesn't have an engagement ring. She'd said, quite emphatically, she didn't need one, that it was just another silly commercial convention and had little to do with real love.

Now, she looks at the glint of Ali's modest diamond solitaire and feels envious of it.

Max says, 'That calls for champagne. Congratulations to both of you, and hello there, my new sister-in-law. Welcome to the family.'

Max slants a smile at Jo and she is already dreading their wedding day, which sounds just like the kind of day she would have turned her nose up at. Before now.

'I'm surprised you came home in a way,' Max says. 'The country is still riddled with unemployment.'

'We couldn't stay in Australia forever,' Finn says. 'I'm hoping to go to drama school and Jo's going to college at night. I'm sure we'll find jobs to support us.'

'Good for you both. Mum and Dad are hoping to see you tomorrow night. They're coming up for the wedding. I can tell them I've already met Jo and she hasn't got two heads.'

'Or horns and a tail.' She finds her voice, making Max laugh.

As the night wears on, she barely tastes her food and almost chokes on her wine. What is happening to her? She has just recently married Finn. What kind of a wife is she, that the sight of his loved-up brother and his fiancée and their conservative and very traditional wedding plans are making her doubt her own decisions? It's clear that Max and Ali are committed to each other, she can see the way Max looks at his wife-to-be and from their conversation they already have a shared history, a life tightly interwoven and a circle of friends that Finn and Jo were never part of and didn't yet have.

❀

Max and Ali's wedding day goes by in a blur, with all of Jo's senses stretched to breaking point as she watches the happy pair go through the usual ceremonial rituals, from the church, to the reception, to Max's face as he stood up to make his speech. 'My wife and I ...' he begins, tilting his head and grinning at Ali, and there is a wave of warm laughter and applause from the crowd of family and friends.

She and Finn had had nothing like this. They'd gone for a meal in Darling Harbour with their witnesses, Mollie and her new boyfriend.

The band arrives on stage and the evening party begins. It is everything she has snubbed and mocked and ridiculed and labelled stuffy and conservative in her efforts to reject her life in County Meath. All the barriers she has erected inside her head to any kind of conformity are tumbling down like a straw house. Towards the end of the night, she feels so fragile and exhausted that she thinks she could snap into pieces, but there is one last spectacle she has to endure.

Max and Ali take to the floor for a special dance of their own. Jo nails a smile to her face as, without taking their eyes off each other, the woman in the lace and silk wedding dress and the man in black trousers and white shirt open at the neck half-waltz, half-sway around the cleared floor and circle of watching guests to the sound of *Dirty Dancing*'s 'Time of My Life', Ali barely up to Max's shoulder, her hands just about reaching up around his neck. And right at the end, Max lifts Ali into his arms and twirls her around as easily as if she were thistledown, as effortlessly as if they have done this many times before. They are both laughing and blend so well that together, they look beautiful.

She can't understand how it makes her life feel somehow lacking.

Ali changes into a pink suit as her 'going away' outfit and in a blaze of laughter and jokes and farewell hugs all around, they press through the throng of family and friends to begin their married life. They are spending their wedding night in a nearby hotel and flying out to Majorca in the morning for a ten-day honeymoon.

And the following week, when Jo contacts her sister and hears about her father's death, she knows that whatever compromises she might have to make, she has to make her marriage work, given the high price it has already cost. She loves Finn. He needs her. However he had felt previously about being shadowed by his brother, those feelings were eased thanks to her, because she makes Finn feel powerful and calm. Nobody ever needed her like that before and in turn it makes her important, useful and valuable.

She tells herself that if she privately feels something is lacking in their marriage, it's the least she deserves for getting married in the impulsive way she did and causing catastrophe in her own family. She can almost hear her mother's voice saying she has made her bed, now she can lie in it. Come hell or high water, she will make it work.

❁

When Jo came downstairs after her shower, Grace was in the kitchen, pouring orange juice.

'Grace! Darling, has Dad told you what happened?'

'Jessica?' Grace looked shocked. 'It's terrible. Ali and Max must be in bits. And Tom.'

'They are, God help them all.'

'I hope Jessica's going to be okay,' Grace said, her green eyes big with concern. 'Dad said she was found on a laneway near the mountains.'

Jo's hands were shaky as she filled the kettle. It was every parent's nightmare. She thought of Grace and the years ahead, when she would make big decisions and small ones, all of which would shape the rest of her life, and she wanted to hug her tight and protect her from any harm, telling her how much she loved her. Most of all she wanted her to be confident with her decisions, so that no one would have the power to shake her self-belief.

Funny how life could be seen so differently when viewed from a mother's perspective.

'Come here to me, sweetheart, and give me a hug,' she said.

'Oh, Mum, I feel so sad about Jessica.' Grace went into her arms and they hugged each other in the middle of the kitchen floor. Finn appeared in the doorway and Jo met his eyes over Grace's head. He stared at her, the bleak look back in his face, before disappearing into his den and closing the door.

Twenty-Five

It was Monday afternoon and they were out in a narrow corridor at the back of Intensive Care. Tom was in school, as they had agreed it was important to keep some normality in his life. Max was going to bring him into the hospital that evening for a short visit and, once again, he was staying the night in Linda's.

Ali looked at the peeling signs on the pale-grey wall, the surplus equipment clogging up the space, an opaque glass door leading to the Cardiac Unit. Anywhere, in fact, but the consultant in the white coat with the brown file in his hands.

'Sorry we don't have anywhere else to talk ... but sometimes this is it,' he swept his hand around the cramped area. 'As you know, during surgery we repaired your daughter's spleen as best we could, but we may have to operate again as there seems to be some slight seepage. It could be some bruising on surrounding tissue and it may well heal. But—'

'What exactly are you telling us?' Max asked. His face was so grim and etched with worry that it looked like a horrible Halloween mask. It didn't resemble the Max she knew any more than the girl inside resembled her laughing, vivacious, beautiful Jessica. Ali moved closer to him and immediately his arm curved around her shoulders.

'If there's a problem in the next couple of days, we have to be prepared to respond extremely swiftly. To put it bluntly, we might have to remove her spleen. Please be assured we're monitoring Jessica and all her vital signs very closely, and in the case of emergency we're ready to act immediately. Jessica lost a lot of blood and needed considerable transfusions. You probably know that her blood group is B, one of the less common ones.'

'No, we didn't,' Ali said. 'She must have got that from Max.'

'Is this a problem?' Max asked.

'No, not at all. We've plenty of stock on hand of the groups Jessica can receive. You can be reassured that the team is doing their very best for your daughter.'

'We do appreciate that, thank you,' Max said.

In the late afternoon, Max insisted that they had a short break and went to the canteen for some food, even though Ali wasn't hungry and didn't want to leave Jessica.

'She's stable for now,' the nurse smiled, a different nurse today, Brenda, and all the names of the people who have tended to Jessica flutter through Ali's head like a roll call. Ali glanced out the windows as they walked down the corridor, blinking at the fresh spring afternoon, the marmalade ball of the sun starting to slide down a western sky, soft banks of puffy clouds licked with a pink tinge. So far removed from where they were right now that it was like a different planet. People outside were going about their business and she wondered what it was like just to be having a normal day. The canteen area was quiet, with just a few visitors and patients getting away from the wards for a while. The air pressed down on her, muggy and stale.

They weren't too long there when Ali saw the police arriving. Fear rose in her throat at the sight of them approaching and the thought that they might know who had catapulted their family into this nightmare.

'Max,' she said, nodding towards the police, her voice coming out in a whisper.

Max half-stood so that they saw him, and they weaved through the tables and joined them.

'Is it okay to talk here?' David asked.

Ali nodded. Their table was out of earshot of the other customers and the wards were so busy that there didn't seem to be anywhere else they could chat in private. 'What's the news?' Max asked.

'We're almost sure we have Jessica on CCTV in the Luas station at Charlemont, just before half past ten on Saturday night,' David said.

Ali gasped. She had slipped out of the house just before they arrived home, and was probably standing in the station as they swung into the avenue.

Paul produced a photo. 'This is a still from the tape. Can you confirm that this is Jessica?'

Ali stared at the grainy black and white image of her daughter and her throat constricted. 'Yes, yes it's Jessica.'

Jessica as she had been then, in her plum jacket and black skirt. Whole. Full of life. A few short hours before she was mangled half to death. Ali wanted to reach into the photograph and haul her to safety.

'And,' he continued in a deferential voice, 'we have a sighting of her getting off the Luas at Dundrum.'

'Dundrum?' Ali couldn't keep the surprise out of her voice.

'Yes, Mrs Kennedy, and she appears to have been on her own.'

Ali sat back, stunned. She could see that Max was as shocked as she was. Where had their treasured daughter been going at that hour? Had she been meeting someone? How come they knew so little about what she'd been up to on a Saturday night?

'We've also confirmed that none of the staff recall seeing her in Johnny Fox's, but we're still making enquiries and checking with all cab companies in the area.'

'Is there anything else you might have thought of?' Paul asked them.

'We can't think of anything at all,' Max said with uncharacteristic pessimism. 'Her boyfriend has been round to see us, as well as her two closest friends, and none of them know what Jessica was doing on Saturday night, but you probably know that already.'

'Yes, we've spoken to them. We also understand that she is no longer in a relationship with Kian?' A question aimed at Max.

If he felt embarrassed at not knowing about Kian, he didn't show it. Instead he said smoothly, 'Yes, so we've been told.'

'You don't think there might have been any problems or tensions between them as a result of the break-up?'

'There might have been, but we didn't know,' Max said. 'Jessica's a very independent young woman. If she had any worries, she kept them to herself and didn't tell us. But if you think that Kian could have been in any way responsible for what happened, forget it,' he continued staunchly. 'He's a lovely guy and wouldn't hurt a hair on Jessica's head.'

Who knows what people are capable of? Ali would have laughed in disbelief at the idea of Jessica getting on a Luas to Dundrum, all alone at half past ten on a Saturday night.

'We have to follow any kind of lead we have, however faint. We need to build up as much information as we can because, somewhere, there may be a link.'

'Well it looks like we'll have to wait until Jessica recovers consciousness before we know anything,' Max said, in a tone of voice that told Ali he was close to losing his temper.

Max rarely lost his temper and she knew it was because he was fearful. Fearful about what had brought his daughter so far from home and why he didn't know. Fearful about the outcome of all this, which was largely out of his control. Fearful when he thought of his precious daughter wandering around Dundrum, while he was joking with Tom.

'We're doing our best to find out what happened,' Paul said. 'We're interviewing all the locals in the area and checking whatever CCTV footage is available between Dundrum and the crime scene. We had a technical team up there yesterday, and they'll be analysing whatever they found. And we're talking to the consultants about the nature of Jessica's injuries, as that could also help.'

Ali didn't want to hear that part. She didn't want to know about the difference between high impact or low impact, or find out in glorious Technicolor exactly how Jessica's beautiful, tall, slender body was mashed and mangled. They shouldn't have been there at all, she wanted to weep. They should be at home enjoying a rather dull Monday evening, Tom grumbling about his homework, and if it was a clear night, itching to get to his telescope, Ali ironing shirts to get them out of the way, Max writing up menu notes, Jessica deciding to take a break from studying to tidy her room, and the blast of music from Jessica's speakers. 'Also, have you thought about there being a second phone?' David asked. 'There are very few women of Jessica's age who travel without a mobile. And it appears, from what your son has said, that she was making or receiving a call shortly before she left home. We think ...' he hesitated.

'Yes?' There was a hard edge to Max's voice.

'Have you considered that Jessica must have used another phone that we haven't yet located, and arranged to meet someone in Dundrum?'

It had been there all along, like a kind of blind terror in the back of Ali's mind, ever since Saturday night. Jessica had let on she was still seeing Kian so she could come and go at will, but all along she had been seeing someone else instead.

Someone she'd kept secret.

Because she knew her parents wouldn't approve.

And why wouldn't they have approved?

Ali didn't want to think about the answer.

'Well obviously she met someone,' Max said, in defence of his daughter, sounding as though it was the most natural thing in the world for Jessica to be swanning around Luas stations late on Saturday night en route to a rendezvous of sorts.

'I don't suppose you have any idea who that might have been?'

Of course they had to ask. It was their *job*. But that didn't make it any easier to have a private family drama dragged out under the microscope, especially in front of the police, no matter how respectful they were.

'At this moment, no,' Max said.

Like we'll know by tomorrow morning, Ali thought faintly.

'Is there anything else you think we should know about Jessica? Even if it's small or insignificant it could lead on to something,' Paul said.

Max exchanged a glance with Ali and she knew what he was going to say next. She gave a slight nod of her head.

'It probably has nothing at all to do with Jessica, but there were a couple of incidents in our bakery last week,' Max said.

David opened his notebook. 'Such as?'

Max briefly recounted what had happened, checking with Ali to make sure he was giving the correct facts. 'There might be no connection,' he said. 'It's just strange that all this is happening around the one time.'

'And you didn't think to report any of these last week?' Paul asked.

Max shrugged. 'I thought that someone was just … acting the maggot with me. Had it continued, I was going to take it a lot more seriously.'

'Mr Kennedy, with respect, do you think there is anyone out there who'd have reason to behave with malicious intent towards you or your family? Business rivals? Anyone at all?'

'No … not at all,' Max said.

Ali thought he hesitated too long in giving an answer. She recalled the look on his face the previous Wednesday. The look that had frightened her. The shadow of it was still there in his eyes.

'We'll have to follow up whatever we can, in case there is a connection,' Paul said. 'If we could talk to those who were supposedly contacted by the bakery, we might be able to obtain some details of where the calls originated.'

'The fake reservations must have been made by the hoaxer, whoever she or he is,' Ali said, trying to think things through, suddenly galvanised by the look on Max's face. 'But while a name and contact number is entered on the system, which in these cases were false, we've no way of knowing what time the person called the bakery to make the reservations. Those calls would be very difficult to trace. However,' she paused, 'the customers caught by the Facebook scam were all called that morning, by a woman pretending to be from the bakery, confirming their appointment. Two of them were so angry, they wanted nothing to do with us, but the third customer was helpful. She was able to tell us that the caller details had been withheld, and I have her contact number, because we've offered her a complimentary afternoon tea to make up for her inconvenience.' She picked up her phone and logged on to her emails.

After they took the details, Paul and David rose to their feet. 'We'll be talking to you again.'

They left then, attracting lots of interest from the other people in the canteen, who were, Ali realised, throwing blatantly curious glances from the police to her and Max. *This is what it's like. We are in the middle of a storm, the life we once knew is shattered and everyone is picking through the broken pieces.*

'Are you sure you'll be okay if I collect Tom and bring him in for a while?' Max asked. 'I don't like leaving you.'

'I won't fall apart,' Ali said.

'I'll call Finn and Debbie, and update them.'

'Good.'

Just as Max kissed her goodbye, his mobile rang. She watched the expression on his face as he took the call and tried to follow the conversation.

'Hi, Kian … yes, I can talk now … Fine. Thank you for that.'

Then Max ended the call and stared at her, his face taut. 'That was Kian. He just thought of something we might want to know.'

'Not something good by the look on your face.'

'No. The night he and Jessica had a row, they were in the foyer of a

Ballsbridge hotel at a twenty-first party. He walked out on her, but he hadn't gone very far when he regretted leaving her like that; they'd both had a bit to drink, he said ...' Max's blue eyes darkened.

'I'll kill him,' Ali said.

'He went back a few minutes later, thinking she'd be at the party,' Max continued. 'But she was gone. He asked the doorman, who vaguely remembered seeing her getting into a taxi with someone, and he thought it was a man.'

'*Thought* it was a man?'

Max looked shaken. 'It was a busy night in the hotel, with an entire rugby team staying with all their hangers-on, so the foyer was chaotic.'

'Great. Do you think it was someone she knew?'

'It must have been. Jessica would never have gone off with a stranger.'

They looked at each other in silence.

'Go on home,' Ali said tiredly. 'Collect Tom, and I'll see you later.'

'Will you be okay?'

'I'll be quite happy to sit by Jessica's bed and not have to talk to anyone at all. Oh, and Max?' she called after him.

He half-turned and smiled at her. 'Yes, boss?'

'Love you.'

His smiled deepened and he walked back to her and, kissing the palm of her hand, he closed her fingers around it.

Twenty-Six

She'd been crying when, purely by chance, he'd seen her in the Ballsbridge hotel. He'd gone to meet some mates for a drink, and he'd texted them when none of them seemed to be around, only to discover he was in the wrong hotel. He should have been in the hotel across from Christchurch. He'd pushed through a bar overcrowded with rugby fans and had come out into a lobby awash with even more people.

Just for a moment, there had been a gap in the weave of party people that gave him a view of the sofas along by the far wall and he saw the blonde girl sitting alone. It was just a quick glance – a moment later, the throng of people had blocked his view, and he'd never have spotted her, but he'd seen enough to make him slip through the crowds and across the foyer.

He'd noticed straightaway that she'd had too much to drink. She was dressed as though she was out for the kill, in a thigh-high mini and clingy top. And she was crying, quietly sobbing her heart out as though it was the end of the world.

I bet your father didn't see you going out like that. And I bet he doesn't know what you're up to. Max Kennedy would have had a meltdown. And she was still under eighteen, as far as he knew. He wondered how she'd managed to get her hands on enough alcohol to make her so tipsy. Still, with the makeup and the clothes alone, and without even looking at a student card with a false date of birth, she could have passed for twenty. And all the girls had little bottles in their bags, didn't they? Neat sizes of vodka or gin to give them a quick buzz.

'Jessica? Are you okay?'

He wondered where her friends were and why she was sitting alone. Jessica gave him a bleary smile.

'Oh, hi. It's you,' she said, slurring her words. 'I guess you're a friend. And I need all my friends now.' She bent her head, her long blonde hair flowing like curtains on each side of her face. She fell into a fresh storm of crying.

'Hey, it can't be that bad,' he said.

'Yes, it is,' she said. 'I've been dumped by my boyfriend. Just now, this very minute.'

He knew that if she'd been sober she'd never had admitted that.

'Oh, dear,' he said, in the warmest voice he could muster. 'That was very stupid of him. I can't believe he'd pass up on a girl like you.'

'Well he did,' she said, patting her face with a tissue. 'We were at Mia's sister's twenty-first party. We had a bit of a row, and he said he was leaving. I grabbed my coat and bag and followed him, but then he said it was over, we were finished, and he walked off on me.'

More information that she'd never have otherwise revealed.

Then, some instinct for self-preservation kicked in. She lifted her chin and glared at him with a touch of defiance in her eyes despite her sorry condition. 'And you haven't seen me like this. No running to my dad.'

'Of course not,' he said, as sincerely as he could. 'I've had my bad moments too. I know what it's like. Will you be okay?'

'I'll have to be, won't I?' she said. Her mouth trembled, tears made her eyelashes spiky and clumpy, her eyeliner was smudged, but her spirit reminded him a little of her mother. He wondered why they took so long to get ready, these lovely young women, spending hours perfecting their makeup, only to let themselves fall into disarray after a few drinks. It seemed ridiculous.

'Are you sure? Is there anything I can do for you?' he asked. He sat down on the seat beside her, strangely reluctant to leave her, finding himself fascinated by the sight of a drunken Jessica Kennedy. She seemed so young, so innocent and guileless in some ways, yet he knew when it came to her studies she was terribly clever. But not clever enough to prevent herself from getting into this wasted mess. 'I'll run after your boyfriend if you like and bash him up.'

'You must be joking,' she said, shuddering dramatically. 'I want nothing to do with him. Nobody lets Jessica Kennedy down and gets away with it.'

'That's the spirit,' he said. 'He must be very short-sighted not to appreciate you, so you're right to want nothing to do with him.'

She gave him a watery grin. Then her smiled slipped. 'You go on, off to wherever you were going. Don't let me hold you up.'

'Are you going back to your friends at the party?'

'I don't think I can face it,' she said tearfully. 'I'd only ruin it for my friends if they saw my face. They don't know me and Kian have had a row.'

'I can see you home,' he offered. 'Make sure you're safe.'

'I can't mess up your night either,' she said.

'You won't be. I was leaving anyway.'

'Sure?'

'Sure. I can be your knight in shining armour.'

In spite of her upset, she laughed as though the idea was hilarious, and that cut him to the quick. 'Right then, come on,' she said, staggering to her feet only to lose her balance and collapse back down to the sofa.

He hooked an arm around her and supported her as she tried to find her balance again. 'Are you okay?'

'I'll be fine,' Jessica gulped.

He helped her through the laughing, chattering crowds milling around the foyer, over to the entrance, and wondered what Max would say if he could see her now, his precious, beloved daughter, looking in tatters as she clung to him for dear life. Max, who was sometimes so irritating, who led such a charmed life, where nothing went wrong.

Except he'd built it on someone else's heartbreak, and had helped himself to something that wasn't his.

Jessica fell asleep in the taxi, her head lolling to one side, her pink mouth open showing perfect white teeth, her coat agape, her top twisted around her so that it exposed a strip of creamy midriff. Then something dark tumbled through his head, an idea that had been fizzing from the moment he'd first spotted her through the weave of people.

He checked his wallet for a spare key.

Twenty-Seven

Jo hesitated in the doorway of the ground-floor den. Finn was sitting at his laptop, staring at the screen. He'd scarcely exchanged a word with her after she'd arrived home from work. He hadn't cooked a meal that evening either.

Grace had put a ready-meal in the microwave.

'Dad's not in good humour,' she'd said, when Jo found her sitting cross-legged on the bed, watching television in her pink and white bedroom.

Jo's heart had clenched and she'd gone straight across the room and hugged her. 'Oh dear, is he having a bad day?'

'He's been very quiet,' Grace said.

'It's not your fault, pet,' Jo had reassured her. She'd sat with her for a while chatting about Grace's hopes to go back to school – please, next week, Mum? – and then she'd come downstairs and made coffee.

She took a deep breath and walked into the den. 'I brought you some coffee,' she said to Finn, carrying a mug.

'Coffee?' He stared at her as though she was a stranger.

'Yes, coffee. I thought you might like some. A touch of milk but no sugar.'

He was still staring at her as she walked across the room and she found his gaze disconcerting in its intensity. Nonetheless, for some reason she needed to connect with him, to try and erase that lost, beaten look she saw in his eyes. She wondered if she was going about it all wrong, trying to recapture the magic in their marriage by looking back on the way they had been, searching for some kind of inspiration. She was older and wiser now compared to the immature, twenty-two-year-old girl whose insecurities had made her question her decisions and find them wanting. What could you know about life at twenty-two? Their marriage might have been impulsive, but so what? No marriage was perfect from the outset and the spark between them had been strong enough to ensure it worked. Over the years of sharing their ups and downs, their hopes and dreams, of clinging together through thick and thin, their love had grown and deepened.

One thing that hadn't changed was the way Finn still needed her. And it worried her to think he was pushing her away. As well as that, she loved him so much that she needed him to make her life complete, just as much as he needed her, for he was her best friend as well as her lover and, over the years, he had come to mean everything to her.

She put the mug down on the desk, at a safe distance from the keyboard. She couldn't help her eyes flicking to the screen, which was totally blank, and when he followed her gaze, she felt as though she'd caught him on the back foot. She waited for him to jump to his own defence, but he didn't.

Instead he threw up his hands and said, 'I can't do this.'

'I'm not surprised. I wouldn't be able to either,' Jo said, her tone comforting. She sat on the edge of a sofa. 'I can't stop thinking about Jessica.'

'Max phoned,' he said.

'And?'

'She's still the same. She might need to have further surgery.'

'It must be the worst of your imaginings. Oh God, you don't expect disasters like this to happen in your own family …' She touched his hand, surprised at how cold it was. 'Gosh, Finn, you're cold.'

He seemed softer around the edges this evening, softer and sadder and far more disheartened.

'What was Jessica doing in that area anyhow?' Jo said, more to make conversation than anything else. 'Ali and Max thought she was spending the night in, with her mocks coming up next week. She won't be sitting them now. Do you know if they've found out anything yet?'

'No,' Finn said.

'God. They must be sick with worry.' Jo fell silent and heard the sound of pop music coming from Grace's television. It was an odd moment, she thought, both of them sitting quietly listening to sounds of normal Monday-evening life coming from Grace's room, whereas Max and Ali were having a very different evening.

His next words came from left field. 'Do you love me, Jo?'

'Of course I do,' she said without hesitation. 'Why do you ask? Is there anything bothering you?'

He shrugged. 'Anything and everything ...'

'Are you that upset about Jessica?'

He shook his head, his face clouded with unhappiness. 'I can't explain ...'

Jo waited, wondering what private hell was driving him. 'I feel it's like a rug has been pulled from under us,' she said. 'It makes me nervous. Max and Ali seemed invincible and if that can happen to them ... well anything bad can happen ...'

'Surely enough has gone wrong with us?'

The ball of anxiety in her stomach swelled. 'Finn,' she said gently, 'we have to look on the bright side, be positive. Something else will turn up for you. You're very talented. You have star quality. It's only a matter of time.'

He gave her a look she'd never seen on his face before. His low spirits seemed to be infused with a fine tension. 'You've no idea, have you?'

'Finn, relax please,' she begged, her head prickling with anxiety. 'I know you don't like being out of work, and it's dragging you down, but wallowing in the dumps isn't going to solve anything.'

It was the wrong choice of word.

'*Wallowing?* So I'm wallowing now?' He looked at her as though he wasn't really seeing his wife, but rather an obstacle in his way. 'You don't understand the way my life has collapsed.'

'What do you mean? Of course I understand. I know you better than I know myself sometimes.'

'No, you don't.'

She watched in astonishment as he picked up the mug of coffee she had just brought in and stalked out to the kitchen. She followed him out in time to see him calmly pour the coffee down the sink.

'Finn. What *exactly* is wrong?'

He spoke without looking at her, his voice so soft she had to strain to catch it. 'Everything is wrong, my dearest, sweetest, darling, beautiful Jo. Life is the pits. The absolute, bloody, crap fucking pits. I'm going out.' He picked up his car keys from the kitchen counter.

'Don't go,' she begged, anxiety making her light-headed. The last thing she wanted was an angry and dejected Finn jumping behind the wheel of the car. 'Stay. Please. We can talk through this. There will be more opportunities for you …'

He ignored her and marched out of the house.

Twenty-Eight

By early Monday evening, Ali felt she knew all the rhythms of the hospital.

There were long periods when nothing much seemed to be happening, and all she could do was sit by Jessica's bed and focus her most positive thoughts on the pale, inert figure almost lost in the forest of tubes and machines. Then there were other times during her long vigil when alarm bells sounded from beds, and staff responded swiftly and urgently, their cool professionalism masking undercurrents of stress and pressure points. Those times she was grateful that Jessica continued to lie undisturbed. Getting better. Getting well again.

Tom arrived, Max remaining in the waiting area while he came through. He looked awkward as he stood there on the other side of the bed, his eyes mirroring the same helplessness and uselessness that Ali felt in the face of Jessica's injuries.

'Dad brought me home for a shower,' Tom said.

'I thought so,' Ali said, smiling at him. He was wearing his new Abercrombie and Fitch tracksuit top, and he was squeaky clean and lemon-scented, vulnerable and innocent, and to Ali, refreshingly vital and alive. Almost a breath of fresh air in the dull oppression of the unit.

'Jess'll get better, Mum, won't she?' he asked, his eyes roving over the banks of machinery as if distrusting them to do such a monumental job.

'Yes, she will,' Ali said firmly, because anything else was out of the question. Thoughts of Jessica not getting well were so far out of her stratosphere that they didn't exist.

'It's amazing what the machines can do,' Tom continued.

'Yes, absolutely,' Ali said brightly, deciding not to acknowledge that too much was expected of the medical profession in these wonder days of science and technology, that not everything was curable, and they didn't have a direct line to God. But in Jessica's case, everything would be fine. 'It might take a little while, but she'll get there,' Ali said. And when she woke up and talked to them, there would be a simple explanation for everything, she added to herself silently.

'Good. I couldn't bear if ... anything was to happen to her,' Tom said, finishing lamely. His face crumpled for a second. Ali reached over and squeezed his arm.

'You don't have to worry about that.' She didn't want to tell him that bad things did happen. Heartbreaking things happened. Young people – sons and daughters, sisters and brothers – got hurt, got sick and died. But it was out there, somewhere. It wouldn't be happening to them. Not their family.

Joanna was on duty and she came over and began to explain what the machines were for, and Tom lost his apprehension and became very interested, asking lots of questions.

'I think it must be good to be a doctor,' he said. 'I might prefer that to an astronaut.'

Ali smiled. 'You've plenty of time to make up your mind. But now I think it's time that you let Dad bring you to Linda's. I'm glad you're sleeping over there tonight cos it means me and Dad can stay here late. Just in case Jessica wakes up.'

'It's okay.'

'Come here,' Ali said, giving him a hug even though she knew he avoided hugs like the plague. She inhaled the clean, sweet scent of him and revelled, for a moment, in the warmth of his slender body in her arms.

Then, with a shy grin, he was gone.

❁

Later, around the time she was expecting Max back, she kissed Jessica's cheek and went outside to meet her husband. Maybe they could go for a stroll outside – she needed fresh air after the claustrophobic day inside – or even a cup of coffee in the cafeteria, where they could be just a married couple for a short while, away from the strain and oppression of the ICU. Max was outside already, leaning against the wall, his mobile to his ear, listening intently. As she drew near him, he ended the call. He looked at her, his face as grey as the wall.

'Max? What's up now?'

'I don't know.'

'You don't *know*?'

'I don't know what's going on,' Max said. 'But I'm going to find out. Excuse me.'

He turned on his heel and marched away so swiftly that Ali was left stunned. She leaned against the wall, losing sight of Max in the weave of people and shuffle of dressing-gowned bodies. Then through a gap, she saw his tall figure in his black jeans and leather jacket. He had passed by the Intensive Care Unit waiting area and was hurrying towards the lift to the ground floor.

Anger gripped her and she followed him, almost running along the corridor, then into the lift and down to the hospital ground floor, which was like the concourse of a railway station. She pushed through the big revolving door at the main entrance and gasped at the cool stream of fresh air. Outside in the gathering evening, she stared around wildly.

The sun had disappeared and the sky was a smoky azure, dotted with shredded, pale-grey clouds. Lights were springing on around the grounds, like chains and loops of bright, gaudy baubles against the smoky sky. Traffic halted in the drop down area, disgorging passengers, and there was the sound of thunking car doors and bursts of laughter and conversation carried on the still evening air.

Max was sitting on a wooden bench. He was leaning forward, his long legs stretched out, his head in his hands.

Ali didn't even know how she reached his side, anger sweeping her along so that her feet hardly seemed to touch the ground. 'How dare you,' she exploded. 'How dare you walk off and leave me, when you know how upset I am.'

He ignored her.

'Look at me! What the hell are you thinking?'

People were walking past, en route to the car park, but she was so incensed she was heedless of their curious glances. She had seen people angry like this, in the city, in supermarkets, so infuriated that they let rip regardless of who was around. She used to wonder why they didn't try harder to control themselves; now she knew they were quite possibly at the end of their tether.

Max rubbed his face, but he still refused to meet her eyes.

'What do you mean,' she shouted, 'you're "going to find out"? Do you know something I don't? And why won't you tell me?'

He was shaking his head. Then he took his hands away and looked up at her. She was shocked when she saw his face.

His eyes were wet with unshed tears. He bowed his head again and his shoulders shook. She could hear the raw, guttural sounds coming from his heaving chest. She couldn't remember the last time she'd seen Max so heart-wrenchingly upset. He had been moved to tears when both his children had been born. He had been upset when his adoptive parents had died, but that had been a more stoic, resigned kind of heartache. Seeing him now frightened her. It made tears spring into her own eyes and her body turn to jelly, and she sat down beside him, the bench hard and cold through the material of her jeans, a hot gush of tears stinging her face. She dashed them away with the back of her hand.

'Max!' she said, her voice faltering. 'What is it? Can't you tell me? I've never seen you like this before. Talk to me. Tell me.'

'You don't know what you're asking,' he said, his voice muffled through the fingers covering his face.

She put her hands on his fingers, without attempting to move them off his face. She took a few shaky breaths and said, 'Max, look at me. *Look* at me. Please. You're scaring me. There's no need to be so upset. We can get through this together.'

'You don't understand,' he said.

'What don't I understand?'

'Everything.'

Her thoughts whirled away like a scatter of sparrows, looping around in her head, searching for crumbs, for anything he might have said before now that would make sense of the depths of distress gripping him, but they came back empty and blank. 'Max, please tell me,' she said finally.

'I can't.' The sound of his voice came out like a groan.

At first she couldn't make out the words. She thought she had misheard. There could be nothing so bad that Max couldn't tell her. They had never kept secrets from each other. 'What did you say?'

'Ali ...' he struggled for breath. Finally, he took his hands away from his face and looked at her with such sad intent that she felt her blood rushing to her head.

She clutched his arm. 'What is it?'

'I can't. I *can't*.' He stopped again and drew a long, shuddering breath. 'I have to do something, but please don't follow me.'

'*What?*'

'I don't want you to follow me.'

'Max, what is going on?'

He shook his head. He reached out and held her face in his hands, and then he kissed her on the forehead, ever so carefully, ever so gently, as though she was made of the thinnest, most fragile, crystal glass and he was afraid she might shatter.

Or as though, she sensed from his eyes when he drew back, he had no right to this kiss.

It was a look that crashed through her head, almost immobilising her, that kept her stuck fast to the bench unable to move, or even mouth his name, as he got up and strode away, weaving through the visitors coming out of the hospital entrance, losing himself in the crowd and the darkening evening.

After a minute, she jumped to her feet and hurried after him, just in time to see him step into a taxi. It pulled away from the kerb and she stood, feeling strangely bereft yet full of rising panic as it swung out onto the road towards the hospital exit.

She fumbled for her mobile, buried as usual in the depths of her bag, and when she finally pulled it free, she could hardly see the display. She had to return to the hospital foyer and the straggle of visitors to key in her pin number. It took her three goes. Then her trembling fingers scrolled through her contacts until she managed to stop at Max's name.

He didn't pick up the call.

❁

In the taxi heading into the city centre, Max stared numbly at his mobile. His head was exploding with Ali's anguished look, her puzzled grey eyes, and the spark of hurt that flashed in them just before he left her. He hoped he was wrong. He hoped it was just his imagination firing off in mad directions, but deep down inside something told him otherwise.

Ali, forgive me.

He saw the glow of Ali's soft blonde hair as he spun her around in his arms, the trusting smile in her upturned face. He took a ragged breath, scrolled through his contacts until he reached a name he'd hoped he'd never have to call like this. Then, his life up to now sheared away from him as he touched his finger to her name and called her. The five or so seconds he waited until she answered, her voice low and cool, were the longest in his life.

'We have to talk,' he said.

'Max?'

'I need to see you.'

The sound of her sharp intake of breath. 'How's Jessica?' she said.

'I must talk to you. I'll be in the city centre in a minute. Can you meet me?'

'*Meet* you? You mean *now*?'

'Yes, now. It's urgent. Very urgent. I have to see you.'

He named a hotel on Kildare Street.

'I can't,' she said. 'I can't just—'

'You have to. Please. I'll wait for however long it takes, but I must see you tonight.'

'Is this – has this anything to do with …?' Her voice trailed away.

'I don't know. It might,' he said, closing his eyes and seeing her silhouetted against a New York night-time skyline, releasing the clasp of a chain holding a silver locket and letting it slide through her fingers.

'But we agreed …'

'I know what we agreed,' he continued, with his eyes closed. He clenched his hand around his mobile. 'But this is an emergency. Make whatever excuse you have to but meet me as soon as you can.'

'An emergency.' Her voice was flat and he knew she was quietly absorbing his words, turning them over in her mind, wondering what had happened to make him call her like this.

Twenty-Nine

Finn stared at his face, reflected in the cheap, harsh light of the pub mirror, turning his head this way and that, wondering if it was just his imagination or if there were fresh lines fanning out from his eyes and newly formed creases mapping their way across his forehead. He wouldn't be surprised. There was certainly more than a sprinkle of grey in his hair. And a thickening around his belly.

'Men get sexier as they age,' Jo had said.

No, they don't, he'd wanted to say, hating the way she patronised him, as if he needed to be coddled. Surely his ego wasn't that sensitive? He'd wanted to tell her to get real, to ask her who in their right mind would prefer a man in his late forties to a young virile twenty-something with smooth skin and an enviable six pack, straight out of a Levi jeans ad, but the words had died on his lips. She'd surely come back with some sickly sweet comment about maturity giving him an edge over all those eye-candy guys.

An edge of what?

Anyway, it didn't matter anymore. He was all washed up. There was nobody running after him to cast him in a perfume or cologne commercial. And he knew Jo didn't really love him the way he loved her. He supposed there always had to be an imbalance in a marriage – one who loved more than the other, one partner who was needier than the other. She stuck to their marriage and did her best to make it work because she was stubborn as hell.

But no matter how hard Jo had tried, she hadn't got totally rid of that empty, insidious spot inside him that whispered that he just wasn't good enough. He thought he had grown out of Max's shadow years ago, but the age-old grudges and deeply held resentments began to eat him up all over again when his career stuttered to a halt, just as Max's began to rise to the heady heights.

And no matter how much he told himself that he was a mature adult and he was foolish to compare his life to Max's, that everybody has a different path to travel and success in life has nothing to do with spurious fame or the accumulation of wealth but everything to do with making the world around you a better place in the way you treat the people who share your life, it didn't help.

And now, the latest blow that had all but decimated his life. No wonder Max still had the power to make him feel like a no-hoper. In an intuitive way, he had known all along that he was only a sad runner-up to him.

Galway, New Year's Eve, 1989

The thunder is cracking all around him as Finn hurries across the bridge and up Quay Street. The carefully wrapped gift box with the silver locket safety nestling in its bed of white silk is tucked carefully into the zipped pocket of his jacket. Despite the inclement weather, there is an air of gaiety about the night. Couples scurrying along together, groups of girls click-clacking along, giggling and laughing, their voices strident as they share their plans for the night. The atmosphere is catching – not that he needs this to feel a lift of excitement.

When he'd phoned Debbie to make arrangements for their night, she'd told him she'd be in the cake shop and to collect her from there.

'The shop?' he'd said. 'You're hardly open on a Sunday, never mind late opening on New Year's Eve?'

'No.' She was silent for a minute. 'The shop's not open but I'll be in there, looking after some business.'

'Is there something wrong?'

'Sort of. Look, Finn,' she went on, 'I'll explain when I see you. I prefer to talk face to face.'

'Now you have me worried.'

'There's no need for you to worry,' she said. She sounded as though there was a smile in her voice and he had to be content with that.

Now he can't wait to see her. It seems like ages since they were together, although it's been barely two weeks. And he's a little early for her, but so what? He can't wait to hold her close, to taste the scent of her, to feel the baby softness of her skin and see her smiling up at him … Although he hasn't a free house tonight. Max went out earlier, in a cloud of aftershave that told Finn he was on the pull, even though he said he was meeting the lads in a pub off Eyre Square, but his parents are having family over for a house party to ring in the New Year.

He aches to hold her in his arms. In his mind's eye, he sees her eyes lighting up as he gives her the present. He's going to hang it gently around her neck and ask her to wear nothing but the locket the next time they make love. He sees it already, lying against her creamy skin just above her breasts, and for a moment he can't breathe. He quickens his footsteps as he turns up a side street where her mother's cake shop is tucked in between a haberdashery and a record shop.

From the top of the side street, it looks as though the cake shop is closed. There are no lights streaming out onto the laneway and the canopy is closed up. When he reaches the door, the lights are off in the front of the shop but there is some light streaming from the back, the kitchen and store room. Debbie is obviously doing some stocktaking, after being away.

He's not too surprised when he pushes the door and it opens. Debbie is expecting him, after all. A roll of thunder booms overhead as he steps through, past the empty counters, their gleam dulled in the shadowy half-light. He walks behind the counter, towards the store room where a shaft of light is spilling out from the open door.

And then his blood freezes and his scalp crawls with disbelief when he sees Debbie curled into Max, clinging to him tightly as if her life depends on it. One of Max's arms is anchoring her securely to him, the other is smoothing her dark, glossy hair. His body is arched protectively over her. Debbie pulls back from the embrace long enough to tilt her face to his, to say something, something that encourages Max to crush her even tighter in his arms and drop a kiss on her dark hair. Such is Finn's shock that he is momentarily incapable of speech and movement. He makes some involuntary sound or something, however, because Max looks up and sees him.

And smiles.

'Oh, Finn. Hi. You're early.'

It is the confident, easy-going smile that lights the spark. That reaches down into the very depths of Finn Kennedy and scoops up long-forgotten childish jealousies and teenage insecurities and injects them with the fresh, new, fragile uncertainties, hopes and dreams of first love and welds them all together so that everything bursts through him like a tsunami. One moment, he is watching his girlfriend in his brother's arms and the next he is throwing himself on his brother, pouncing like an enraged animal. He manages to land a punch on the side of Max's face, and although Max is solid and strong, the surprise of it makes him stagger back against a shelving unit. It gives Finn enough time to summon all his strength, draw back both arms and hit him again, twice, one blow connecting with his jaw, the other landing in his chest.

'Finn! No!'

Blood is drumming in his ear and he hears Debbie's protest as if from far away.

He sees Max looking at him wide-eyed, as though he can't comprehend what Finn is up to, almost like a child who is taken by surprise by an angry adult, and it heightens his anger. He lands a couple of more punches on Max's hard frame, and then Max's eyes turn cold and he straightens up. In moments, they are tussling with each other, Max now defending himself against Finn's punches. Somewhere a tub of flour is knocked over, the contents pouring out like white sand, releasing a small cloud of dust motes dancing in the air. There is another clatter as a swing of Finn's arm sends a pile of cups and saucers smashing to the tiled floor. Through a red mist, Finn is aware of Debbie's silent, open-mouthed shock. Her brown eyes are pools of tears, which slowly slip down her face.

The sight of her tears stops Finn in his tracks long enough for Max to pin him to the wall.

'I don't know what the hell is wrong with you,' Max says, his breathing ragged. 'How dare you upset Debbie like this, never mind toss me around. Look at the mess you've made – the damage to the bakery. I've a good mind to frogmarch you to the nearest station.'

'Max, leave it,' Debbie implores, wringing her hands. She is keeping her distance, Finn notices, and then her eyes dart towards him and it feels as though a knife has plunged into his belly. They are scared and apprehensive as they fasten on his and he knows, in a sickening moment, that he has lost her trust and her love.

'You two,' he sneers, his defences rising up around him. 'I might have known you'd be up to something behind my back. You've had plenty of opportunity, all lovey dovey, I'll bet, between the shop floor and the store room. If I hadn't arrived early tonight ...' His chest heaves and his voice trails off because he cannot continue. He notices that Debbie is wearing her best Pepe jeans and a white blouse he hasn't seen before with some kind of embroidery on the sleeves and ruffles down the front. He can make out the contours of her lacy bra underneath and a tiny hint of cleavage is visible just above the closed top button. He wonders if she was thinking of Max when she put it on.

'You have it all wrong, bro,' Max says.

'Don't call me brother,' Finn rages.

'Finn, listen to me,' Debbie implores. She has found a tissue and she dabs at her streaming eyes. 'Max was just giving me a hug.'

'Oh yeah, I could see that all right.'

'Because I was upset. I—'

'Well, of course. That's what other guys are for. Handing out free hugs. It looked like more than that to me, the way you two were locked together. How long has this been going on?'

'Will you shut your effin' face for a minute,' Max says. 'You might learn something if you had the manners to listen to your girlfriend.'

Something in his heartfelt tone of voice quietens Finn. As he looks from Max to Debbie, he begins to realise that maybe something else is going on here, beyond a lovers' assignation.

'Let go of me,' he says to Max.

Max releases his hold and Finn takes a few breaths.

'Tell him, Debs,' Max says.

Debs. Finn had never called her that. Not once. It implied a familiarity.

'Tell me what?' he asks. 'The reason I caught you in a clinch?' *They've fallen in love*, he thinks. Debbie is bored with him. Max is more attractive, better at fun and jokes, less serious about life, easier to be around … maybe, even, better in bed. Rage burns a trail in his stomach.

'I've been here all day doing an inventory,' Debbie says, speaking quietly, her troubled eyes meeting his. 'I went home to get changed for our night out, came back to finish off some figures and on the way back I met Max heading to the pub, so I brought him in and told him why I was doing an inventory.' Debbie pauses and looks at Finn as though he's let her down big time and Finn is afraid to ask why she was caught up in such a boring job on New Year's Eve.

She lifts her chin. 'We're closing … we're already closed.'

'What's closed?' At first, he doesn't grasp what she's saying.

'The shop. The business. We're all washed up. The past couple of years have been too tough, we've been losing money, and Mum just can't hang on any more. She's been trying to ride out the recession but she owes too much money and I don't even know if the sale of the premises will cover all our debts. Probably not.'

Finn feels an ache in his chest.

Debbie continues, in a soft voice that tears at his heart. 'We went to Dublin, to my aunt's, for Christmas so that Mum would have time to think and work out what's best and get a break from it all. My uncle went through all the books with her and that's when she knew it was hopeless. So the cake shop is officially ceasing to trade from midnight tonight. Happy New Year, I don't think.'

'Why didn't you tell me?'

'I didn't know how bad things were, Mum kept most of it to herself. She thought if she stayed cheerful and optimistic and put on a good face that she'd pull through. But business is business and no matter how fanciful or optimistic Mum is, the figures don't add up any more. I've had to tell Max he's out of a job from now, and the others … Mum will tell them on Tuesday.' Her voice thins out and breaks and Debbie begins to cry again. Max's arm goes around her.

Much as he longs to, Finn knows he has given up the right to that privilege with his hasty and fearful behaviour.

'We'll sort it out somehow,' Max says.

'We can't,' Debbie wails. She looks around helplessly. 'Everything has to go, all of it.'

'I'm sorry, Debbie.' Finn knows his words are useless, but he says them anyway.

'And so you should be.'

She stares at him as though he's someone she doesn't recognise. As though he means nothing more to her than a clumsy stranger on the street who has bumped into her and caused her to lose her balance. There is a momentary silence and Finn realises that the storm has passed. Strains of revelry can be heard from outside, as the New Year's Eve partygoers crank up the merriment. He also sees that Max's face is bruised in two places and he will most likely have a black eye in the morning. Max picks up a dustpan and brush and begins to sweep up the broken crockery and the sound of it jars Finn's senses like chalk on a blackboard.

He doesn't want to tell Debbie his news now, that he has been offered a place in drama school in Dublin and he was going to ask her to come with him. That dream has soured on him. He stands by helplessly as Debbie pulls over a bin into which Max can dump the broken shards of cups and saucers. They work in unison as though they are used to working together.

'I didn't mean … all this,' he says, his words paltry offerings against the upset he has caused.

'Just go, please,' she says to him, her face expressionless.

Moving deftly and efficiently, Max turns his attention to the spilled flour.

With a last look at the two of them, tidying the mess he has made in his anger, Finn walks out. Outside, the night-time air is laced with a thick kind of energy, from the residue of thunder as well as the fizz of a New Year's Eve excitement. He passes jam-packed pubs with people spilling onto the pavement outside. He walks down by the Spanish Arch, down to the dark glittering river; the wind whips up again, tossing his hair and slithering coldly down behind gaps in his upturned collar.

He stares into the oily black water and the swiftly moving current for a long time. He is tempted to jump in and end this pain in his chest. Then his hand closes around a small jewellery box in his jacket pocket; he takes it out and stares at it for a moment, before hurling it into the middle of the Corrib with all his might.

He walks home, letting himself quietly into the house, hearing party noises from the front room, his uncle's annual rendition of Rod Stewart's 'Maggie May' while his father struggles to keep up with his key changes on the piano. He moves quietly upstairs to his bedroom, closing the door. He hears the sound of the women downstairs singing a raucous version of 'Sweet Caroline'. He lies on the top of his bed long after the chimes of midnight have sounded, the conga on the road outside is finished and the visitors have left; long after his parents go to bed, their whispers of surprise that he is obviously home and in bed echoing in the now quiet night.

Long, too, after Max eventually arrives home, scraping his key in the lock so noisily that Finn knows he has had too much to drink.

The following day, Finn doesn't go downstairs until he is sure that Max has gone out. He doesn't know what Max has said to his parents to explain his bruised face, but it's doubtful they know what has happened as they talk to Finn as normal. If they think he is a little on the subdued side, it doesn't matter. They are full of the bad news about the cake shop because it means Max is out of a job. And to hear that news on top of being set upon by muggers meant it had been an unfortunate New Year for him.

'Muggers?' Finn says as he busies himself pouring milk into his coffee.

'Yes, he was set upon down by Eyre Square,' his mother says. 'He said it was more high jinks than anything else, but I think it was muggers. Wait until you see his face. High jinks! But the saddest thing is that – even though it means he won't be out of a job for long – Max is leaving us.' His mother's voice shakes.

Finn puts down his coffee cup without tasting it. 'Leaving?'

'He's moving out. He's going to Dublin to look for a job.'

'By himself? Or is he going with anyone?'

'By himself, I'd say. Sure who'd be going with him anyhow? We're going to miss him, though. The house will seem empty without him. Still at least he's not going further away like a lot of his generation did. Pray to God the nineties will be good to us all.'

❁

Max accepts his apology, but Finn knows he is doing this simply to keep the peace in the house. He is full of plans for his life in Dublin and the new job he'll be starting in a bakery on Abbey Street and his enthusiasm helps to mask the chilly politeness between them.

Debbie, on the other hand, will have nothing to do with Finn. The first two times he calls to her door, her brothers come out and tell him she doesn't want to speak to him. On his third attempt, her mother answers the door and starts to cry when she sees him.

'Finn, I don't know what's gone wrong, but Debbie's left for Liverpool.'

'Liverpool?'

'She's gone over to my cousin and her daughter. I know something happened with Max, the boys heard something about him breaking you two up … Why did you let him do that? I thought you two … I can't believe my lovely Debbie's gone,' she says, her tears pouring down her cheek.

He doesn't know what to say. He turns on his heel and walks away. As he makes his way through the city, his attention is grabbed by a poster in a travel agent's window. It shows the Sydney Opera House and the long golden curve of a sandy beach.

Australia.

Thirty

As soon as the taxi turned onto St Stephen's Green, Max paid the fare and jumped out. He strolled up around by the park, pausing at the northeast corner to glance at the brightly lit Shelbourne Hotel, and groups of happy laughing people enjoying a night out, framed by the big bay windows.

He'd brought Ali there to sip champagne and celebrate when they'd opened Booth Street Bakery. She'd smiled with an almost childlike delight.

'Here's to your dream, Max,' she'd said, clinking glasses. 'I knew you'd do it.'

'You did it for me. I'd never have got this far on my own.'

He wouldn't have got anywhere without Ali at his back. He owed her so much it hurt. He turned up the collar of his leather jacket and passed by the front of the hotel, feeling removed from his body and unable to think, such was his wave of regret.

He had just reached the hotel in Kildare Street when his mobile beeped with a text message: 'I'll be with you in less than an hour.'

The hotel was quiet. He ordered a sparkling water and sat at a table in a corner, ignoring repeated calls and texts from Ali, trying to breathe slowly so that some part of him would stay calm. But any scrap of calmness that he had managed to muster deserted him when he saw her hesitating at the entrance to the bar.

Snatches of their murmured conversation came back to him, the conversation that had begun the morning after the night before. They had sworn never to be alone together. It was part of their agreement. It was the only way they could live with what they had done. It had been a terrible mistake, they had agreed, something that had happened through destiny or fate, whatever. Unusual, once-off circumstances had thrown them together, circumstances that would never be repeated. They didn't want to hurt anyone else. They didn't *have* to hurt anyone else. No one else had to know. All they had to do was pretend it had never happened. There was safety in numbers and, from then on, they would make sure there was always her husband or his wife around. But never just them, alone.

Looking at her now, her eyes scanning his, wondering anxiously what had caused him to contact her, reminded him forcibly of what exactly he had done. What they had both done.

He wanted to run away and hide, but instead he stood up as she approached his table, her lovely face wreathed with concern, the elegant way she moved across the space plucking a distant chord in his memory. The memory of a woman coming towards him across a bedroom floor, silhouetted against a window. The warm feeling of her crushed in his arms on a night filled with icy terror.

'Max. Is something wrong?'

'Jo. I'm not sure,' he said, feeling suddenly overwhelmed by the depth of his fear and exhaustion and quite unable to have this conversation. 'There could be. Thank you for coming.'

New York, 12 September 2001

When Jo wakes up and sees Max in bed beside her, she sits bolt upright, startled with shock, grabbing the bedsheet against her nakedness. The curtains are open and the sky outside the wide, picture window holds the grey, pre-dawn lightness. Then everything from the day before, from the night before, crashes into her head and she is trembling with a swell of emotion so strong that it overwhelms her. She starts to cry, almost choked by her deluge of tears, her chest so sore and pained that she is convinced her heart is about to break. She presses her hand against her mouth and bites down hard on her finger to prevent herself from screaming.

Instantly, Max is awake.

'Hey ...' He sits up and she feels his arm tentatively sliding across her bare shoulders but she shakes it off.

'Oh, Max, what did we do?' she says through her sobs.

There is a silence that tells her Max is struggling for the right words. 'Jo. It's all been unreal ... like the world came to an end or something,' he says in a subdued voice. 'Yesterday was a nightmare. But Jo—'

She waits, conscious that everything has changed between them and they are in a dangerous place. The wrong move, the wrong words, can send them reeling into a lifetime of regret and unhappiness. Although they have already made all the wrong moves. Her sobbing intensifies, and she is crying as much for the victims of yesterday's atrocities as for what they have done.

He says, 'Don't be upset. What we did was wrong, but it made some mad kind of sense last night.'

She cries into the bed sheet, wiping her streaming face with it, and nods her head. She had needed to cling to another human being, to dissolve into someone's arms, to be held and comforted, and who better than the solid, reliable Max. Still, she must have been insane.

'But that's as far as it goes,' Max says. 'I didn't see you last night, this never happened.'

She nods again. 'Yesterday ... I still can't believe it. But last night ...' her chest heaves as her tears fall harder now. 'Finn must never know.'

'He won't. Neither will Ali,' Max says.

'We can't go back home and act as if nothing happened. Are we kidding ourselves?' Her eyes scour his face.

He gives her a look full of certainty. 'We can. We have to. My marriage is important to me, as yours is to you. I love Ali and Jessica. It shouldn't have happened, then again lots of things shouldn't have happened yesterday.'

'It'll show in my face. I know it will.'

'We'll just have to keep away from each other as much as we can.'

'If Finn ever found out ... Oh God, this would kill him.'

She teeters on the brink of hysteria at the idea of both of them in bed, together, like this. What had they done? What had they been thinking? Although yesterday had been the kind of day when hell itself had walked the earth and good people clung together in its ugly wake. Not that their actions had been good – far from it.

'For what it's worth,' he says, 'thank you for taking me through a horrendous night. I think you're beautiful, Jo, there's something sensual and very lovely about you, and Finn is a lucky guy. The first time I saw you I couldn't believe he'd married you.'

'Why not?' Her voice is thick through her tears but somewhere beyond the drama of where they are now, out there on the horizon where she exists as a wife, she needs to know the answer.

'You're different—' he hesitates. 'You're almost too classy for us Kennedys.'

'Classy. I sound like my mother and my sisters. So in other words, I've reverted to type.' She gives a harsh laugh. 'It was there all along, there was no getting away from the blueprint of me, under the false bravado. Even though I ran halfway around the world.'

Max shakes his head. 'You've lost me.'

'Don't mind me. I've just realised I've become what I was running away from in spite of my need to thumb my nose at it. The girl who met Finn in Australia wasn't exactly classy. More like a defiant, overgrown teenager.'

'Well you took me by surprise. You seemed so full of life that I couldn't believe you'd hooked up with my reserved brother. And we were all gobsmacked at the way you two came home married and all.'

'Sometimes, so was I.'

'Were you?'

She lies back down again, hugging the bedclothes to her, letting the back of her head sink into the pillow. It's far too early to get up, and she feels jaded in her soul and spirit as well as her body. Although she feels she'll never sleep peacefully again.

She starts to talk, as much to sort out things in her own head as to explain. It is easy in the semi-darkness of the room, the morning after the night before, before the sun comes up and the spreading light illuminates the broken city and the dust clouds still clinging like ghostly sheets to the shattered remnants of buildings. Easy too to talk like this, to bare her soul when she is still numb with the shock of what they have done.

'I couldn't believe I had done something so life-changing in such an impetuous way,' she says. 'Couldn't believe I was actually *married*. In the days after the wedding, it felt strange and unreal. So much so that when I came back to Dublin with Finn, and I met you and Ali, I was all over the place.'

'Like what?'

'You both seemed so settled, very much part of a couple, as though you'd known each other forever. I felt I hardly knew Finn compared to the life you two seemed to share.'

'And Ali and I thought you and Finn were so romantic, marrying on a beach, miles from everyone. We all thought it was true love.'

'I thought it was too, until I met you and Ali and there was something so solid about you two, it stopped me in my tracks at the time and made me wonder if I'd been ridiculously foolish for getting married so impulsively. Oddly enough, I envied all those traditional wedding fripperies as well, simply because I'd turned up my nose at all that and deep down I was terrified I'd done the wrong thing. Here I was, newly married, we were barely off our honeymoon and I thought it meant I didn't love Finn anymore. Or that I had never loved him in the first place.'

'Marriage isn't a great sticking plaster that prevents you from having doubts and insecurities. If anything it throws up more perils.'

'I copped on to that eventually,' she says. 'It got more complicated when the following week I found out my father had died while I was on honeymoon, and my sisters made out it was partly my fault for giving the family a shock with my hasty marriage. So that didn't help my confidence either.'

'I'd say not. Yet you're still together, and happily married by the looks of it.'

'Nine years. I can't believe it.' Her tears are flowing freely, sliding across her face so that they trickle into her hair and onto her pillow. 'I didn't love him then anything like the way I do now. It's deeper and it's steadier. But that's what love is, isn't it? It's being with someone, sharing your life with them, putting up with their foibles, sharing the ordinary, the everyday. It's not always the grand passion, with dramatic music and sparkly fireworks. Sometimes it's just quiet and steady and it hums along in a way you might take for granted. We've settled into a marriage that works, I guess. I think we prop each other up in a funny way. He needs me and I need him to need me. Does that make any sense?'

'Yes, Finn was always short of confidence himself.'

'Growing up with you I'm not surprised.'

'Why me?'

'You're larger than life, Max, in every way, and very secure in your own skin, so much so that you'd overshadow a fainter soul. You bowled me over a little when I met you first. Good job Ali's well able for you – she's so sparky that she almost eclipses you. As well as that …'

'As well as what?' He is still sticking safely to his side of the bed and for that she is grateful. She turns carefully in bed so that she is lying on her side facing him, her cheek pressed into the pillow, the sheets up to her neck.

'Years ago, Finn was bullied in school.'

'I didn't know.'

'You would have been very young. He told me, just once. He didn't realise what was going on for a while. Then your parents found out and moved him immediately. But, sometimes, I think a seed of it is still there.'

'Oh, my God …' Max falls silent. 'You're right about one thing. He can't find out about us.'

Despite everything, Jo's eyes feel heavy, and warmth steals around her body. She allows herself to close her eyes, and she feels herself drifting away. She sleeps for a while and when she wakes up, it is morning time and bright daylight floods through the windows.

Max is gone. She lies in bed, blanking her mind against the past twenty-four hours, erasing every trace of it from her memory. She picks up the locket from her bedside table and thinks instead of the weekend she'd spent in Paris with Finn, celebrating their fifth wedding anniversary.

He'd wanted to buy her a piece of jewellery. 'I never got you an engagement ring,' he'd said. 'I want to make up for that now.'

'Once upon a time that might have bothered me a little,' she'd admitted, remembering her sudden and inexplicable desire for an engagement ring. 'But since then I've realised love isn't about things or jewellery. It's about …'

'What?' he'd asked gently.

'It's about us together. It's about the way you look at me. It's wanting to wake up beside you every morning, thinking of you as I go through the day and storing up pieces of my day to laugh and joke about with you later, sharing the good and the not so good things, knowing you will always listen, and at the end of each day, lying in bed beside you at night. Sometimes, even …,' she'd paused, 'listening to you breathe.'

'Thank you,' he'd said.

He'd still insisted that five years together deserved some recognition. He'd put the locket around her neck in the jeweller's shop and bade her look in the mirror.

'It's beautiful,' she'd said. 'Are you sure?' she'd continued, mindful of the hefty price tag, conscious also of the history behind his gesture, and the other locket he'd bought, years ago in Galway.

He'd told her the story one night on their honeymoon when she'd asked him what had happened with Max. He'd told her about Debbie, the girl he'd thought he'd been in love with, but it had been more about being carried away with sex and the romantic idea of falling in love than love itself. Then the big row he'd had with Max, the anger that had bubbled up inside him until it spilled over. How ashamed he'd felt afterwards. But it would never happen again, he had vowed, except on the stage or television screen, for Jo by his side had quenched his anger and filled over his pockets of resentment with her soothing love.

'I'm very sure,' he'd said, his eyes meeting hers in the mirror. 'I don't think you realise how beautiful you look to me, Jo Kennedy.'

Afterwards they'd made love with a passion that took her breath away.

Jo hugs that memory close to her in the following days as she waits for a flight home along with thousands of other stranded travellers, in a city that is already emerging from the ashes and regaining its indomitable spirit in the face of so much sadness. She thinks of Finn, superimposing the pictures of Max in bed with those of her husband, recalling good times, holidays they have shared, recalling the early days of their marriage when she and Finn started building their lives together.

By the time she gets back to Dublin later that week, tired and emotional, throwing herself into Finn's arms at the airport, the haunted look in her eyes and her restrained mood is put down to the horrendous experience she has come through.

Thirty-One

'I don't know how to put this,' Max said, swallowing back the anxiety that had consumed him since the call from the police earlier that night, when Ali had found him in the hospital corridor.

He'd quickly brought Jo up to date with Jessica's progress. He'd ordered two brandies, telling Jo she'd need it. Now he swirled the golden liquid around in his balloon glass as he grappled with words, unable to meet her eyes, knowing that what he was about to tell her would alter their lives.

'I've never known you to be lost for words,' Jo said, attempting a poor joke.

'There's no other way to ask you. Do you think – is there any way that Finn could know about us?'

Alarm registered in her eyes. She pushed her fingers through her hair distractedly. 'Jesus – God – I should hope not.'

'Are you sure?'

'Positive. I never breathed a word. I was always very careful to look neutral whenever your name came into the conversation. Why do you ask?'

'There's something weird going on, and I don't understand it. Where was Finn on Saturday night?'

'At home, as far as I know. You don't think—' Her eyes were fearful.

'I don't know what to think. I wanted to talk to you first. Ali doesn't know we're even having this conversation. Where is Finn tonight? You hardly told him you were meeting me, or did you?'

'I had to get my babysitter in because Finn has gone out.' She took a gulp of her drink. 'We had an awful row. He was in a crap humour and said his life was a pile of shite at the moment. I think he's really upset because he thinks his career has gone down the tubes.'

'So it's true that his contract wasn't renewed?'

She sighed. 'Yes, and it's eating away at him. How did you know?'

'I heard rumours.'

Max was silent for a while, his mind churning.

'What makes you think Finn might know about us?' Jo asked.

'Before Jessica's accident, we had a mad week in the bakery,' Max began. 'My notebooks went missing, there was a Facebook scam … other stuff, as though someone was trying hard to rattle me and the business. We gave the police some details to follow up, in case there was any connection with Jessica's accident, and I had a call from them this evening to say that the mobile phone used in the Facebook scam was bought two weeks ago and is registered in the name of Finn Kennedy.'

Jo's face went white. 'I don't believe you.'

'I find it hard to believe too. The police will be checking to see if there's a connection between what happened last week and Jessica's accident.'

'You're not suggesting …' Her eyes widened. 'No way, Max. Finn wouldn't hurt a hair on Jessica's head. He was very upset to hear of her accident, there has to be another explanation.'

'What, though? Even when Ali asked if I had any enemies or anyone with a grudge against me, the only person I could think of was Finn. There has always been resentment between us.'

'I think some of that is a hangover from years ago. He might have resented your easy charm and confidence, when he was more wary of life, in part after being bullied in school, but he's hardly resentful enough to do anything so stupid.'

'If he found out about us, on top of his career crash, God knows what way he'd be feeling.'

Jo shook her head. 'Finn wouldn't hurt Jessica,' she said in a slightly hard voice. 'You're off the mark there.'

'I can't help remembering that he got stuck into me before, over an incident with Debbie Dillon …'

'I know all about that.'

'You do?'

'We don't keep secrets from each other, except when I …' Jo stumbled over her words. 'That's why I'm finding it so hard right now, because he is keeping stuff from me, he won't talk about his career and he's been like a devil these past few weeks. I can't get through to him at all. I don't know where we're going to end up. Finn is going through a bad patch, but this …? No way. There's no way he could have found out about us. I've always been very careful.'

'If he found out about us he'd go ballistic.'

'He'd go crazy if he knew, but surely it's me he'd be targeting.'

Their eyes met and held. He hated the look of anxiety in her eyes, powerless to take it away.

'I hope this is just your imagination running away with you,' she said quietly. 'Finn's dejected enough over his career right now, without this bomb going off.'

'Then how do you explain his phone calls?'

She shook her head. 'I don't know. Even though it's hard for him to see your success in the face of his expired contract, I can't imagine he'd target your bakery, let alone Jessica.'

'The police will want to talk to Finn, as part of their general enquiries. They'll probably ask him where he was last Saturday night, after we all left.'

'What are we going to do?'

'I don't know. You've no idea where he went tonight?'

'No. He took his car, he could have gone anywhere.'

'Does he tear off in his car if you guys have a row? Is it normal enough?'

'No, I told you, he was very angry, I've never seen him so angry. Dear God, Max, I hope you're wrong and that he hasn't found us out.'

'We can do nothing at the moment. I'll leave it up to the police to talk to him. Once you're happy there's no way he could know about us ...'

'Definitely not.'

'Go home, Jo,' Max said, feeling exhaustion ripple all about him. 'Forget we met. I'd better get back to Ali. I left in rather a hurry without saying where I was going and I'm sure she's out of her mind by now.'

Jo stood up and put on her coat, smiling at him in a fond way. He had the sense that both of them, separately, had come a long way from the couple who had slept together that night in a New York hotel.

He said, 'Take care of yourself, won't you?'

'I will, and you. I hope things work out for Jessica. And I hope there's a proper explanation for those phone calls.'

'So do I.'

He saw her into a taxi, blew her a kiss, and then flagged down the next one for himself. En route to the hospital, he was filled with a marginal relief. Whatever had been going on in the bakery, there had to be a rational explanation. Even though he couldn't visualise Finn setting up a Facebook scam, maybe he was just getting back at him in some way because he was bored at home and looking for mischief. If he'd found out about him and Jo, he's the person Finn would be after. And maybe Jo.

Whatever about him, his family deserved to get their lives back on track. Ali, Jessica and Tom, the people he loved with all his heart. They were entirely innocent and had done nothing wrong.

He was just beginning to wonder what exactly he could tell Ali about rushing off earlier tonight, what he could say to explain his strange comments and equally strange absence, when his mobile buzzed.

It was a text from Finn.

Thirty-Two

In those first few moments after Max left Ali in the shadowy hospital grounds, all kinds of anxieties coursed through her head. Her legs felt like water as she went back into the hospital, so that she thought she was gliding through space, and when she reached the foyer she stared around at the brightly lit area, as though she couldn't figure out how she'd got there.

She had never seen Max like that before. So upset as to be almost broken. Unable to talk to her. Hiding something from her, something big. Her thoughts crashed about wildly. It had to be the bakery. If it had anything to do with Jessica, she'd know. If it had anything to do with her accident, she'd know. The doctors and the police would have told both of them, wouldn't they? If it had anything to do with Max himself, she'd know. After twenty years with him, and two children, she knew all of him, from the way he breathed when he was asleep to the neat, economic way he moved around the bakery; she knew all this as well as his thoughts and feelings in the way you know the shape of your own fingernails. So it had to be something outside of him, something to do with Booth Street, and whatever had been going on the previous week.

He doesn't want to worry me on top of the worry with Jessica. That's all.

It was a relief to come to this conclusion; it saved her from having desperate thoughts spiralling around in her head. Somehow she retraced her steps to the ICU and went through the procedures of ringing the bell, donning a plastic apron, washing her hands, normal things that quietened her a little, and it was another funny kind of relief to find Jessica much as she had left her.

'Not much change,' Joanna said, smiling at her. 'Except Jessica seems to be breathing a little easier.'

'Is that good?'

'Yes, it's a step forward. All her vital signs are improving; it's just tiny increments, but it's good progress for her.'

Ali stared at the screens and monitors, but they were just a jumble of coloured lines and figures. Then she sank into a chair and rubbed her face with her hands. She leaned closer to the bed, resting her face against the green blanket covering Jessica. To help soothe her ragged nerve endings she reached inside herself for a happy memory, something her mother had always told her to do when she was having a tough day. A good memory would always cheer her up, Clara had said, and help Ali realise that everything in life was fleeting, even the bad days.

October 1992

Ali tilts her face to the darkened sky, and feels so full of happiness she could burst.

'Look at them, Max! Hundreds and thousands of stars … Oh, this is really special.'

She hurries farther down the shadowy garden, trailing a path through the long grass, the hem of her nightgown catching on clumps of weeds and wildly growing shrubs. She is wearing a bomber jacket over her nightgown and a pair of wellies. When she gets to the end of the garden she turns around.

'Are you glad I dragged you out here?'

'Of course I am,' says Max, stamping down some of the tall, rampant weeds as he follows her down the garden in his hooded parka jacket. 'I'm delighted you've dragged me out of a warm, comfortable bed into this jungle of a garden at almost midnight.'

'Yes, but I couldn't resist it. Look at that sky. It's beautiful. I wish I knew what they were all called. Still, it's a good omen, isn't it? We're not even living here a week and we have a starburst right on top of our first ever home. It can only mean good things. Brilliant things.'

He reaches her side, his breath coming out in little frosty puffs.

She looks at the outline of the roof of their home darkly angled against a glittering, star-lit sky and says, 'Make a wish – now.'

'I wish I was in a nice warm bed making love to you.'

She wraps her arms around his waist. 'Where's your romance?'

'I thought that was very romantic.' He kisses the top of her head.

'It is, but you're supposed to make a wish for something marvellous and wonderful.'

'I think it's marvellous and wonderful when I make love to you.'

'Yes, but how about – I'm making a wish for both of us – that you'll get out of Nolan's and into a bakery of your very own.'

'Hey, hold on a minute, we've just taken on a mortgage. We'll be up to our necks in it for the guts of twenty-five years.'

'So? You have to have some ambition. Surely you want to go bigger and better? Look at that sky up there, don't you feel our lives are like that? Full of infinite possibilities? Mum used to—' All of a sudden she gets a lump in her throat and her voice thins out.

'What, love?'

Ali shivers for a minute. 'On starry nights like this, she'd wake me up and wrap a blanket around me and bring me out onto the balcony. Even if I had school the next day. She'd hold me tight as I sat on the edge. Then she'd tell me to wish upon all the stars in the universe. That I was to wish for whatever I wanted in life. And then work hard for it. I felt there was magic in the stars.'

'And what did you wish for on those nights, Ali?'

She looks up at him and smiles. 'Someone like you.'

Thirty-Three

Another bar. This time a bar in Dundrum Town Centre, quieter than usual at the start of the week. Max's legs were stiff and heavy as he finally clambered out of the taxi into the cold night air. Dread of the unknown and anxiety of what he might say to Finn had hardened the edge of each and every cell in his body. He was fearful too that some imprint of Jo might cling to him, some resonance of her perfume or her reflection in his eyes. Silly and stupid but, still, a fear coiling in the pit of his stomach.

Finn was waiting inside, sitting at a table up near the window, where Max could see the Mill Pond outside and the rise and fall of the dancing water fountains. His brother was wearing a dark-grey pullover. His jacket and scarf were folded beside him, a pint on the table in front of him. He remained seated on the banquette and his eyes gave nothing away as he watched Max pull out a chair opposite him. Max thought of the possibility of Finn being involved in Jessica's accident and he resisted an urge to grab him by the throat.

Jessica had been close to here too on Saturday night. He wondered if she'd met someone here – the area with the bars and restaurants and theatre was a popular haunt – but he still couldn't for the life of him figure out how she'd ended up where she had.

'Max. A drink?' Finn asked pleasantly, giving nothing away as he signalled a bar girl.

'Water, sparkling, please.' Coupled with his exhaustion, the brandy with Jo had mudded his head slightly, and he needed to hang on to every atom of control in front of his brother.

Finn raised a mocking eyebrow. 'You might need something stronger,' he said. Still the pleasant tone of voice, but his eyes were so hard as they flicked across Max's face that he felt the top layer of his skin had been scoured.

'And why is that?' Max asked equally pleasantly, under no illusion that an invisible battle line had been drawn.

'Because I'm about to blow your whole life out of the water,' Finn said, smiling an empty smile. Max wondered oddly if he thought he was playing for the cameras in an episode of *Reprisal*. Acting a part. If so, how much of this was Finn and how much was Larry Boland?

'Don't you think,' Max said, struggling to maintain an even voice, 'that it already is?'

Finn shook his head. 'Uh-huh.'

Max leaned across the table. 'For Christ's sake, don't play games with me. My daughter is seriously ill, and I'm not in the humour for any shite. But I'd like to know why you were behind the scams in the bakery last week.' Immediately he was annoyed with this lack of control – he hadn't meant to blurt it out quite like that, and he thought he saw a spark of unease in Finn's eyes but it was gone as quickly as it had appeared.

'That's bullshit.'

'Not when the mobile phone used to make the calls was registered in your name. The police are trying to establish if there's a link to Jessica's accident.'

Finn looked dismissive. 'You don't seriously think I'd have any hand in that bakery crap? As for Jessica's accident, you're out of your mind. Thanks for your rotten opinion of me.'

'Then why did you want to see me? Why did you text me?'

Finn's lip curled. He looked at him with narrowed eyes, his expression unreadable. 'Don't pretend you don't know. I bet you've been afraid of having this conversation for years.'

Max's heart flipped. He had the odd sensation Finn was acting a part, not for the effect of it but purely because sliding into someone else's skin was the only way he was able to bring himself to have this confrontational exchange. Because he, too, was scared of something.

'I don't know what you're talking about,' he said.

'The hell you don't.' Finn lifted his pint, knocked back a large quantity of beer, and thunked his glass back down. He sat back and folded his arms defensively.

He was playing with him, Max realised. But he still wasn't exactly sure what Finn knew. He felt giddy because his mind was racing furiously at the same time as fragments of his life began to crack and shatter just beyond his reach.

'I think I always knew,' Finn said.

'Knew what?'

'That when you came on the scene I was only going to be second best, like I have been all my life. I knew. In here.' He pointed to his heart.

'This is ridiculous. The only person who's making you feel like that is yourself.' Max began to rise to his feet, trembling inside, not wanting to hear any more.

'Sit down,' Finn said. 'I've only started. The problem with you, Max, is that when you wanted something, you invariably got it. You seem to forget that I couldn't have anything without you wanting it too. All those growing-up years, we all had to be extra nice to you, to smooth your path through life and give you whatever you wanted.'

Max stayed silent. Finn was in full flow, talking about someone Max didn't recognise. 'We all had to put you first and make extra allowances in case you ever felt hard done by. Hell, even I felt sorry at times for the guy with the big blue eyes whose mother dumped him when he was just a newborn. I mean, how do you make up for that, let alone live with it?'

Max's hands clenched into fists. He had to restrain himself, even though every bone in his body wanted to wipe the smug smile from Finn's face. He still wondered what Finn knew or didn't know, hoping against hope that maybe he was just shooting in the dark.

Jo's words came back to him: *There's no way he could have found out about us. I've always been very careful.*

He too had always been careful when the four of them were together. Especially in those first few times after New York. He'd been ultra-careful not to allow his eyes to linger on Jo, to keep his distance from her, silently shocked at what they had done, horrified at the mess they could make of both their families. Not wanting to hurt one soft hair on Ali's gorgeous head. Never mind his beautiful children.

Ali. Jessica. Tom. Ah, God. Don't do this …

'What do you want?' Max asked.

'I want to ask you something.'

Their eyes locked. There was a loaded pause, a moment when everything was full of anticipation and pregnant with possibilities. A moment when it seemed even fate was holding its breath.

'Go ahead,' Max said, feigning indifference.

'Where and when did you sleep with my wife?'

'I don't know what you're talking about.'

'Did you lust after her because she was mine? Because you couldn't bear me having something you didn't have?'

'You're being ridiculous.'

'How did you feel afterwards? Triumphant? Happy? That you'd scored a point?'

'This conversation is crazy.'

'Or did you convince yourself, in that moment, that you were in love?'

'Finn – I'm not listening to any more of your shite.'

'Yes, you are. I'm not going anywhere until I've had my say. And guess what, it is a load of shite and bollocks.' For a nanosecond his guard slipped, and the look of pain in his eyes was more than Max could bear. It told him that Finn wasn't just shooting in the dark, that somehow he knew the truth.

'Maybe you told yourself that you needed her. You just had to have her.'

'Finn ...' Max shook his head, words failing him through the wall of anxiety rising inside him.

'Or did you think ... no one need ever know. No one will get hurt. It'll be our secret. We needn't tell a soul.' He paused, and then continued, his voice laced with steel. 'Did you look at her across the table, when you were a guest in my home, and remember how it was with her? Did you picture what it had been like to have sex with her? Did your hands itch to hold her body again? To touch and feel her?'

The air around Max was suddenly icy cold. 'Shut up,' he said.

Finn ignored him. 'I was a bit nervous of introducing you to Jo,' he went on remorselessly. 'I thought you might want her, like you took for granted that everything I owned was yours. But I said to myself, "Nah, Max would never betray me like that, never mind Jo. Jo loves me enough to resist any pull she might feel from him. Besides, Max loves Ali and he'd never betray her." That's what I said to myself, thinking we could all live happily ever after. But I was wrong. And don't tell me it "just happened" or it was "a mistake" or you "didn't mean to have sex" with my wife, because I know you did.'

He stared at Max, his eyes veiled, but his tight face and clenched muscle in his jaw told Max he was at the edge of his composure.

'I know what you did,' he continued. 'I'm asking you where and when? Where and when did you betray your own wife? And how long has it been going on?' His last few words were tagged on so softly and swiftly that they caught Max on the hop.

'How long?' he echoed.

Finn grunted, as though Max had finally and unwittingly admitted something. 'You see, I *know*, Max. I *know*.'

Another deep silence. As Finn eyed him coldly, holding himself in check and waiting patiently for the right moment, Max saw all the pieces that made up his life – all the love, all the joy, all the ordinary precious moments – trickling through his fingers and falling slowly into that silent chasm.

'I wasn't a hundred per cent sure until this week,' Finn said. 'I kind of feared, in a way that I might lose Jo because I needed her so much, that deep down inside I wasn't enough for her. But then, earlier today, my worst fears were realised. And I'm going to tell you all about it in a minute. I'm going to blow your whole life out of the water, just as you blew mine.'

Max didn't reply. He couldn't. Shell-shocked, he was unable to figure out what Finn knew and how he had come by his information. He was frantically wondering what this meant for him and Ali.

Ali. Oh God.

Love means doing everything to protect the person you love. Right then, he wanted to put his hands around Finn's neck and squeeze tight. The realisation almost deranged him.

'What do you want?' he asked, his voice thick.

'I want an answer. You haven't been listening to me. Where and when did you have sex with my wife?'

'I didn't …' Max said brokenly. 'It wasn't like that.'

'No?' Finn's eyes were dark with anger. 'I think it was. Don't give me the it-shouldn't-have-happened crap. And don't tell me you couldn't help it. You were hot for her. So where did you and Jo have it off?'

'Look – it was just—' He stopped.

'A once-off? A quick shag?'

'No, Finn.'

'A slake of your horny desires?'

'For God's sake!'

'Yes? I'm waiting, Max.'

Fear made Max close up inside. 'I've nothing more to say,' he said, knowing he'd already been goaded into saying too much. His mind felt eerily blank, unable to work out what had to be done next, unable to even consider how he might begin to defend the indefensible in front of Ali.

'Aren't you curious as to how I know?' Finn asked.

Max stayed silent.

'Aren't you asking yourself exactly what I do know?'

Still Max didn't reply.

'Or are you trying to figure out how I managed to stumble across a twelve-year-old secret?'

Twelve years. Something exploded at the back of Max's head.

'Was that the start of it all?' Finn probed.

Max stared at him helplessly.

'I found out Jo had slept with someone other than me,' Finn said in a heavy voice. 'I knew there had been someone else. I found out quite by chance, just three weeks ago. Funny how a casual remark can bring your world tumbling down. So while I knew Jo had been unfaithful, I wasn't sure it was with you. When you were over on Saturday night I brought up Debbie Dillon and history repeating itself to see how you'd react. I was going to shovel it on further only you weren't drinking and then we finished up early ... But I found out by chance again, this time with Jessica's accident.'

'What had you got to do with that?'

'Nothing. I'm still appalled that you think I did.' He shifted in the chair, sitting up in such a way that Max knew his punchline was coming. 'Unfortunately, Max, bonking my wife was one thing, and it was very wicked of you, but it's only part of the problem you have.'

'The only problem I have is getting Jessica back on the road to recovery,' Max said tersely. 'And finding out who caused her accident.'

Finn stared at him for a long moment. 'Shagging my wife was bad enough, and I'll never forgive you for that, but,' Finn jabbed his finger in the air, 'if you think it's a nightmare to have a daughter in Intensive Care, just think how you'd feel if you found out she wasn't yours at all.'

Max's head whirled. The bar spun around him and he thought he was going to pitch forward. 'What do you mean?' his voice whispered. 'What are you saying about Jessica?'

Finn said tersely, 'I'm not saying anything about Jessica. It's Grace I'm talking about, because Grace is *your* biological daughter. She's not mine.'

Max closed his eyes. When he opened them, Finn was still staring at him, breathing hard. 'You're joking.'

'I wish I was. You don't know how much.' Something passed across Finn's face. A veil of utter sadness. But it vanished as swiftly. 'And I'll tell you exactly how I know.'

In a slow, sombre voice, Finn told him exactly how he knew. By the time his brother was finished talking, Max felt winded. 'This is … unreal.'

Finn looked at him as though his world had come to an end. 'It is. It's a nightmare. I don't know how you're going to explain to Ali that you've well and truly stitched me up, but it might be best if you tell Ali before I do.'

'Tell Ali?'

'Yes, you'll have to tell her that you knocked up my wife.'

'How can I tell her?'

'So you're not denying that Grace could be yours?'

Max couldn't breathe for a moment. 'I think this conversation is off the wall.'

'I agree with you. The whole thing is nuts. Who would have believed that my own brother, not content with everything he has, would covet my wife? Who would believe that my own brother, and my wife, having had carnal knowledge of each other – I love that word 'carnal', don't you? It's a slutty word – would then conspire to pass off a child of theirs, the fruit of his fucking dick and her—'

Max pulled him by the arm. 'Shut up, Finn. The cameras have stopped rolling.'

'Not in my head, they haven't.'

'We have to talk about this.'

'*We* don't have to talk about anything. But *you* damned well have to talk to Ali.'

'What's the point in upsetting Ali? Especially right now?' Max knew he was grasping at straws and they were slithering through his fingers along with his life as his mind grappled with the full implications of what Finn was saying.

'Oh, you're being facetious, now, are you? *What's the point!* I'll tell you what the point is'– Finn stabbed a finger into his chest – 'if you don't tell Ali, I will. Only I'll not just tell her, I'll do exactly to her as you did to my wife, whether she wants it or not.'

'Are you threatening my wife?'

'Oh no, I'm making a promise to you. In the words of Larry Boland, "I promise vengeance. An eye for an eye." You won't know when or where, Max, but however much you look over your shoulder, I'll find a way to get to her, and I'll do to your wife exactly what you did to mine. So go home like a good little boy, like the kid who knew how to sweet charm everyone to get his own way, and try sweet charming your way out of this mess before I go looking for your wife.'

Thirty-Four

Jo had just walked out of the kitchen and was in the hallway when her mobile rang.

Max. Her pulse accelerated. *There can't be anything amiss*, she prayed. He was just calling to say Jessica had recovered consciousness. He was calling to say it would be okay to visit her in the hospital. She swallowed hard, pitched her voice high and welcoming. 'Hi. Everything all right?'

There was a short, heavy silence and in that silence she knew everything was wrong.

'He knows, Jo.'

'What?'

'I'm at home. I've just come from talking to Finn,' Max went on, his voice faltering. 'He knows. He said terrible things … he thinks we might have been having an actual affair … and not just …'

'Sweet Jesus.'

'What is it, Mum?' Grace appeared at the top of the stairs. She was wearing her pink dressing gown over her PJs. She looked the picture of innocence and Jo's heart melted.

'It's fine, darling, go back to bed,' Jo said, looking up at her. 'I'll be up very soon.'

Her hand clenching the phone, she moved into the front room and sat down on the cream sofa. It was a beautiful room that she and Finn had just had restyled. Restful, spacious, with silk wallpaper, stylish cream drapes and family photographs in crystal frames on a table in the corner. Its ambience was one of success, prosperity and a happy family life.

'Jo ... it's worse.' Max's voice was soft, too soft. 'It's not just that ... he knows about us, and he says – oh God, he says that Grace is my daughter, not his. Jo, how could this be? Did you know? Why didn't you tell me? This changes everything ...'

The beautiful room spun around her so wildly that her stomach was nauseous. 'Christ, Max! What are you saying?'

'He says Grace is our daughter. *Ours!* Didn't you know?'

'What? No! Of course not. Although ...'

'Although what? *Tell* me, Jo. This is no time for pussyfooting around.'

'Once or twice, I wondered,' she gulped, shivering. She held the phone in one hand and put her other arm around herself, but it was cold comfort for her shaking body. It was no comfort at all against the way her life was unravelling or the chilly grip of fear. 'Once or twice ... I thought she had a look of you?' Her voice was thin. 'It was just an expression, a kind of ripple across her face when she smiled. But it was so terrifying a prospect that I convinced myself it just couldn't be. I thought I was just being ... fanciful. And anyway the odds were against it. Weren't they?'

'Were they? We didn't think about protection, did we? I think I stupidly assumed you were on the pill. When Grace was born I never in a million years suspected that she couldn't but be yours and Finn's.'

'I had just come off the pill the week before New York, because Finn and I had agreed to start trying for a baby. All the advice I had read suggested that it could take at least a couple of months, or maybe even longer, for everything to adjust.' Her throat closed over. 'She was two weeks later than her scheduled date, so I was positive she could only be Finn's.'

She had thrown herself into Finn's arms on her return home from New

York, still shaken with all that had happened. They had made love for seven nights in a row, and regularly enough in the following weeks, so when she had discovered she was pregnant, naturally it had been very easy to believe that Finn was the father. Anything else would be catastrophic.

'Finn said the idea that Grace wasn't his crossed his mind a couple of times,' Max said.

'You're joking.'

'It was more from the point of view that he thought Grace was too good for him, too brilliant, too special, that he could hardly believe ...' Max faltered.

'Hardly believe what?'

'That she was actually his. That he had fathered her.'

'Finn said that? But what makes him so sure she's not his?'

'When Grace got sick ...'

'He looked after her doctor's appointments,' Jo said, something sparking at the back of her head.

'Grace is blood group B. Your doctor said it to Finn in passing, during a recent call about her blood test results. Finn looked it up on Google and knew she couldn't be his daughter because apparently both of you are type O?'

'That's right.' Jo's heart was sinking even further.

'Finn said that as you're both type O, then Grace should have been that type as well. So he knew you'd been unfaithful.'

'He did?'

'He also suspected it was me. He had us over for dinner last Saturday, because he was hoping to ply us with enough drink and see how we reacted, but I wasn't drinking, we left in a hurry, and anyway it all blew up in his face when I talked to him earlier this evening about Jessica, and the possibility of further surgery and blood transfusions. He went so quiet I was just trying to make conversation and I happened to mention her less common B blood group, which she partly inherited because I'm AB.' Max's voice was in her ear. 'Grace is B and, according to Finn, this can happen when the two parents are AB and O. He said he's looked it all up on the internet and is sure of his facts . . .' he broke off. 'Jo – what are we going to do?'

'Jesus, I don't know. Where's Finn now?'

'I guess he's on his way home to you. He's mad with rage. Maybe you shouldn't be there. I'm worried for your safety. He went for me before when I hugged his girlfriend, for God's sake.'

'That was years ago. He won't hurt me. Finn can be a moody animal at times but he wouldn't touch a hair of my head. I'd rather talk to him face to face, even if he is very angry. I'm not about to run out on him. He must be in as much shock as I am. And he knew all this earlier this evening and he didn't breathe a word, let alone touch me.'

'I have to tell Ali . . .'

'God.'

'He said if I don't tell her, he's going to—'

'He's going to what?'

'He threatened to more or less do to her what I did to you. Whether she wants it or not. Somewhere, sometime, he'll get to her. God, Jo, I can't . . .'

'He's bluffing, Max.'

'That's what he said to me, that he would do a Larry Boland.'

'Finn would never . . .' Her voice trailed away. How did she know what he might or might not be capable of, if he was enraged enough? Especially where Max was concerned. And he had been in a downward spiral ever since his contract had expired. And on top of that, he had had suspicions about her after Grace's blood test. She could see it all now with the clarity of hindsight, his strange moodiness, his reluctance to talk about himself, his distance from her both in bed and out of it.

'We can't just take Finn's word for this,' Jo said. 'It'll all have to be checked out by experts.' She wasn't really saying these words, was she? What kind of nightmare was this?

Grace. Dear God. Her heart plummeted. Could it really be that she was

Max's daughter rather than Finn's gorgeous girl? Her heart went out to her husband. What must he be thinking? Or feeling?

Max was talking. 'Finn seemed to be very sure of his facts. Ali hasn't a clue. What am I going to say to Ali? How can I devastate her life? This is going to kill her.'

'It's going to kill me and Finn. We're all in this shitty mess together.'

'Ali did nothing to deserve this. Jesus, how can I tell her?'

Jo's heart clenched. 'Finn did nothing to deserve this either. I'm so sorry.'

'It wasn't your fault.'

'It was both our faults,' Jo said.

'There's no point in arguing about that now,' Max said, his voice muffled. 'What a rotten mess.'

Jo gave a harsh laugh that turned into a sob. 'There are no words to describe it. No words whatsoever.'

'Somehow or other,' Max said, sounding bewildered, 'and I don't know how, but I have to find the words and sentences to tell Ali what has happened.'

Thirty-Five

It was over two hours after he'd marched out of the hospital before Ali heard from Max.

She'd gone out to the bathroom, her limbs cramped and stiff, and once outside Intensive Care, she'd switched back on her mobile and sent him another fruitless text. Then on her way back to ICU, her mobile beeped and her heart galloped so much that, at first, she couldn't read his text.

He was at home.

That was all it said, but she felt a huge wave of relief. Everything was all right if Max was at home. At the back of her head, when he'd walked away from her, she'd been filled with a momentary, irrational panic that she might not see him again, that he was leaving her, and it was as though half of her body was missing. She left the hospital shortly afterwards, Monica, the nurse on duty, promising to call if there was any change in Jessica's condition.

'I'll be back first thing in the morning,' Ali said, kissing Jessica's cool forehead.

Outside, the damp air was chilly on her face, the breeze coming in flurries. She jumped into a taxi, realising afterwards that their car was probably still in the hospital car park. It could stay there for now, she was tired and emotional and had more important things to concern her.

'Max?' She called his name as she came into the hall and closed the door. She hung her coat up in the cloakroom and toed off her shoes, pulling on a pair of flatties. She walked through to the kitchen, but he wasn't there nor was he in the downstairs study or sitting room. Funny, all the way home she had pictured him in the sitting room relaxing with a glass of wine on their stone-coloured sofa and she had intended joining him, leaning into him as they chatted about the bakery and whatever had gone wrong.

'Max?' She called again, knowing he had to be at home because the security system had been disarmed. She went upstairs, wondering if he had already gone to bed. Surely not before she had come home, though.

He was in their bedroom all right. But not in bed. One of the side lamps was on, bathing the room in soft, glowing light. He was sitting on the sofa in the bay window, looking out onto the canal, still wearing his leather jacket. There was something about the rigid way he was holding himself that put her on guard. Yet nothing could be that bad. Not after Jessica. She flew across the room and put her arms around him. 'Max! What's the matter?'

He shuddered, drew a deep breath. Then he looked at her. And she knew then there was something very wrong. She knew it wasn't going to be all right. Instead of sitting curled beside him, resting her feet in his lap as she sometimes did, she drew away from him.

'There's something I have to tell you,' he began, his voice wooden.

Her heart faltered. 'Is it the bakery?' Wishing, hoping, praying it was just Booth Street, but knowing by his face it was far more serious.

He swallowed. 'Yes and no.'

'What is it, Max?' she whispered.

'First up, the police called me last night to say that the mobile involved in the Facebook scam was registered to Finn Kennedy.'

'I don't believe you. *Finn*? But why would he—' She broke off, recalling Max's scared face of the week before, the feeling that he was keeping something from her.

'I don't know what to think,' Max said.

Her eyes searched his. 'Neither do I. Finn would have no reason to cause trouble for the bakery. For us. For you.'

He didn't answer her immediately. He stared into space and she knew then that for some reason Max had already considered Finn might be responsible. As for why, she didn't understand.

'You haven't done anything to annoy Finn, have you?'

His shoulders sagged and he rubbed his face.

'What's going on, Max?' she asked, something beginning to tremble inside her.

'Years ago ...' he began.

Years ago? So it wasn't just now ... What did he mean, years ago? Like when? Images of her life with him spiralled through her head, blurring around the edges like a faulty photograph, but nothing jumped out at her.

'When I was in New York ...' He paused.

Her brain froze over. It was curiously blank. She didn't know what he was talking about. He'd been to New York a few times, just as he'd been to London, to Paris, to Rome.

'It was 9/11 ...' He bent his head, slowly rubbing his forehead.

What could have happened to make Max so agitated? she wondered, her words echoing back to her as though they bounced off a sheet of thick ice.

'I remember that time,' she said, recalling the horror of those days, and the way she'd cried at the sound of his voice as he'd said he was safe and sound. She'd given Jessica an extra hug and kiss from him. Then the wonderful days when he'd first arrived home, and soon after she'd found out she was expecting Tom.

Max was talking. 'So you see, I was all over the place, although that's no excuse ...'

No excuse for what? she wanted to say, but the words froze on her lips. Because she didn't want him to answer. A cold blade of fear ran from Ali's head down to her toes. She leaned forward and put her hand across his mouth. 'Don't say anymore, don't say another word,' she begged. 'Please don't say anything that will wreck what we have.'

His eyes stared at her, full of sorrow. He lifted her hand from his mouth and kissed the palm, closing her fingers over the kiss. She pulled her hand away, feeling stung.

'Ali – God. I'd give anything to turn back time. But I can't and it's too late.'

She began to shake, feeling it rippling out in waves from her stomach. She wrapped her arms around her middle, holding herself tightly, but she couldn't prevent cold chills from running up and down inside her.

'Max, please, I beg you, don't do this.' Her words tumbled wildly. It was terribly important that he didn't speak. Whatever it was, leave it alone, don't give it life, don't give it air time, don't make it real. Don't let anything terrible come between us.

She looked out the window beyond the passing red tail lights of traffic, where the canal gleamed darkly. She saw a man taking a dog for a walk along the canal path, heedless of the drama going on in the second-floor room of the house across the road. She would have given anything to have had his innocence.

Max shook his head, looking beaten. She had never seen him looking beaten, until now.

'You need to know …' His voice was low, a monotone.

'*I* need to know?' Fear lent her a momentary anger. 'Why should I *know* something? Maybe I just want things to stay as they are? My life just to be the way it is? With Jessica getting better and Tom and you …'

He stared at her silently, his eyes so sad that she felt herself crumpling. She wanted to shut him up, to prevent horrible words from shattering their lives. She could see by his face it was too late. Tears gathered behind her eyes, scalding hot.

'Not here,' she said wildly. 'Don't tell me anything in this room. I beg you not to spoil this room, our special place.' They weren't supposed to bring sour words into this room. Some couples made a pact that the sun would never go down on an argument. Max and Ali had agreed that they would never bring an angry word over the threshold of this room, their haven. But if he had done something terrible, what difference should it make where she heard it? In a funny way, she hoped it might stop him from talking. That he might say, all right, I'll leave it, I'll let it be. Instead he got up and walked out, and she listened to his heavy footsteps going all the way down to the kitchen.

She followed him down, her legs like water, so fluid that she seemed to float, so dizzy that she had to cling to the banisters and the hallway rushed up to meet her. He was standing in the kitchen staring at the crammed corkboard as though he was trying to memorise the daily minutiae of their lives.

'What are you trying to say?' she whispered, the blood thumping in her ears.

'New York.' He didn't look at her. 'The time of 9/11 … I went looking … for Jo …'

Her world stopped.

'Jo …' The knowledge stunned her. Now it had come out of its hiding place, there was no putting it back. In the enormity of what he was saying, everything Ali had ever known of their lives together was sucked up and snatched away from her, leaving a black void.

Max made a terrible sound and buried his face in his hands.

She looked at his hands and almost doubled over with pain when she thought of them on Jo.

'Why?' she whispered. '*Why* did this happen? *Why* did you have to tell me?' she cried, heedless of how ridiculous her words were. '*Everything* is ruined.'

She began to hit him, her arms flailing about, connecting with his shoulders, his back, his chest, anywhere she could reach. He stayed still, like a stone, doing nothing to stop her, nothing to defend himself, because, she realised bitterly, he knew what he had done was indefensible.

'Oh, Max, dear God! How could you? *How?*' Her tears began to fall, streaming down her face, the strength of them causing her to catch her breath. She dashed them away with the back of her hand. '*Why?*' It was a scream, wrenched from her heart, scorching her throat as it burst out of her.

He shook his head.

'What about Jessica and Tom?' she asked raggedly. It wasn't just her, she realised in a cold white heat; he had done this to Jessica and Tom too. It was to all of them.

'It's not just – Oh, Ali, forgive me ...' Now his shoulders were shaking and she realised he was crying his heart out.

'It's not just what, Max?' She didn't know where she summoned the words from. Surely there couldn't be more? In some far-off distant corner, she wondered why he was telling her this now, years after the event? Or was it over? Had it been going on since then? Her mind jabbed through images of them all, gathered together around dining tables, in conservatories, at family parties but, again, nothing untoward jumped out at her.

She refused to consider any other images. She couldn't bear to think of her or even conjure up her name. Not knowing how she managed to formulate the words, she said, 'Has this been – how long ... is it an affair, Max?'

'No, God no! Just ... once.' His voice was muffled.

Once. It felt like a stab wound.

'You've wrecked everything just for a *once*-off?' she said, her voice rising. 'How could you have been so selfish? So unthinking?'

'It was the day that was in it,' he said. 'It just—' He shrugged, helplessly.

She could see it. Oh yes, the day that was in it all right, the horror of it all could easily have sent vulnerable people into the wrong pair of arms, seeking refuge, seeking escape. The need to give and receive comfort, an overwhelming desire for love and reassurance to help obliterate the awful tragedy, on a day when the value of life itself had been cheapened so appallingly.

But Max? They *loved* each other. He knew he'd be coming home to her later that week. He had just called her that day and told her he loved her. They were Max and Ali, Ali and Max. Surely that had meant something to him? And all these years it had been there, lurking in the background, like a kind of poison, both of them knowing what they had done, hiding it carefully from everyone else.

She couldn't bear to think of them in the same breath, but beyond that she was horrified to realise she didn't know what to do, what to think. It seemed everything inside her had shut down, swamped under the huge wave of sorrow that coursed through her at the realisation that their marriage and their lives would never be the same again.

'I don't want to know,' she said. 'I can't ... cope with this, with what you've done. And I don't know why you suddenly decided to smash up our lives with this ... this shit. Especially now, with Jessica. What made you decide to confess? Why couldn't you have kept your guilty conscience, your dirty little sin, to yourself for a little while longer?'

'I had to tell you,' Max said.

'You *had* to? You hardly needed to square your conscience, or decide you suddenly wanted forgiveness? Which, by the way, you aren't going to get.'

He made no reply.

She pushed on. 'Why now? When we're already on our knees with Jessica? Unless ...' she faltered, her mind spinning. 'Is there a link? Had this – God, Max, don't tell me what you did had anything to do with Jessica? I don't understand.'

'I had to tell you because, if I hadn't, Finn was going to tell you, only he wasn't going to put it as politely as me,' Max said.

Finn. She'd lost sight of him for a moment. The cuckolded husband. It was a label that Finn would find unforgiving. She could easily imagine him wanting to kill Max.

'So the reason you had to tell me your crappy little secret is because Finn found you out.' Funny how painful it was to realise she'd been the last to know.

Max nodded.

'And what way was he going to tell me?' Ali asked.

'It doesn't matter,' Max sighed. It was such a defeated sigh that Ali felt shivers up her spine.

'How did Finn find out? Did he catch you at it with his wife?'

'No. I told you, it was just the once. Oh, but Ali, there's more …'

He started to cry again, so brokenly that all her nerve endings ached with the sound of it.

'More what?' she asked.

'It's not just – us. Finn found out when I told him – about Jessica's … her blood type.'

She was disconcerted. 'So? What's that got to do with anything?'

'He'd already found out, recently, that Grace—' He couldn't continue.

The air around Ali was sucked away, as though a bomb had gone off.

'Grace what?' she whispered.

Max's face was white. 'Finn found out when Grace was sick that she has a blood type that meant she couldn't be his biological daughter. Then when I was talking to him about Jessica … it turns out …'

'It turns out what?' She knew, but she still couldn't believe, couldn't accept the enormity of what was happening to them.

'Grace's blood type is the same as Jessica's, which is inherited from mine. Oh, Ali, it's all such a mess.'

She backed away from him. Crossing the room, she collapsed on the edge of a chair. She stared into space for several moments, blinking hard, trying to get a grip on her dazed thoughts and the nausea that rushed into her throat. 'A mess? I can't – oh God. Get out. Go away. Leave me, now, this minute.'

'Ali, I—'

'You heard me. *Go.*'

'But, please, we have to …' He got up and began to walk towards her, and she saw him in another time and place, reaching for her to lift her into his strong arms and twirl her around. She recoiled.

'We don't have to anything. I hate you. I never want to see you again.'

He stared at her for long moments, then without saying another word, he got up and left the room. After a while, she heard the thud of the front door closing. She sat, immobile, as the house settled into a silence so heavy she could hear it roaring in her ears.

Majorca, 1992

On their honeymoon, they rise early to watch the sunrise.

Max is bemused when Ali suggests it, as they lie in bed the night before.

They have just had a deliciously long love-making session, after a drinking session that went on into the sultry late evening and involved too much iced sangria on a terrace overlooking the sea. Back in their hotel bedroom, Ali is in a giddy mood and keeps rolling around the bed away from Max, twisting out of his grasp, laughing so much that she even falls through the gap in the middle of the beds and all he can see is her tousled mop of blonde hair and outraged expression suitable for a six-year-old child, as her face comes up through the gap. Like most continental holiday hotels, their honeymoon bed is two single beds pushed together. It works most of the time and they usually end up cuddled tightly together on one or the other, except when they are horsing around and the beds separate. Ali only quietens down when he corners her in the bathroom, and lifting her easily, he balances her against the tiled wall. As he holds her still and slides inside her, he watches her eyes soften luminously and he loves the way her breathing becomes raggedy and her white teeth bite down on her red lower lip the deeper he goes.

He loves the way her soft eyes widen as she stares into his when she comes. Trusting, honest, totally vulnerable in that moment.

There was more when he carried her back to the bed, Max drawing it all out, slowly and luxuriously, holding on to the soft curve of her waist as she rocked on top of him, turning her over and drawing a pillow under her hips to make it more intense for both of them, teasing her and playing with her until she whimpered for mercy.

Now they are more than replete. There is only a sheet covering them in the warm humid night. Through the open window of their balcony, four floors up, occasional snatches of conversation and revelry drift up from passers-by, and now and then a scooter stutters along the street. Ali is tucked into the crook of his arm and he feels the press of her soft breasts against his chest. Her hair is still damp at the temples, and there is a sheen of sweat on her brow. He knows exactly how it tastes, muskily sweet, with a minuscule trace of coconut suntan oil. Her scent is all around him and even though they are lying side by side, his skin is still tingling so much after their love-making that he feels he is joined to her still, hips to hips.

'Hey, missus,' he says, teasing her with her new title.

She lifts up a slender arm and flexes her hand, inspecting her wedding band. It is a narrow, plain band of gold, all they could afford. He told her he'd buy her an eternity ring when they'd been married ten years. Ten years sounds a whole lifetime away, she'd said. But spending ten years with Max, being married to him, starting a family, sounds like heaven, she'd qualified hurriedly.

'Yes, master,' she jokes.

'Glad you remembered who's in charge.' He puts his hand up against hers and it is twice its size. He interlinks their fingers, loving the feel of her hand in his.

'Oh, you're in charge all right, you're in charge of carrying out my orders.'

He tightens his hold. 'Do you think there's any chance we can get some sleep? I'm knackered. I was awake at the crack of dawn this morning.'

She turns in bed and traces a finger across his chest. 'What were you doing awake at the crack of dawn?'

'I was looking at your lovely face and thinking we're a whole week married tomorrow.'

She wriggles in bed, moving in closer to him. Her soft blonde hair tickles his nose. 'A whole week. Tomorrow. I hope you're not suffering from a seven-day itch. Or having regrets already,' she laughs.

'Nah. We had left the curtains open, remember? So we could see the stars last night. Only when the sun rose it sparked right into the room.'

'Ooh, that's so romantic. Why didn't you wake me?'

'I was afraid to move. You were burrowed right into me and I didn't want to disturb you.'

She tilts her head back so she can look him in the eye. Her eyes are clear and trusting, and the way she looks at him sears into his heart. 'But I'd love to watch the sunrise,' she says, 'especially on our honeymoon. And you're in charge of carrying out my orders.'

'Mmm.' He is starting to drift into sleep.

'So if you're awake.'

'Yeah …we'll see.'

She gives him a nudge early the following morning. He watches through half-closed eyes as she slides out of bed, pulling on a lace-edged cotton wrap that is part of a negligee set she bought especially for their honeymoon. She'd already laughed that it had been a waste of money as he hadn't given her a proper chance to wear it. She'd already told him he seemed to be more passionate than ever, more hungry for her, since their wedding day, whatever had got into him. If this was what marriage was about, it was going to be brilliant.

'I knew you'd find some use for that eventually,' he says, as she pulls him out of bed by the hand and draws him across to the balcony.

Down below, the streets of the Majorcan resort are so hushed and empty of life that the ochre and whitewashed buildings are like a vacant movie set. If they turn their heads, they can glimpse a corner of the satiny sea. Up above, the pale pewter shadows are slowly draining out of the never-ending bowl of the sky. Then from the brow of the hills rimming the far horizon, the light begins to spread. He stands behind her, his arms clasped around her, and together they watch the new day begin. She leans back into him, the back of her head resting on his chest, the warmth of her body seeping into his cool skin, and after a while she twists around in his arms and tilts her face up to him.

'Thank you. Thank *you*! Oh Max, this is perfect. Us, now here. In this moment. I want to stay here forever. I love you so much.'

Her face is washed in pale yellow light, her hair is a glittering halo around her head. Her eyes are bright with laughter, like a child's eyes. He wants to crush her to him so that they are inseparable. He wants to keep her safe forever.

'Are you glad you persuaded me to marry you?'

She punches him playfully. 'I seem to remember *you* asked *me*.'

'Did I?' he jokes, recalling the cake he had baked for her, with his proposal traced in silver icing. Ali had cried when he'd surprised her with it; then again, he hadn't expected anything else.

'Max! You're ruining the moment.'

'We'll have more perfect moments,' he says, as he bends to kiss the tip of her nose. 'We're just at the beginning of it all.'

'Whenever I close my eyes, no matter how long we're married, even ten years, I can think of this, us, at the start of it all.' Ali throws out her arms. 'I'm so happeeee!' She spins around in a circle and falls into Max's arms.

Chapter Thirty-Six

Max woke with a jolt. He'd been dreaming about Ali and their honeymoon, and she was still there with her fluffy blonde hair and her curving smile, laughing at the edge of his consciousness. He didn't know where he was. Even though it was in shadows, the room was unfamiliar. He made out the glint of a mirror, but it was in a different place and it wasn't the Victorian gilt-edged mirror that hung over the mantelpiece in their bedroom, the one Ali had picked up in a car boot sale, knowing it would be perfect. This was a long mirror, of the kind ubiquitous to bland hotel rooms. He lifted his head from the pillow and looked down at his fully clothed body, sprawled on top of the bed.

Then he remembered everything and the room shifted sickeningly around him.

After he'd left the house, he'd wandered up along the canal in a daze, recalling other walks along its banks, with Ali, with the children, sometimes all of them together when the kids were younger, Tom in his buggy getting excited about the swans, his words tripping over themselves in his enthusiasm. Pain sliced through his chest so deeply that he imagined this must be how it felt to be knifed. He had to hold his breath for a minute and he was so disorientated that he was almost run over by a taxi accelerating to catch the traffic lights on the bridge. Realising that he couldn't spend the night wandering the streets, he'd booked into a hotel, feeling panicked as he walked into the cold, thick silence of the plain, no-frills bedroom.

How could this be? How on earth did he think he was about to sleep here? And how did he end up here anyway, with all the possibilities of his warm, rich life with Ali and the children suddenly reduced to a beige room with beige carpet and a matching duvet cover.

He'd called the hospital. Jessica's vital signs were good and she was comfortable, they'd said. If there was any change at all they'd contact him. Then he'd lain, fully clothed, on top of the bed for what seemed like hours, and somewhere in the middle of all the images screaming in his head – pictures of Ali, and then the way she'd looked at him tonight – he'd obviously dozed off.

He sat up and put his face in his hands. She'd never forgive him. Neither would Finn. He didn't think he'd ever be able to forgive himself and he wept silently at the realisation of the incalculable damage that had been inflicted on the two families thrown into a nightmare scenario, damage that would have to be somehow sorted and managed through endless red tape, the repercussions stretching far into the future.

And Grace, his. *His* daughter, all these years unknown to him. The night with Jo, that impassioned, needy night, where they'd clung to each other in the face of terror and sadness, had resulted in Finn's beautiful, darling Grace.

Only she wasn't Finn's.

Other images crowded his mind: Finn and Jo announcing their pregnancy soon after he and Ali had broken the news about their second child; Finn smiling proudly that Christmas as he'd put his hand on the tiny swell of Jo's tummy, Grace's christening day, her first birthday, photographs Finn had produced of the day she'd started school, a succession of family Christmases – and Finn there, always, his eyes alight with pride and love.

And now Max had taken that away from him and robbed him of all his past memories and his future joys.

He tried to imagine what it could have been like for him if things had been the other way around and it had suddenly transpired that Ali had slept with Finn and Finn was Tom's biological father, and it was ridiculously impossible to grasp, let alone understand, let alone come to terms with. If their situations were reversed, Max could easily see himself landing a few enraged thumps on his brother. How much could you ask of a human being?

He sat up and put his feet over the side of the bed, but he couldn't get off the bed, couldn't feel his feet and couldn't put the weight of his body under him because he was paralysed with fear. He was frozen and immobile, stuck fast to the bland, beige coverlet so that he thought he would be stuck there forever. It was just after eight in the morning. He didn't know how he was going to get through the next hour, let alone the day ahead. His mobile rang and his fingers skittered across the screen as he took the call.

Jo

'Max, where are you?'

It was an effort to talk and his voice was rough. 'I dunno ...' He couldn't remember the name of the hotel, just that he was in room four hundred and something. 'I'm in a city hotel, I stayed here last night.'

'You've talked to Ali?'

'Yes. She told me to leave. She doesn't want to see me anymore. So I left.'

'Was she very upset? No, don't even answer that, of course she was. She must be devastated. We all are.'

Jo's voice was hoarse, as though she'd been crying all night. He tried not to think of the night she'd cried in his arms. He tried not to think of Ali's tears. His conscience pricked at him yet again. How could he have just left, leaving her alone to face the ruins of their marriage? He shouldn't have listened to her. He should have stayed.

Yet the time she most needed love and comfort, he couldn't give it to her because his was the face she least wanted to see.

'And this on top of Jessica,' Jo went on. He stared at an insipid print on the wall and felt his stomach heave. 'Oh God, Max, what are we going to do?'

'I don't know. Where's Finn? I presume he's not there. You'd hardly be talking to me if he was around.'

'He didn't come home last night, so I don't know. Max ...' she hesitated. 'How was he, last night? Was he quietly angry or in any way depressed?'

'He was upset, but more angry than anything else. Angry with me.'

'I'm afraid of what he might do ... hurt himself ... or something stupid. I waited and waited, I sat up for hours but he didn't come home. And I have to go into the office this morning, I've conference calls lined up that are critical so I'm leaving Grace over to the childminder, although she's not happy about that. Little does she know it's the least of her problems. Oh, Max, what will I tell her?'

'Nothing for now.' He had to remind himself she was talking about his daughter. It felt all wrong. As though life itself was out of synch. And Grace was the innocent in this, unaware that her world had shattered. 'We have to think about this,' he said. 'We need to work something out.'

What, though? *Hello, Grace, by the way, I'm your dad after all.*

Jesus. Yet apart from a brief biological impulse, Grace was totally Finn's.

'What are you doing today?' she asked.

He laughed hollowly. 'I don't know. Right now Jessica is my first priority. I can't hide in this room indefinitely. I need to go home to shower and change my clothes. Then the hospital. If I can go there, of course, and risk meeting Ali.'

'And what's happening with Booth Street?'

'Debbie's holding the fort. But that can't go on indefinitely either.'

'God. Any more word on how Jessica is or what might have happened?'

'No, not yet. Looks like we'll be waiting for her to wake up and tell us.'

'I have to go. Keep in touch with me, Max, I'll be checking my phone as often as I can.'

'Good luck. I don't know how you can go to work.'

'I don't know either but the bills and mortgage still have to be paid, and Finn has had no income for the past four months, it's a no-brainer.'

'Christ. You have your own worries too.'

'I have to go. Keep in touch, won't you?'

'Of course. Take care, Jo.'

He went across to the window and pulled back the curtains. He stared out at a medley of Dublin city rooftops and chimney pots, jostling for space under the pale-grey sky. It reminded him of the view from the window of the flat in Larkin House where Ali and he had made love for the first time, and he was gripped with a bolt of sickening nostalgia.

October 2001

They are leaving a twenty-first birthday bash, a crowd of them jostling together, fixing scarves and jackets, swapping last-minute, boozy repartee as they spill out of the nightclub into the cold October air. Max is so busy saying goodbye and exchanging final jokes that Ali grabs her opportunity to slip away from him and walk off in the direction of Dame Street.

After a short while she hears his voice calling behind her.

'Ali! Wait!'

She ignores him, and continues marching down towards the front of Trinity College. She blinks hard at the sudden mist in front of her eyes, and as she weaves through the late-night strollers she feels sharply alone for a moment.

His voice comes again, a little closer this time. 'Ali? What's up?'

She sticks her chin in the air, tightens her hold on her shoulder bag and quickens her pace. He finally reaches her, and she feels his touch on her shoulder as he swings her around to face him. 'Ali! Why did you race off? What's up with you?' he says, slightly out of breath.

'Go *away*. Leave me alone.'

In nine years of marriage, they've had differences of opinion and silly rows, but she's never walked away or spoken to him like this before. He shoves his hands into his jacket pocket, clearly baffled by her behaviour. 'What is it?'

'You mean you don't *know*?' She's annoyed with the shake in her voice, when she wants to sound firm and in control.

'Know what?'

'I don't believe this.' She's furious with him now and feels like stamping her foot, only she's the grand old age of thirty, and not three. She'd fully expected that he'd know what was wrong, and she had pictured him sweeping her off her feet and apologising profusely by the time she reached the cobblestoned path to the gates of Trinity College. But not this complete and utter lack of understanding. It starts to rain and she has no umbrella. Her hair, which had been styled and blow-dried for the evening and was supposed to last the whole weekend, is now getting ruined. She feels cold drips slipping down beneath the collar of her red jacket and she hates the man she has married.

'I can't believe you don't know,' she says, her voice still wobbly.

Outraged, she turns away and ignores him, and marches as best she can in her silvery high heels up to the pedestrian lights. She crosses the road and goes over to the taxi rank, her hair getting wetter and raindrops sliding down her face.

Their taxi finally arrives and he slides in along on the seat beside her. All the way home, she ignores him, feeling as though she will be wrapped forever in this black fury. In the porch, she fumbles for her key, her hands shaking as she scrabbles in her bag, raging that he leans in over her and smoothly opens the door. She steps into the hall, the knowledge that she looks like a drowned rat adding to her misery. Just before she thumps up the stairs, he turns her around to face him, as he had done outside Trinity.

'What the hell is up with you?'

'Funny,' she says heatedly, 'that's what I'd like to know as well. What's up with *you*?'

'What did *I* do?'

His incomprehension is so great that it fuels her indignation.

'It's what you didn't do. I might as well not have been there tonight,' she says furiously. 'You seemed to forget I was with you.'

'No, I didn't. You're exaggerating.'

She stares up at him. 'You were so busy flitting around everyone except me that I hardly saw you all night.'

'Hey, come on, it was my cousin's birthday party. It was good to catch up with people I haven't seen in years.'

'That didn't mean you had to neglect me.'

'*Neglect* you? Come on, Ali. Anyhow, you were as thick as thieves with Jo all night. Every time I looked across you were busy chatting to her.'

'What else could I do? That bloody awful party was more like a stag do and I hardly knew anyone else … As for talking to Jo? That's rich. We're chalk and cheese. I had a pain in my face trying to drag words out of her.'

She thinks she is going to cry from frustration.

❀

Max had introduced her to everyone, to his cousin who was celebrating his birthday and what seemed like an army of strapping friends and relations who had come over from Galway for the celebrations. Then she had sat down beside Jo and Finn, fully expecting Max to join her.

But he had mostly ignored them, drifting from one back-slapping group to another as the night wore on, barely coming back to see if she needed a fresh drink. She had gone over and joined him a couple of times, but he had looked distracted and she felt in the way and out of place, having no reference points in his conversation with old friends and relatives from Galway, so she had ended up sitting back down beside Jo for most of the night.

Worse, even during the few times that Max had come back to the table, his eyes had slid over her and Jo and back to his raucous cousins hanging around the bar, and when Ali had suggested he sit down, he'd looked hunted, as though a seat between her and Jo was some kind of electric chair.

Then Debbie had arrived, slithering coyly through the group at the bar just as easily as she slithered into the susceptible parts of Ali's heart. How come she had turned up here, coming from Liverpool for a party? She didn't even come over to say hello to Ali but had hung around the bar too, along with Max and a guy Ali recognised as one of Debbie's brothers, making Ali feel on edge.

'If you think it's okay to ignore me all night, we're finished,' she says, letting the words trip out of her mouth, even though she knows they are ridiculous. He laughs, his eyes gleaming, his shoulder shaking. She feels like slapping him hard across the face. Head high, she marches up the stairs and into the spare bedroom, slamming the door.

It is a decision she immediately regrets. She needs the loo, she needs to clean her teeth and clean her face, but her stubbornness prevents her from backing down and leaving her little haven. She waits, her heart thumping, listening to the sounds of Max moving around downstairs and at long last coming up to bed.

Deep inside her, she is crying like a baby. Tonight should have been so different. For once, Jessica is staying over with Mia, her friend. Mia's mother, Carol, had winked at Ali as she had dropped her daughter off, telling her to make the most of the free night as they don't come along that often. She'd felt heady with expectation as they'd left for the party, looking forward to an undisturbed night in Max's arms and a leisurely lie-in the following morning.

Instead she is hiding out in the spare room with the lumpy single bed she'd brought from Larkin House, while Max has the comfort of their double bed all to himself. With a cry of frustration, she throws herself down on the bed.

Surprisingly, she sleeps.

They avoid each other the following morning. Ali nips into the shower when Max goes out to the shops for the paper. She hides in the box room when he comes back, feeling that she has never hated anyone more than she hates Max at that moment. Times passes, and the house resonates with silence. She strains her ears wondering what he's up to.

Around midday, tempting smells rise up from the kitchen. Thick, sweet scents of baking. Stealing up the stairs and under the gap in the door. Ali feels her stomach contract with queasiness. She's gone too long without food. After a while, she feels prickles of sweat on her brow and her mouth tastes stale. Nausea grips her stomach, and she tries to breathe lightly, holding off the waves of nausea as long as she can.

She almost leaves it too late, wrenching open the bedroom door and dashing to the bathroom. She's barely inside the door when her stomach heaves and the full contents of whatever she ate last night and yesterday are spattered all around her; the tiled floor, the wash basin pedestal, the side of the toilet bowl, the bath panel. She reaches to grab a towel, but in her haste she slips, searches futilely for balance before she falls into the regurgitated mess, hitting her head off the bath panel so that vomit is even smeared across her curly hair.

She is too astonished to cry.

'Ali! What the—' Max stands in the doorway, taking in the situation with a keen glance.

Don't laugh, she silently begs.

He doesn't. He doesn't even speak a word. He steps into the room and gently picks her up, heedless of the vomit getting on his clothes. He grabs a towel and wipes her face and wraps another one round her hair. He fills the bath with warm water, pouring in lavender gel, and he removes her soiled clothes, peeling them carefully off her as though she is a baby. He sits her in the bath while he cleans the floor, the pedestal, the side of the toilet bowl, drying the floor afterwards with another towel. When that is done, he turns his attention to her, sponging her down, using the shower hose attachment to wash her hair, tilting her head back and drizzling the warm water through it gently.

Afterwards he wraps her in towels and dries her carefully, swaddling her in another towel before picking her up and carrying her into the bedroom so that she can get dressed.

'I need to clean my teeth,' she says, shaking in the aftermath, finding it difficult to meet his eyes.

'Okay.' His voice is gentle. 'I'll make some tea and toast. Come down when you're ready.'

When she goes down to the kitchen, Max pops some toast and pours her a cup of weak tea. There is a warm scent of baking, but the kitchen is gleaming spotlessly and the counter top is clear. She looks around suspiciously. 'What's been going on?'

'Nothing.' His face is innocent. 'How are you feeling?'

'Don't ask.' She feels on the edge, her upset over the night before now layered with a sudden achy vulnerability. Now she knows why her hormones were all over the place. She sits down at the table and picks at her toast, takes a sip of tea. He sits down opposite her, angling his elbows on the table, his chin in his hands. She looks everywhere except his eyes.

'Well?' he asks.

'Well what?' she counters.

'Have you anything to tell me?'

'Have you anything to say to me?' She finally risks looking at him, giving him a glare. His eyes are soft and apologetic.

'I didn't mean to upset you last night,' he says.

'Is that all?'

'I'm sorry that I ignored you, I guess I got caught up with the craic. But I missed you in bed, my love, I missed your hair tickling my nose and the warm glow of your cosy body when you sleep curled into me – sorry, your sexy, curvy body with the fabulous boobies.'

'Go on.'

'I love you to pieces, Ali Kennedy, and I need you in my life. Do you forgive me?'

She feels her mouth relaxing and a corner of it tilting upwards ever so slightly.

He sees this and continues, a grin on his face. 'And I didn't mean to laugh you off either.'

She flashes him a stern look. 'Didn't you?'

'But I think that because I didn't laugh when I saw you covered in your own goo, it cancels that out. So am I forgiven?'

'Well maybe, just this once. But that's all, and I mean it.'

'So now that's sorted, what else have you to tell me?' He gets up and comes around to her, putting his arms around her, stroking her back and kissing the side of her face. She revels in the warmth of it all, his face close to hers, and lets it fill up her raw, vulnerable spaces.

'I suppose you've guessed,' she says.

'We're having another baby?' His eyes are warm with happiness.

'I think so. It's early days, and I never got sick so soon with Jessica, but it's like I kind of know, Max? On instinct?'

He smiles at her.

'I know we've been trying for months,' she says, 'but I even think I know when it happened—'

'Yes?'

'That first night, after you came home from New York, remember?'

He says nothing, but hugs her tightly against his chest in reply.

'We couldn't—' she laughs, the sound muffled against his jumper. 'We couldn't stop. Remember? All night. We didn't go to work the next day. And I felt so loved up by you.' She gulps. 'So glowing with life and love down to my fingertips that I sensed something brilliant was going to happen. I wasn't sure until I got sick this morning …'

She draws back and shakes her head in wonder, tears pooling in her eyes. Without saying a word, he pulls her close to him again and holds her for ages, his hands slowly stroking up and down her back.

That afternoon she finds a cake hidden in a press in the kitchen. It's covered with a thin layer of icing on which Max has piped in red, 'I'm sorry.' He had hidden it, Max explains, in case the look of it made her feel sick again.

'I was thinking,' he says, 'maybe next year we'll start making plans for our own bakery? Maybe with a view to opening one the following year? A baby and a bakery in the same year might be a bit of a challenge, one at a time might be more workable.'

'Oh, Max. Really?'

'It'll be a lot of hard work, Ali, no holidays for ages, full hands-on, we'd have to talk very nicely to bank managers and accountants, look for suitable premises, hire staff, we wouldn't make any money for the first few years, but we've always wanted it.'

'It sounds perfect.'

Later again, after an excited Jessica has arrived home, brimming over with her time on the farm, Ali stretches out on the blue sofa, still feeling a bit peaky. Max fixes a cushion behind her head and another one at her feet. He and Jessica sit on the carpeted floor in front of her, leaning back against the sofa, watching the telly, sharing popcorn and laughter, turning their heads every so often to make sure she's all right.

Ali looks at the two heads in front of her and down at the still slim body and, in spite of her tiredness and queasy tummy, she feels enveloped in a glow of love and comfort from the top of her head right down to her toes.

This is happiness, she thinks. Pure unadulterated contentment.

Thirty-Seven

The first thing Ali remembered when she woke up was the warm, happy feeling of being loved and in love.

Unable to face the big, wide bed she'd shared with Max in the room overlooking the canal, she had spent the night in the spare bedroom. She'd lain awake staring at the ceiling, her eyes wide open. She hadn't thought of anything at all. Least of all Max. It was great, really. A blessing in disguise. Her mind felt blank, like a frozen canvas, with no feeling, no pain or hurt. Just this emptiness. She wondered what it would be like to live out your life feeling like this … feeling nothing at all. It would be great. You could live like this and it would save a lot of heartache.

Then she'd dozed off and despite her determination not to think of Max, she'd been dreaming of him and the time she'd found out she was expecting Tom. Now the cold hard reality that it was all gone, all torn away, hit her like a sledge hammer.

She pulled a mental shutter down over it.

The morning was still dark and shadowy when she got off the bed. Feeling as if she was floating, such was her detachment, she went downstairs and switched on the kettle. She took out a mug and spooned in instant coffee, just a slight shake of her hand betraying the deep unease.

She brought her coffee into the conservatory and, releasing the blinds so they sprang upwards, she looked out into the back garden. The day was starting and no matter how much she longed to wallow in the dark night and stop time from rolling forward into the harsh reality of this new dawn, glimmering light was already dancing across the feathery bamboo bushes bordering the stone walls. Max had planted them the autumn they'd moved into the house, digging the ground and turning the sods with ease, letting Jessica and Tom help him as Ali watched, smiling, from this very window. She was glad she was able to recall it and stay completely numb. Even then their marriage had been soured, and Ali had been blissfully unaware of it. All this time, the years between then and now, it had been there, like a silent black shadow, lurking behind all those moments that made up their lives together, including wedding anniversaries when she and Max went out to dinner and he toasted her with champagne, not to mention family gatherings, when Jo and Finn were also present.

No wonder, occasionally, something dark had clutched at her, a fear that everything would be taken away. Now her fear had been realised, and the pain was far worse than she'd imagined. And this time Max couldn't rescue her.

Stupidly enough, she'd thought that if there was going to be a threat to her marriage it might come from Debbie. Now she knew that the night of the party, when she'd been in the early stages of pregnancy with Tom and they'd had a fight, Max hadn't neglected her because he was more interested in his Galway mates and Debbie, but because he was keeping away from Jo. A Jo who was afraid to drink too much in Ali's presence in case she lowered her guard.

She made a second cup of coffee, and then she went upstairs and into the room she'd shared with him. A wave of painful memories and the familiar scent of her white jasmine diffuser threatened to break through her icy calm. She didn't want to set foot, let alone sleep, in this room ever again. She went straight to the drawers, pulling out some underwear, stuffing her arms with jeans and tops, before bringing them down to the spare room. She made one more trip into the en-suite for toiletries, afraid to breathe in lest she inhaled a whiff of Max's aftershave. Then she put her lotions and cleanser into the bathroom that Jessica and Tom shared.

Next up, the hospital and Jessica.

She was coming up through the hallway when the front door opened and Max walked in.

Thirty-Eight

He was wearing the leather jacket and black jeans he'd had on the previous night. Every cell in her body froze. She stared at him, unable to grasp the reality of him, let alone grasp what he had done. He was her husband of over twenty years and every inch of him was as familiar to her as her own body, except in another way he was a stranger to her. Her senses flooded with panic when she looked at him in all his familiarity and thought of the way he'd collapsed her life around her.

'I didn't think you'd have the nerve to come through that door,' she said, her voice choked.

'I want to talk to you.'

She'd never seen him so grey-faced with exhaustion. Fresh lines scored a trail fanning out from his eyes and in spite of everything, her heart bled for him. The Ali of yesterday, when she'd been innocent of his betrayal, wanted to take him into her arms and kiss every inch of his face. This morning she didn't want to look at it. 'No.'

He moved up along the hall, invading her space, taking off his coat and scarf. In her shock, she felt powerless to stop him.

'I shouldn't have left you on your own last night,' he said. 'It was wrong of me. I should have stayed.'

'Stayed?' she echoed, unable to understand. 'You must be mad. What are you doing back here?'

'I'm staying here for now.'

'I can't believe you think you can sleep here. You must be deluded.'

'Who said anything about getting a night's sleep? Ali—' There was a catch in his voice that pricked her icy calm. His blue eyes were deep pools of concern that threatened to unnerve her. He ran a hand through his hair and she felt sick when she saw the glint of his wedding band.

'Were you wearing it that night?' she asked.

'Wearing what?' His face was guarded.

'Your wedding ring,' she said bitterly, choking over the words. 'Were you wearing it that night or had you taken it off and dumped it somewhere?'

Something flickered in his eyes and Ali's stomach lurched. She hated herself for asking that question, for surely now he was thinking back to that night and remembering everything that had happened.

'Jesus, Ali, does it make any difference?'

Her mouth trembled. 'No, I don't suppose it does. Who cares after all? It was just a bloody wedding ring and not terribly expensive. It doesn't mean anything anymore. And neither do you. I want you out of here.'

'Of course you do,' he said. 'But what I meant was, I'm sorry I left you on your own after getting such a shock. I should have been here, just in case.'

She laughed shortly. 'In case what? In case it was all just a fairy tale? I'm just going to have to get used to it, aren't I? I presume you've come back to collect your stuff?'

'Collect my stuff?'

'Our marriage is over,' she said, the words sounding so hackneyed and ridiculous they came straight out of a soap opera. They didn't belong anywhere near Ali and Max. They didn't reflect the depth of the love they'd shared or all the blended intricacies of the life that had held them together.

If she'd thought he was going to be cowed by her words she was mistaken. He gazed at her steadily, and once again she was subject to a warm, solicitous look from those blue eyes that could have melted an iceberg. 'I understand how you feel,' he said, his voice gentle. 'I know I gave you a terrible shock last night and I can't even begin to tell you how sorry I am. There are no words capable of explaining how much I regret what happened or how much I regret shattering our lives. We have lots to sort out, and it's all a horrible, ugly mess, but for now can we put this to one side until Jessica is on the mend? I know you're hurting badly and I'm sure you hate me, but she's the priority right now.'

'*We* won't be putting anything anywhere. And you don't understand how I feel. If you did, you wouldn't be here now. I don't want to have to look at you. And neither do I want to watch you pretending to be a devoted father.' She knew by his recoil that her remark hit home, as she had meant it to.

'That's not fair, Ali.'

'Oh, yes it is and it's only the start,' she said bitterly. 'You've messed it up for all of us Max, not just me.'

'I know.' He gave her an anguished look that wrenched her heart. 'And I'm going to do my damnedest to fix it for all of us.'

'Don't bother,' she said, little shivers running around her body. She tried to recapture her composure. She didn't want it to crack in front of Max. 'I don't care. I'll never trust you again. I'll never forgive you and I'll never forget. I'm going into the hospital now and I don't want to see your face there.'

'You can't stop me from visiting my daughter.'

'Worried, are you? Huh, it seems you've been neglecting one of your daughters all her life.'

The flicker of agony across his face hurt her to the quick. That was the nature of love, Ali realised, with a flash of insight. You couldn't turn it on and off at whim like a tap. So she was struggling with all his distress as well as her own. And if you loved someone with all of your heart, your heart belonged to them, it wasn't yours anymore, and true love persisted no matter what awful things they had done. She knew even then that learning to unlove Max was going to be the hardest thing of all and would probably take the rest of her life.

She ignored his white face and ploughed on remorselessly. 'And if you have any consideration for Jessica, you'll stay away.'

'Please, I can't do that,' he said brokenly. 'I have to see her.'

She had to shift her gaze because she couldn't bear to see the wounded expression in his eyes. 'Whatever you do, make sure I'm not around when you visit.'

'How am I going to manage that?'

'You'll find a way.' She shrugged, feigning indifference to his plight. 'We can't have Jessica's progress upset by the atmosphere between us. And if you'll excuse me,' she said with cold politeness, 'I'm off now.'

He was blocking her path to the door. He stepped back to allow her pass and as she went by, her chin in the air, careful to avoid any contact with him, she heard his quiet words, 'I'm so sorry, Ali. And I'm scared to death at the mess we're in. Scared I'll lose you, scared what will happen to the kids. I can't live without you.'

She ignored him. She fixed her gaze on the midpoint of the front door and let herself out of the house.

❀

Booth Street Bakery was empty without Ali.

As Max walked in that morning, he knew that although he might be in charge of the kitchen, Ali was the heart and soul of the business. She had made the bakery what it was. Now he had ruined that too.

'Max!' Debbie saw him first. 'We didn't expect you in this morning.'

He had hardly expected to be there either. He'd left the house and his footsteps had led him there.

'We thought you'd be up at the hospital,' Debbie went on. 'How are things?'

'Jessica's stable for now. I just wanted to—' He looked around at the busy tables, with their arrangements of bud flowers and beribboned menus, the pristine condiments and china, and beyond them the counters, displaying a mouth-watering assortment of bread, cakes and pastries. It meant nothing without Ali's presence, her smiling face, the way she skipped down the stairs, fluid like quicksilver, her enthusiasm and energy that bubbled over, her love and attention that flowed through every nook and cranny of their lives together, including here.

'Yes, Max?' Debbie said.

The floor staff were all gathered round him now, their faces full of concern. Even Daniel came out of the kitchen, looking very subdued, which was a change from his usual flirty demeanour. Max was overwhelmed at the show of solidarity and solicitude. He pulled himself together. 'I just wanted to make sure you were all okay here. I don't know how long—'

'It doesn't matter how long,' Debbie said. 'You've enough to be worrying about without us. We'll cope. Will you have coffee while you're here? We can go up to the office, where it's quieter.'

'Great, thanks.' His voice was as wooden as he felt. He wondered why he'd bothered to call in as everywhere he looked he saw Ali in happier times. He walked upstairs with Debbie, but found he couldn't go through to Ali's office.

'I won't stay for coffee after all,' he said, changing his mind.

'Any idea of who?' Debbie asked him quietly as they stood on the corridor.

He shook his head. 'It's all in the hands of the police. I just . . .' He sighed, took a breath, knew it was okay to talk to Debbie, that she was the big sister he'd never had. 'The police have discovered that the mobile used in the Facebook scam was registered to Finn.'

'Finn?' Debbie's face paled. 'He's hardly – God. I know we had trouble before but that was a lifetime ago.'

Max was startled for a moment wondering how much she knew, until he realised she was talking about the New Year's Eve night in Galway years ago, his arms around Debbie and Finn's twisted face, his explosive anger. How they'd all scattered to the four winds afterwards.

'Don't remind me. God knows where we'd all be now if that row hadn't happened,' Max said.

'I would have been married to Finn, maybe running my own place, if my mother had got her way,' Debbie said, giving him a wry glance.

'Really?'

'My mother had high hopes for us, you know. She was very disappointed when I went off to Liverpool. Anyhow, it's all ancient history.'

'They're trying to find out if there's a link between Jessica and what happened here last week,' Max told her.

'I hope not. But there couldn't be. Not Finn.'

'I should have called them in last week. God only knows what I might have prevented.'

'You can't torment yourself like that, Max.'

'Can't I?' he said, going back down the stairs.

He walked out the door of the bakery, feeling as if he was in a trance. Beyond picking up the car from the hospital park, he didn't know where he was going to go, or how he was going to fill in the time until he could collect Tom from school. And after that he had to figure out how he could visit Jessica without upsetting Ali any further.

❈

The call from the nursing home came through on Tuesday afternoon, just as Jo was finishing her final conference call about the jewellery launch. She didn't know how she'd held it together all day, getting through the hours on some kind of autopilot, while her mind churned with thoughts of Finn. The call told her that her mother had sunk quite low. They didn't want to move her anywhere. Jo might want to pop in later and have a look.

Jo phoned Maeve immediately and asked her to keep Grace for an extra couple of hours.

'Don't tell her about her granny being low just yet,' Jo said. 'It might be nothing, another false alarm.'

'There's no rush,' Maeve assured her. 'Take all the time you need. Grace is happy enough watching the telly with Karen. I'll tell her you were delayed at the office.'

'Thanks a mill,' Jo said, grateful that Maeve didn't ask any questions. Like where was Finn. No doubt she assumed he would be accompanying Jo to the nursing home in order to support her. She certainly wouldn't have guessed that Jo hadn't seen him since he'd walked out of the house the previous evening, suspecting Grace wasn't his daughter after all.

The idea of it all shocked her again.

Finn was probably right in his assumptions. It didn't take rocket science to compare the various blood groups and come up with a conclusion. She sent him a text, telling him what had happened, explaining that Grace was being looked after, but there was no reply. Maybe, she thought bleakly, he didn't want to know about Grace anymore. *Because in a way she is no longer his responsibility.*

Yet how could he turn his back on Grace when she was the beautiful princess he'd loved with all his heart? Images of the fun they'd had together as a family crowded her mind, together with pictures of the way Finn's eyes used to light up whenever Grace came into the room, the way his gaze softened when he looked at her in sleep. She'd had her photo taken with him every birthday and every Christmas and on the first day of each new school year. He kept copies of them along with all her Father's Day cards tucked away in a desk drawer.

She felt nauseous. How could all that be wiped away? Or count for nothing?

❖

It was amazing how empty a house could feel, Max thought as he walked aimlessly out of the bedroom that evening and came downstairs. Even with all the family photographs scattered here and there, reminders of all those happy times, and his wife and children just a couple of miles away, the house was flat and lifeless with a horrible kind of silence. He didn't know where the day had gone, he'd wandered aimlessly around the city centre, then arrived home before lunch and finally slept for a couple of hours, making up for all the hours he'd stayed awake the night before. Now it was early evening and he'd already collected Tom from school and dropped him to the hospital to be there with Ali. He'd told his son he'd pick him up at seven o'clock and bring him home.

'Tell Mum I'll be in then,' he'd said, pausing in the drop-off area outside the main hospital entrance. 'I can bring both of you home before I go back in myself for the evening shift. We're taking it in turns, you see, me and your mum.'

At least he hoped they were.

It was unfair to be using Tom like this, as a sort of go-between, but with the need to power off mobiles in the ICU there was no other way. Tom hadn't seemed to find anything unusual about it all, thankfully. 'I'm bringing in my school bag,' he'd said, hauling it out of the car, suddenly seeming too small for the bulk of it. 'I've loads of homework including yucky maths and I might get some of it done while I'm sitting there. Oh, and, Dad,' he'd said, looking back at him a little dejectedly before he closed the passenger door, 'it's okay if we can't go on Saturday night.'

'Saturday night?'

'You know, the trip to the park,' Tom had prompted him. 'To see the meteor shower.'

'Thanks for reminding me,' Max had said. 'Of course we'll go. You can't miss that. We'll sort something out. Promise.'

Tom's face had shone, as though his father had performed a miracle. 'Oh wow, thanks, Dad! They'll be coming every three or five minutes. And even the moon will be out of the way.'

Thinking of Tom's face now, and the omnipotent power possessed by parents, made Max's heart clench. He had an hour before he was expected at the hospital and he didn't know what kind of reception he'd get from

Ali, or if he'd even manage to see her, but he wanted to make sure she was home safe, just in case. On another level, he was nervous and on edge, in case Finn tried to get to her in some way, considering the way Max had torn his life apart.

He went on down to the kitchen and his mobile rang as he turned on the coffee machine.

It was Paul. The police were checking activity on Jessica's phone, and in the days before her accident, a couple of calls had been made to her from the phone registered in Finn Kennedy's name, the phone used in the Facebook scam.

'I'm just letting you know,' Paul said. 'We'll want to talk to him, the way we're talking to everyone connected with Jessica, to see if it can help establish what happened.'

'When will this be?'

'I expect it'll be tomorrow sometime. It's not a priority because it's not as if the calls were made on Saturday night.'

'I see,' Max said slowly. The air around him seemed heavy and weighted. All of a sudden he didn't see. When he thought about it in the cold, clear light of day, he just couldn't see how this made sense. Whatever about his brother's behaviour, which was crazy in a way and absurd for a man like Finn, no matter what Max might have done on him, surely Jessica would have talked to him or to Ali?

Thirty-Nine

At first he didn't think it was going to work. At first he'd thought Jessica was too drunk.

When he'd realised he still had the spare key to his mate's apartment, he directed the taxi to go there. A spare key just in case the opportunity ever arose and he needed a bed away from home, his mate had said, winking at him. His mate who was safely tucked inside the bar of a Jury's Christchurch Hotel at that moment. Who wasn't around to see him hauling Jessica through the entrance hall of his apartment and into the bedroom.

Lifting her onto the bed and taking off her jacket was harder than he had thought, but the photos were worth it.

She looked smashed – her eyes unfocused, her face smeared, her hair tangled. Her boobs were spilling out over the top of that tube thing she was wearing, and whatever way she was lying and that short skirt had ridden up, her legs were splayed suggestively.

Jessica Kennedy, as she had never been seen before. Her father would have a seizure.

He wondered if she had much sex with her boyfriend.

Then he picked up his iPhone.

Afterwards he brought her into the living room, letting her flop across the sofa. He made coffee and the scent of it disturbed her and she roused, muzzy and upset, holding one side of her head as she sat up.

'Wha— How did I get here? Jesus, where is this? What am I doing here?'

'This is my mate's place,' he said. 'I thought it was best to get you sobered up a little before I bring you home,' he said.

'I don't want anything,' she whimpered, looking vacant and lost. 'Where's the bathroom?'

'It's just across the hall.'

She kicked off her heels and made a dash for it; when she returned, her face was pale and shiny and he guessed she'd been sick. He'd left her jacket over the arm of the sofa, and she picked it up and huddled into it. Then she slid her feet into her shoes. 'I just want to go home.'

'And how about your parents, if they see you like this?'

'They're out, at a party, and Tom is staying with his friend.'

'So the coast is clear,' he said.

There was something in his gaze that unnerved her for she ignored his comment, bent down carefully and picked up her glittery bag.

'I'll call a taxi,' he said. 'Will I see you home?'

'No, thanks,' she said, her in-bred good manners coming to the fore. 'I'll be fine. It's just ...' she lifted her chin.

'What is it, Jessica?'

'You haven't seen me like this.'

'No, I haven't.'

'I'm not usually like this. I just had a couple of shots too many because I had a feeling my boyfriend was about to – oh, God.'

He didn't want her to start crying again. 'Hey, shush, it's cool. I never bumped into you tonight and we weren't even here. Are you sure you don't want me to go with you in the taxi?'

'I'm sure.'

He took her mobile number and called a taxi and escorted her out to it when it came, giving the driver her home address. He asked her to call him as soon as she was home.

The following week, the fun began. She contacted him, knowing something had happened that night, but not quite sure what. She was stunned when he met her after school and showed her the photographs of her drunk and disorderly, stretched across the bed. He felt a slight pang when her eyes widened in shock, and as though a light was dimming, some of the innocence went out of them forever.

'What are you going to do with these?' she whispered.

'Nothing for now,' he said. 'They might come in useful, though, but I won't do anything without telling you first. Promise.'

Her eyes narrowed and he knew she'd recognised it as a threat. He met her a couple of evenings, bringing her out for a drive, knowing she didn't want to be with him, but too afraid to say no in case she found her photographs splashed across Facebook or handed to her father. She talked about the bakery and the incidents, as though she suspected him but was too nervous to confront him. And he relished the sense of power it gave him, the sense of having one over on Max.

So it was fun until the Saturday night, when it all went horribly wrong.

Forty

Jo's heart was lodged inside her like a stone as she drove to the nursing home, wondering what she'd find there, wondering if Veronica had slipped away already, far out of Jo's reach, denying her the chance to make some kind of amends. But she hadn't gone anywhere just yet, it seemed, for Kylie was much as normal when she answered the door.

'Your mother is very weak,' she said, accompanying Jo down the corridor to her room. 'She seems to be sinking lower all the time.'

'How long … do you think …?'

'It's impossible to say,' Kylie said. 'Days, maybe a week or two. Sometimes they just hang on, lingering in a twilight, I dunno. I guess they're afraid to go or they need to be told to go …'

'*Told* to go?'

Kylie smiled. 'I've been working in various nursing homes for three years and you see lots of things at the edge of life and death. Not everything has a rational explanation. Sometimes people cling on stubbornly, refusing to give up their hold on life, others hang on because they're afraid to let go of their loved ones, then there are more who give in without a whimper.'

'Even if their minds are not their own?'

'Who knows what's really going on in anyone's head?' Kylie said. 'The longer I'm here, the less I understand.'

'I guess that comment could be applied to life in general,' Jo said drily.

'I'll leave you to it,' Kylie said when they reached Veronica's room. 'Ring the bell if you need anything. And you might want to put your sisters on standby. They're abroad, aren't they?'

'Yes, they are. Thanks.'

Veronica Harper looked as though she was asleep. Tiny, frail, bird-like, with strands of white hair the colour of cotton wool, she seemed to Jo's eyes to have shrunken further in the bed. *Weeks, maybe just days*, Jo thought. Her mother's life, finally at the end of it all, reduced to this. She sat down by the bed, close to her mother's face, conscious of time slipping through her fingers. Unless there was an absolute miracle, Jo would never have the reconciliation she craved.

They'd never resolved it – the Tuesday afternoon Jo had come home early from college that had precipitated her departure for London and Australia. What could you say? How could you voice the shock you'd got from finding your mother in bed with another man? A holier-than-thou mother, who'd applied strict rules to her daughters yet a different rule to herself.

Jo hadn't even noticed the car parked down by the side of the house. It had been pouring rain and she'd got off the bus at the end of the road, hurried up the garden path and let herself into the house. She was just walking into her bedroom when she heard sounds coming from the spare bedroom at the end of the corridor. Sounds that made her stand still, frozen with disbelief. Then she heard her mother's laughter and the voice of a man who wasn't her father.

She crept into her room, the walls swaying around her. She got into bed, fully clothed, and pulled the duvet over her head. An hour later, she heard the click of the guest-room door opening and she tip-toed across to the window in time to see a grey car come up from the side of the house and accelerate out the driveway.

It was hours before she ventured downstairs. Her father had come in, late as usual from his surgery. He had fallen asleep in front of the television.

'Where were you all this time?' her mother asked.

'I was upstairs studying,' Jo said.

'How long have you been home?'

'A couple of hours,' Jo shrugged, hardly able to meet her eyes as an angry red stain coloured her mother's face.

Her twenty-first birthday party had been arranged for the following Saturday night. It took Jo three days to sort out her plans and she left on Saturday morning while her mother was collecting her cake and her father was on a house call. She left a note saying she was sick of college and wanted to travel the world. She left her mother to cancel the party and tell the neighbours and friends. Still, it was a lot better than trying to explain to her father why she suddenly detested her mother. A lot better than souring her sisters' worlds with their illustrious marriages to very eligible men.

Then the self-righteous Jo had messed up everything anyway, by helping to trigger her father's early death, something else that had never been resolved between them. Not by a look or a glance, or even a stray comment, did Veronica even hint that she might have held Jo in any way responsible for helping to hasten her father's death.

Veronica had never been her superior self again, it was as though she had crumbled, and Jo was in no doubt that whatever had been going on that wet afternoon, her mother had loved her father deeply. To Jo's surprise, her mother had tried to talk to her about it, once, five years after Jo came home.

'I know why you went off that time,' she'd said one Christmas when they had a moment alone. 'I want you to know it never happened again. I loved your father.'

Jo could only imagine the cost of that confession to her once-regal mother – but she had just turned her back and left the room. Only after the hard-learned lesson of New York and Max had she realised she was no one to judge, yet she still continued to skirt around Veronica with stiff politeness, avoiding any confrontational subjects.

In time, Veronica had picked up the pieces of a radically changed life, mellowing with the years and becoming a besotted grandmother to her five grandchildren.

'These little people are the best gifts in the world,' she'd said, taking Grace to her heart with the same measure of love with which she cherished her other grandchildren.

Jo tried to imagine what her mother might say to her now if she knew the predicament her daughter was in. It was doubtful she would ever open her eyes again. She would certainly never talk again, never tell Jo she just wanted her to be happy, and Jo felt overwhelmed. There was no chance now for setting the past to rights and Jo would have to live with that.

But didn't they say that hearing was the last to go? Her mother couldn't talk to her, but maybe Jo could talk to her mother – and tell her things she should have said years ago, before it really was too late. Like, for instance, she forgave her mother for giving her such a shock, that now she understood how these things could happen, and she hoped her mother would forgive her for all the upset her impulsive behaviour had caused. Things like, she loved her mother and wanted her to be at peace. Jo leaned forward and took her mother's frail hand in hers, and with tears slipping down her cheeks, she spoke from the bottom of her heart.

Jo didn't know if Veronica heard or understood one word. She sat for a long time, hearing footsteps pass outside, a name being called, a phone ringing, sounds of everyday life. Inside the room all was quiet. She watched her mother's unresponsive face, the shallow rise and fall of her chest as her breath came and went. She talked some more, repeating a lot of what she'd already said, and then she left, kissing her on her thin cheek, saying she'd be back tomorrow.

She drove home, parking her car outside the garage, as after a quick shower and phone calls to update her sisters she'd be going out again to collect Grace. She let herself into the house, taking off her gloves and overcoat and switching on lights as she moved down the hall. With a start, she realised the house alarm hadn't beeped when she'd opened the hall door and guessed she must have forgotten to set it when she'd left the house that morning. No surprises there, considering the state she'd been in. She kicked off her high heels and slipped up the stairs, pulling off her jacket as she went into her bedroom, and then she jumped, startled.

Finn was sitting in a chair, silently watching her.

Forty-One

'Finn. What are you doing? Why are you sitting in the dark?'

'It's my home, you know. As for what I've been doing, I've been waiting for you,' he said.

'I didn't see your car outside.'

'It's in the garage.'

She wondered how she was going to erase that look from his face. She didn't think she could cope with this now. She knew what she wanted to say, what she wanted to tell him, it was all caught in her heart, but she was scared of getting it wrong. 'Where have you been?'

'Do you care?'

'Of course I do.'

'Did you ever care? Or was I always only second best?' He leaned back, crossing his arms, his eyes absorbing her. His tone was casual and she wondered if he was acting the part of the spurned husband and she'd be able to get through to the real Finn Kennedy.

She swayed, putting her hand up to her head. Sometimes Jo felt she was the only one who knew the real Finn, the soft, sensitive and deeply romantic person, buried deep behind that guarded exterior. The actor who confounded his fans by being so different off-stage. The brother who couldn't seem to get away from the notion that he was always second best. The husband who needed her to validate his sense of self.

The father who loved Grace with every atom of his being.

She also knew that what she said, or didn't say, would direct the course of all their lives – hers, Grace's and quite possibly Finn's.

'Finn, please, I know we've a lot to sort out between you, me and Grace, but I don't think I can start right now. I'm nervous of saying the wrong thing.'

'So you admit it. I knew Max would call you straightaway. It's all very simple really. You had sex with my brother and passed Grace off as my daughter. You betrayed both of us. End of story. End of marriage.'

'I thought Grace was *ours*, Finn. And in all ways possible she is ours, yours. You've been there for her from the moment she was born, remember? Holding her in your arms, walking the floor with her at night, answering her cries anytime she called out "Daddy", watching her in the school play, *being* there for her for all the little things and the big things that truly matter.'

'You bitch. I bet you've been squaring your conscience with that crap all these years.'

'I thought she was ours. She *is* ours. In all the essential things, she's your daughter.'

'Except the most essential thing of all,' he shouted. 'It's not my blood running in her veins.'

'We don't know for certain.'

'Jesus bloody Christ, I do know. And you're forgetting something,' Finn said.

'What?' she said, her voice raw.

'You slept with Max. That's how all this happened.'

'What happened between me and' – she had to take a deep breath – 'Max was a once-off. We both bitterly regretted it.'

'When and where? At least have the decency to enlighten me, unlike my brother.'

'It was New York. The night of 9/11.' Even thinking of it now made her shake.

He stayed silent.

'I'm not making excuses but I wasn't myself. If I'd been on time for the meeting that morning, I could have been another statistic, blasted into powder. So I wasn't thinking straight.'

A muscle jerked in his cheek, but he went on as though she hadn't spoken. 'You must have had a great laugh at my expense. Both you and Max. Sneering and laughing behind my back.'

She stared at him. 'No, we didn't. If your main concern is us sneering and laughing, it sounds to me that your pride is hurt more than anything else.'

'Of course my pride is hurt, but that's nothing compared to the pain in my chest. Did you enjoy it?'

'What?'

'Did you enjoy having sex with Max? Was it better than with me?'

Jo felt shivery. She couldn't look at Finn. 'That didn't come into it. It was just, I dunno, a shock reaction to the situation we were in. I was just grateful to be alive,' she said. 'I was horrified at what had happened, and my narrow escape, and so scared I just needed someone, something to cling to.'

'See, I can't stop thinking about it. I'll never be able to stop imagining you two together. I can never go to bed with you again without wondering if you're thinking of him, comparing me to him. It's fucking up my head,' he shouted.

'Please don't shout.'

'I'll shout as much as I want to. You were the only one who made me feel calm inside and that's gone now. All *gone*.'

'I didn't *make* you feel anything, Finn. You don't need me to validate you. I don't have power over you. That was how *you* decided to feel,' she shouted back at him, warning herself to go very carefully.

'You have an answer for everything, don't you?'

'I don't. I wish I had an answer for *us*.'

He laughed. 'That's easy. We're all fucked up.'

She bit her lip.

'You won't have to pretend to love me anymore,' he said.

'I never pretended.'

'Sometimes, Jo, I was afraid you stuck by me all these years because you felt you had to, not because you wanted to.'

'Sometimes I was confused and unsure about life and love,' she admitted. 'Who isn't? And, yes, I wondered if I would have done things differently. But listen to me, Finn. Do you think I would have stuck around if I hadn't really wanted to? I only did things that made me happy, Finn. I married you because it made me feel happy.'

She stared at him for a long time in silence, seeing echoes of the young man who had stared into her unguarded eyes in a pub in Coogee, who had cradled her face gently in his hands and kissed her slowly and carefully that very first time. She recalled the man who had made slow, tender love to her in a tiny flat on a hot Sunday afternoon. She knew now they could never go back to that carefree young couple on the beach. Too much had changed. But now, she didn't want to go back. The life they now shared was bigger, richer, more complete, but she hoped the essence of Finn and Jo was there somewhere, buried beneath the complex layers and myriad threads of family and friends, hopes and ambitions, duties and obligations, passions and fears that were the day-to-day reality of their marriage.

'Maybe we didn't marry for the exact right reasons,' she went on. 'Then again, what are the right reasons? The day I married you I was the happiest person in the world, and I felt important and valued and that my life was bursting with promise.' Her voice shook. She swallowed. 'When we came back to Ireland I thought we were going to start afresh, and then, I don't know – life got complicated. Things got muddied. I was upset and guilty over my father's death. Riddled with self-doubt that I didn't trust my instinctive decisions. The day we got married I loved you, Finn, in a young, optimistic way,' she said. 'I love you now but in a different way. A far richer, deeper way. Then, I was young and foolhardy, and what I felt for you was one-dimensional compared to the breadth of what I feel now. But I don't know if *you* really loved *me*.'

'What do you mean?'

'I think you needed me to shore up your life, and that's different. You wanted a girlfriend and then a wife, to bolster you up.'

He shook his head. 'That's not true. You excited me then, you still excite me. Which makes me realise what a perfect fool I am. When I look at you I ... oh, Christ, forget it.'

'You what, Finn?'

He looked at her, his dark-grey eyes suddenly tender, so that she felt a sudden curl of desire for him. 'I want to lose myself in you, just as I wanted to last month, last year, always. That will never go away.'

'Why do you want to "lose" yourself?'

'You take away my fears and fill me with peace, but that's all over now,' he said.

'It was one night. Twelve years ago. I was in shock. We both were. I know it was wrong, I'm not making excuses. I'm just trying to explain the way it was. You can set that one night against twenty years. I can't change your thoughts, only you can do that. I can't change what happened either. It's your choice, Finn, whether you fall into a pit of revenge and recrimination or decide to make something positive of your life. *Our* lives. My mother is dying,' she went on. 'I saw her this evening, that's why I'm late. She has days left. Then her life will be over. It makes me realise how short life is, how important it is to make the most of every day, and I know I want to spend it with you.'

'The problem is,' he said, 'as well as sleeping with Max, I can never forgive you for Grace. All along I found it amazing to believe I'd helped to create such a beautiful human being. I marvelled that she had come from a microcosm of Finn Kennedy. I was so wrong. So fucking wrong. Deluded beyond belief.'

'You're forgetting something vital. Grace has been nurtured by Finn Kennedy since she came into this world. Blood is only a DNA element, or something,' Jo went on. 'A sperm is only the tiniest of microscopic matter. It may not be your blood running in her veins, we don't know for sure, but it's your love humming through every pore of her. We're her parents, us, together. What's important is love and caring, understanding and nurturing, and you lavished that on Grace. In every sense of the word, you are her father. And you've been a great father to her, you're her hero.'

'Yeah, right,' he said tiredly.

'You are,' she insisted. 'I want you to keep on being her hero. I want you to be there for her through those teenage years, a strong protective father keeping an eye on the boys who are bound to come calling for her. I'll need you for that, Finn. Very much. I want you to bring her out for driving practice, because I'd never have the nerve. I want you to be there for her when she eventually meets a man she loves and needs you to walk her up the aisle. And then … and then,' she started to cry, and took a gulp, 'in time, I want you to be the grandfather she will need for her babies. Most of all, I want to see you two having fun and games, dancing around the kitchen again, even if it is that awful MGMT song …' she said, hoping to give him something to latch on to, an image of him and Grace in happier times. 'It can happen again, you know.'

'No.'

She swallowed at the sound of that word, the resolute way he uttered it. 'Finn, listen to me …'

He shook his head and his shoulders sagged. 'It's over. It's too late. Don't try to salvage what's impossible.'

'We can try,' she whispered, going over to where he sat. Tears coursed down her face. 'All of this has come as a shock to me as well. But who says we can't start again? We can find the spark again, I know we can.'

'No.' He shook his head. 'Even your precious Max seems to think I could have been involved with the pranks in his bakery last week and that

I could have been out for revenge – that there's a link between them and Jessica.'

Jo shook her head. 'I told him no way. I told him you'd never stoop that low or hurt a hair on anyone's head. And he's not "precious" to me. You are. We can move. Start again somewhere away from here. I can't imagine my life without you. I'll go anywhere with you. There's nothing to stop us from going, say, to America, San Francisco. You'd be on the doorstep of LA. I know we need to confirm who Grace's father is, and if your guesses are correct—'

'Go on, I dare you, say it – if she's Max's daughter – as she most likely is.'

'She's *your* daughter, Finn, in everything that counts. She doesn't need to know anything otherwise until she's eighteen and able to handle it maturely.'

'I can't, Jo.' He got to his feet and walked out of the room.

'How do you think Grace would feel if our marriage ended now?' she said, following him out to the landing.

'How do you think she'd find it living with warring parents? I'll always be screaming inside at the thought of you with Max.'

She looked at him and felt a lump in her throat. 'I know you will for a while,' she said softly. 'But think, Finn. What did I do after that night?' she asked, not knowing where the words were coming from, for they hadn't been in her head. He started to walk down the stairs and she walked down after him. 'Did I stay away? Did I reject you? Did I find you wanting? No, I didn't. I came home to *you*, Finn. Remember? I ran into *your* arms. Because it was the only place I wanted to be.' She knew then that, once more that night, words had come from her heart. 'You can make of that night what you like,' she went on raggedly. 'I can't change what happened, but you have a choice. You can play it out on a loop system in your head, over and over, that one night, driving yourself mad. Or you can think of all the hundreds of wonderful nights we've shared.'

He paused in the hallway and stared at her before opening the door.

She was shaking. She grabbed his arm, not wanting him to walk out the door. 'Finn, please, I'm not asking you for forgiveness – I know that's impossible for you right now – I'm asking you for another chance.'

He brushed off her arm and strode out into the garden. She followed him, forgetting she was in her bare feet until she felt the ground wet beneath her. It had started to lash rain. He marched down the path, heedless to the deluge, and leaving the front door wide open, she hurried after him trying to grab hold of him again while the rain soaked her clothes and flattened her hair.

'I'm asking you to have faith in us. Please, Finn. To believe in us, together. I said to you years ago, when we left Australia, that we were starting afresh. We're not those two young people any more, we're wiser and stronger,' she cried. 'And I love you more than ever. We could turn our lives around again.'

He stopped at the gate and she held her breath. Then he shook his head and strode out into the night. She ran after him and caught his arm again, but he brushed her off once more, walking away so swiftly that she had no choice but to turn back.

'Finn,' she called after him, 'please, please come home.'

Forty-Two

Ali had sat by Jessica's bed for most of the day. She'd been unable to eat very much, her stomach tight, her appetite non-existent. From time to time, her thoughts had drifted to Max but, whenever she pictured him, the pain was so intense that she felt cut into ribbons. Those times she had to sit upright on the chair and breathe very slowly. She thought of Finn and Jo, her mind so jittery that she had to tell herself to concentrate on Jessica and forget everything else for now.

Then Tom had arrived in the late afternoon.

Innocent, beautiful Tom.

'I'm going to do my homework,' he'd said, 'so by the time Dad comes to collect me at seven, I'll have most of it done. Then I can watch telly in Linda's – or at home, if you come with me.'

He'd told her a few minutes ago that he was almost finished his maths. The concentration on his face together with the tip of his pink tongue poking from the side of his mouth, along with his bent head showing the back of his thin, pale neck, were touchingly vulnerable to Ali. Oblivious to the hiss of machines or bleep of monitors, he was kneeling on the floor beside Jessica's bed, the side opposite the bank of machines, using his jacket as a kneeler, balancing his copy book on the seat of a plastic chair. From time to time, he threw an eye to his sister, in between his books.

So far, he seemed unaware of the tension between his parents. Ali was grateful for that. His world had been rocked enough already. She didn't want to think about how much more frighteningly it would be rocked as soon as she and Max went their separate ways. Tom absolutely idolised Max.

And vice versa.

'We can get a taxi home,' Ali said. 'There's no point in dragging your father out and back.' If they left the hospital before seven o'clock, she'd avoid Max completely. She'd have ample time to make some supper and be settled in the guest room before he arrived home. If he did come home.

Even though she didn't want to see him or talk to him, knowing he was upstairs in their room made her less vulnerable in case there was a call from the hospital.

When it happened, it was so quiet and natural that Ali thought she had imagined it.

It came again, a flicker in Jessica's eyes, and Ali's heart flew into her throat.

'Nurse?'

Monica was beside her in an instant.

After a short while, Monica said, 'She's coming back to us, your little lady.'

'Do you think so?' Ali asked, one hand stroking Jessica's forehead, the other hand rubbing her arm.

'Her breathing is stronger, we can probably take her off the ventilator tomorrow. All her signs are positive. She'll be right as rain in no time.'

Ali looked at Jessica's face and wanted to bawl her eyes out from pure relief. She felt a few tears escape and hastily wiped them away.

'Hey, that's allowed,' Monica said, smiling at her, passing Ali a handful of tissues.

'Is she waking up, Mum?' Tom squeezed his slight figure in between Ali and the bed and began to rub Jessica's hand. Ali had to fight hard to resist the temptation to reach out and stroke his dark hair. Even in this emotional atmosphere, Tom, in his fledgling, pre-adolescent independence, would shrug it off with embarrassment.

'She could be waking up very soon,' Ali said, with a shake in her voice.

'She could even be sitting up in another couple of days,' Monica said brightly.

They were so busy watching Jessica's face that Ali lost track of time until Tom reminded her.

'Hey, Dad should be here,' he said, fixing her with blue eyes that were the replica of Max's, only his were filled with boyish innocence. 'What are we going to do?'

❖

Ali almost didn't recognise Max, sitting slumped in a chair in the waiting area. She watched her husband unobserved for a few moments. With his hunched shoulders and pained, exhausted face, he seemed to have aged ten years in the past couple of days. He bore no resemblance to the Max of the ready smile, who could carry the world on his shoulders, never mind the Max who lifted her easily into his arms. She wanted to fly into those arms and make it better, until she reminded herself that he had caused the chasm between them with his actions and she couldn't see how she would ever be able to forgive him for the way he had ripped their lives apart.

He must have sensed her there. He looked up and smiled automatically at her, his face warm and gentle, forgetting that they were at war with each other. Then like a shutter coming down, his features grew taut and wary. He stood up and walked across to her.

'Did Tom explain ...?' he said.

'He did. We were going to leave before seven and be out of your way, but something has happened ...'

'What?' Anxiety sparked in his eyes.

'It's good,' she said. 'Jessica seems to be waking up.'

A hint of joy flitted across his face. Then he looked subdued again. 'I suppose you want to stay.'

'Of course I do,' she said.

'I know you don't want to see me or look at my face but is there any chance I can come through?' he asked, his voice raw with exhaustion. 'Could you just, please, give me that? A chance to be there when she wakes up?'

'How can you ask this of me?' she hissed, conscious of curious eyes watching them. 'How can I sit there with you beside me?' She hated what he had done, and she hated this place, where the most emotional moments of their lives were being played out in front of strangers, who were now privy to their deeply private business. This was what hospitals were like, though. The most important elements of all were played out here: life and death.

'Please, Ali, I beg you,' he implored. 'I promise I'll keep as far away from you as I can. You don't have to look at me. I'll be very quiet. I'd give anything for a chance to be there for Jessica. Just tonight. Please.'

Max had never grovelled before. It made her shrink a little inside, to see how far he had been reduced. Then again, they'd all been diminished by his reckless actions.

'Tom's inside,' she said coldly. 'He can't stay here indefinitely.'

'I could call Linda,' Max offered. 'I'm sure she'll look after him. I could drive him over to her and be back here in no time. Ali? Please?'

She couldn't look at him. She wanted to tell him that too much humility didn't suit him. She felt cut adrift, giddy with hurt, unable to pull the various pieces of herself together.

'Ali ...' It was a plea. 'I need to be in there with you, in case something happens.'

'Jessica seems to be out of danger now,' she said.

'Yes, but—' He searched her face, looking as though he was about to say something else and thought better of it. 'In case anything else has to be signed, or the doctors need to talk, it's best if both of us are around.'

He was right, and she hated that too. Hated the way she had to be the one to give in. 'Okay,' she said tiredly, 'just for tonight. Call Linda. See if it's okay for her to take Tom. But don't ask any more of me. The answer will be no.'

❧

'I like being in Linda's during the day and after school,' Tom said as Max drove them home, 'but I kinda prefer my own room and my own telescope at night. But if it means you can be in with Jessica then that's okay. I hope she wakes up soon. I miss her even though she was always annoying me.'

'I'm sure you do,' Max said. 'And it's important that me and your mum are able to be there for Jessica. Hopefully she'll wake up soon and be on the mend.'

And be able to tell us exactly what happened ...

They picked up a change of clothes and overnight stuff for Tom. Max dropped him off at Linda's, going into the house with him and realising his mistake as soon as he stepped in the door. Linda's house was madly chaotic and her three lively boys so full of noise and mischief that it brought home to him how deathly quiet their own house now was.

He had just jumped back into the Voyager and was about to gun the engine when his mobile rang. It was Debbie, and what she had to say made him turn the car in the direction of Booth Street instead of the hospital.

Forty-Three

He couldn't find the right moment. Three times he tried to start, taking a deep breath as he walked into the kitchen, coming out again when his courage failed him. Now the bakery was closed and he and his mother were setting it to rights for the following morning. They weren't sure when Max would be back, so as much advance prep as possible was done to make life a bit easier for the busy morning rush.

Max had been in that morning, a grey-faced, exhausted Max. Later that evening, near closing time, his mother told him quietly that the police suspected Finn Kennedy of being responsible for the incidents in the bakery the previous week and they were now trying to establish if there was a link between those and Jessica's accident.

'I hope this all gets sorted,' his mother had said, her face creased with worry. 'Max and Ali don't deserve this, nor does that sweet innocent girl. And it couldn't have come at a worse time for me.'

'What do you mean?'

'I didn't want to say anything yet, and I haven't said it to Max, but my friend Thelma has offered me a great job in Liverpool. She's opening a café down near the Albert Dock and wants me to go in with her as a business partner. It's a fantastic opportunity but I wouldn't leave Max in the lurch, and certainly not at the moment, with all his family in disarray.'

'You never told me,' he said.

'I had to wait until it was definite,' his mother said.

When they were nearly finished their prep work, the dough was resting in the fridge and all the dry ingredients were weighed out, he knew he couldn't delay any longer.

'You'd better sit down, Mum,' he began.

'Are you finally going to tell me what's up?' she said, looking at him in exasperation. 'You've been going around like you've ants in your pants all afternoon.'

'Yeah, I'm jittery about something.'

'What have you done?' she asked. There were shadows under her eyes and his conscience pricked him. She'd been working flat out covering for Max, as well as worrying over Jessica's accident. What he had to say was going to make things a whole lot worse for her.

'I've been stupid,' he began.

'Oh, I'm sure,' she smiled, as though it couldn't be all that serious.

'No, really, I have.'

Her smile faltered. Her face changed. 'Don't tell me you've got a girl into trouble?'

'Into trouble? Nah,' he said. 'It's something else – to do with the bakery.'

'What to do with the bakery?' she asked in a flat voice.

It was a lot more difficult than he'd thought it would be.

'It was me,' he said. 'I was behind the stuff that happened last week. Here. In the bakery. It wasn't Finn Kennedy.'

His mother stared at him for ages, and then he saw something in her eyes he never thought he'd see. Disappointment. His mother, who usually looked at him as though he was the sun, moon and stars, all rolled up together.

'I need a drink,' she said. Her hands shook as she took a glass out of the press and opened a bottle of wine. Then she pulled out a chair and sat down heavily as though she was suddenly deflated.

'Run that by me again,' she said, giving him a cold look. 'Because I can't believe what I'm hearing.'

'It was only supposed to be a joke—' he began.

'A joke.' Her voice was deadpan.

'Well, sort of. I just wanted to give Max a bit of a kick up the ass ...' Even now, it sounded infantile.

'Are you telling me you were responsible for all the crap that happened here last week, because you wanted to give Max a kick? Seriously?'

He stared down at his feet and then he nodded.

'Would you mind telling me why?'

Forty-Four

Daniel loved coming to Galway on his school holidays. To his uncle's house, with the big, sprawling field beside it. Acres of space, high blowy skies and gallons of fresh air. From the time he was seven or eight, until he was thirteen or fourteen, he came over every August for a month, his mother bringing him across on the boat in the earlier years, then flying over from Liverpool in later years when air fares had come down and there was more spare cash. His mother would stay with her brother for a few days, and then go home to her job in the hotel kitchen, returning to collect him at the end of the month.

They were the golden summers of his childhood. From early in the morning until late at night, he played with his cousins, hiding in the tall grasses, climbing the trees, play wrestling, running and racing, playing cowboys and Indians, playing football, then coming home starving and wolfing down huge portions of food at his aunt's big farmhouse kitchen table.

'We'll put some colour on yer face,' his uncle would say. 'Set ye up for the winter.'

Sometimes they went fishing in the glittering River Corrib, out beyond the city boundaries, into the sprawl of the green countryside where the air was like a gulp of fresh water, and sometimes the grass smelled warm under the August sunshine and he loved those kinds of days too.

It was a world away from the granite jungle he lived in with his mother in a council flat in Liverpool where the kitchen was the size of a box room and the table had just enough room for the two of them. His cousins thought it was very cool that he lived on the doorstop of the greatest football clubs in the world. He never told them that it wasn't so great in a way. Or that he'd rather have lived with them in the big muddle of the Galway house – only with his mum, of course – for it was a world away from the school yard where he was teased and mocked for being half-Irish and having no father.

Best of all, in those early years in Galway, there was his granny.

She was old. Her skin was all wrinkled but her eyes were like the currants she used to put in the buns she baked. Even though she was old, she was able to bake lovely cakes and she lived in a very small house near a big cathedral with flowery curtains and a flowery sofa. She even had flowery cups and saucers and lacy things to cover the plates. He loved going to visit her, and sometimes when it rained he was brought to his granny's and he even stayed over occasionally with one of his cousins and they were properly spoiled, because his granny always baked lots of goodies for them, cakes and apple tarts and cookies, and she let them stay up late and watch whatever they liked on her small television. So they were happy then, even if the rain was bucketing down outside, bouncing off the road, and people were afraid the river might burst all over the warren of streets behind the Spanish Arch.

She told them stories of growing up in Galway and it was like a different world. She told them they were living in the good times and that life had been hard, even when Daniel's mother had been young.

But the worst time had been when her cake shop closed.

The year he was nine, he was staying with her for a couple of nights when she talked about it. He'd helped her with her shopping, carrying it up from the market for her, and that evening she'd poured herself a whiskey and opened the bottle of Coca-Cola for him.

'When the shop closed, your mammy went across to England,' she told him, her warm brown eyes a little clouded.

'Why didn't she stay here? I want to live in Galway. I asked her already but she said no.'

'You're not to let on I told you, or there'll be hell to pay, but your mammy's heart was broken.'

'Cos the shop closed?'

'Because there was boyfriend trouble,' his granny said, her eyes looking far away into the distance. 'Your mum was a beautiful lass, she still is, but in her twenties she was my gorgeous daughter, and I thought she'd marry her boyfriend and settle down in Galway and she'd be near me with her family, but it didn't happen.'

'Had she a different boyfriend instead of my dad?' Maybe that was why his dad went away. Maybe his mum had loved someone else all along and that was why his dad got angry with her and had rows and left. His dad had a new wife now and another baby son. He was living in London and Daniel only saw him occasionally. Sometimes, he heard his mum crying in the night when she thought he was asleep.

'She was in love with Finn,' his granny said. 'Finn was a lovely man, quiet and mannerly ...' She gave a deep sigh. 'Then everything went wrong when I had to close the shop.'

'I'd bash his head in if I met him,' he said stoutly, thinking of his comic book hero defending the beautiful princess.

'I don't think it was Finn's fault.' His granny sounded a little confused. 'Your mammy never told me what happened, but the lads heard stories and something went wrong with Max, his brother. He broke them up and took my recipes.'

'Then I'd have to bash his head in,' Daniel declared.

'Max went away too,' his granny said, her voice sounding thin and frail.

'He went to Dublin with all my recipes. The shop closed. Oh dear, I don't want to talk about it. When I think of the lovely cake shop I had and the way I had to close it, I feel sad.'

'Cheer up, Granny,' he said, a little alarmed. 'Will I put on the telly?'

'Yes, please dear, and pour me another drop of whiskey, and don't let on you heard my silly talk. Our secret, okay?'

The smile had returned to her creased face and he felt a bit better.

He never spoke of it. Then he was home for his granny's funeral a year later and, in the churchyard, between his tears he saw his mother talking to a tall man as though she knew him very well. She seemed happy for a moment, throwing back her head and laughing at something he'd said. And not only happy but beautiful. The man had a wife, because a small lady with hair that reminded him of frilly corn walked up and tucked her hand into the man's arm. She looked very young to be a wife so he thought she might be a girlfriend until he saw a small blonde girl, who had been picking daisies along the grass verge, run up to them and the tall man lifted her into his arms.

'Who was that?' he asked, as they got into the mourning car and his mum waved at the tall man as they slid away from the kerb and followed the coffin.

'Oh, just an old friend,' his mother said, reaching for her tissues and wiping away some tears.

His uncle said, 'And fair play to the bould Max for coming down to show his respects.'

Max. He knew that name. He remembered. He wondered what sort of a friend Max could have been if he'd robbed his granny's recipes and she had to close the shop. Then he had broken up his mother and her boyfriend. Daniel looked at the hearse in front carrying his granny in her coffin and his heart felt so scalded at the thought of what was coming next that everything else went out of his head.

❋

Years later, when he was working his way around the world, it all came back to him again.

'I'm moving back to Dublin,' his mother emailed. 'The hotel is closing and I think it's a good time for me to go back to Ireland and my roots. The world is your oyster, and you can go anywhere or be anyone but, me, I'm way past the settling down stage. And thanks to the new motorway, Dublin is just over two hours from Galway. But the best bit is, I have a job already! I bumped into an old friend – Max – he worked with me years ago in your granny's cake shop. Anyway, he runs a very successful business here and has won awards for – guess what – your granny's cranberry bread. (If only she knew.) He's expanding his bakery and has offered me a job ...'

His mother was too soft, he decided. Too soft and too good for the likes of Max Kennedy. But it was only when his girlfriend ditched him in Ibiza and he arrived back in Dublin with all his savings gone, and started to work in the bakery – until something more suitable came along, of course – that he realised how much his mother had lost out on. And it wasn't one bit fair.

He hated working as a lowly kitchen porter, at everyone's beck and call. The Kennedys got up his nose – they were so full of it. It should have been his mother's name over the door. It should have been Debbie on the television and in the magazines. Feck it, a lot of the awards Max won were based on his granny's recipes. Then there was Finn. That prick she had loved until Max had split them up. He was now a well-known actor. So far, he hadn't met Finn but he knew from the internet that he lived in an upmarket part of Dublin, and he was married to Jo. They had a daughter, Grace. How come Finn hadn't had the guts to stand by his mother all those years ago?

And she must be still hurt by whatever had happened because she never watched *Reprisal*.

He watched it himself, on his iPad, studying the hard, aggressive character who was all too quick to punish his enemies. The only thing he couldn't get his head around was how come his mum had gone to work for Max. All she said was that she was lucky to have a job in the recession and wasn't it great the bakery was doing so well. She was far too soft and forgiving, and sometimes it wrecked his head.

But now, on that evening in the bakery, he hoped she'd be as soft and forgiving with him.

❁

'... so you see, Mum, of all this, the bakery, the business,' he said, throwing his arms out in a sweeping gesture. 'It should have been yours. Max took stuff that should have been yours by right. He helped himself to Granny's recipes and she had to close up. Only for Max, you could be running a show like this, winning the awards, appearing on the telly.'

He stopped because his mother was shaking her head. She put a hand up to her forehead and closed her eyes. When she eventually opened them, they were so flinty it clenched his heart.

'You're talking rubbish, Daniel,' she snapped. 'You stupid gobshite, you only know half the story. Do you think I'd be working here if Max had ...' She stood up abruptly and went over to the sinks, breathing hard. Then she turned around to face him. 'My mother's cake shop had to close, there was no choice. There was a recession and she was up to her neck in debt, and the night I broke the news to Max in the store room of the shop, I got very upset. He was giving me a hug when Finn came in and saw us and jumped to the wrong conclusion. Finn went for Max without giving us a chance to explain that it had just been a hug and left him with a big black eye. Jesus, Daniel, I felt so bad about it all, so heart-sickened, that when Max was helping me clear the rest of the shop and the mess Finn had made, when I came across my mother's tattered recipe book I told him he could have it. So I *gave* the recipes to him. See?'

He was aghast to see his mother crying.

'Your gran was finished with the business,' she continued. 'I didn't want anything to do with it either. We all went our separate ways, then when I came back to Dublin, I was only too glad when Max offered me a lifeline and a job.' Suddenly she made a grab for him, and began to stab him in the chest with her index finger. 'And why in the name of holy fuck you didn't ask me about all this before you began your dirty little tricks I don't understand. How could you have done this?'

He couldn't answer her. She folded her arms and stood in the kitchen, and he thought of the way she'd been there through all the ups and downs of his childhood and adolescence. The mother who had seen him off with a big false smile pinned to her face when he'd left England to travel the world. The mother who had been overjoyed when he'd announced he was finished with his travels for now and would come to live with her in Dublin, little knowing he was stony broke and had no choice.

'There's more …' he said.

He looked at her, watching her eyes grow wide with alarm. She backed away from him and he never felt more ashamed of himself as he did right then.

'Please don't tell me,' she said in a tremulous voice, 'that this has anything to do with Jessica.'

'Yes and no.'

He watched her face crumple. She put her hand up. 'Don't say any more, you little shit. Not another word.'

She rummaged in her bag and plucked out her phone.

'What are you doing?' he asked.

'I'm calling Max,' she snapped. 'I hope I can get him and he's not gone through to ICU. You deserve to be locked up, you ungrateful little brat.'

Forty-Five

It had been one thing to play the part of the vengeful son, Daniel decided, to mess around with a Facebook page, and sneak into the office to move Max's notebooks, and make hoax reservation calls, driven by his conviction that his mother had been robbed of her legacy. Even messing around with Jessica had given him a bit of a power trip – ordinarily, she wouldn't have given him a second glance. But when Max walked into Booth Street, a Max with tiredness rimming his face, it was another thing entirely, it was a load of shite having to explain his stupid actions.

Max watched without moving a muscle, his stare becoming more and more implacable, while his mother wept quietly. Daniel stumbled over his words, explaining how he'd bought a pay-as-you-go phone in Finn's name, and had involved his new girlfriend as well, as she worked in a modelling agency, knew her way around Facebook, and helped to target women whom they'd believed would cause the most fuss.

Then his mother explained why he'd done it, and Daniel wasn't sure if he imagined it or if Max's unrelenting stare softened a little when he looked at her. When he stared back at Daniel, however, that iron gleam was in his eyes again, and Daniel realised that underneath his friendly, laid-back disposition, Max Kennedy could be a formidable enemy.

'Why Finn?' Max asked, before he'd finished.

'Because—' Daniel floundered, 'because he let you bust up him and Mum.'

'Finn did try to talk to me,' Debbie said to her son, her voice husky, 'but I didn't want anything to do with him after I saw the way he went for Max.'

'I didn't know that,' Daniel said, hating the defensive note in his voice.

'Your notebooks are in the pantry,' Debbie said to Max. 'He hid them behind the flour bins, in a tomato box. Max, I can't begin to tell you how sorry I am.'

Max put his hand on her arm. 'Shush, Debs, it wasn't your fault.'

'If I hadn't asked you to give Daniel a job, this wouldn't have happened.'

'You are in no way to blame,' Max said firmly, looking at Debbie.

'I'll hand in my notice, of course, immediately,' she said, mopping more tears.

'No, you won't,' Max said. 'Not yet, anyhow. Both Ali and I need you. Especially now.' He turned to Daniel, 'As for you, you little—'

His mother looked at him. 'Daniel, didn't you say this had something to do with Jessica?'

'Sort of ... there's more,' Daniel said, hating himself at that moment.

Max's face tightened. 'What "more" do you mean?' he said in a quiet voice.

Stuttering and stammering in the face of Max's fixed stare, he told them about Jessica, meeting her in Ballsbridge and bringing her back to his mate's apartment. Before he was finished talking, Max had taken his phone out.

'I'm calling the police,' he said.

'I didn't run her down,' Daniel blustered. 'Honestly. You have to believe me.'

'You can discuss that with the police,' Max said. 'Because I don't trust myself to continue this conversation and leave you with any recognisable features.'

'I didn't mean for this to happen,' he said pleadingly. 'My girlfriend stood me up in Dundrum last Saturday night and I face-timed Jessica ...'

'Face-timed?' Max's voice was icy.

'Yeah, on her iPad cos her mobile was off, so I said if she met me I'd talk about deleting her photos. I was acting the fool ... I brought her for a drive. I was going to bring her to Johnny Fox's for a drink, but I took her the long way around and it got too late and she got upset and I let her out of the car ... then when I cooled down and went back for her ...' His voice trailed away.

The thump to his head came out of nowhere.

'You stupid, stupid ... look what you've done,' his mother cried, wringing her hands.

Max was standing over by the far wall, as though he needed to be as far away from Daniel as was physically possible. One hand was holding his mobile to his ear, and he was leaning against the wall with his other hand, as though it was the only thing keeping him upright.

Forty-Six

Ali thought they looked like a perfectly normal couple, sitting by the bedside of their daughter, Max sitting on the chair that Tom leaned on to do his homework what seemed like hours earlier.

Jessica appeared as comatose as she had been that afternoon. According to Monica, there was no way of predicting when she'd actually recover full consciousness, but her vital signs were improving all the time. Max had filled her in about Daniel Dillon when he'd arrived. He told her he'd sent a message to Finn's voicemail apologising for asking him if he'd had anything to do with the bakery incidents or Jessica, but after that he didn't talk to Ali at all, or look in her direction. He just held Jessica's hand, his thumb stroking backwards and forwards across the back of it, and he made occasional comments to Monica.

Ali was shocked at the news about Daniel, but she couldn't give it any head space yet. She found herself sneaking glances at Max. However hurt she was, Ali could see by his face, by his eyes, and the bowed stance of him, that behind his careful attentiveness towards Jessica, he was locked into his own private hell.

A hell of his own making, she reminded herself, hardening her heart.

Still, that didn't stop her from letting her eyes drift in his direction, running over his face, from the shape of his forehead, to the trim cut of his dark hair, to the lines fanning out from his eyes, and his full-lipped, generous mouth; she knew how it would all feel under her touch, under her lips because there wasn't a part of this man's face she hadn't held or kissed before, she knew it like the back of her own hand. She glanced at his face as unobtrusively as possible until she felt choked and full to the brim with everything it had meant to her.

Once, he caught her looking, in an unguarded moment. He stared back at her silently, his eyes telling her how much he wanted to wrap her in his arms and hug her, how determined he was to make this better, but she deliberately glared at him before breaking contact.

As time went on, most of the visitors left and the unit seemed to be a little more hushed, with just the nursing staff moving quietly around the beds. Up in a corner of the ward, they seemed to be in a world of their own. Jessica's eyelids began to flicker again and both of them leaned forward, anxious to be there for her, to calm and reassure her.

'Go on, talk to her,' Monica encouraged.

She must have thought they were a strange couple, Ali realised, scarcely talking to each other let alone their daughter, both of them caught up in a nightmare where the bottom had fallen out of their lives.

From the other side of the bed, Max gave her a searching look, his eyes sweeping longingly across her face. 'Is it okay if I talk to her?' he asked.

'Talk away,' she said, as nonchalantly as she could.

'Thank you,' he said.

Then, he leaned a little closer to Jessica and began to talk. Ali would have given anything to be able to sit back, close her eyes and let his warm voice wash over her. Instead she listened with growing heartache as Max spoke. He told Jessica how much he loved her, how much she meant to him and her mum and Tom, how precious and valuable she was to them. He chatted fondly about her as a baby, how he had felt holding her for the very first time, and the joy she had brought them, the way she had altered their lives for the better. He chatted about the funny things that had happened along the way as she grew into a beautiful young woman, the life he was so glad to have shared with her, and how much she meant to him and her mum.

Ali knew he meant every word he said. So why, oh why, had Max managed to put all this wealth of love and happiness under threat? How could he have been so careless with himself, and Ali and the children's love for him? Why had he ruined everything for them? She felt the sharp prickle of tears at the back of her eyes and she willed them to stay there. She couldn't lose it now in this room.

She understood the private hell he was going through and knew that he realised just how much he'd broken their trust. Still, she was glad he was there when Jessica finally opened her eyes, alarm and fright mirrored there as she looked from one to the other. Ali was so overcome she was speechless, but Max, sensing this, kept on talking to Jessica, calmly and reassuringly. He was on his feet by now, leaning over the bed, his body angled towards her like some kind of caring angel, as he clasped her hand in his, telling her she was in hospital, she'd been in an accident but would be fine – she was going to be fine, she was going to be well again.

The frantic look in Jessica's eyes eventually faded away. She couldn't talk properly because of the ventilator, but she took her hand out of her father's grip and gave him a thumbs up. At that point, Ali allowed some of her tears to fall.

Eventually Monica moved in. She'd allowed them precious time with their daughter, but said she could see from the monitors that Jessica was already tiring.

'My name is Monica and I'll be looking after you for the next few hours. I'm going to send your mum and dad home,' she said to Jessica. 'You're a brave lady, and you've done so well to come through this. But you need to get some proper rest and we'll have to run some tests to make sure we fix you back even better than the way you were before. Okay?'

Jessica gave a small nod of her head and smiled.

'Your mum and dad will be back in the morning. They have to get some rest too, so they can look after you properly when you go home.'

By the time Ali had given Jessica a gentle hug, mindful of all the tubes and wires, her eyes were already closing and she was sleeping peacefully before they left.

Ali was overcome with a mixture of exhaustion and relief as she and Max made their way out of the ICU, past the huddled groups in the waiting area, down the brightly lit corridor, past the shops closed up for the night. They walked in silence across the eerily quiet foyer and out into the night. It had rained earlier, and the ground was wet with puddles, the air coldly fresh.

'I have the car,' Max reminded her.

She didn't want to travel home with him, stuck with him in the close confines of the car, but she was too tired to care, numb with exhaustion and relief. He led the way across to the car park, and only when he opened the passenger door did she say automatically, because Max always forgot it, 'The car park ticket?'

He gave a wry smile. 'Back in two secs.'

She sat alone for a few minutes, staring into space, her gratitude that Jessica was on the mend mixed with sheer exhaustion. The main thing she needed was sleep, blessed sleep. Max and all the heartache he had caused could wait for another day. She tilted her head back against the headrest and closed her eyes.

❁

Max was walking back across the car park when his mobile rang.

The police. 'Max,' Paul said. 'Can you talk? I know it's late.'

'It's fine. I'm just on the way to my car. Did you get the statement from Daniel Dillon?'

'Yes, he's just left the station,' Paul said. 'But that's not why I'm calling. As a result of Daniel's statement and the time frame he gave us, we called in the couple on the lane, the couple who found Jessica ...'

'The couple who were out walking their dog?'

'Turns out they weren't — walking their dog.'

'You can't mean—'

'It seems they were coming home from a night out, the husband was driving, and when they saw Jessica up close in the headlights, he got such a shock he accelerated instead of braking. They're an elderly couple who need the use of their car to go anywhere as the wife has mobility issues, and they panicked because they were afraid he'd lose his licence. Forensics will be examining their car in the morning. And then he'll be charged.'

'With what, exactly?' As if it made any difference.

'Dangerous driving causing serious bodily harm, failing to stop, perhaps failing to stay at the scene because he went home first with his car.'

'Was their car not checked out already as part of your routine enquiries?' Max asked.

'The car in their garage was looked at, but it turns out that was their son's car, and he's in America on a year-long visa. We would have twigged that in the next day or two when we cross-referenced all the details. In their panic, they had parked their own car in a barn at the end of their garden.'

Max sighed. 'An accident. A stupid, bloody accident. Look what it has caused.'

The repercussion of the previous Saturday night tumbled through his head, making him dizzy. He saw Jessica as she had been in the emergency unit on the night of the accident; he thought of his call to Finn, when, unknown to Max, he had confirmed the worst of his brother's suspicions. He looked across to where Ali sat in the car, vulnerable in her exhaustion, her head tilted back against the headrest. He didn't know how he was going to tell her this. *An accident*.

'That's how most things go wrong,' Paul said. 'Split-second distractions. Silly mistakes.'

'Tell me about it,' Max said bitterly, the dark night heavy around him. 'Thanks for letting me know.'

'We'll call you tomorrow with an update,' Paul said.

Forty-Seven

Ali cried all the way home, soft tears slipping down her face. They drove up along the canal and turned in towards their avenue, the route so familiar that it could have been an ordinary night, her and Max on their way home after being out, before going on upstairs to their room, their private space. As they turned in to their avenue, a figure walked out of the shadows around their porch.

Ali gave a little cry.

'It's Finn,' she said, forgetting she wasn't really talking to Max. 'What's he up to?'

Max drove into the garden and jumped out of the car.

Their voices were loud in the cool night air.

'What are you doing here?' Max asked.

'What are *you* doing here?' Finn said.

'This is my home.'

'Well then, you mustn't have told your wife as I asked. Otherwise she'd have thrown you out.'

'She did. I came back.'

'Why?'

'Because I was afraid you'd show up at some stage.'

'What for?'

'What for? Once upon a time, you bashed me up when I put my arms around your girlfriend. So now, I probably have a far bigger bill to pay.'

'This might come as a surprise to you, but I'm not the person I was then.'

'Really?'

'If I was still that guy I would have killed you by now. With my bare hands.'

'And what about your nasty little threat to my wife?'

'I said that in the heat of the moment.'

'We're not having this conversation out here,' Ali said, taking control, realising that there was something going on that she wasn't aware of, something that had made Max come home and brave her wrath to ensure her safety. She rummaged for her keys. 'If you want to snap at each other or bash each other's brains out, you'd better do it inside.'

She opened the front door and marched down to the kitchen, turning on lights as she went. It still amazed her that the kitchen looked the same as ever, considering the way their lives had been torn asunder. *Their* kitchen, the corkboard jammed with notes, the counters needing a good tidying, Tom's rugby boots dumped at the back door. The place where so much of their family life had been played out that the very walls seemed to resonate with fun and laughter.

'What do you want?' Max growled.

Ali poured a glass of water, knowing she would far prefer a big glass of wine. She turned around and almost gasped when she looked at Finn in the bright light – he was even more grey-faced than Max. His hair was wet and his coat damp from the earlier rain.

'I want an apology,' Finn said. 'How could you think I had anything to do with your bakery problems, never mind your daughter's accident?'

'I apologise, unreservedly,' Max said.

'I want a DNA test as soon as possible,' Finn said. 'So that I know for definite.'

'Know what for definite?' Ali found herself challenging, even though she'd fully intended to stay out of their particular argument. She was weary to the bone and the news about how Jessica had been hurt had sucked any remaining energy from her. She was conscious suddenly of their body language, both she and Max leaning against the kitchen counter in a mirror image of each other, the way they had often stood when they'd chatted about their day. Looking at them, you'd never think Ali was going to spend the night in the guest room, crying until dawn.

Finn laughed hollowly. 'What do you think? Who Grace's father is, of course. Max has told you, hasn't he? All the gory details?'

'He has told me,' Ali said. 'I've been thinking about it – even thinking of you, Finn, believe it or not. I've had rather a lot of time to think today about the complicated mess we're all in – but the answer to that side of it is very simple.'

'Oh yeah?'

'What difference,' she asked, 'is a hospital test going to make to all those years you've spent loving and caring for Grace? A test will prove the clinical biology of it all, but that's not what being a parent is, is it? Being a parent is something that comes from the heart and is the greatest love and the greatest hard work, starting as soon as that baby is born.'

'Spare me the psychology.'

'It has nothing to do with psychology. It's all about what you do and how much you love.'

Finn shook his head. Max was very still.

'I know what has happened is a load of shite,' Ali said. 'And I don't excuse my French, because I mean it, and I'll never forgive Max. I want to kill him. But Grace is the innocent here and she's the only part of this whole mess that's any way straightforward. Answer me something off the top of your head, Finn,' she said, pausing long enough to make sure he was paying attention. 'Who was Max's mother?'

He stayed silent.

'Come on, who was she?' Ali pressed. 'What's the first answer that comes into your head?'

He still didn't speak but there was a glimmer of something in his shadowed eyes.

'Was Max's mother the person who left him in the basket at the back of a church when he was a tiny baby? Or was it the person who cared for him day after day, year after year, who made sure he had his homework done, who wiped his nose, picked him up when he fell, walked the floor with him when he was sick, organised his birthday parties, shared his little triumphs ...?'

Out of the corner of her eye, she saw Max looking at her in appreciation. She glared at him. This wasn't about getting him off a hook, or about the look in Finn's eye. It was about an eleven-year-old girl who may or may not have been given life on account of Max, but who didn't deserve that precious life to be pulled apart.

'So who was Max's father?' she asked. 'His *real* father?' She waited a beat or two before she went on. 'I'm not saying you shouldn't have a test done. And Grace will have to be told at some stage if the answer is what you suspect, and then Max too might have some responsibilities, but only what is agreed with you.'

Finn shook his head.

'Think about it, Finn. Because if you are Grace's *real* father, you won't walk away from her,' Ali said. 'You'll continue to love her all the days of her life. And now, if you'll excuse me, it's been a long day and I need some sleep.'

She walked out into the hall, too exhausted to feel anything else. She stepped out of her shoes and started up the stairs. Then halfway up she paused when she heard Max talk to Finn, their voices floating out through the partly open door.

'Go on home, Finn,' Max said tiredly. 'It's late, and this is for another day.'

'Thanks to you I have no home to go to,' Finn said.

'Yes, you have. Jo loves you. So does Grace. No more than yourself, I wish – I wish all this had never happened,' Max said. 'Too many people have been hurt and lives messed up. It was a mistake, but one that was all too easy to make in New York that day.'

'And that's your excuse.'

'I have no excuses,' Max said. 'There are none. But if you'd been there, been in that beautiful morning, and then the horror of it all, the unreality – ah, Jesus, the terror, the grief, the devastation, the heartache and despair that gripped the city that day … the lives lost, and then like the best and worst backing track, the messages of love from phones before they went down, from people who were trapped …' Max paused, before continuing in a bleak voice, 'I thought Jo had been killed. If you'd seen her when she came through the hotel lobby, covered head to toe in white ash, if you'd *seen* the look on her face … in her eyes … if you'd *been* there … scared shitless like us. We didn't know if there were going to be more bombs or carnage. We comforted each other. A little too much. We haven't talked about it since. We agreed it should never have happened. She told me how much she loves you. For what it's worth, I'm sorry.'

'Sorry! You're *sorry*.'

Finn sounded so full of wounded rage that Ali thought he was about to hit Max. He didn't. The kitchen door slammed back on its hinges and he marched up the hall, then slammed the front door behind him as he went out into the night.

Ali crept up the rest of the stairs and went into the spare bedroom. Despite her tiredness, she lay rigid in bed long after she heard Max coming up the stairs and his footsteps overhead.

He'd spoken to Finn, so honestly and simply that if you looked at it as a stranger might, it was easy to understand how he and Jo could have ended up comforting each other in those circumstances. She thought about what he had said, his bleak voice telling Finn how scared they'd been that day. She twisted and turned as she remembered the images on the television and the heightened emotions they'd caused, but she could only imagine how terrifying it must have been in the devastated city that day.

Would Finn be courageous enough to go home to Jo and forgive her? If not, there would be three lives shattered. In the next breath she laughed at this; how could she expect Finn to do what she wasn't prepared to do? She couldn't forgive Max, ever. It was too much to ask. Whatever fears she'd had that something might damage their world, she'd never expected anything of this magnitude. Yet all those years since it had happened, she'd been living quite happily with him in blissful ignorance. Working together, laughing together, making love. There was a lot to be said for not knowing the truth.

She gave up trying to sleep and lay on her back in the darkness, her mind filled with the way Max had looked in the hospital waiting area earlier that evening, shoulders sagging, and then at Jessica's bedside, there was no sign of his dejection. He'd put that to one side and had been steady, calm and reassuring as a loving father might be.

Jessica was something else again. It dismayed Ali that she'd got into such trouble despite her parents' attempts to keep her safe from harm. She was so grateful that Jessica had turned the corner – they were lucky.

From the room upstairs, she heard Max pace the floor. She longed for everything to be all right again, she wished he hadn't broken her heart, because she wanted more than anything to curl into him and feel his arms around her, protecting her. Instead, she lay in the loneliness of her bed, stuffed her fist into her mouth and began to cry.

Forty-Eight

Jo got out of bed at the first pale light of dawn. She showered, then she wrapped herself in a cuddly robe and went downstairs to the big silent kitchen where she opened all the blinds and made some coffee. She went into the conservatory and opened all the blinds there too, and sat in the cushiony armchair by the window, her hands laced around her mug. She took a sip, feeling the hot liquid thaw out some of the chill in her bones.

She'd stayed up the night before, after she'd collected Grace and tucked her up in bed – a Grace who'd asked anxiously about her father. Jo did her best to soothe her daughter's fears, her words sounding false to her own ears. She'd waited up to see if there was any sign of Finn coming home. There wasn't.

She'd eventually crawled upstairs, and put her head on the pillow. She must have dozed, because it was soon after four in the morning when the call had come from the nursing home to say Veronica Harper had passed away peacefully in her sleep. Jo stared around the shadowy bedroom, stilled with the finality of it all. No hospital dash this time, or last-minute resuscitation. No death-bed resolutions. Veronica Harper had slipped away quietly, catching Jo by surprise. It was over.

'I'll be there first thing in the morning,' she'd said, knowing there was no point in dragging Grace out of bed at this unearthly hour, whatever about herself. 'And thank you.'

She sat by the window, watching the morning light steal slowly across the garden, wondering where Finn was and thinking of her mother. She had a short space of time to absorb the knowledge that her mother would never talk to her again, never listen to her or speak, never answer a phone call or even open her eyes. Never say she just wanted Jo to be happy. As soon as Grace got up, it would start – phone calls to her sisters, extended family and friends; funeral arrangements would have to be made, the ritual of the funeral itself and a gathering of the Harper clan. Finn and their problems in the middle of all this.

And somewhere in the days and weeks beyond all that, getting used to life without her mother and the gap Jo already felt in the fabric of her life. There would be no second chances and no reconciliation.

Yet already Jo knew that her words of love to her mother the previous night had freed her troubled heart. She wished she could ease Finn's troubled heart. She wanted to soothe him with her love, fill him with hope again, help him see that he had a life worth living, that they had a marriage worth saving, and a love that deserved a second chance. She needed him too, to be there for her over the next few days. She knew she would never get used to a life without him in it. After a while, she made another cup of coffee and sat quietly, soaking up the thin, early-morning light that slowly deepened, chasing away the shadows of the night.

Then she heard a sound she hadn't expected. The sound of a key in the door. Footsteps came slowly down the hall, into the kitchen, and paused. Her heart began a slow thump as Finn walked into the conservatory. His face was deathly pale and sombre. His hands were in the pockets of his navy overcoat and his shoulders were slumped.

'Jo ...'

Joooh. It sounded just the way he'd said it long ago, in a bedroom in

Coogee, and her heart turned over. Silence stretched between them, Jo's cup of coffee suspended in midair. She stared at him, afraid to think, to feel, to voice anything, to even move.

'I've been … walking around most of the night,' he said. 'I talked to Max and Ali,' he went on, his voice so quiet she had to strain to hear it. He looked everywhere except her face. 'Then I wandered up the canals as far as … as far as the dock. I sat there for a long time, staring into the water at the deepest point …'

Jo caught her breath.

'I didn't know what to do or where to go,' he said. 'I didn't have the energy to go anywhere or even do anything.'

Somewhere beyond the constriction in her throat, she managed to make what she hoped was a soothing sound.

'Do you know that four in the morning is the blackest time of all?' he said, staring out into the garden, where the angle of the sun was softly falling across the dew-damp garden. He looked as though he was surprised to see it there, as though he hadn't ever seen it before.

'I do,' she said. She put down her mug and clenched her hands tightly to stop them from shaking too much. She'd had those moments after coming back from New York.

'Things can seem bleaker then than at any other time.'

'Yes, they can.' *Keep talking*, she urged silently.

'So dark that it can suck all the life and energy out of you and make everything seem heavy, pointless and utterly crap.'

'I know.'

'It was the worst moment of my life. And then …' He paused, rubbed his face.

'Then what?' she murmured.

'I dunno … I sat there, unable to do anything, even move, and it just passed, that time, that horrible dark hour. Because I did nothing, it seemed to flow through me, somehow, and then I was on the other side of it, and the sky had started to lighten and my heart was still beating, I could hear it thumping in my ears. I can't explain how it made me feel …'

'You don't have to,' she said soothingly. 'I understand.'

'It made me feel that … well, there could be, maybe, a tiny bit of hope for us.' He looked at her, a quick glance, so fast she might have missed it, and then he gazed out into the garden again.

'There's always hope,' Jo said, her voice soft. When there was the breath of life, there was hope.

'Then I thought … that maybe, seeing that I'd nowhere else to go, nowhere else at all that I wanted to be, I'd just walk home.'

'Good. I'm glad you did.'

Thank you, thank you, thank you. She sent up a silent prayer. She didn't know if there was any connection between the time of her mother's last breath and Finn's moving on from his dark, dark night. She didn't know what she believed in any more. She didn't know what the future would hold for them but, right now, that didn't matter.

The most important thing was that he had come home with a tiny bit of hope in his heart.

She stayed where she was, seated by the window, unable to bring herself to cross the room and close the chasm between them. Something in his face told her not to make any presumptions, let alone a move towards him; they still had a long way to go.

But there was someone else who had no such inhibitions. There came the sound of footsteps running down the staircase, and then the pitter-patter of bare feet in the kitchen. Finn lifted his head, suddenly alert. Then Grace whirled into the conservatory, a ball of life, love and energy.

'*Daddy!* You're home!' she squealed, running towards him.

Finn opened his arms and she ran into them.

Forty-Nine

On Friday morning, Jessica was sitting out of bed, her injured leg propped up in a cast, when her mother came up the ward.

'Hey, look at you,' Ali said, coming around the bed to give her a hug. 'You look a million times better than you did yesterday, and the day before, never mind before that again.'

'I feel I'm coming back to the land of the living at last,' Jessica said, trying to quell her rising panic. There were questions to be asked and lots of things she had to sort out with her mum and dad. Like where she'd been going, late on that Saturday night. Like what had been happening with Daniel. And the bakery. And the photographs he'd taken of her, which she wasn't sure he had deleted. Most of all, how come she'd managed to put herself at risk, in spite of the way she'd always confidently dismissed her parents' cautions to keep herself safe by telling them she wasn't that stupid.

Only, of course she had been.

When she'd come around properly, she'd been shocked to hear it was Wednesday morning and she'd been in hospital for three days. She'd also been shocked to hear the extent of her injuries, and knew she was lucky to be alive.

She'd thought her dad might have been cross with her when he'd visited her the previous night. Instead he'd seemed to be quietly sad – which was a million times worse. He hadn't asked her any questions at all. His mouth had smiled, but his eyes had been very unhappy. He had new lines around his eyes and it made her feel bad about all the trouble she'd caused. He'd squeezed her hand and reminded her of the golden rules of the house: to say where she was going and bring her mobile phone with her always, to stick with her friends, and if the least little thing went wrong, to call him day or night, anytime, and he'd come for her, no matter where she was. Then he'd kissed the top of her head and told her how much he loved her in such a way that she felt like crying.

Her mother would come in every day, then Tom would come in after school, then he and Ali would go home together and Max would come in to visit in the evening.

'You have my visits all sorted out, like a proper shift,' she said to her mum.

'This way there's always one of us around to keep an eye on you.' Ali smiled, but it was a strained smile. Her face was pale and blotchy, her eyes rimmed with red fatigue, as though she'd been crying on and off for days, much like her dad had looked the night before. *I've done that*, she thought uncomfortably, *with my stupid behaviour.*

After Ali had chatted away about how she was feeling and the nurse had said Jessica would more than likely be moved to a regular ward the following day when she'd been assessed, there was a silence. Jessica didn't know where to start, there was so much to say.

'I suppose we'll have to talk about … how I ended up here,' she said worriedly.

Ali put her hand on her daughter's arm. 'We know, darling, all of it. Daniel talked to your father and the police. And the police have caught the man who ran you over.'

Jessica shivered as her mother filled in all the blanks on what had happened during the week. The police, Daniel and the bakery, and the couple who lived on the lane.

'Debbie assured Max that Daniel doesn't have your photographs anymore. She—'

Jessica shook. They all knew. 'She what?'

'She took his mobile and smashed it up with the heaviest pan in the bakery.'

'I'm so sorry, Mum,' she said, unable to hold back tears. 'I was so stupid.'

'I think that's one lesson you learned the hard way,' her mum said, patting her hand.

'What's going to happen now?' Jessica asked.

'As soon as the doctors give the all clear, the police will talk to you and you'll have to give them a statement. The man who knocked you down will be charged with dangerous driving. I'm not sure what will happen to Daniel yet. There are a few things he could be charged with – theft of the notebooks, impersonating Finn, blackmailing you …'

'He didn't come right out and say it, but the idea was there. He was playing with me because he just hadn't decided what he wanted me to do,' Jessica said. 'From the sound of it, he managed to upset the bakery enough all by himself.' She couldn't help her tears falling again and she grabbed a tissue.

'Shh, it's okay. Don't upset yourself,' Ali soothed. 'Right now you just need to get well.'

'It's been terrible, Mum,' Jessica wept. 'A nightmare. I couldn't believe the mess I got myself into. I've been so scared.' She plucked more tissues from the box.

Ali shook her head. 'That's the thing I can't understand. If you were that scared, why didn't you tell Dad or me?'

'I couldn't.'

'But why not, love? You're hardly afraid of us.'

'It's not that.'

'Thank goodness.' Ali gave a laugh that didn't reach her sad eyes. 'You and Tom mean everything. I'd hate to think you couldn't confide in us.'

'It's because we mean so much that I didn't want to let you down, I didn't want to wreck our happy family,' Jessica said, relieved to be having this conversation even if it was difficult. 'Can you imagine Dad's face if the photos had been posted on Facebook? Or Twitter? His princess? The thoughts of it sickened me. Everything would have been ruined for us, even Tom would have hated it. It would have been awful.'

'Still, sweetheart, if we'd known what was going on, we might have been able to halt Daniel in his tracks and spare you all the heartache. And no matter what happened, we would have supported you.'

'I was afraid to take that chance. I was terrified of letting you down.'

'You could never let us down, Jessica. You might have been a little foolish, but we still love you the way we've always loved you.'

Jessica felt a weight off her chest. 'I never really appreciated our family until I thought our happiness was under threat,' she said. 'I know we have our off days but mostly you and Dad are brilliant parents, and I love you both so much. I'm so proud of you.'

'Hey,' Ali said, looking embarrassed.

'I don't care if I'm being slushy. I'm so relieved the nightmare is over that I have to say this. I'm even proud of Tom, he's the best. But you're especially great, the way you manage us and Booth Street.'

'Booth Street's a success on account of your dad,' Ali said.

'The food is only half of it,' Jessica said. 'You're one of the most amazing people I know.'

'One?'

'Dad is the other amazing person, of course. How you guys managed to get together I don't know.'

'We were both far too young, as you've pointed out.'

'Nah. It was fate. There must have been something in the air, some kind of destiny that made your paths cross and made the immoveable force, as in our big, strong Dad, meet an unstoppable object, as in go-getter you.'

'It was a cake, actually,' Ali said, looking as though she was a million miles away.

❀

Later, Ali walked down the hospital corridor, as familiar to her now as her own hallway. Her heart felt shredded into a million pieces. Jessica had been scared at upsetting the family, a family unit that meant everything to her. She didn't know that the worst had already happened, that her mother's dark fears had materialised in a way she'd never expected and the future happiness of her family was teetering on the brink.

What would happen to Jessica and Tom and their precious family life if she couldn't forgive Max? They'd be broken-hearted. As would Max.

Ali loved her daughter with a strength and depth that took her breath away. Ali could forgive Jessica's foolish mistake. Max had made a foolish mistake as well. She still loved him, but was it enough to accept what had happened and put it behind them?

She went across to the cafeteria, feeling dizzy as she remembered the way Max had run out on her just a few nights ago. Jessica thought that destiny had brought them together. Ali couldn't stop thinking about that first time, when her life had collapsed after her mum had died, and Max had taken care of her. Ali wondered what words of wisdom her mother would have for her now.

'I can't live without you,' Max had said earlier that week. She knew by his face that he'd meant every word. But a quirk of destiny had ripped them apart and she didn't think she had the strength or the courage to put them back together again.

Fifty

'We're all going,' Max said to her, very quietly but very firmly, in the kitchen on Saturday night.

'You can count me out,' Ali hissed, her heart bleeding as she thought of Tom in his room getting together his clothes for his big adventure. 'I can't bear the thought of even sitting in a car beside you. No way. I'd feel sick.' She tossed that last remark in for good measure, her fleeting triumph mixing with a pang of sorrow when she saw his face flinch as though she'd slapped him.

'Do you think I don't know that?' he growled. 'This is the greatest adventure of Tom's life so far. Can't you put his feelings before your disgust of me? You can't let him down. You can sit in the back of the car and avoid the remotest possibility of any form of bodily contact with me.'

Bodily contact. Her senses swam.

She'd hardly spoken to Max since Tuesday night, she'd avoided him as best she could, but they couldn't go on like this. She'd heard him pacing the floor again as she'd lain awake the night before, the upsets of the past few days surging around in her head. It had taken her a long time to finally admit to herself that she wanted everything to go back to the way it had been before, with no knowledge of what Max had done, so that she could lean into him, be wrapped in his strong arms, be hugged in bed at night in their room overlooking the canal, and have him soothe her fears. She wanted to hear him say, 'Hey, Ali,' when he popped his head into her tiny office in Booth Street. She wanted to feel the touch of his hand on her waist when she passed him on the stairs. The ordinary trivialities that were so precious. She wanted to talk about Jo and Finn, and even Grace. That made her remember what he'd done, and in the next breath pain sliced through her.

They couldn't carry on as though it had never happened. Yet in a funny way, she wanted him to make it better, make up for it, love her more than ever before and do everything in his power to redeem himself and put Max and Ali to rights again. Because as she'd lain in the darkness, she'd looked into the still depths of her heart and known she couldn't live without him. But she still couldn't see the way forward.

So she was scared of watching the stars with Max just a few feet away. Scared of where their lives were going, and what the future held for all of them.

'Mum!' Tom shouted down the stairs.

She went out into the hallway and looked up into his concerned face peering down over the banisters. He looked so like Max that she felt dizzy. What if, in future years, happily married Tom took another woman into his arms to console her on a day when the world itself seemed to crash to an end? If asked, she would tell him that he had been very careless with his wife's love and trust, and he should spend the rest of his life making it up to her. And she would pray that Tom's wife might find it in her heart to give him a second chance.

'What is it, Tom?'

'I can't find my torch.'

'Your *torch*?'

'Yeah, I need it to guide us from the car to the viewing site.' His voice was high with excitement.

She couldn't admit that she didn't think he'd need a torch to light the way from the car park to the area in front of the Papal Cross. His face was so full of trust and innocent expectancy that she couldn't but go along with him.

'Did you try the utility room?' she asked, knowing also as she looked at his face that it would be next to impossible to tell her son she wasn't going to go with him. It would surely deflate his enthusiasm like a pin stuck in a bubble.

'Yeah, course.' He tore down the stairs, a streak of energy and excitement. 'And I have some Snickers bars for our picnic,' he said, his face alight with hopeful eagerness. 'I've been saving up my pocket money. I hid them in the fridge cos I know you like your chocolate out of the fridge. Has Dad made the sandwiches yet? He said he'd make a flask as well. Although I mightn't be hungry cos it's gonna be awesome.'

'Yes, I'm sure he has all that sorted,' she said, feeing faint. She was being sucked along, like a piece of flotsam being whirled helplessly towards the long drop of a mighty waterfall.

Tom was doubly excited to be leaving the house at a time when the streets were quiet and he would normally be tucked up in bed. They drove through the city centre and up the quays towards the park, Ali sitting in the back with Tom, as he went through everything he expected to see that night.

'When we can make out the Big Dipper, we'll know our eyes are adjusted to the night light,' he chatted brightly.

Just once, Ali saw him pause in his chatter long enough to throw a puzzled glance between his dad in the driver's seat and his mother in the back seat as though he knew something was wrong between his parents but was afraid to think of it.

'Tell me about the meteor shower and how it comes about,' she asked brightly, her chest pained with the knowledge that Max's soft blue eyes were constantly glancing at her through the rear-view mirror.

'It happens when the earth moves into a cloud of celestial dust left behind by a comet,' Tom said knowledgeably. 'We don't even need binoculars or a telescope tonight as they should be visible to the naked eye.' He grew silent and he sat forward expectantly as they turned in at the park and drove up along Chesterfield Avenue. They parked the car and Max and Tom went around to the boot and took out rugs and the picnic hamper. A number of other cars were already parked and others pulled up close to them, doors slamming and voices calling across the still night-time air. Ali pulled on her woollen scarf and gloves and followed Max and Tom, listening to the excitement in Tom's voice, his pitch softened in honour of the momentousness of this occasion. They led the way to the viewing area, which was the wide-open acres of space in front of the Papal Cross, where groups were scattered about, all set for the night-sky extravaganza. The cold night air was infused with a low buzz of conversation, a festive atmosphere, the feeling that anything could happen.

'Guess what?' Tom said suddenly. 'I forgot my torch.'

In the shadowy darkness, over their son's head, Max's eyes met hers in shared amusement and Ali's heart lurched.

'Though I guess we didn't need it after all,' Tom said.

'I guess we didn't,' Max said, ruffling his son's hair.

Max spread a plastic sheet, some travel rugs and cushions on the ground and he and Tom lay down, the better to watch the night sky than getting stiff necks from craning to see. Ali sat down a little away from them and hugged her legs and rested her chin on her knees and listened to her husband and son talking softly as their eyes adjusted to the darkness.

'I can make out the Big Dipper,' Tom said, and then a short time later, 'Wow, Dad, did you see that?'

'I did. Look, there's more stars.'

'There's gangs!' Tom said, his voice rich with happiness and contentment, 'Millions!'

Ali reluctantly tilted her head heavenwards and then she sucked in her breath at the beauty of the sky, the deep, black, velvet backdrop a perfect foil for the stars twinkling from the heavens. She didn't know the technicalities – no doubt Tom could have given her a lesson – all she knew was that some of the glittering stars seemed to be putting on a show especially for her, reaching down inside her, playing kiss chase with her and with each other as they darted off.

Something stilled and quietened inside her and the anxieties that had gripped her for the past few days loosened. She thought of her mother bringing her out to watch the stars when she was very young, and she could hear her voice again, as though it was now, telling her that their lives were full of infinite possibilities, that there was magic in the stars and she could wish for whatever she wanted, then work for it.

❦

Later that night, after Tom had gone to bed, overcome with excitement after his adventure, Ali slipped quietly into the spare room and lay sleepless on top of the bed, her emotions so raw at missing Max that every time her heart beat, it sent shockwaves around her body.

She had made a wish, years ago, for someone like Max and he had come into her life. She had hoped they would all live happily ever after. But life wasn't like that. People made mistakes, accidents happened, some with silly inconsequential results, others with far-reaching repercussions. Life didn't come with a guarantee-of-happiness tag.

The inescapable truth was that only one person could ease the pain that pounded her body from head to toe. Only one person could soothe her hurt. But in order for him to do that, she had to rise above what had caused that hurt. Was there any possibility she could be big enough to give him a chance, or brave enough to risk going after what she wanted?

Where was can-do Ali in her own hour of need?

Yeah, where was she? Go-getter Ali? She almost heard the words swirling in the air around her.

Something bubbled up inside her, something that drove her off the bed, so that she stood there in her striped socks, her jeans and velour jumper, her hair mussed up from tossing in bed. It propelled her out onto the landing.

Tom's bedroom door was slightly ajar and she peeped in. He was sound asleep, a small gap in the curtains open to the night sky, and she wondered if his excitement earlier that night was fizzing through his dreams. Jessica's door was wide open, the room a comforting confusion of clothes and books and makeup.

She passed a mountain of shirts slung over the banisters, waiting to be ironed, and Tom's grey tracksuit abandoned in a heap halfway between his room and the laundry basket, fully confident that the laundry fairy would do her thing. She stopped at the framed collage of photos that had pride of place on the wall leading to the next floor, a jumble of memories spanning twenty years. Beside it, there was space for other frames, for the years ahead that hadn't yet been written or recorded. She wondered how it would look.

She went upstairs slowly, her heart thumping, her mouth dry. Her fingertips shook as they connected with the door. She pushed it open. A lamp cast soft light across their room, the big, high bed with the patchwork quilt was tossed, plump pillows scattered.

Max sat by the window, looking out onto the canal. She stared at him for a long, frozen moment and then he must have sensed her presence because he turned around. Their eyes locked.

Ali stood on the threshold. One step was all it would take. She knew by the way he was looking at her that he was holding his breath, waiting to see if she would take that step, for both of them knew there could be no sour words in this room, all arguments left at the door. She swallowed, trying to get rid of the roaring in her ears and the feeling of suffocation in her throat caused by her fluttering heart. She couldn't move.

He stood up and came towards her. He was wearing a soft navy jumper and she gazed at it because now it was impossible to meet his eyes. He stood facing her and then he reached out his hand as though to help her into the room.

'I need ...' she began, her voice hoarse.

'Yes, love?' He waited expectantly.

'I need you to bake a cake,' she said, risking a glance at him.

He dropped his hand, his eyes tinged with disappointment. 'Sure. What kind?'

'Any kind.' She paused. 'So long as it can be iced. With a message.' She stole another glance in time to see his eyes light up and a slow smile spread across his face. Her heart quivered. God, she loved this man. Every bit of him. She wanted to be wrapped in his arms forever.

'What do you want me to say on it?' he asked, his voice thick with emotion.

'I want you to say …' she tilted her head, thought for a minute, the air between them buzzing with anticipation.

'Please forgive me?' he asked hopefully

She shook her head. 'No.'

'I'll love you always?'

'Go on.'

'To Ali, the best wife in the world?'

'Not that either. Keep them coming.' She felt weak. He was so close, every cell in her body was thrumming.

'I love you, Ali Kennedy, from the bottom of my heart and my soul. I'm going to spend the rest of my life making sure you know this.'

'You're beginning to get warm,' she murmured, gazing at him now.

His eyes were dark, liquid pools. 'I'm not sure if that'll all fit on the cake.'

'I think you'll have to practise it a lot.'

'I'll give it my very best and most careful attention.'

'Is that a promise?'

'Cross my heart. Why don't you come in so we can talk about it more?' He lifted her hand and dropped a kiss into her palm, wrapping her fingers around it. He didn't let it go, but held it securely in his own and she felt a warm glow spiralling all through her body.

She hesitated, for just a moment, their hands joined, her eyes searching his face. Then she stepped across the threshold and into the room.